The Tymorean Trust
Book Five

ALIEN CONTACT

By

MARGARET GREGORY

TAT Publishing

Also by Margaret Gregory

TYMOREAN TRUST SERIES:

Book 1 - Power Rising
Book 2 - Great Ones
Book 3 - The Return to Earth
Book 4 – Earth Mission

ATAPI SORCERESS SERIES:

Book 1- The Wild One
Book 2 – Atapi Sorceress

THE THIRD GENERATION SERIES:

Wanda – From Bad to Worse

Cover designed by msgdragon
Images by:
© Can Stock Photo Inc. / alphatucana and © Can Stock Photo Inc. / Digitalstudio

For permission requests, address the request to the author c/o
Permissions,
C/o TAT Publishing
PO Box 150
Glen Waverley, Victoria, 3150

www.tatpublishing.com

ALIEN CONTACT

Part 1 - Chapter 1

From a distance, the forty storey glass fronted building was reminiscent of the 20th Century space shuttles. The central tower tapered gracefully to a domed peak and the lower levels fanned out like wings. It was a familiar sight in Washington DC, and worldwide to everyone with an interest in science.

That morning, as the rising sun began to reflect off the glass, the World Science Research Authority headquarters was already a subdued hub of activity.

An estimated ten thousand hopeful applicants, who had successfully passed the first selection stages for positions within the organisation, would pass through the massive double doors during the next few days.

Tymos Ward and his twin sister, Kryslie, joined the steady stream of people walking across the wide, open courtyard from the street. They passed and ignored the outdoor exhibits provided for tourists without actually looking at them, but their eyes caught the flashing messages on the 16 frame organic LED screen that were incorporated into the windows of the building. The message, "Welcome to our esteemed applicants," was scrolling through different world languages, changing every 30 seconds.

Then a movement caught Tymos's attention, and he looked to see a camera, attached to an extendable boom, scanning the courtyard. A media reporter was standing on an elevated scissor lift platform, talking into a recording device.

"I guess it's not surprising that this is a media circus," Tymos mused aloud.

Kryslie, whose attention had returned to observing the multitude of ethnic groups represented replied, "Well, it is the first time in forty years that this many people from countries in the Imperium have been in one place in the American Convocation at the same time. Definitely a first for Washington."

"At least this time, they are all friendly, aren't they?"

"The overwhelming emotion is excitement," Kryslie told her twin. She hadn't been trying to pick up subversive thoughts, but as an empath as well as a telepath, she would be more sensitive to such considerations. "This is a historic event. The first time that any organisation has advertised for applicants on a world wide scale as well as offering a chance for ordinary people to work on the moon."

Tymos chuckled, "The WSRA universities may turn out highly trained specialists, but they don't train people for the mundane support roles."

The graduates from the six American, and twelve foreign, based WSRA universities would all be vying for the senior positions.

Tymos and Kryslie had opted to apply to the entry level invitation via an on-line portal. They received an applicant number, uploaded a minimal amount of personal information, a sketchy outline of their educational background, and played up their real experience - without including dates for any of it. The documents contained carefully inserted power keywords for the massive WSRA computers to scan and pick up on. Their replies were quick and there had been no error messages relating to the scarcity of personal information. The message sent to the contact email contained only the directions relating to the next phase.

They had successfully distracted the computer, for what really mattered would be the ability of each applicant to do the work required in the various roles. They had used the 'educational records' created for them when they had applied to the WSRA Washington University, seventeen years before, only this time they had not needed to have a personal recommendation to support them. It was the fact that they had actually attended the university that they were intending to hide.

During the following months, the million or so on-going applicants attended sessions at their nearest WSRA University, undergoing a range of aptitude and psychological tests that weeded out the less suitable candidates. Having given an address in California, Tymos and Kryslie went to the Pasadena campus. Those that passed that stage, were asked to undergo a thorough physical examination, to determine if they were suited to work on the moon.

Only the top point one percent of the original millions of candidates were invited to attend the advanced testing at the WSRA headquarters.

The Ward twins passed through the massive double doors, paying no attention to the cameras and reporters set up just inside. They noticed, in a single glance around, the two huge wall screens showing scenes from the building of the WSRA's Lunar 1 base. Any voice over accompanying the videos was lost in the babble of hundreds of applicants.

The voice announcement system was, however, loud enough to be heard, and the messages being replayed every two minutes were for the attendees to check the overhead boards for directions to the rooms they needed, or to request help from the uniformed ushers, and to keep proceeding in an orderly and timely fashion. Kryslie and Tymos already knew where they were meant to be and how to get there.

Several more news cameras were set up amidst the crowd. Tymos and Kryslie split up to edge around their field of view. Together, their dark red hair would draw attention, apart, they were less noticeable amongst the taller, more exotic looking people.

The twins moved back together, but before stepping onto the upward glide-walk, Tymos paused and gave the vaulted entrance hall another, longer look. Being there was a bitter sweet experience. For although the year was 2095 and Tymos himself looked only to be in his mid-twenties, he had been in this very place when it had still been just a convention centre. He had witnessed the World Peace Treaty being signed in 2057, ending a particularly nasty war between the Eastern Alliance (now referred to as the Imperium) and the Americans. He had also been there a few days later when the WSRA and the United World Nations were born.

Kryslie sensed her brother's thoughts of that earlier time, and it roused others in herself. At that time, she had been a virtual captive in the country of the real leader of the Eastern Alliance. She'd had a child there, a boy she had seen only for a brief time, and who would be much her current age and look older than her apparent visual age.

She tugged on her brother's arm. "Come on, we have things to do."

Without replying, Tymos obeyed the suggestion, and together, they stepped onto the glide-walk and began to move up. As they rose, keeping their eyes directed upwards, passing the vaulted ceiling of the entrance hall to reach the next level, Tymos revealed that he had been aware of his sister's thoughts.

"I wonder if he is here."

"He won't need to be," Kryslie thought her reply to Tymos. "He went to one of the WSRA universities."

With a purely mental chuckle, Tymos countered, "So did we, but we are here."

He glanced to his right as the glideway took them upwards, and saw his sister's pensive expression. He knew she often thought of her son, even when she didn't speak of him.

They didn't need to remind each other why they had chosen to apply for junior roles with the WSRA. The paradox of Kryslie having a son, who looked to be a decade older than she did, exemplified their reasoning.

Earthborn they were, but their nativity had been back in the late twentieth century. Some of their antecedents had been alien – missionaries from the distant planet of Tymorea. No one had expected them to inherit the special aptitudes of the royal Tymoreans, but when they had begun to exhibit the signs of those abilities rising, they were taken to Tymorea to be trained and now considered that world, their home.

The Guardians of Peace, the mystical beings who had first bestowed an elite power on the Tymoreans, had chosen them to be their Advocates, and to wield some of the Guardians own power when there had been a need to cleanse Tymorea of the radioactive contamination caused by a deadly war. When the Tymoreans had emerged from stasis within protected cities and taken up their lives again, the Guardians had new work for their Advocates who now bore the title of Great Ones.

While their brother and fellow Great One remained on Tymorea, they returned to Earth, leaving with the Tymorean missionaries chosen to establish an Earth Mission. Only, they didn't arrive with the others. The Guardians took them back in time, to pivotal points in Earth's history, and finally brought them to a time, years before their kin were due to arrive. This was so that the work of one of the previous missionaries, who had not obeyed the summons to return home, could be found and used to prepare the final protections needed for the base.

Kryslie's son, had been born during one of the short periods when they had work to do in the past. It had not been her choice to leave him, but the will of the Guardians. They had been in Earth's present for seventeen years now, but still looked only to be in their mid-twenties.

Their travel through time had been linked to Tamir Grainger, the son of the Tymorean scientist and the founder of the WRSA. He had prepared the way for them to attend the Washington University, so they could recover his father's work.

They had studied at the university for five years, distinguished themselves, had offers of high paid jobs, and another from the WSRA – but they had not graduated. They had left, without accepting the proof of their qualifications that would allow them to apply directly for senior positions with the WSRA.

That decision had been made even before they had needed to attend to their true work – the safe guarding of their kin, and the protection of the Earth Mission. Working full time for any organisation would not have been possible. With their known intellect, so much would have been expected of them, they would be too well known, and their seeming agelessness remarked upon.

Now, they could almost be the children of one or other of their younger selves. Better to be unobtrusive, become merely two more junior support staff – less noticeable, able to blend in to the crowd, observe and watch, to be ready for the future time when they would need to act to ensure Earth's peace.

Room 3 delta was more of a hall or auditorium, and it was filled with row upon row of three metre long, upward sloping tables. An usher told the arriving queue of people to move forward, to be directed by the ushers standing to the left and centre of each row.

At the front of the desks was a vacant podium, with a backdrop of the rich red drapes that covered the windows. All the light in the area came from down lights.

Kryslie followed her brother along one row, near the centre of the room. She stopped at the next free position, pushed the seat down and adjusted it so the desk was at the right height for her. A man of middle age stopped after her, saw what she had done, and adjusted his own seat for his greater height. More people sat beyond him, and then the row behind them began to fill up. When all the attendees were seated, the section of table in front of each candidate rose and rotated, revealing data pads inset into the surface. A stylus and a digital pen, were attached to each data pad.

Once everyone was seated, the candidates received instructions from a recorded voice that came over a speaker. "Please input your name and applicant number and check that your preselected areas of interest appear and are correct. This session lasts for two and a half hours. Answer the questions in the order they are presented, and according to your listed first and subsequent preferences. If you have completed all questions before the end on the time period, you may select another area of interest to be considered for. You may begin."

The murmur of voices that had ceased when the instructions began, now became an almost audible thrum as digital pens wrote, or styli tapped keypads.

Tymos and Kryslie were not competing against each other, and had intentionally chosen different but overlapping interest areas. They set to work with focussed concentration, the answers coming fast and quick from their retentive memories. They intuitively knew what keywords to include in their answers. Well before the end of the time allowed, they had finished their ten sections, and set about completing more to fill the time.

They each had a thorough knowledge of subjects relating to the astro-sciences, but they could answer questions on science topics from biology to zoology, from the various engineering, information technology, electronics and computing fields, to mechanics and maintenance. They could have aced any of the hundreds of available interest areas, but concentrated on those that were most vital on a lunar base.

The people in the room were a random selection of ethnic origins and interests. While Kryslie was answering questions about tracking astral objects, she was aware that the man beside her was answering questions about vehicle maintenance, and someone else nearby was answering questions about first aid and medicine.

The most difficult part of the tests for both Kryslie and Tymos, was the need to play down the extent of their intelligence, their expertise and experience, to a level just below that which would be required to enter the WSRA universities.

When the end of time chime sounded, the recorded voice instructed the candidates to save their work, sign off and leave the room in a timely manner as the room was needed for the next group of candidates.

As Tymos followed his sister back along the aisle between tables, the sections containing the data padds rotated once more.

The lower level was still as busy as it had been on their arrival, and crowded with the next batch of candidates waiting to go up and those that had finished for the day pushing through to reach the outer doors or taking time now to take in the ambience of the entrance hall. Tymos and Kryslie eased their way through the milling people with the fluid grace of skilled fighters, and finally reached the less crowded courtyard.

"I'm for food," Tymos announced, once they were walking back along the main road towards their rented apartment.

"It's your turn to cook," Kryslie reminded him.

"We can find a street vendor to patronise," Tymos suggested. "Then if we were every other hopeful candidate, we'd be hurrying back to our lodgings to prepare for the practical assessments."

"The hands-on stuff won't be hard. I can't see them letting us build a generator or something similar from scratch," Kryslie predicted. Before they had left the WSRA University, she and Tymos had been able to design and build highly specific power generators.

Tymos laughed aloud. "You know, I have decided that as all-encompassing as this testing procedure has been designed to be, whoever designed it seems to be assuming that the greatest brains all went to the universities."

"When you think about it bro – they are looking for lowly grunts of the highest possible quality. Can you see any of our peers from the university, who graduated into high salaried positions, accepting a lowly tech-3 position?"

"Not after five years at an elite university," Tymos agreed.

"Well, that gives us a huge advantage," Kryslie pointed out.

Tymos and Kryslie, kept to their compact rented apartment while waiting for the notification of the next stage of the process. They were neither studying hard, nor idling, simply taking the opportunity to sift through information that was available on the electronic information web. Pausing occasionally to have a drink or a meal or a few hours sleep.

The timetables for the practical assessments were sent to each candidate's digital mailbox, two days later.

The Ward twins each had devices that looked like the latest palm sized computer phones with all the capabilities of the commercially available ones, but also other apps that the general populace of Earth, had not yet considered possible. They received the electronically mailed instructions, indicated by beeps from their devices, at almost the same time.

Each read the generic information that preceded the details, which indicated that practical sessions were not scheduled if the candidate's written results for an interest area were scored at less than 80 percent.

Tymos stood and walked to where he could compare his schedule with Kryslie's. They were not in the same group for any of the practical sessions, because they put their interest areas in a different order. That was what they had hoped. However, each of them had been included in fifteen interest areas, had two practicals on the first day, and then one every other day. The prospect didn't discourage them, as it would give them fifteen chances at a position with the WSRA.

Kryslie's prediction that the exercises would be set at a level that didn't require expert knowledge, proved to be accurate. Her engineering practical required only that she followed directions, understood concepts and applied them correctly. The small scale exercises were done within a laboratory on the 27th floor, but then the initial group of sixty candidates was split up into groups of twelve for team assessments.

Her group went to a workshop area down in one of the basement levels of the WSRA building. There a lab coated supervisor instructed them to work together to assemble an all-terrain vehicle in the quickest possible time. The man wore casual clothing under the lab coat, but he had several badges on the collar of his white polo top and Kryslie's keen eyes recognised them as designating him to be a senior engineering officer.

"All the parts and tools you will need are supplied," the man told them, with a trace of condescension, probably unconscious, but typical of many WSRA graduates. Something about him was familiar to Kryslie, and it only took moments for her to recognise the face as a student from the Washington University, who had started four years after she had. Even though it was unlikely he would recognise her from back then, she chose to glance around the windowless space, identifying the air conditioning vents that introduced a steady flow of fresh air and giving thought to the reason for the tunnel in one wall that had a metal grid over it. She listened with her face averted until he finished his speech and had turned to leave them to work. By then, she had decided that even with the concrete walls painted white, and a comfortable level of light from warm white LED lamps, it wasn't somewhere she would prefer to work day after day.

Like the rest of the group, Kryslie scanned the laid out parts and schematics occupying several tables and the floor, and scanned the neatly racked tools on the wall. In her survey, she also noted some apparently un-related materials. In her mind, she decided that they had not been put there by mistake, or left there carelessly, but she made no comment. Around her, her teammates were getting started and a tall Italian man decided to usurp the position of team leader.

Half an hour into the hour allowed, when the chassis of the vehicle was assembled and jacked up to enable the wheels to be slipped into place, a strident alarm began. The white light dimmed and went out, to be replaced by flashing red emergency lights.

Everyone stopped and looked around, nearly deafened by the noise, and wondering what they should do. Next moment, a tremendous wind blew across the workshop, wrenching even the heaviest of the tools from the wall rack and flinging them across the workspace. Someone grunted in pain, and another yelled, "Get down near the floor!"

The self-proclaimed team leader, grabbed onto the half assembled vehicle, even though it was rocking ominously, and pulled himself along it and then forced himself to the door. He tried to open it, and found it stuck shut. As he turned to return the group, he was plucked off balance and ended up sitting on the floor.

Kryslie realised instantly that it wasn't a wind pushing on them, but an incredibly powerful vacuum pump pulling air from the room. When the Italian, simply swore in his native language, she took control.

"We need to seal the outlet. Tip everything off the table and help me manoeuvre it over the grid." She needed to yell to be heard by the nearest people, and when that didn't get them moving, she forced the message into their minds, along with an image of the grid.

Once the others knew what to do, they acted in concert, and when they had moved the earlier projectiles that were now clinging to the grid, held the table level with the tunnel beyond. Kryslie, recalling what she had noticed earlier, crawled against the suction effect, until she reached the 'conveniently placed' bag of instant cement that was sliding slowly along the floor, and the sealed plastic container of water in a rack on the wall. There was no time for finesse, when she returned to the table, she forcibly ripped off the seal and shoved the cement bag over the opening to stop the water being sucked out. She then tore a section of the bag and used her hand to begin mixing the cement. The force of the outrushing air was reducing, and that meant time was short. She began to seal the table to the wall with the cement, and everyone not holding the table helped her. The noise of the rushing air diminished to a whisper and the alarm finally stopped. For a moment, the workshop was silent.

As soon as the vacuum pump could no longer suck air, it switched off, and the lighting returned to normal. The air pressure in the room quickly stabilised as supervisors came in to check the candidates. These were not engineers, but doctors, according to the collar devices.

Kryslie assured them that she was fine, but she could see that several of the group were pale and shaky. The man who had been hit by a spanner had blood running down the side of his face from a cut on his forehead. The Italian was scowling, and casting irritated glances her way. No doubt he had been hoping for extra points by putting himself forward as the leader. He had not expected such a realistic, sudden emergency. His mind was seething at the idea that they might all have died of suffocation, but Kryslie was sure it would not have come to that. If they had not solved the emergency, the vacuum pump would have been turned off. All the candidates had passed the physicals, and were in good condition, so a few moments of minimal air should not have harmed them greatly.

They were not required to finish assembling the vehicle, and Kryslie decided that the real test had been to see how they worked together under normal conditions, and in an emergency.

Pre-warned by his twin's experience, Tymos wondered what emergency they would create for the systems programming assessment. The individual tasks of debugging code, creating subroutines to control machinery and the like had seemed childishly easy to him. The group task was to locate the subroutine that was causing a machine to run in a dangerously erratic manner, isolate that section of code, rewrite the faulty code, and restart the system.

He suggested that each of his group of twelve concentrate on a separate part of the algorithm. He wasn't the one to find the problem, but he quickly isolated the faulty piece of code while two others re-wrote it. Their first attempt failed, but the second worked. The machine restarted, and ran better, but still not smoothly. Tymos urged the group to keep checking the code, and he found where certain pre-sets had been altered from figures stated on the machine casing. One of the other candidates knew where to adjust these and did so. This time, the machine purred along like new. The supervisors entered and congratulated the group on a job well done.

Later in the day, ensconced in a virtual reality lunar shuttle simulator, Tymos expected to have to deal with some kind of system failure, which he would need to handle so that he and his passengers didn't crash into the moon. It was a full on exercise, that was as exhausting as the real thing would have been. The controls in the simulator were as sluggish as the controls of a real shuttle would be in similar circumstances, and it had required strength to hold the controls steady.

Shuttle pilot had been one of his lower preferences, but he spared a thought for how well mere human pilots managed sluggish controls. They would have to have strong arm muscles, to handle one in an emergency.

Kryslie returned to the apartment first, and since she was aware of the concentration Tymos needed for the shuttle exercise decided to swap cooking duties with him and had a high protein - high carbohydrate meal ready when he returned.

"You must be getting soft," she challenged when putting the plate of pasta marinara in front of him. "Fancy not being able to manage the shuttle controls."

"I didn't want to make it look like it was too easy for me," Tymos protested. "Anyway, how did you go this afternoon?"

Kryslie sat herself at the table before answering.

"I was going fine. They kept adding aircraft to my holding pattern. I was up to nineteen, without the option to send them to land elsewhere. Then they revealed their little emergency…some out of control shuttle, hurtling towards the landing area. All I had to do was redirect the other aircraft out of the way of the calculated trajectory, so the shuttle pilot could totally wreck his craft."

"Glad I was in a different shuttle," Tymos grinned before beginning to eat. When he'd swallowed the first mouthfuls, he remarked, "You know, I can recall a newsfeed from several years ago. One of the shuttles transporting stuff to the moon, almost crashed because of a systems failure. I'm wondering if all of these disaster scenarios are based on actual ones."

"They may well be, but it hardly matters. We both still have another thirteen disasters to survive," Kryslie pointed out.

The hectic month of testing and evaluation halved the number of candidates, many chose to drop out of the process, and others were advised to do so. The remaining candidates received email notification that there would be a two week break in the proceedings so that the computer could shortlist candidates for all the available positions. The final appointees would be selected after personal interviews.

So many factors had to be considered in addition to mere ability. Some of these were diplomatic, some were psychological. Terra 5, the newest Earthside base, had been constructed within the Imperium, the coalition of countries that had chosen not to join the United World Nations. A large proportion of the lesser ranked staff would be selected from the Imperium countries. The others would need to be able to work there without friction.

Similarly, the staff sequestered on the lunar base, would also need to work in harmony. Lunar 1, the first of two moon bases to be completed, had other unique requirements, the personnel needed to be comfortable living within an enclosed dome, and able to tolerate a lower gravity, and the spectre of exposure to vacuum if the integrity of the base was breached.

Tymos and Kryslie had rarely socialised with the other candidates, but on the last day, they made an exception. Everyone at the campus outdoor café had the right to be proud of reaching this point, they were each literally one out of millions, but there were not as many places to be filled as candidates. It meant though that there would be many disappointed people, and the group was tense with the need to wait for results, too stressed and edgy to relax.

Kryslie had to tighten her mental shields to block out all the emotions. Tymos, sensing the pressure she felt through their twin bond, decided to reveal some gossip he had overheard.

"You know, I heard that there is quite a turnover of staff within the WSRA," he began. "I checked, and nearly a quarter of the positions they need to fill are at the already established bases."

He had the interest of the people around him and went on, "I wouldn't be surprised if they don't keep the names of the extra candidates on a waiting list or in some file, for future openings."

Kryslie added, "And they have another two bases under construction. A second moon base and that one down in Australia."

"Yeah, so they do," one of their companions agreed.

The general tension eased, but only slightly. Tymos caught his sister's attention and mentally suggested leaving.

"Why don't we go home and visit Daniel?" Tymos suggested. "I don't feel like idling away the next two weeks here, do you?"

"No, because I think most of the crowd back there will be too tense to relax until they know if they have been short listed. I do need to get away."

Unspoken between them was the belief that they would not need to wait for a later opening, and would be chosen as part of the staff of Lunar 1.

The place they called 'home' was not any usual kind of middle American residence, but an extensive underground cavern system, located under the site of a missile crash. The land above was still hotly radioactive, even after nearly forty years and as no humans were able to penetrate to ground zero, it was the perfect place for a secret base.

Tymorean technology protected the cavern living space from the effects of the radiation, and enabled the radiation to be transmuted into electrical energy to supply their power. Water was available from underground springs, pure and untainted, and the air was refreshed by an underground garden.

It was the support base for all the Tymorean-born missionaries, and like a second home to those living in scattered locations all around the world.

From their rented apartment in Washington, Tymos contacted the base using his communicator. These portable Tymorean devices transmitted messages in a way not yet known on Earth, and so were impervious to being intercepted by human radio receivers or scanners. They could be mistaken for a generic version of the latest smart phones, having the capability to access the world communication and data web, store data and transmit images and voice, and had many other uses. In this instance, Tymos only activated voice mode.

"Earthbase, this is Tym."

He expected to hear Lexina, one of their Tymorean friends, but it was a young male voice that answered.

"This is Earthbase, how can I help you?"

Kryslie grinned suddenly. "Daniel said there were a few new faces, and I think I know that voice…"

Her twin had picked up her thought and was matching her grin.

"I'll go easy on the lad," Tymos claimed, then answered the question. "I would like the long range beam set to Washington, locus …" He gave the coordinates of the apartment.

"Right, um…"

Through the speaker, they both heard, "How do you adjust the beam generator?"

Moments later, a glowing mauve line appeared suspended in the air, and then it widened open into glowing mauve oval. Tymos and Kryslie were already stepping into the glow and activating their transmitters when they heard, "The beam is active."

Their personal transmitters enabled them to teleport from place to place, although without the long range beam, the distance they could move was limited by their personal energy, and the strength of their Tymorean power. On Earth, most of the missionaries were limited to moving line of sight, Tymos and Kryslie were powerful enough to be able to transmit through several thickness of wall.

As soon as they had materialised in the arrival cavern, Kryslie sent the deactivate signal to the beam generator, and the mauve glow faded out. She took in a huge breath and released it slowly, letting her tense muscles relax. "I'll be in the garden. Coming?"

"In a bit," Tymos told her. He stayed where he was and let his mind take in everything around him. His eyes flicked around the huge cavern, passing the vehicles parked just beyond the protective force field that protected the living areas from the tunnels leading to the surface. All four vehicles were there, so no one was out getting supplies. The two vans were transported in and out by the long range beam, usually to a point just outside the fence around the exclusion zone above ground. The two open jeeps, were used when they needed to move around within the radioactive zone. They were decontaminated in the outermost cavern before being bought further in.

His ability to sense the aura, or energy field, of the Earth reassured him that the air within the caverns was still pure, as was the water. He didn't need to do a personal check, there were instruments to warn them if something went wrong, but it was a habit. Now he trotted across the cavern, following his sister to where he could just see the refreshing greenery of the garden.

Kryslie was already sitting cross legged in one of the small clearings. Tymos took off his boots and socks, and made use of a rock outcrop nearby. He began to feel a refreshing breeze on his face, which was actually the way he sensed the energy of Earth.

"If you are drawing that much energy, sis, you must have been using a lot. I could have helped you…"

"I managed just fine," she said without opening her eyes. "The worst of it was this past week, and today – everyone was like taut springs."

Tymos studied the garden, considering how he could improve it further, may be changing some of the plants… At the moment, it gave the impression of a forest glade above ground - the high rock ceiling had been painted a pale blue, and indirect lighting gave it a daylight effect. The day cycle above was mimicked here by lights changing to sunset colours and then fading to dark. The plants here had taken time to grow and begin to thrive, but now the light and temperature settings were just right. New plants would take time to adjust, so maybe that was a task for another time.

His mind wandered from the garden to other chambers within the system. Partly because the manufactured breeze that recycled and refreshed the air brought a whiff of something cooking.

"At least we won't have to cook while we are here," Kryslie echoed his thought. She had offered to help every now and then, but the Tymoreans assigned to the domestic tasks were horrified at the thought of a Great One – cooking and serving them. She had stopped offering.

The missionaries that were actual field agents, had long since accepted the Great Ones presence on Earth, and worked easily with them. It sent Tymos thinking again of the new arrivals, and his mind went to sensing them.

Aloud, he said, "It was Morin who answered me."

"I knew that rascal had potential, but if he is here now, he must have really applied himself to his studies." Kryslie was impressed.

They had met Morin when he was perhaps only ten years old. That had been in the early stages of the war on Tymorea. They had met him again after the cities had woken up from the long stasis sleep. He had wanted to serve the Great Ones then, but he was a commoner, the son of a mutant, and hardly literate. He was however, one of the rare mutants that were telepathic.

Kryslie let her mind seek the boy, no, he'd be a young man now. "He's had enough training to have developed adequate mind shields," she remarked.

"But has forgotten that other telepaths can pick up the cheeky thoughts that keep bubbling out of his mind," Tymos countered. "I don't think he realises that we are here."

"We were both tightly shielded when we arrived," Kryslie reminded him.

A voice spoke to them from a short distance away. "Welcome back, Great Ones."

Both Tymos and Kryslie turned to look at the owner of the voice, not surprised that it was Vincent, the second in charge of the base, and the Tymorean chief medic. He gave them the traditional bow, of one greeting a person of higher rank.

"Is there anything here that needs doing?" Tymos asked.

"Nothing that requires the presence of a Great One. We were not expecting you to return yet."

"We needed a break and the WSRA computers need two weeks to run their various algorithms on the results of all the tests," Kryslie told the older man. "Where else would we go?"

"I am sure that there are many places on this beautiful world that you haven't seen yet."

"We need to keep available," Tymos shrugged. "What else brings you?"

"Some messages have arrived from His Majesty and your friends," Vincent revealed.

"Good timing," Kryslie commented, then said, "You've some newcomers."

Vincent, who was a tall man, in his seventh decade, with dark hair greying at the sides, smiled and reported. "Three. Harlo and Tennic are with Olassa, doing a training placement. And my brother sent a young aide to assist Daniel. I believe that you recommended him."

Tymos grinned, and asked, "What do you think of him?"

"He is an excellent choice. Has an insatiable appetite for knowledge…of any kind." Vincent was smiling. "He is just what Daniel needs. However, he is currently fretting because he thinks he lost someone along the path of the long range beam. Perhaps you can reassure him when you go to see Daniel to get your messages. They are in the communications room."

Even though Vincent was the brother to one of the Tymorean Governors, he technically had no authority over Great Ones, except when acting in his role of mission physician. However, both Tymos and Kryslie were still in the habit of listening to their elders, so they accepted the suggestion. Now, at least, the calmness of the base had relaxed them. Vincent, no doubt, had sensed the tension in them both as soon as they had arrived.

The communications cavern came off a rock passage that led off the arrival cavern, but on the far side from the garden. They could have walked the distance easily enough, and usually did, but sometimes, like now, it amused Tymos and Kryslie to transmit the short distance, or 'flit'. Their teachers back on Tymorea had usually frowned on the practice.

Daniel was talking on the video communicator link to a mature blond haired woman. Kryslie recognised Olassa, Vincent's niece and daughter of Tymorean Governor Xyron. She and Tymos waited by the entrance, not wishing to disturb the conversation. She noticed that the rock walls in here had been painted in a light pastel shade of green. It was restful, and she wondered if it had been Vincent's idea.

Since the missionaries had finished setting up the basic facilities, gradual improvements had been made to the caverns she and Tymos had created. The lighting in here was indirect, originally powered from the local power grid, but now generated using the radiation outside.

Unlike Vincent, Daniel hadn't sensed their presence. He had none of the Tymorean power, even if he was the coordinator of the missionaries.

"I thought Morin was meant to be in here?" Tymos whispered.

Kryslie let her empathic senses roam, since Morin might have been shielding his mind. "Kitchen. Seeking consolation in food."

They heard Daniel suddenly spin his chair around on its wheels. Olassa was staring at them from the screen, eyes wide with surprise.

"Finish your conversation, Daniel. We are in no rush," Kryslie told him.

"We have," their father told them. Olassa had already closed the connection.

"So, what's doing? What did Olassa have to say?"

"It was a routine report," Daniel Ward brushed the question aside. "I have private messages for you both from His Majesty and your friends. Will I route them to your personal chambers or do you want to read them here."

"Here will do," Tymos decided, going to a spare terminal and brushing the activator plate.

Daniel used his portable data pad to effect the transfer. He put the one from the Tymorean High King Governor, his children's foster father, at the top of the list. Once he saw that their attention was on the messages, he hustled out to attend to other matters.

After a short while, Tymos's attention wandered from reading about events back on Tymorea. "I'll read these later," he decided. "Will you send them to the data pad in my chamber?"

Kryslie glanced at him, knew what he was thinking, and said, "Ok, but I don't think you need to worry about the WSRA computer losing us – or it would have done so as soon as we applied."

Tymos gave her a sheepish grin. "I know, I know, but this process is too important for us to get careless."

"Well, don't let Markus think you don't trust his programming. He and Arnuth did a massive job, helping the WSRA to program that algorithm, and they must have added the subroutine you wrote."

"No, I will tell him he did a great job," Tymos assured her.

Kryslie was preparing return messages when a voice greeted her.

"Krys! I saw Tymos so I figured you were here."

Lexina was one of the first friends Kryslie had made when she had first gone to Tymorea, and she had wrangled a place in the Earth Mission when Daniel had requested domestic staff. Now she was helping to create space scanning capabilities for them.

"How are things going?" Kryslie asked.

"Once you and Tymos helped solve the glitch that stopped us linking to the Earth satellites, we've really progressed. We have access to the Tymorean out-system probe drones – they were placed a few days ago. It gives us coverage within this solar system and a few light years beyond." Lexina had trained under her father and was a qualified astronomics specialist. "Do you want to come and see what we've got?"

In the huge operations cavern, Tymos was in one corner, head close to that of Markus, looking at something on the computer there.

Lexina led the way to another of the dozen screens, one showing the blackness of space, and began manipulation a touch pad.

"Probe one is out beyond the transuranic zone, I have it waiting for a comet that is due to pass close to Earth. Probe two is in-system, orbiting the moon. The first of the two bases is ready to be commissioned. Shuttles are coming and going every day. Want to look?"

Lexina easily programmed the probe to show the shuttle landing pad, where pods of supplies were being dropped from the cargo hold onto motorised wheeled trolleys and driven off by figures in EA suits.

She moved the focus to a point several miles from the base, where a structure was being assembled.

"Radio telescope," Kryslie identified. "There are meant to be radio spectroscopes and several other receivers."

"How soon will you go up once the staff are appointed?" Lexina asked.

"Since the majority of the staff have never been in space, I expect there will need to be a period of training," Kryslie proposed. "I wonder if there have been volunteers from the media to go up for the commissioning."

"Knock your best friend out competition," a voice stated.

Kryslie turned and grinned at the pale featured young man, who was standing quite formally, but to her senses seemed to be a bouncing bundle of excitement.

"Great One, I am ready to serve you," Morin greeted her with the traditional bow, but it was quickly completed. He was grinning with self-satisfaction.

"Morin, you've done us proud," Kryslie greeted him. "I am told that you are Daniel's chief aide."

"Yes, and I really want to thank you for giving me this chance. Do you think I can ever get into space, too?"

Tymos wondered over. "Morin, it's great to see you."

The young man bowed to Tymos with the same enthusiasm as his previous gesture. "I'd really like to go into space…"

"You already have, you know," Tymos told him. "You must have, to have got here."

"Um. We went from the spaceport at Reva to some big chamber somewhere, and then a few blinks later we were here, and all I wanted to do was heave…oh, um, sorry."

"Quite a few of those who try out for the Tymorean Space fleet have that trouble too. They usually decide they'd rather stay planetside," Kryslie suggested. "Besides, you have only just got here – there must be so much you still have to learn about Earth."

"If you stop seeming to be bouncing around like a kangaroo," Tymos teased.

"What's a kangaroo?" Morin asked immediately.

"See? Something you haven't learnt yet," Tymos challenged. "Anyway, before you can change postings, you need to learn the job you were given, and know it so well that you can train a successor."

Tymos grinned again, Morin's enthusiasm was a pleasant change from the months of full on testing and taunt nerves of the WSRA applicants. He moved back to the computer terminal in the corner, and pulled over a chair and his fingers began to type on the press pad.

Kryslie sat beside Lexina, and felt Morin almost leaning on her to see over her shoulder.

"Morin?" Daniel called impatiently.

"Yes, Boss. " Morin jumped up and looked at the speaker,

"Didn't you pass on the message? Larissa has dinner ready, and she doesn't want it to get cold."

"Sorry. Great Ones, I had to tell you dinner was ready. And she had made a surprise since she heard you two were back here."

"I smelt something delicious," Kryslie admitted, rising.

Lexina put the probe into a higher orbit and set the scanners to ring an alarm if anything needed attending. "Hey, Markus, get your head out of cyberspace and come eat."

Vincent and several other missionaries were already in the dining cavern, waiting for Larissa to serve them. Vincent seemed relaxed, but two of the other four people present seemed to be ruffled by having to wait to eat. However, as soon as they saw the Tymos and Kryslie walk in, they rose, bowed, and murmured, "Great Ones."

Tymos spoke to them, since he knew all the missionaries personally. "Congratulations, Ethan. I hear your wife had the baby. Give her our regards when you see her."

"I will, Great one," Ethan smiled.

To one of the others, he said, "You did a great job with that environmental campaign, Kevial. I believe the pygmy possum population is on the rise."

"It is Great One, but I am taking a sabbatical back home to see if I can find ways to make them safer."

"Tymos, why don't you sit down? Larissa is waiting to serve," Daniel said pointedly.

Vincent, watching quietly, saw an expression of mild outrage come over the domestic manager's face. She was a stickler for protocol, and felt the Great Ones should be treated like gods.

She made her feelings plain by dishing food the Tymos and Kryslie first, making sure they had enough, then coming to him, the other missionaries and base staff, and finally to Daniel and Morin.

Daniel seemed oblivious to the implied disrespect, and simply began eating. Vincent noted that Kryslie did not, and was sure she and Tymos were talking silently to each other. He knew that they missed very little.

"This is excellent, Larissa," Kryslie said, still having not touched her food.

Larissa's smile of pleasure turned to a look of concern, when she realised that Kryslie was making no move to eat.

"I am thinking that you do such a good job managing the domestic side of things, that you are the perfect person to take over from Daniel. I think he's been working too hard, and I am going to insist that he has a two week break."

Daniel stopped eating, his fork half way to his mouth. He would have spoken, but he saw Vincent make a slight hand gesture indicating for him to say nothing.

Kryslie was watching Larissa, who seemed to be trying to talk, but not quite knowing what to say. "Surely you don't think it beyond you, since you seem to think that Daniel is the next to least person around here."

"But…I can't give you orders, Great One. I can't tell you what to do. And who will cook and keep things running around here?"

Kryslie shrugged. "I can do that."

"I can't let you do that…"

"Are you telling me that I can't? That I am incapable?"

"No Great One of course not," Larissa was fighting tears now.

Kryslie relented. "I don't know if you make a habit of serving Daniel last, but from now on, I expect you to treat him with the respect due to his position as Coordinator of the Earth Mission. When Tymos and I are not here, he is the highest ranking member of the mission."

Her mind was saying, "But he's not a Tymorean. You should be in charge, or Vincent."

Kryslie made no apology for seeming to read her mind. "No, he's not a Tymorean, but he is a damn good coordinator. Actually, he's a brilliant one. Do you know why? And do you know why he is able to find you all the high quality Earth food stuffs for you to do your magic on? He was born on this world. He knows the people, knows the different cultures. The Governors could not have chosen a person better suited to the job."

"But he treats you like…"

Tymos interrupted. "Don't say it! Krys and I might out rank everyone here, but we are not administrators and we do not have the time to do that job any more. And you can be perfectly sure that if we have an issue with anyone, we will deal with it."

While Larissa's attention was on Tymos, Kryslie began to eat. The domestic manager glanced from one to the other, guessed she was dismissed and walked back into the kitchen alcove.

"You didn't need to make an issue…" Daniel began. He stopped when he saw the determined expression on Kryslie's face.

"Yes I did. But I won't make her do your job."

Kryslie turned her attention to eating, and everyone else kept quiet and copied her example.

Lexina, sitting next to Kryslie, murmured, "She's good at what she does, and she isn't a bad person."

"I know that – you notice I didn't say I'd send her home. I just wanted her to think…"

"You haven't been around much since she took over from Jenala and Beth. And I doubt that she knows he's your natural father. Though it might amuse you to know that all the newer missionaries, the ones you haven't worked with much, and who still look at you with awe, wouldn't change places with Daniel for anything. They can't imagine being in charge of a mission that has two Great Ones dropping in at odd intervals."

Kryslie had to laugh. "Put that way, you make us sound like ogres."

Morin, whose eyes were like saucers, because he was privy to the exchange, dared to ask, "What are ogres?"

After dinner, Kryslie outraged Larissa again by helping to bring the dirty dishes back to the domestic cavern for washing. The area had the feel of a big airy kitchen. You could forget the fact you were underground, as there were screens on several of the walls that projected Earth landscapes, and mimicked the time of day, the same way as the garden did.

"I should be doing that, Great One," she protested again.

"Larissa, Tymos and I would get awfully bored and awfully out of condition if all we did all day was stand on a pedestal and have servants do absolutely everything for us. We'd get so fat and full or ourselves…not a very great image to strive for."

Even while stacking the dishes in the dishwasher, Kryslie had been building a mind picture and sending it to Larissa. The woman was horrified at what she thought was her own imagination, but trying not to giggle aloud. "Besides, who do you think gave your predecessors all the recipes you have been improving on? Anyway, the people of Earth don't have any conception of what we are, so we have to be able to look after ourselves. When we are away from here Tym, and I alternate cooking."

Larissa's eyes were wide as Kryslie blithely went on, "When we are working with the humans, we have to act a part – we can't just do what we like then."

It seemed now, that Larissa had finally understood the point that Kryslie wanted her to see, and now she was to be rewarded with a special task.

"I have a favour to ask of you, Larissa."

"I'm here to serve Great One."

"You are probably not aware that Tymos and I were born on this world or that Daniel is our biological father."

Larissa's eyes had grown huge again and she was unconsciously shaking her head.

"I'm sure you have noticed how hard he works."

The head movement of the other woman changed to nodding as Kryslie went on, "What I would like you to do is to see that he has regular meals, takes breaks every now and then…"

"You can rely on me, Great One."

Larissa beamed with pride and took amusement from the fact that Kryslie did know how to use the amazing chamber that washed dishes for her.

Tymos was seated in front of a computer screen, scrolling through search results when he sensed Kryslie's return. She gave his screen her attention, long enough to deduce what he was searching for, and then looked at the screen Markus was looking at.

"So bro, what's the conclusion? Is your little scavenger program still active in cyberspace? And is the WSRA computer immune?"

"Seems to be," Tymos confirmed. "I can find no mention of you, or me, in the world cyber archives. I have been looking as far back as the archives go. However, it doesn't affect images."

"Does it alter or adjust the names in any captions?" Kryslie asked.

"Mostly deletes the captions. Any way – for the WSRA computer, I have added a subroutine so that it won't give out info about us."

"Should be enough," Kryslie decided, not admitting to relief. "So, no one should be able to link us to ourselves of past times."

Daniel bustled in and spoke to Markus. "What's the status?"

Markus merely handed Daniel a data padd, and let the coordinator read the information there for himself.

When he had finished, he saw both his children looking at him and he gave them a cryptic smile. "The WSRA computer will need a major service after this effort," he said wryly. "It has completed three sorts and has another fifty-seven variations to go. You will pleased to know that you did not come out on top of those three."

Tymos knew Daniel was teasing them. "What were the first three looking for," he asked, as expected.

"Floor sweepers, paper shredders and clerical staff."

Kryslie snorted. "I knew that program was detailed."

"Now, those remaining sort algorithms are going to take time so, are your Greatnesses going to spend all of your time here watching our computer monitoring the WSRA computer or will you finally take a holiday?"

"We've scarcely been here an hour. Are you tired of us already?" Kryslie teased her father.

"It has occurred to me that, in the decade since we arrived here, and in all the time you were here before that, neither of you have had a vacation. I take one every year, and the others who work here have taken twice that."

Markus, still watching the computer, was chuckling.

Kryslie knew her father was leading up to something and waited.

"Have you researched an appropriate vacation spot?" Tymos asked, standing up and stretching, while playing the game he also perceived.

"I thought, perhaps, Florida," Daniel began. "Lots of water sports, natural water habitats, lots of flora and fauna to study, fishing etc."

"Have you perhaps a suggested itinerary?" Kryslie grinned.

"Well now," Daniel seemed to consider. He turned to a pile of data pads next to a computer screen, and seemed to shuffle them. "I think I have seen one around here."

Morin trotted in with a data padd and handed it to Daniel.

"Thank you, Morin," he said and then added an aside to his children. "Best assistant you could have recommended. Don't know what I would do without him."

Kryslie grinned. Daniel was probably unaware that Morin could pick up on his preoccupied thoughts. Daniel checked the padd before handing it to Kryslie. She held it so her twin could also read it.

"Seems interesting," Kryslie murmured, reading what read like a detailed tourist spiel for the Everglades in Florida. "Terra 1 is down that way…we've never been there."

In Morin's mind was the amused thought that Daniel wanted them to check out the Chief of the WSRA, who was having a break and visiting the area.

"You will probably see more than enough of that place, shortly," Daniel said quickly. "Since all the lunar shuttles come and go from there."

Tymos couldn't sense the full reason behind the suggestion, only that Daniel wasn't sure enough of his reason to state it openly.

"Why are you suggesting we shadow Basoli?"

Daniel relaxed enough to grin faintly. His children always seemed to know more than anyone else. The Commander-in Chief of the WSRA was not even mentioned on the screen.

"Nothing definite," he said, becoming serious. "Basoli will be your boss. Things I have read about him, things he's said in interviews, and things young Bynan, his PA, has said about him, make me suspect some latent xenophobic tendencies. I might be wrong there, but there are also some subtle undercurrents in political circles about the WSRA expansion."

Kryslie commented. "The WSRA is a politically and geographically neutral body. It funds itself, and no one country has any control of it."

Daniel shrugged. "Like I said, I am not expecting any trouble. So – have a nice vacation."

Within hours of arriving at the resort in Everglades City, and settling into the small guest cabin that Morin had booked for them, Tymos had used the free Wi-Fi to link his data padd to the resorts computer system. Even though the computer had the latest cybersecurity protocols, it was no barrier to one with Tymos's skills.

He knew which rooms the government party were assigned, where they had booked to eat, what meeting room they were using, and the names of all the party, including the security team that travelled with Florida's Governor. He inserted a program to alert him when any of the party arranged any kind of activity.

Then, he and Kryslie set about learning their way around the resort, splitting up to cover the extensive area in a shorter time. When they settled into one of the restaurants for an early dinner, they compared notes, and mental images of strategic places. From those images, they could, if needed, transmit themselves in moments to the respective locations.

The restaurant they had chosen was the one where the Government party would be dining, later in the evening. It looked out over the golf course, and beyond that glimpses of the Gulf of Mexico were visible.

They were just starting their dessert when the flurry at the entrance caught their attention. One glance that way was enough to confirm that the Governor's security were checking out the area.

"Former military," Tymos remarked. "Makes you wonder why the Governor thinks he needs the fuss."

"Daniel didn't mention any concerns about him," Kryslie remarked in turn. "He's more likely to need someone to warn him when he might hit his head. He's tall enough."

They recognised the Howard Treswick from his appearances on the televid broadcasts, but it was the first time they had seen him in person.

"You didn't mention that the Secretary of State would be here, bro."

"He must be just here for the day – there is no suite booked for him."

"Would he be using an alias?"

"I don't think so – he's too well known. Though the security might be for him."

Tymos's data padd pinged, and he checked the message. "Change that – the room booking just went through the system."

Kryslie gave him a mental nudge. "Basoli just came in. He's shorter than I expected. He can't be much taller than you."

"Then the other one must be the environment minister," Tymos remarked. He stopped looking at the group and turned his apparent attention back to his cheesecake dessert.

He and Kryslie didn't linger over the rest of their meal. She went directly back to the cabin, but he detoured to the meeting room that the official party had booked and slipped inside. The room was deserted at that hour and he was able to place an unobtrusive listening device in one of the decorative side tables. It was of Tymorean make, and would be undetectable should the security men scan the room for such things.

Kryslie had usurped the reclining chair and was watching the tri vid news when her brother returned.

"I feel we should be doing something more than just lazing around," she admitted, when Tymos flopped into the other chair.

"This beats fretting about test results. And it was a reasonable idea for us to observe Basoli." He was putting his data padd down as it dinged again.

"We can't exactly find out much by just watching and eavesdropping. He is hardly going to casually say he's xenophobic, on a world where aliens are just science fiction."

"Yeah, well, that's true, but we might be able to get an idea of his attitudes to other things. Anyway, he and the others are safe enough in the hotel, and we can enjoy ourselves for a bit. Surely the Guardians don't expect us to work all day every day."

"Maybe not," Kryslie finally admitted. "The news just mentioned that there is a lottery for places on the moon shuttle when Lunar 1 is opened - and a fee of one thousand dollars just for the chance of a place."

"Did they say when it was to be officially opened?"

"New Year's Day, so just over three months from now. Time enough to get the lucky attendees some training. And guess who will be officiating?"

Kryslie had shielded her mind before asking the question – forcing her twin to guess.

"Basoli?"

"He'll be one. Who else?"

"UWN President Hughes?"

"And?"

"Your friend from the Imperium?"

"His alleged Eminence, bin Halil, is not my friend, and yes. Diplomatic of the WSRA though. But I am hoping that the new WSRA grunts won't be established at the base by then."

"I might see what I can find relating to the training for Lunar 1 personnel," Tymos mused. "I know the senior staff for Lunar 1 have been training for a while."

"So, what do you plan to do tomorrow?" Kryslie asked.

"I'll mingle with the guests. What about you?"

"Well, since Daniel forced this vacation on us…I think I might spend the day in or around the pool. I'll monitor the meetings while I appear to be asleep. Tomorrow, I will mingle!"

Kryslie floated on an inflatable raft in the small lake that was the resort's swimming pool and listened with some interest to Basoli's presentation to the government representatives. He was proposing an expansion of WSRA's Terra One base, located on the site of the old NASA rocket launching facility and the former air force base. He had a strong case for his proposals. As he pointed out, once the lunar base was operational, regular shuttles would be launching, and these were not silent events. She couldn't fault the research that had been done, and the environmental impact studies. He believed the idea was feasible, although there would likely be opposition to the WSRA acquiring more land to use as a sound buffer and fear about possible contamination from the shuttle exhaust and fuel storage.

For now though, he was sounding out the other men and soliciting their support. These were informal discussions, and no decisions would be made until his formal presentation to the President.

Four days of listening to talking, even while enjoying the attractions of the resort, made both Tymos and Kryslie feel the need to do some vigorous activities. Their personal energies had been restored, and more. So when Tymos's computer spy program showed that the Governor, and Basoli were booked on a tour of the Everglades the following day, they made their own plans. They organised a rental powerboat from Everglade City and arranged to pick it up at a dock not far from where the Linus Mc Lellan, an elite cruising power boat booked by the Governor, berthed overnight.

Instead of trying to sleep, they packed some snacks and water in their small back packs and chose to jog from the resort to the dock, so they would be on the water before Basoli and the Governor arrived.

The night was still warm, and they both wore shorts and short sleeved polo tops – casual but not too touristy, and rubber soled sport shoes. They kept their speed down to a jog as they followed the road since they weren't in a hurry, and there were still cars coming with relative frequency. As it grew later, the traffic lessened, and they allowed themselves to run. There was no one to see how fast they moved, which was faster than most Olympic sprinters.

They slowed every now and then, to drink some water, or get a feel for a new section of the route. Neither of them was breathing hard, or even sweating much. Keeping fit had been trained into them when they were still students back on Tymorea.

As they neared Everglades City, they slowed their pace to a walk, and felt the sea breeze beginning to strengthen. They both began to sense the updrafts that presaged a thunderstorm. The clouds that came over to hide the night sky, were already thickening.

When the first fat, heavy drops of rain began to fall, and then became a torrent, they didn't try to find shelter. The storm was moving quickly and within minutes it had passed. In its wake, the air was pleasant and cool and for a while, the humidity was gone. The sky was already beginning to clear again.

They continued walking towards where they knew Captain Stanley's Boat Shed was located. The map they had studied back in their cabin at the resort, was clear in their minds. The street lighting gave them enough illumination for most of the way, but once they were near the area where the tour and hire boat docks were located, only a few lights were on.

One light was at the berth of the Linus Mc Lellan, and Tymos paused to study the features of the boat while Kryslie read the board that showed images of the boat's interior and maps of its usual route.

At that time, an observer – had there been one – might have noticed a change in Kryslie's eyes. The board wasn't getting much of the light, and she adjusted them to see better in the dim light. This caused the shape of her eyes to alter subtly, and her eyes now glowed faintly as different wavelengths of radiation reflected off them.

As she studied the sketch diagram of the boat's interior, and the images, her mind was correlating them with details her twin was noting from his external look, and his mind knew what she had read and memorised.

The Linus Mc Lellan had a crew of four, and was able to take groups of up to six people in comfort. Unlike most of the local tourist boats, it was glassed in on all sides and covered over so that air-conditioning was possible when the boat was under way. The board gave its length as 18 foot, so when it travelled, it needed to keep to the wider channels, even with its flat hull and twin jet engines.

When they had seen enough, Tymos and Kryslie headed for Captain Stanley's boat shed, and decided to sit on the associated dock and wait for morning when the place would be open.

"It's not exactly the best time of year to come here," Kryslie commented, more for the sake of hearing something other than the silence. Her eyes were watching the distant flashes of sheet lightning, as another storm passed to the south of them. She and Tymos were sitting on the edge of the dock, legs dangling just above the water, slowly drying out after being doused by the earlier heavy rain.

"Less tourists," Tymos shrugged, "And I suppose, if you rarely have time for a break, you make do."

"So we have that in common with Basoli," Kryslie shrugged. "I wonder if that was why he and the Governor are taking that air-conditioned gin palace."

"Might be to protect them from the mozzies," Tymos suggested.

Kryslie laughed. The little flying pests had tried to swarm them, but with their personal energies at a high level, and enough free energy remaining in the wake of the storm, they were both emitting some of it like a repellor field around them.

"It should be settled and more pleasant for a while, this morning at least," Kryslie predicted. It had been quite a while since they had been able to sit and simply feel the flow of energies around them.

They watched the eastern horizon start to get lighter, and waited for the boat rental shed to open. Two four seater airboats roared past, polluting the air with noise, before they stood up and walked to see about their own rental.

The boat hand, who was wearing camo-patterned cargo shorts and a white tee shirt under a dark hoodie, took them to a four seater centre console power boat, that was tied to the dock and gently rocking from the wake of the airboats.

"You've driven one of these boats before?"

"A few years ago," Tymos claimed. "Not here though. I don't expect to have any trouble."

"It's only got a 6 horse motor. That'll only let you go up to the max allowed speed. Don't want to go fast, might hit some critter in the water. A gator or a manatee. How far to you want to go?"

Kryslie inserted, "We want to see what we can of the different environments, make some sketches, take some photos."

"You greenies?" the boat hand asked. He had stepped down into the boat and putting the key in the ignition. He gestured for them to come down.

"We wouldn't like to see this environment damaged," Tymos told him. "But we're not irrational about it."

The man gave a snort that might have been smothered laughter, as if he remembered an amusing incident, but he kept to his business. "Got four floatation jackets under the front seat. The fire extinguisher is under the back seat, usually keep it in the clip in between the seats while the boats on the water."

He raised the padded seat cover on the rear seat and pulled it out as well as two plastic paddles. "There's a bucket under there too, and an anchor and line. Not an idea to anchor anywhere, but if you pull into a bank, it'll hold you there if there's a wind blowing."

Tymos and Kryslie were instinctively balancing the boat, even though with its flat bottom, it was quite stable, even with their instructor moving around.

"There's a torch and navigation chart, and the other needs in the console, and the radio. Put it on once you get under way – keep it on channel B – that's the one I listen out on. You'll hear warnings if there's a storm coming up. Weather can change awful sudden in these parts – specially this time of year. You got insect repellent? You'll need it – or you'll be eaten alive once the sun warms up."

"In our bag," Kryslie took hers off her back and rested it on the front seat, taking out a folding wide brimmed hat and sunglasses. "Sun screen too," she claimed, although that was something else she and Tymos didn't need.

"Right then," the man said, more to himself. "Boat's meant to be back before dark. If you're going to be late, call in. But the boat isn't set up for night – hasn't any lights, so you'll need to have the torch on so other boats can see you."

"Thanks," Kryslie said, as the man returned to the dock, hardly making the boat rock.

He paused to watch them as Tymos started the engine, Kryslie freed the mooring line from the metal cleat on the dock. He seemed satisfied that they knew what they were doing, and turned to return to the shed.

Kryslie decided to play passenger, and as Tymos took them out into the main channel at idling speed, she took his bag and retrieved his hat and glasses. The little motor barely intruded on the silence, nor did it frighten the now waking birds into stopping their morning song and chatter.

Tymos let the boat direct itself while he donned the hat and glasses. Now he, and his sister looked like the twins they were, and at a distance, might have been taken for two men.

Daylight was increasing, but the sun had yet to rise above the trees and low buildings, as Tymos motored past the Linus Mc Lellan at its dock. On the landward side, a van was unloading insulated ice boxes and these were being passed on board. On the water side, a crewman was leaning out one of the starboard windows and using a long handled window brush on the outside of the glass. He called out a greeting, and Tymos cheerfully returned it. Kryslie had a pocket sized camera out and snapped a picture as they went past, then waved and grinned.

The quiet noise of their motor was suddenly masked as the Mc Lellan's motor burbled into life. It was a diesel, unlike their motor which ran on a synthetic biofuel. It wasn't scheduled to leave until nine o'clock, but its passengers might be arriving at any time.

"If you do a slow circuit around this inlet, I'll take photos," Kryslie suggested.

They didn't want to be hovering near the larger boat when the governor and his guest arrived, just where they could keep it in sight without their interest being obvious.

The inlet that formed the marina basin was quite large, as it also accommodated charter boats that took groups out to fish in the Gulf, or in along the 10,000 islands.

One of the charter companies had a dockside store, and Tymos pulled alongside and let his sister clamber off the boat. While she went in to buy some more bottled water and fresh packaged sandwiches, he had a perfect excuse to look around, although his attention was on the Mc Lellan's dock where a white limousine had just pulled up.

Kryslie returned and passed her purchases to her brother before climbing back down to the boat.

"Governor Treswick, his wife, and Basoli went onto the boat," Tymos told her. "Only two of the ubiquitous men in black shades were with them. One went on the boat – the other returned to the limo and went off in it."

"Since we know where the boat will go, do you want to head out in front of them?" Kryslie proposed.

Tymos didn't bother verbalising his agreement. When Kryslie cast of the mooring line, he backed away from the dock and headed towards the channel heading towards the Everglades Waterway. He maintained the slow speed, and she made a pretence of pointing at interesting things and taking photos. They had only gone a short distance down the water way when the Mc Lellan passed them, the rooster tail from the jet engines just breaking the water surface.

Without looking at the larger boat, Kryslie thought at her brother. "They are all getting nice and comfortable, the men are having a light lager, and the Governor's wife is drinking fruit juice."

Tymos chuckled. "I'd rather be out in the open air. We can see more without the glass and roof."

A boat, similar to their own, went past and caught up to the Mc Lellan. Tymos commented, "So that is where that guy went. Is he an escort, or a scout?"

"Who is going to try and annoy either of those important men out here? If the news media were in the know, they would have been at the dock. Were they?" Kryslie asked.

Tymos gave the negative as a thought. He kept the boat near the edge of the channel, as the sound of an airboat grew louder. The Mc Lellan had disappeared around a bend in the channel, and was hidden by a grove of mangrove trees. The sound of the airboat decreased after it had passed them and turned the same bend.

Kryslie said, "I reckon it was Vincent who gave Daniel the idea for this enforced holiday."

"Probably, but he was right. We haven't had a chance to see much of Earth's natural places. And the Earth's aura is very strong here. We haven't had time to really refresh our energies lately."

"And lazing in the pool these last few days was doing what?"

Tymos shrugged. "Tymorea has nothing like this area."

"This feels like make work all the same."

Kryslie stopped speaking the rest of her thought, as a shiver went through her. It had nothing to do with the cool breeze their passage was creating. Tymos half turned, and met her gaze. He shared her sudden foreboding.

"Did you sense anything?"

"Nothing definite…but maybe you had better turn on the radio."

"We'll both know if a storm is coming…" Tymos considered, but he was doing as his sister suggested.

The channel meandered, sometimes there was a straight section and they had sight of the Mc Lellan. At other times it was lost behind trees, cedar now, or visible across a section of

Sawgrass prairie.

Tymos let Kryslie take the helm, and he sat on one of the seats and brought out his palm computer and connected it to the satellite news and weather service. He found little of immediate interest, and the weather forecast had not changed.

By eleven thirty, they were approaching the private island where the Mc Lellan usually docked for lunch. Kryslie motored past, giving the larger boat only a passing glance of recognition.

Tymos brought up a navigation chart on his computer, studied it, and then studied their surroundings. "There," he pointed to a narrow channel, heading into the cedars, about thirty metres ahead.

When they were level, Kryslie decided, "That will do." It wasn't really a channel, as it didn't go very far, but was big enough for the boat, and provided shade. She turned the boat and backed it into the opening. Once in, she let the boat drift to one bank, and used the short mooring line to snag an overhanging branch and stopped the motor. There was very little current, so they wouldn't drift out.

"So, is there anything happening that concerns us?" Kryslie asked her brother, who had finally closed his palm computer.

She had caught movement in the water and now, something that had two eyes and two rows of scaly humps was looking their way.

"Not really. The storms they are forecasting shouldn't happen until late evening. The Mc Lellan should be back by then. I really don't know what gave you the shivers earlier."

The feeling hadn't been strong enough for a premonition, but Kryslie took it as a warning of danger, and a need to be alert. Tymos didn't dismiss it, but they had nothing to act on. He put his palm computer in his pocket and lay down on the seat along the port side of the boat.

"Wake me when it's time to leave," he said, tipping his hat over his face and pretending to sleep.

Kryslie moved to the other seat, and sat looking out into the channel. Part of the view beyond it was hidden by trees, the rest was open sawgrass prairie. Except for the distant drone of airboats, all seemed still and quiet. She took off her hat and fanned her face, for without the breeze caused by the boat movement, the day was warm and humid.

She heard the drone of mosquitos, hovering no closer than three inches from any part of her. She tuned out their buzzing and listened to the other little sounds of life around her – the occasional chirp of a bird, or the splash of some creature entering the water.

Then she opened her mind to seek the Mc Lellan, where the passengers were starting to eat an alfresco meal. The insects were being kept at bay by use of a number of low power ultrasound devices. It reminded her of her sandwiches and she dragged her pack closer to get them out, As she did, her brother's hand reached out, so she could get him his.

Even though she tried to concentrate on the things she had seen as they travelled along the waterway, her mind kept returning to the airboats that had passed them. Some of them had packs on board, so the current operators of those boats were intending to camp overnight – perhaps taking their time to get down to the southern end of the waterway. After a while, she managed to put herself into a kind of meditative state, hyper aware of everything around her - until a sudden jolt, like from a low energy electric fence startled her.

Kryslie instinctively checked the area immediately around her, stretched her awareness to the Linus Mc Lellan. Basoli and the Governor were talking softly and having an after lunch drink. Whatever her senses had detected, it wasn't nearby. She glanced at her twin. He had sat up at the moment she had felt the tingle. Now he was using his palm computer, checking to see if there was any information available on the newsfeeds.

"Smoke," Kryslie finally announced, having smelt the faintest trace on the fitful breeze.

Tymos in turn sniffed the air. "Yes, but there is no report of a fire."

They both scanned the small section of the horizon that they could see, for the breeze had come from there.

Kryslie pulled he rope free from the branch, and started the motor, she could move towards the opening of the tiny inlet without needing to turn. As they emerged, they could see more of the horizon beyond the sawgrass. Now they could see a narrow column of smoke, rising up and beginning to spread out.

"I can't sense a storm," Kryslie spoke aloud, knowing her twin would take her meaning as, "the fire wasn't stared by lightning."

Tymos reached for the radio and sent out a call on the emergency frequency. A coast guard operator picked it up and switched him to a different frequency, but not the other one marked on the radio. Although he could not give the exact location of the fire, he gave the operator his position from the GPS built into his palm computer, and the direction from there to the smoke column, and received assurance that the information would be passed on.

Kryslie watched the smoke as she emerged into the channel, aware that fires in the Everglades could spread fast. It was a wise idea to begin heading back towards the city, particularly as the breeze was strengthening and bringing a stronger smell of smoke.

A warning was being broadcast over the radio, the position of the fire and the direction it was heading.

In only a fraction of a minute, Kryslie had pinpointed the location on a mental map of the area and calculated, "That's only twenty miles."

"The sea breeze should start to come in soon," Tymos predicted, "Though the air is unstable."

They motored past the island, noting that the crew of the Mc Lellan were trotting back to the boat with the folding table and chairs, and the three guests were walking quickly, urged on by their two escorting guards.

"So long as we don't get a storm here," Kryslie commented. "There must be at least fifteen airboats on the water, and not all of them will be continuing south."

The airboats were taking turns to report their position and intentions to the base stations of the hire companies. Some were even now making for the nearest refuge – safe areas prepared for emergencies like this. Those continuing south, were moving at their top speed to get out of the line of the fire.

The sound of the diesel jet engines of the Linus Mc Lellan carried to where Kryslie was idling their boat forward, but soon it was overwhelmed by the first of the airboats returning. She let them go past, intending to stay just ahead of the Mc Lellan.

Already the smoke was thickening as the breeze from the fire increased in strength. Visibility was getting poorer, so the boats would need to slow down as they navigated the channels. Added to that, the steering of the Mc Lellan would be harder at lower speeds and it would need to stay mid channel to avoid hitting the bank, or the overreaching trees.

The nimbler air boats required less water and could go closer in, so they passed the larger boat in the wider sections of the channel.

Most of the passengers on the airboats had tied makeshift masks across their nose and mouth, to try to filter out the smoke, although there was quite a bit of coughing from some passengers. They had some small relief in the sections of channel that were between thick groves of cedar, but not once they were back in the open savannah.

Kryslie emerged into one such open section, where the visibility was down to about ten feet. She could tell where the fire was for the horizon was indicated by a faint, glowing, orange line.

"Where is that sea breeze, bro?"

She had been too busy steering to try to sense the air currents, but she knew Tymos had been concentrating on the natural energies.

"I don't want to meddle, even if a sea breeze pushing back on that fire would help us," Tymos told her. "The energies around here are finely balanced. If I start to change them, I am likely to cause a thunderstorm."

Thoughts, more like vivid mental images of possibilities, passed between the twins. Finally, Tymos verbalised. "If all the boats keep moving steadily, they should all get back safely."

Awareness of their position, the whereabouts of the other boats and the fire were instinctive, for all of their senses were adding to the overall picture. Two more airboats emerged from the tree lined channel, and headed north, passing the little powerboat without seeming to notice them.

"Where is…" Kryslie was expecting the Mc Lellan to emerge next, and let her mind concentrate on it. It was in a narrow section of the channel, and seeming to be having steering trouble. The increase in motor noise suggested that another boat was held up behind it. That engine reduced revs to idle, waiting for the larger boat to move.

When the noise of yet another engine carried out of the tree tunnel, Kryslie began to turn their boat around — some instinct was warning her of trouble.

A sound like metal dropping on metal, had her speeding back up the channel, knowing that there were no boats between her and the Mc Lellan, and even so, being able to adjust her eyes to see in the murk — seeing the energy auras of the trees and the water — and then the heat signatures of the boat engines.

On her face, she felt the breeze from their passage, but now, a stronger breeze was blowing from her right. An instinctive awareness of her twin, told her that he was 'borrowing' a breeze — making small local changes in the air pressure — aiming to blow the smoke away, to increase visibility.

As they neared the Mc Lellan, Kryslie slowed the boat and studied the chaos she sensed. Voices called out, loud and frightened — but they were the relatively unscathed victims — there were two that were screaming with their mind, trapped under water.

Without needing to warn her brother, Kryslie turned their boat into the bank, and tethered it loosely by throwing a line over an overhanging branch. In a fraction of time, she had her sandals off her feet, as well as her hat and glasses, and performed an efficient horizontal dive that had her sliding into the water like an otter.

Tymos took a moment to get an overall picture of the accident, the wreckage and the damage. The Linus Mc Lellan was pushed into one bank, an airboat was leaning towards it at a crazy angle, and pieces of fibreglass from what might have been a jet ski, were on the air boat and in the water.

People had been thrown from the airboat, and these were mostly standing in water that was up to their necks. Tymos suddenly thought of the little power boat used by one of the Governor's security guards. Knowledge seemed to come to him in a flash, and he didn't question it — the escort boat was trapped under the airboat, the guard driving it…

Tymos could only faintly sense the man, and without wasting another moment, he matched his sister's dive into the water, but he stayed on the surface, propelling himself faster than an Olympic swimmer, but with very little splashing.

He approached from the bow of the Mc Lellan, able to see that two of the crew were trying to push the airboat off the escort boat, so they could get to the trapped man. Without asking for permission, he pulled himself onto the tour boat, moved along the narrow deck next to the windows, and added his strength to the effort.

Although he could easily have shoved the boat away, he was aware that his sister was below, and timed his effort for when she was ready to pull both trapped victims free.

He let the Mc Lellan's crewman hop down and lift the injured guard up. He helped the second crewman receive the man, even as he saw his sister bob to the surface.

She was nearer the stern of the tour boat, and towing the two casualties towards the Mc Lellan.

"Krys?" he thought at her, needing to know if she could handle both casualties.

"Go to the guard," was her terse reply. "I can keep these alive and make them cough up the water, until you are free."

Tymos took her evaluation as fact, and moved quickly after the injured guard, not waiting to be invited down into the cabin. He pushed past the hovering Governor, and WSRA Chief Basoli as if ignorant of their identity. He sensed the latter jerk away from him, and stored the reaction away for later thought. All his energy at the moment was directed towards the badly injured man.

"I have had first aid training," he stated, meeting the eyes of the Governor's wife and seeing relief appear there. "Do you have a first aid kit aboard?"

She pulled it into view with her free hand, her other one was keeping a wadded up sling in place over a bad head gash. The kit wasn't nearly adequate, and she knew it. However, her next comment proved that she wasn't just decoration for her husband.

"The captain is cutting the table cloth into strips."

Tymos nodded and glanced at the two hovering men. "I need clean water, and a towel or something."

Basoli, went immediately, even though he had a bandaged cut over his left eye. The Governor glanced from his wife, to the direction where Basoli had gone. Tymos brushed his mind, he was feeling the need to be involved, and was at a loss of how to help.

"Sir, someone needs to help my sister, she is bringing two victims across – they nearly drowned."

For a moment, the Governor looked into the eyes of the young man, who seemed to have read his mind. The eyes were blue, but a shade that seemed to glow with mauve light.

"I'll see she has help," he agreed with no trace of self-importance.

Tymos forgot him, and turned his full attention to the injured man. While he waited for the water, he gently examined him for other injuries.

As he moved the man gently, he spoke in a low voice, explaining what he was doing. He kept his eyes down, so that the woman wouldn't see how they changed when he looked at the energy flows in the man's body.

The energies were sluggish; a bad sign.

"We need to keep him warm," he inserted into his monologue, and as the water arrived, the Governor's wife went to find a blanket, and Tymos took over the pressure on the wound. While most of his hand was on the pressure pad, one finger touched the man's face, and he sent a trickle of healing energy into the man. Once that was established, he turned and took the cloth from Basoli, and gestured for the water to be placed nearby. "Thanks."

Using his free hand, he dipped a corner of the cloth in the water, and used that part to gently wash the blood away to see where any other wounds were.

The Governor's wife returned and carefully covered the man with the blanket, then when the cloth needed rinsing and re wetting she took it from Tymos.

"What's your name," she asked, as she watched him work.

"Tym," he admitted, so softly that only she would have heard. She said her name was Imogen but he gave no sign of hearing her. He concentrated on gently dabbing an area above the man's right ear, where his adjusted eyes saw an oddness in the energy flow. It was opposite the bleeding gash, and was probably a bruise, or internal bleeding. He risked using more of his power, seeing his hands glowing faintly, but hoping no one else saw it. The man was barely alive, and if he did nothing, would be dead before a helicopter could get him to hospital.

The captain arrived, carrying looping strips of cloth. Imogen took some and began rolling it ready for use.

"How is he doing?" the captain asked, anxiously.

"Pretty bad," Tymos told him. "Have you called to seek assistance?"

"Yes, the Coast Guard will try to get a helicopter. They will call back when they find out what can be done. Can you manage here – I need to help fix the leaks in the bilge. When the boat landed on the side we split a few welds."

"You see to that," Tymos spoke without turning. "If the smoke stays thick out there, the helicopter might not get here. You might have to limp back to the city."

That thought had already occurred to the captain, and he was hiding his fears that they might not make it. He trotted off, leaving Basoli watching, not knowing how to help.

"Ron, can you roll another strip up?" Imogen invited, gesturing to the rest of the fabric strips.

Tymos risked using more power, while the others were busy. His hands glowed even more, and finally he began to see improvement in the man he touched. From watching the energy flows, which related to blood flow, he could see them slowly speeding up. The pad under his hand was soaked red, but he left it there. Under it, torn blood vessels were beginning to mend.

When he sensed Basoli looking at him, he eased of the amount of power he was sending the man, and readjusted his eyes to normal.

"Do you have a bandage roll ready?" Tymos part turned to take the roll from Basoli. "I need someone to take over the pressure here."

Basoli stepped back, and Imogen leant forward. She cast a look at him, before doing as Tymos had requested.

Before starting the bandaging, Tymos checked that the unconscious man had no apparent neck injury. He felt it very gently, and as a precaution, supported it with one hand as he unrolled a short section of bandage.

"Can you hold the end there," Tymos asked Imogen, and once she put other hand on it, he began to wind the bandage strip around the man's head, bringing it to a firm, but not over tight tension, and enabling Imogen to remove her hand. He got her to hold the roll so he had a hand free to pull out a packaged gauze pad.

Basoli saw him struggling, to open it, and gently took it and cut it open with scissors from the aid kit. Tymos gave him another terse, "Thanks" and tucked the pad where he had seen the swelling by the right ear.

He continued the bandaging, covering most of the man's head, and when he had used up two of the strips, it seemed the bleeding from the gash had stopped.

The other two rolls of cloth strips he used to support the man's neck, and he rested the head on the carpeted floor of the cabin. He then felt for the man's pulse by resting a finger on his carotid artery and then checked the man's breathing by having his hand lightly on his chest. The pulse was far from strong, and ragged; the breathing was shallow. Tymos wondered how long he dared stay there, seeming to do nothing. No longer…had the man stopped losing blood, he was still serious, but no longer in danger.

Tymos stood up, and staggered slightly. Basoli steadied him, and asked, "What now?"

"Hope the helicopter gets here. He should be moved as little as possible. Oxygen would help since there is smoke even in here, but boats don't usually carry that."

Tymos wanted to leave, before Basoli had a chance to study his face. Imogen spoke up, giving him a reason to turn away.

"I'm glad you were around. I was afraid that Gerald wasn't going to make it. Now I think he has a chance. Hopefully he didn't get any infection in the wounds, and get sick in spite of your efforts."

"I hope so too. But I need to see if my sister needs help."

Tymos gave a slight bow to Imogen Treswick, and walked towards the tiny outer back deck.

When Kryslie slid into the water, she went under the surface as if it were her natural element. She adjusted her eyes to sense heat, so she could avoid the legs of the people in the water. They did not need to panic further thinking her a crocodile or alligator. There were a few of the creatures gathering, but she sent a surge of energy at them, and they moved off, reading the sensation as a warning of danger. She went directly to where she could see two glowing shapes struggling to get free from under the edge of the airboat.

In her head, she was aware the Tymos was going to push on the airboat, so the injured escort could be freed. He was waiting for her, to be ready, and as soon as he sensed she had a grip on both victims, he acted.

The smaller glowing shape came free easily, it was a child, already unconscious. Kryslie sent a surge of energy into her, enough to make her blood flow, but not enough to make her try to cough. The other figure was an adult, and not as slender as the child.

"Tym, push a little more."

The mental request was acted on immediately, and the larger figure slid free. Kryslie wasted no more time kicking to the surface. The water was four foot deep, so she was able to stand with her head above water, and once she did, she took deep breaths. No one around her would realise just how long she had been under the water, holding her breath.

As she half walked, half swam to the Mc Lellan, she sent a surge of power through both victims, the larger, a woman, began to cough up water. The child stayed limp.

"Krys?" She heard Tymos think at her and sensed that he needed to help the trapped guard escort and needing to know if she could handle both casualties.

"Go to the guard," was Kryslie told him. "I can keep these alive, make them cough up the water, until you are free."

She couldn't heal like her twin, but she could keep them alive and start to help them. Hands helped her bring her victims onto the rear deck of the boat, and then helped her from the water. She was surprised to see Governor Treswick, without his jacket, kneeling down starting to do resuscitation on the woman. One of the Mc Lellan's crew was trying CPR on the child. He was muttering, "Come on, Kid, breathe."

Kryslie slipped up beside him and murmured, "Let me."

She would seem to be doing no different to the man, but as she breathed air into the child's lungs, and gently but firmly compressing the chest, she was sending some of her energy into the little body. She felt the heart give a kick when the energy acted on it, and the lungs heave and force up some water. She turned the child's head, so the water drained away, and then felt another cough building up.

The crewman gave an audible, "Thank the gods."

"We'll need some blankets if you have some," Kryslie suggested, glancing to where the woman was trying to sit up, while still coughing. She wasn't recovered enough to realise who was helping her.

Kryslie kept a hand on the child, a girl, as she kept coughing, in spite of being barely conscious. Her personal energy was helping her blood to circulate oxygen to the brain and extremities. By her estimate, the child had been in the water for about five minutes…but she could not tell if there was brain damage from the experience. All she could do was keep her breathing, keep her circulation working, and wait until her twin could take over, and do more to heal her. When the coughing eased, Kryslie began to massage the girl's arms and legs, explaining to the quizzing look from the governor, why she was doing it.

"To help improve circulation," was her claim, and the governor accepted it as logical. He wasn't to know that all that was keeping the child 'alive' was her Tymorean power, acting on the body like a pacemaker would for the heart.

The crewman brought blankets for the woman and child, and glanced at Kryslie to see if she wanted one, but she shook her head and took one to cover the child.

"How is she?" the woman managed to ask in a rasping voice, before more coughing overcame her.

Kryslie wasn't going to say how bad she really was, so all she said was, "She seems to be breathing. Is she your daughter?"

The woman nodded, and pulled the blanket more tightly around her.

"She will need to be checked over by doctors," Kryslie advised, but her brother would come soon, and his healing gift would make a difference.

Moments later, Tymos emerged, glanced at the woman, who was well enough, and squatted next to his twin. He already knew how the little girl was, and what he needed to do. Mentally, he said, "Move around a bit."

Kryslie knew he wanted her to shield his hands from view, as he began to do as she had before. No one seemed surprised, as he took over the massaging. His hands were glowing faintly, as he willed the child to recover. After a few moments, the child began to stir, and the coughing started again.

"Most of the water is out," Tymos spoke to his sister's mind. He was nurturing the spark of life that his sister had preserved. "How long do you think she was breathing water?"

Kryslie estimated, "Four or five minutes. She was still moving just before I got her free."

Tymos kept up the massaging, that covered his use of power to help the child. Kryslie risked adjusting her sight to see the energy flows. They were looking better, and more importantly, brighter.

Sensing the Captain approaching, Kryslie stood up, and Tymos reduced the amount of power he was using so that his hands no longer glowed. He kept his hands on the girl, but stopped moving them.

"The Coast Guard are going to try getting one of their helicopters in. They will land at Heccles Island. It isn't far."

Tymos's mind instantly recalled a map of the area, located his current position, and the island. It was privately owned, and had a small jetty and was probably only a hundred metres from where the channel emerged back into the open savannah.

"Great. Couldn't be better. I think the little one will be fine, but the sooner a doctor sees her the better." Tymos was aware that his sister's attention had wandered. She seemed to be trying to locate the source of a niggling feeling of concern. She sensed more injured people, but had ruled out those from the tour boat who were still trying to get out of the water. He decided to ask, "What happened here, anyway?"

With a growl, the Captain vented some of the anger he was holding in. "What happened is some fool on a jet ski was coming flat out – even though the smoke was as thick as thick. Worse than it is now. It hit the airboat as it was taking the bend, and that skidded into us and ran up over the escort boat."

All eyes were on the captain, including the Governor and Basoli, and no one saw Kryslie climb back off the Mc Lellan. Tymos asked, "Are all your crew and guests okay?" He had a sense of the memory of the incident in the captain's mind and shared it with his twin.

"Shaken, and a few bumps and scrapes. Not sure how we can get out of this mess to get to the island though." The captain looked at the girl and her mother and suggested, "We should get these two into the cabin, out of the smoke."

"I have an idea to get that airboat righted," Tymos proposed. "If it still goes, and doesn't sink – we can get the people back to the city."

"You are a man of many talents, Mr…." the Governor noted, leaving the sentence unfinished, hoping Tymos would give his name.

He didn't, and after a moment, the Governor seemed to lose interest in the question. Tymos turned and saw Basoli studying him, and reinforced the thought he was sending at them, "My name and face are not important."

Tymos turned to study the airboat, and the people still clinging to the seats, even though it was at a crazy angle. Behind him, the woman was being helped inside, and the little girl was being carried. No one paid attention when he climbed across to the high edge of the airboat.

Kryslie sensed the image Tymos received from the captain's mind of the events that led to the accident. Possible scenarios flashed through her mind, as she played with various angles of impact. The Jet Ski rider…riders…she corrected herself, were somewhere close – not in the water, but were rousing and in pain. She swam to the bank, helped a few people from the water, and then walked amongst the trees. Why the Jet Ski had been going so fast, when the visibility was poor was a matter for the authorities to work out, but the men were injured.

She heard slithering nearby, and heard a moan, and she sensed one of the crocodilian species. The moan came again, and she went off to her left. Lying amongst two of the huge cedar trees, to where he had been dragged, was one of the missing jet skiers. A reptilian tail flashed out of sight, but Kryslie had seen enough of it to identify a crocodile. The man was bleeding from teeth marks in his leg, and all but unconscious, but not critical.

He would be safe enough there while she followed the large creature, who she hoped would lead her to the other man.

It did, but it saw her as a threat and turned suddenly and charged at her. It was fast, but Kryslie was faster, reacting by kicking out at the creature and sending it three feet off the ground before it crashed back to earth. Once it recovered from the fall, it moved off as fast as it had approached and slid into the nearby water.

The second man looked to be lying where he had landed after the impact, for they were within sight of the awkwardly leaning airboat. She could see her brother moving people upward, trying to alter the boat's centre of gravity. He would have to shove the boat away from the Linus Mc Lellan, and off the crushed escort boat, to get it to sit flat in the water again.

No one was looking her way, so after checking him for possible neck and spinal injuries, seemingly by running her hand along his length, she simply lifted the man over her shoulder and began to take him back to his friend. Had anyone seen her, they would have been astounded at her strength, for the man was a good twelve inches taller than she was and twice as solid. She put him down by his friend.

While she looked at the wounds of the first man, Kryslie allowed the Earth's aura to fill her, and then she let it emanate from her to act as a deterrent to the wildlife. The bite marks were not as deep as they might have been. When the croc had him, he must have been unconscious, unresisting. She ran her hand slowly along each row of puncture marks, and sent some power there to seal the wounds and kill infection. As she was doing that, she checked the man's pupils, and pulse, and adjusted her eyes to see the energy flows. He probably had concussion, but it wasn't bad. He didn't look to have neck or spine damage either.

The idea of, 'The devil looks after his own', came into her mind, and she wondered if the men had been drunk, or on drugs when they hit the airboat.

One began to try to speak, the words were garbled, at first, but then she caught snippets. The men, she guessed from what she understood, had seen the fire and were trying to get away from it.

In the back of her mind, she heard Tymos comment, "No excuse. Do they need me?"

In her turn, Kryslie sensed he was about to finish righting the airboat. She heard a very loud splash, and vocal complaints from the people who had just received a soaking.

"No," she sent to her twin. "I think they will survive without our help. When you finish there – want to help me get them to our boat?"

"I was going to suggest we tow the airboat," he sent back.

"Ask the Mc Lellan to do that…"

Her twin didn't ask why, simply picked up on her reasons. One, she didn't want these men with the injured or the official party if they roused and were violent. And she'd sensed that the fire was now only five miles away. The smoke was building up again, since they had been too busy trying to help the injured. It would affect the chances of the helicopter being able to come and land and evacuate the seriously injured.

"I'll do that," Tymos promised.

Tymos helped the people from the airboat that had been flung into the water, to return to the boat, and when none of them went to the driving seat he asked, "Where's your tour leader?"

"Tha's me," a voice said from nearby. The man had been helping with the passengers. Tymos turned and looked at the man who had spoken, whose eyes seemed unfocussed.

"Don't think the motor will go. Might need a tow."

"I don't think you should drive if it did," Tymos decided. "I'll help you to the Mc Lellan, and ask them about towing you."

The Mc Lellan's engines started up as they approached, but one of the crew saw them coming. The airboat driver was helped aboard, and the crewman went to talk to the captain. The reply was an affirmative, and Tymos swam downstream from the jet engine before climbing onto the bank to help his sister.

Kryslie hefted one of the men, and Tymos took the other, and they moved silently through the trees to where they had left their boat. They sat the men on one of the long side seats and secured them to the rail that ran the length of the side of the boat. Both men were still too dazed to struggle.

Tymos started the boat, but they did not move out until the Mc Lellan, with the airboat in tow, had passed them. Kryslie tuned the radio to the frequency on which the tour boat could talk to the Coast Guard helicopter. It was hovering just out of the worst of the smoke, unable to see where the island was.

As they idled in the wake of the larger boat, Tymos only had a small part of his mind on steering. Most of it was sensing the air currents, and drawing fresh air from over the Gulf, towards them.

To the pilots of the helicopter, it seemed that the sea breeze came in at the right time. The smoke cleared enough for them to see their intended landing place. The landed quickly, just as the boats they were to meet prepared to dock. They saw the larger boat drop the vessel they had in tow. A smaller vessel took over the tow, and by the time the paramedics jumped down from the helicopter's side door, the airboat was docked on the other side of the wooden jetty.

While the paramedics were checking the injured on the Mc Lellan, a Coast Guard officer requested a report of the accident from the crew. A short time later, he strode to where Tymos had nudged their boat into the bank.

"Are these the jet ski riders?"

"Yes," Kryslie agreed. "Do you want to take them as well? They knocked themselves silly."

"I'll have the paramedics check them," the officer decided. "If they aren't too bad, we will take them on the second trip."

"What if you can't get back," Tymos asked. "That fire is getting close."

"There's a water drop coming," the officer revealed. "Although if we can't get in we will call you and you would be wise to head back as fast as you can."

When the officer had gone, Tymos used the anchor to hold the boat into the bank and both he and Kryslie went ashore.

While the breeze was blowing the smoke away, it was also making hot air from the fire rise up. Massive cumulonimbus clouds were forming.

One of the paramedics detoured to check the men in the small boat. The other casualties were already being taken on stretchers to the helicopter.

"What is the story with these two?"

Kryslie filled the woman in, and she checked their vital signs and their eyes.

"They are well enough for now," the paramedic decided. "We will off load the others and come back."

"If the fire or those clouds don't stop you," Tymos suggested. "If they do, it will take us about an hour to get back. Will that be a problem?"

"Not if they don't try to do anything. Why do you have then tied to the boat?"

Kryslie remarked, "I think the police will want to talk to these men. One was muttering about a fire starting and I think the Jet Ski was stolen."

"Will you be able to handle them if they wake and become violent?"

"We will manage," Kryslie assured him.

When the woman had re-joined her partner, Tymos and Kryslie walked to the dock. They stayed off it, since most of the air boat passengers were in huddled groups there, as were the Governor, his wife, and Basoli.

The roar of the helicopter engine powering for take-off made hearing any of the passengers' voices impossible, but Kryslie felt empathically, the fear amongst the passengers as they watched the fire approaching from beyond the helicopter.

It would look like they were also watching the helicopter for they covered their faces with an arm when it took off in a cloud of rising dust.

However, once the helicopter was out of sight, they stayed there, as if watching the fire, but in fact they were studying the lines of energy around them, and the air currents that were still disturbed by the helicopter's rotors which were visible due to the smoke, that was thickening again due to a lull in the breeze.

Working like a practiced team, Kryslie began to create an area of higher pressure, as Tymos began to create a breeze, pulling air from behind them and pushing it towards the fire. The building storm responded, and the centre of the cell changed direction, and began to move towards the fire. The clouds grew blacker, as if full of rain that was being held from falling.

Quick footsteps, of someone running along the dock, were ignored until they realised that the man was coming to them. Kryslie withdrew her attention from the storm, allowed her eyes to normalise before she turned, and hoped the power she was holding did not make them seem too bright.

"You need to get your boat under way," one of the Mc Lellan's crew men gasped. "The water helo can't make the drop, and the coast guard helo can't get back in."

"Surely the fire bomber can get in…" Kryslie used the question to delay leaving.

"Normally, yes, but the updrafts and down drafts near there are something fierce," she was told.

"Oh! Right. Tym?"

Her brother ignored her, but that was expected, so she said, "We will follow you and the airboat, although someone will need to steer that."

"We'll see. Come on now."

The first fat, heavy drops began to fall, and Tymos's rigid stance relaxed and he turned. "Yeah, we'd better move."

He spoke silently to Kryslie as they trotted back towards the boat. "The bulk of the rain should fall on the fire."

They returned to their boat, retrieved the mooring anchor, ignored the glares of the now conscious prisoners, and started the motor. They didn't reverse out into the channel right away, but waited until the towline from the tour boat was passed and the Mc Lellan had begun to tow it up channel. One of the passengers was in the steersman's seat.

Basoli watched from the rear window of the tour boat. The Governor was standing by the Captain, listening to the reports of the fire. His wife was sipping water, and wiping her eyes with a damp cloth. She had been coughing a lot from the smoke.

The people on the airboat were trying to cover their heads with jackets or towels, in a futile effort to shelter from the downpour. He was glad he was under the cabin roof of the Mc Lellan, and only a trickle of water was coming in through the covered over portside windows. He would be even gladder when he was finally back in Everglades City. It had been disappointing that the helicopter could not return due to the storm cell.

He considered that the storm, with the heavy rain, had come at an advantageous time. From the voice traffic on the radio, it had slowed the fire, and if it rained for long enough, it might even put it out.

Movement aft of the boat caught his attention. The little punt with the red heads and the two prisoners was coming alongside the towed airboat. Those two didn't seem to mind the rain, although the two men on the seats were holding their free arm over their heads.

He wondered why one of the red heads was crossing to the airboat, but before he could think of a reason, except that he might be able to steer it better than whoever was at that task, his attention was caught by the voice of the Captain who was speaking to the Governor.

"We are still taking on water. At this rate, we may not make it back to the dock."

Basoli walked over and invited himself into the conversation. "What if we drop the tow?"

The Captain smiled grimly. "I have thought of that, but we have a duty to help those in distress. I have tried to raise someone back at the base, but there are no vessels able to come that are large enough to tow us, and the airboat."

Just then, as if she had heard the conversation, a woman's voice came over the radio. "Linus Mc Lellan, this is tour boat TB156."

The captain let his first mate answer the call.

The woman continued, "My brother just went across to the airboat. He is going to try and see if it will start."

After a startled glance at his captain, the man responded, "Good luck with that. Let us know if you need any tools."

"We will, thank you," the woman agreed.

Governor Treswick commented, "Useful pair, those two. Lucky they were around."

Basoli gave a gruff reply, reminded of the odd feeling he'd had when the man brushed against him. "A jack of all trades it seems, but I don't think I would have left my sister alone on a boat with two jail escapees though."

"Those two seem docile enough."

"I wouldn't want to trust appearances."

The two men lapsed into silence, watching the airboat and trying to see what the red head was doing, but he was crouched down behind the last row of passengers, and they had turned to watch the man working.

"How will dropping the tow help us?" Treswick asked. "I'm not a nautical man."

"We can travel faster without the tow, and I believe that will help – it will allow more power for the bilge pumps at least," Basoli explained.

Shouts from across the water, distracted the observers from watching the airboat. In the little punt, the two men had roused fully and were trying to stand and get to the woman. She had turned to glance at them but was now back steering the boat and ignoring their increasingly crude threats. They were both trying to jerk themselves free, or untie the binding on their tied up arm. Their actions were so frenzied, that the normally stable boat was rocking wildly.

The boat slowed, to idling speed and the red headed woman turned to face them, hands on hips like an irate mother. Her voice didn't carry but the response of one of the men did, or at least the, "…you effing bitch…" did.

The watchers guessed that she might have been suggesting that they take a swim, for she gestured to the water, and the men subsided.

Kryslie slowed the boat and turned on the two men. "Sit down!"

"Untie us you effing bitch!" The men stopped trying to jerk free

"No. You both knocked yourselves silly when you drove full speed into the airboat. You have been unconscious for over an hour. You need to go to hospital and get checked out."

"What have you done with our jet ski?"

From the man's unguarded thoughts, she knew he had stolen the Jet Ski…appropriated it.

"In umpteen pieces several miles back down the channel."

The man seethed, and made no effort to hide the fact that he was checking his pockets. He thought he had a sharp knife that could cut the rope that tied him to the boat.

"What do you hope to do?" Kryslie asked. "You want to go swimming in the channel? Let the gators or crocs finish what they tried to start?" She gestured to the water. "Or are you fool enough to think you can get to the bank and try to out run the fire?"

The second man nudged his friend, and hissed, "Shut up you idiot. We will have a better chance when we get taken off this boat."

The first man wasn't listening, he was on one foot, kicking out with the other, but Kryslie was just out of reach. He swore more vile curses and threats, when the focus of his rage turned her back and went to the console.

Kryslie spoke to him before revving the engine, "Please do your best to fall overboard. I will be happy to trawl for gators."

His next words were drowned out by the abrupt start-up of the airboat's engine, and the cheering of the passengers. Her brother stood up and glanced her way. She gave him a fist in the air gesture of triumph, even as she was answering his mental questions.

"I can manage them. Although they will try to get free when transferred to official custody. So, if you need to stay and steer that noisy airboat, go ahead."

The next moment she heard Tymos's voice on the radio, talking to the Linus Mc Lellan. "If it stays running for five minutes, you can drop the tow."

Once the three boats were underway again, Kryslie thought at her twin, "These two were somehow responsible for the fire. It wasn't deliberate, but they were too doped up to try to put it out when it was small. They were in a stolen car, but they got it stuck on a mud track that led to where someone had left a jet ski. When they saw the fire, they panicked."

Tymos thought back, "They will be held on charges of escaping custody. It shouldn't be too hard for us to suggest to the police that they listen out for a report of a stolen jet ski, and an abandoned stolen car."

Police were waiting in force at the Mc Lellan's dock, but Kryslie idled out in the inlet until the sluggish tour boat had docked, and then came in to throw a line about the bollard on the end of the dock. Tymos had kept going, heading for the airboat's normal docking place.

Two officers, looked down at her. "How did you manage to tame them, miss…?"

They hoped she'd give her name, but she answered their question instead. "They aren't tame, and they will try to escape as soon as you release them from my knot work. I was able to do that while they were still knocked silly. Where do you want them?"

"Where did you hire your boat from?"

"Captain Stanley's Shed. It isn't far from where my brother has taken the airboat."

"Can you take them there? We have colleagues waiting to talk to the tour group."

Kryslie nodded. "No problems."

The two officers had a quiet discussion, and one of them decided, "If you don't mind, I'll came with you."

There was no reason to say no, and once the man was aboard, and he gave his name as Jerry Pell, Kryslie unhooked the mooring line and backed the boat away from the dock. She glanced over her shoulder as she reversed, and saw the more aggressive prisoner eject a glob of spit at the shoes of the policeman.

Their thoughts were informative — they'd both been in custody for robbery with violence, and has escaped from a place near where the fire started. Likely, she would not need to say anything.

At Captain Stanley's Shed, extra police met the boat, and took the mooring line from her. Then the men were handcuffed before being released from the ropes, and their blatant attempts at escape were easily thwarted.

Pell requested that she, and her brother came to the precinct building in Everglades City to make a report. He asked her name and she said, "Krys Ward," and gave her address as the resort.

Once he went off, Kryslie made sure all her things were in her bag, then checked her brother's. She was about to toss her bag up onto the dock when the boat hand from the hire company arrived, wide eyed at the unexpected activity.

"Do you know who those two men were?" he asked. He didn't seem to notice that she was alone, when she'd had Tymos with her before.

"Two idiots who rammed a jet ski into an air boat," Kryslie claimed, and she saw the man's expression change. "The coast guard helo took several people off to hospital."

The man reverted to businesslike, and took her bag and then the other. "You had someone with you before. He's not hurt is he?"

"No, he's fine, he was steering the air boat, since the skipper was hurt. I need to go and meet him. Do I need to do anything else here?"

The media had flocked to the dock, having scented a sensational story. Tymos did not want to be interviewed or made out to be a hero. So, using the excuse that he needed to go and meet up with his sister, Tymos slipped away from the tour boat dock. He had agreed to the request to make a statement to the police in the city, as soon as he was able.

He had seen the Governor's limousine arrive, and though his wife and Basoli had gone to wait in there, Treswick himself was busy talking to the media. When he spoke of the two amazing red heads, and all they had done, Tymos and Kryslie were long gone.

Basoli sat in the air conditioned coolness of the limousine, his clothes still reeked of smoke, but at least the air was fresh. He listened to the Governor talking of the events of the day. Mention of the two red headed Samaritans drew his mind back to them, and to the oddness that he had felt when they were close. He recalled the tingle, like of electricity, when the man had brushed him aside as he went to help the Governor's guard. That man had seemed completely confident of his skills, and indeed had probably saved the guard's life. The woman too, had seemed absolutely confident when she had faced down the dangerous escapees in the boat. Admittedly, they were partly tied up, but they might have got loose.

Governor Treswick, finally seated himself in the limousine. As the driver started off, he said, "You will be my guest at the official residence tonight." He was looking at Basoli, who murmured, "I would need to collect my things from the hotel."

"So will I," Imogen Treswick reminded her husband. "So, what's the reason?"

"The police will be sending over one of their senior men, so we can tell all we can of the events."

"We really don't know all that much," Imogen reminded him.

"They should talk to those two young people," Basoli suggested. "Did you get their names?"

Treswick looked startled. "You know, I meant to ask them, and each time I thought of it, I forgot. However, we can find that out from the police."

Imogen said thoughtfully, "The young man told me his name, now what was it? Jim? Tim? Something like that."

Tymos and Kryslie walked to the main road, and waited for the taxi they had requested. Once back at the resort, they went directly to their cottage. While Tymos used his communicator to hook into the hotel computer, Kryslie headed for the shower.

When she returned, refreshed and in clean clothes, Tymos greeted her with, "The Governor's party are checking out, and the times for the interviews have been sent. We have to be back to Washington the day after tomorrow."

"So, we head back, after detouring to give the police out report. Do you think Basoli noticed us particularly?"

"He saw me when I went to help the guard, but I paid him no particular attention. I was projecting a suggestion for him to forget my face. We will need to do that when we report. The last thing we need is for the media to focus on us."

"Why don't you put the newsfeed on?" Kryslie suggested.

Tymos picked up the remote control for the televid screen and flicked through channels, stopping on a news channel.

"I've notified the hotel computer that we will be leaving tomorrow, and sent the final account to Earthbase to deal with," Tymos added, before he went to have his turn in the shower.

Kryslie prepared a light snack from the food they still had in the cottage, and then packed her bags ready to leave in the morning. She would only have a few things to add at the last minute.

Making a report to the police was a mere formality. They hadn't seen the accident, only the aftermath, and were told they would not be needed for anything else. Naturally, they had to provide their names, but could not give an address since they would be leaving the rented Washington apartment once they passed the interview stage and became a member of the WSRA.

They returned from the police building to the cottage to collect their things, and then requested a long range beam from Earthbase.

Morin met them on arrival, still a bundle of excitement. "You aren't meant to be back yet."

"Our interviews are the day after tomorrow," Kryslie said, grinning as his face changed to disappointment. "Besides, we had enough excitement yesterday to last a while."

"That was you! I knew it. The Governor guy was praising these two people, but he couldn't give their names."

"Just as well," Tymos murmured. "I'm going to check the police computer."

"Boss wants to see you, Great One," Morin was suddenly business, remembering how important Tymos and Kryslie were.

"I'll fill him in," Kryslie offered.

"And I'll tell Larissa you are here. You are staying for lunch," Morin said in a rush. "Did you have a good holiday?"

"The holiday was fine. Where's Daniel?"

"Comms room."

"Thanks. We'll need the long range beam after that. We have lots of loose ends to tidy up in Washington."

As she left the arrival chamber, she heard Morin's unguarded thought that she and Tymos were going to be 'escaping back to work'.

The pace of activity at the WSRA headquarters was less frantic than the week before. This time the invited candidates were escorted to the first floor where a comfortable lounge was assigned for their use. Snacks and drinks were available, as were screens set to the world news feeds.

Tymos and Kryslie arrived in the early afternoon, after spending the morning arranging for one of the missionary Tymoreans to take care of their apartment. They saw a group of candidates bunched around the vid screen, and heard enough of the voice over to know that the topic was the events in the Everglades and the involvement of Florida's Governor who was rumoured to be planning to run for President. His tour down in the Everglades with the Commander in Chief of the WSRA, had some observers speculating as to whether Ron Basoli was being groomed to be his running partner and potential deputy.

Tymos didn't think the article was more than idle speculation, and was glad that the focus of the media had turned from the two people who had helped at a boat accident. He gestured to two empty chairs, and said, "I'll grab a drink for you."

He recognised some of the group sitting nearby, but didn't attempt to join them. He listened, hearing, "…found out two days ago that he didn't make the cut. He was really disappointed until he had a call from Extech Scientific. He…"

The speaker stopped talking as the announcement system called a new name, he slumped back into his seat as another man, nearer the door, stood and went to where a uniformed usher waited to direct him.

That was the pattern for the next few hours. Names were called, people disappeared through one of the six doors, but did not return through the lounge. Newer arrivals arrived to replace the ones who left.

Late afternoon, when people had stopped arriving and the number of people in the lounge had dropped to about twenty, instead of the average fifty, Tymos and Kryslie noticed that one of the ushers was going from group to group, speaking briefly to each one. The path the young woman was taking would bring her to their corner, last.

They were not surprised, for they recognised the woman as Bynan, the personal assistant to WSRA Commander in Chief, Basoli.

Kryslie smiled as the woman approached. "Bynan," she greeted softly. "What's going on?"

"The voice over system has stopped working," she admitted candidly. They were trying to call you next, but are now setting up to send SMS messages."

Tymos suddenly chuckled. Those near him heard, "All that talking must have given it a sore throat."

Then he said, more softly, "That's something I didn't consider."

Bynan spoke softly, "Great One?"

"Forget the title. It has no place here."

Kryslie answered the question Bynan had not uttered. "Tymos inserted a program into the WSRA computer, so that it wouldn't give out information about us. Seems that includes mentioning our names in public." She gave her twin a grin.

Tymos deflected the teasing his sister was doing mentally, by asking, "How was Basoli when he got back from Florida?"

Bynan was startled by the question.

"Daniel made us take a vacation. We saw him down there," Kryslie explained.

"Oh, the media have been trying to get hold of him all day. He has escaped them by being here for the interviews. He has a spray sealed cut on his forehead and a large bruise, and has needed analgesic tablets."

Bynan didn't consider that she was being indiscreet, she was answering a question from a Great One.

Just then, both Tymos and Kryslie felt their communicators vibrate as they announced a phone page.

"Well they must have realised that we are related," Kryslie murmured, as she confirmed that they were both to proceed to the same room.

Bynan murmured, "Follow me."

She led them to one of the doors and down a short passage, and finally gestured to a partly opened door. She stayed back and let them continue. Her assigned task was simple - to direct the interviewees for the Lunar 1 positions, and remain at the lounge door, but these two were Great Ones and respect for them was ingrained in every Tymorean.

Tymos knocked, announcing their presence. His keen hearing had picked up that the three men in the room were talking amongst themselves, and this stopped and a voice called for them to come in.

This smaller room was an office, but three men were seated on the far side of a large desk. They were all wearing formal WSRA uniforms.

Kryslie studied their collar insignia, and ignored the view out of the picture window behind them. Basoli, seated in the centre position, had a black uniform with plenty of gold braid – his insignia was of a rocket overlaid on a round planet. The colour made his skin seem pale, and his thinning hair greyer than it was.

On his right, in a deep maroon coloured uniform of a similar style to Basoli, and with the rocket insignia of a Commander, was a brown haired man in his fifties. The man on the left was younger, about forty, with dark hair. His uniform was also red, but a brighter shade, and his collar insignia was of some kind of satellite.

The three men were, in their turn studying the two red heads who entered, making their own first impression.

The concept of a Great One did not exist amongst the human population, and since they had elected to apply for relatively lowly positions with the WSRA, Tymos and Kryslie were giving the impression of being slightly awed by the important men they were meeting. Their posture, was more casual than formal, but giving the impression of vague hesitancy. They intended to be the opposite of their selves of two days before. It seemed to be working, for there was no instant recognition from Basoli.

The youngest man spoke first. "Please be seated. I am Ray Burton, Deputy Commander of the Lunar 1 Base. I'd like to introduce you to the Commander in Chief of the WSRA, Ron Basoli, and Commander Adam Landin, Commander of Lunar 1."

Rather than moving to shake hands, Tymos and Kryslie gave each of the men a slight bow of acknowledgement.

Commander Landin spoke first. "Congratulations." He moved his gaze from Kryslie to Tymos as he went on, "I am delighted to be able to offer you both a position at the new Lunar 1 base. Now, I may have been presumptuous – do either of you object to working at the same base?"

"No, Sir," Kryslie said immediately.

"We are used to working together," Tymos confirmed.

Landin went on, "Good, because when your names topped more than a dozen categories, I simply had to have you both. However, my counterpart at Terra 1 would not have objected if you had wanted to be apart."

Kryslie let her head slant to the left as she gave him a questioning look.

Landin smiled and explained, "As Lunar 1 is a new base; I was given first choice of staff except where the specialties overlapped with the needs of Terra 5."

Basoli inserted a comment, "We do reserve the option of rotating staff as required. Do either of you have an issue with that?"

"I understood that would be the case," Tymos said soberly. "It would give the WSRA incredible flexibility."

Kryslie merely said, "I would be happy to serve wherever I was needed." She betrayed no trace of reluctance to work at Terra 5, located as it was in the country ruled by Abdul bin Halil.

Landin began to quiz them about themselves, their interests, experience and questions to get a feel for their personality. This was something a computer couldn't do. Basoli sat back and continued to study them.

As Tymos was explaining that their education had been unconventional, Kryslie thought at him. "Basoli is finding you vaguely familiar. I don't think your suggestions the other day are holding."

Kryslie took over the conversation to allow Tymos to reinforce his mental suggestions.

"We like to keep fit, and find things we don't know and learn all about them from basics up."

"You have proved successful at that," Landin agreed. "How did you manage to work in so many places without official educational results?"

"We targeted our employers, and most of them were impressed by our demonstrations of competence," Kryslie grinned faintly, allowing the three men to see how it fit with their current position.

Unfortunately, her words seemed to be the trigger that caused Basoli to recall where he had seen them before. Kryslie sensed the moment, and his confusion. He was irritated because he had forgotten the face of the Samaritan who had saved the life of one of the Governor's guards, and wondering about the distinct difference in behaviour of the two people now in front of him to what he had seen two days ago.

Kryslie had no time to explain what she had sensed, so she simply projected two images at her brother – him, in command, acting as he had needed, and them to day, playing hesitant.

Tymos gave up trying to repress Basoli's memory when he said, "You did an exceptional job two days ago, Mr Ward."

"Thank you, Sir."

Kryslie detected a hint of wariness in Basoli, as he looked at her twin. Something she couldn't find more about without probing his mind, and she had no reason to do that. She decided to distract him.

"We couldn't just do nothing, Sir. We were there and were able to help. Do you happen to know how the injured people are doing?"

Basoli now focussed on her and for some reason, his uneasiness had increased. "The guard is still in an induced coma, but the swelling in his brain is decreasing. The doctors have given a favourable prognosis. The little girl and her mother are fine. They told the police that they were trapped by the airboat until you released them. How did you know they were down there?"

She shook her head as if implying that she hadn't known, but said, "Those airboats can hold up to 20 people, there weren't that many in the water or clinging to the boat."

It wasn't a lie, nor was it fully the truth. "I feared there might have been more people." She let them assume that she had dived down to check.

"Is all this relevant, Sir," Landin found himself saying.

Basoli glanced at his subordinate, "Landin, you have two good ones here. They were calm and efficient in a crisis – something our computers cannot necessarily predict."

Burton pointed out, "They did well in the testing, Sir."

Giving that statement a waving off motion, Basoli said, "Those exercises were such that any reasonably observant person could do well. Sanitised emergencies, since the candidates would rightly know they would not be greatly harmed."

He pushed himself to his feet, and announced, "I'm pleased to have you as part of the WSRA. Landin will give you instructions for the orientation phase."

Landin and Burton rose as their superior walked around to shake hands with the new staff members.

Tymos rose as Basoli extended his hand and studied him; Kryslie only had time for a quick warning. "Power down!"

She was ready when it was her turn, and used the touch to try to read him. This politeness was a test. He had expected to feel something when he shook hands but he hadn't.

Kryslie stood up as Burton followed Basoli out of the room. She didn't know what was now expected of them.

"If you are not in a rush," Landin claimed their attention, "I'd like you to remain." He was moving into the central chair.

"No rush, Sir," Tymos assured the Commander. "You were going to tell us about orientation?"

He gave a good impression of being relaxed, but his mind was busy talking to Kryslie. "He must have felt the power I had in me when I went to help the guard."

"He expected to feel it again, and didn't, but I don't think that will be the end of it," Kryslie warned him. "I had the sense that he thought there was something odd about us."

"Well, we were not acting shy two days ago, we were being our natural selves. He would not expect grunt level staff to have such obvious self-assurance."

Landin leant back in his chair, noticing subtle body language cues that suggested that his two new staff members were not as relaxed as they had been moments before. Were they wary of him? Surely not; he had given them no reason to be.

"I'm going to be open with you," he said candidly. "These interviews," his hand made a circling gesture in the air, "the last dozen at least, were simply a means for me to get a feel for how the successful candidates – my new staff – will interact. I have no doubts that both of you will fit in just fine."

"You imply that some of us didn't need to be interviewed," Kryslie questioned her perception.

"Quite true," Landin smiled. "You see, I have to build my team from nothing. Oh, I have selected a senior team, consisting of experienced specialists and promising recent graduates, but I don't have specific niches to fill. So, without specific jobs in mind for each new staff member, I have been selecting people skills and knowledge in more than one area. I hope this will give me the most flexibility while I determine what skills I need at Lunar 1. Any skills that I have not foreseen, will be filled with the next intake."

Kryslie gave him a smile and a shrug, while admitting to her brother his method had merit. She was wondering what he was leading up to, but his mind was giving her no clues.

"I did wonder, since you did so well in the preliminary and advanced testing, why you never applied for a place in one of the universities."

Kryslie noticed that Landin's gaze was flicking between her and her twin. She repeated the shrug. "Lack of opportunity and proper records."

In that instant, she sensed his disbelief, even if nothing showed in his expression. She risked a slightly deeper probe, and encountered a strong mind shield.

Tymos shifted his position and drew Landin's attention. "It's true, although maybe it isn't meant to be. Our initial tentative enquiries to the University were turned down, due to lack of official records. What is required is given clearly at the cyber portal. It was moot, anyway. We have had too much personal business these past few years to have the luxury for formal study."

He flicked a mental question at his twin. "Well?" He hoped he had deflected the question, for it was the one they did not want to answer.

Landin straightened, stood and invited, "There is a small meeting room down the corridor. We can make coffee there and continue this discussion in greater comfort."

As Tymos rose, almost exactly at the same time as his sister, he met her gaze, although his face didn't change from its neutral, 'new employee' expression.

He thought at Kryslie, "I can't probe him either, though I can't imagine what he could possibly know about us. Maybe Basoli's odd attitude to us rubbed off on him?"

She replied the same way, "Basoli was fine until he remembered us, so his attitude is from the boat accident. I think this is unrelated. Landin seems very keen to have us, not just because of our skills. He is almost....I'd say "possessive.""

The meeting room wasn't far, and probably doubled as a staff break room. It had a door leading out into a small garden, with benches under shady trees. An oddity, since they were on the first floor, and another 39 stories towered above.

Tymos returned his attention to the room when Landin asked, "What will you have?"

Their new boss was standing by the kettle, reaching into a cupboard for three cups.

"Coffee thanks," Tymos agreed, but he stayed back, flicking a mental, "Keep him busy," to his sister.

Knowing what her twin intended, Kryslie followed Landin and asked, "Do you have some kind of chocolate powder?"

While Landin was checking various cupboards, Tymos took out his communicator, selected a particular function, and did a slow circle of the room. He glanced at the screen, understood the message, and returned the device to his pocket. He had been wary of recording devices in the other room, even though no mention had been made of recording the interviews. He had just confirmed that there were no passive, or active, listening devices in this room.

"I'll take those, Sir," Kryslie offered, picking up her cup of drink as well as her twin's. She followed Landin to one of the groupings of table and chairs. Tymos, took his cup, but after a sip, put it one the low table, and waited for Landin to sit although he gestured for Kryslie to sit first.

She accepted the old fashioned Earth courtesy with a smile, and relaxed into one of the leather armchairs, saying, "We are really excited that you picked us to work for you."

She made her posture relaxed, and Tymos followed her example, and let his sister continue her intended dissembling.

"Is it really an issue that we didn't have any fancy academic records, like from the Uni? I mean, you'll need people who can do the hands on stuff, not just spout the theory."

Landin laughed a natural laugh, "I have tried to weed out that sort. Everyone at Lunar 1 will need to pull their own weight, and work with everyone else." He paused to sip his own drink, and then glanced at both of them as if wondering how to approach an awkward question.

"There was something you want to ask us?" Tymos asked, making eye contact.

The direct question surprised Landin, but he answered at once. "When this recruitment phase began, the WSRA computer was programmed to look for certain things. Once basic identifying data was entered, it was stored and virtually ignored. The exception was in regards to selecting staff for Terra 5. We want a higher proportion of personnel there that come from the countries that are not part of the UWN."

Landin saw the two red heads nodding politely, sipping their drinks and waiting for him to continue. He couldn't tell that Kryslie was thinking at her brother, "What's his point?"

"When your results came through, and your names topped so many lists, I did look at the data you provided, and found it confusing."

Landin was concentrating on watching Kryslie now as he went on, "Your resumes gave no dates, nor where you gained your experience. The computer didn't need that, and your test results prove your claims…"

He held up a hand to forestall the comment Kryslie opened her mouth to make, and went on, "Forty years ago, I had the pleasure of meeting a woman, whose name was …like yours…Krys Ward. I was visiting my grandfather at an informal occasion at the White House. It was a decade before I went to the university in Washington. I learnt from my grandfather, that the woman I mentioned was a formidable bodyguard and that he had known her during the war. You, Kryslie Ward, are the image of that woman, and look to be much the same age as she was at that time. I wondered, are you related?"

His question caused an instant stillness in both of his listeners, and even though they didn't glance at each other, he had the strangest feeling that they were communicating.

"I trust him," Tymos told Kryslie silently. Her instincts were telling her the same and she mentally shuffled memories of that time until she recalled the meeting.

"President Wallis," Kryslie admitted obliquely. "December third, in the first year of his first term in office."

Landin's face betrayed surprise. He understood what she had not said directly.

"So, how old are you really?" he asked with commendable poise. He was tense, suddenly excited.

Tymos did some mental calculations. "We have been on Earth for something like thirty-eight years..." He shrugged at Landin. That could make them the children of the earlier Krys Ward.

"How about telling me, in your own way, how you could have known my grandfather at a place called Rapid Creek." Landin didn't mention the time period – he knew they knew when it was.

He sat back and waited. When neither of his two new technicians spoke further, he prompted, "That was sixty years ago."

Kryslie shrugged. "Did your grandfather tell you anything else about me?"

Landin glanced at both of them. "He said he met you first at Rapid Creek when he was still a very young man. I thought then, that you did not look old enough to have known him years before."

Kryslie tried again to reach his mind. He was still not letting his thoughts leak into his public mind.

"Are you willing to trust us?" Kryslie asked quietly.

"I have the word of two men that I admired and whose integrity I believe in. Both of them trusted you and your brother without reservation," Landin admitted.

"Your grandfather and Tamir Grainger," Tymos stated.

Landin nodded.

"Have you heard of Tymoreans?" Kryslie asked quietly.

"Yes, Grandfather Wallis told me they were a dedicated group of people who were working for peace. Grainger agreed, but once added that they were more than that."

"We are," Tymos confirmed. "What do you think he meant?"

They were verbally fencing. Landin guessed that these two had secrets that they needed to protect. If he wanted them to tell him what he wanted to know, he would have to admit his thoughts and risk being thought a fool, or mad.

"That you are from an ethnic group not originating on Earth," he finally admitted.

Kryslie smiled wryly.

Tymos asked, "If we were, would it bother you?"

Landin relaxed and let his mind shield drop. He thought, in his mind, "Grandfather felt you could read his mind...can you read mine?"

Kryslie looked at him and nodded. She sensed his excitement and no trace of fear at the idea of talking to two probable aliens. He knew only good things of them and that they were highly intelligent.

Tymos went on as if continuing his question, "You said you read our application details. We were born in Australia, in a suburb of Melbourne. You can check if you like."

His mind told them, "I did. I could find no mention."

Kryslie answered the same way. "You probably did not go back far enough. We were born in the latter half of the 1900s. I was Cynthia Ward, back then."

Landin's eyes widened and Kryslie shrugged again.

Tymos took his device out again, not concerned if Landin saw it. He stood and aimed it around the room. He smiled, and adjusted something on the device before placing it on the table. He sat back in his chair. He could talk freely now, without risk of being overheard.

"We were born here," Tymos said quietly. "But we are also Tymoreans. There are things about us that we still can't explain. We didn't know of our heritage until we were sixteen and had turned into total brats. The cause was our Tymorean heritage surfacing. It was unexpected. We were, apparently, descendants of Tymorean missionaries, but since those antecedents had interbred with humans, no one expected us to inherit any Tymorean...abilities."

"Telepathy?" Landin guessed, thinking mentally.

Kryslie thought back, "In my case, yes. Most Tymoreans are not telepaths, and are pretty ordinary. At best we should have just been more intelligent than average and have better physical abilities."

Landin's mind thought, "Supermen" and Kryslie gave her wry, amused smile while shaking her head.

"No, just a bit above human average," she thought back.

She was not going to imply that she and her brother were not 'most Tymoreans'.

Tymos coughed politely, as if noticing his audience was talking among themselves. He was intending to subtly imply that he wasn't a telepath.

"Go on," Landin invited.

"We were fostered by Tymoreans, and had the brattiness trained out of us. We were taught to make the best use of our intelligence and trained to hone our physical abilities. Then we came back here to be missionaries."

Once more, they were only telling a fraction of the truth. Their Tymorean power was stronger than that of all other Tymorean missionaries, and they both had additional gifts that were amplified by their power.

Landin made some guesses of his own, some correct, some not quite. Neither Tymos nor Kryslie chose to correct him.

"So, how old are you really?" he asked again.

Tymos shrugged. "As old as we look, I guess. The truth is - we can't say exactly. While we were away with our foster parents, there was a war there. Many, many thousands of people were placed in a kind of stasis for no one knows how long. Once the war was over, the missionaries that were recalled to help fight, were sent out again. We were old enough then to become missionaries and allowed to return here."

"But still – you were at Rapid Creek..." Landin began.

Kryslie sighed, "Yes, and for other brief periods before that. However, for reasons we don't understand, our return was ... unique. We should have arrived ten years ago."

She used the action of drinking to organise her thoughts, and decide how much to tell him. She had told him the truth, and if Ladin considered it, a perfect reason why they would have been unable to attend one of the WRSA universities. However, their admission confused him.

"Here you will have to suspend your disbelief," Tymos urged. "We returned the day after we left, seeming to be just as we were, but not quite. When we realised that we shouldn't be there, we were moved somehow, about twenty years ahead in time."

"Time travel?" Landin thought excitedly.

"Not that we could duplicate," Kryslie thought back, quashing his sudden thoughts of the possibilities. "We had no control. I think, we were being moved by the Guardians of Peace, to witness pivotal moments in Earth's history."

Landin thought on what he knew of her and her brother and had to agree that seemed to be so.

Tymos went on, "We were only in each time for a short period, until about twenty years ago."

"Are there others like you here?" Landin asked, changing topics abruptly.

He meant, other Tymoreans, but Kryslie and Tymos deliberately took it to mean – like them, specifically. And since they hadn't admitted how special they were amongst Tymoreans, were not lying when they answered.

"No. Usually only two missionaries go to any world. They are to observe that's all. But in times of war, they will try to nudge events towards peace," Tymos finished.

"My grandfather mentioned a group of people," Landin remarked, watching Kryslie and Tymos. This time he noticed no change in expression or body language. They kept meeting his gaze.

"We encountered two Tymoreans during the war, before we helped your Grandfather. We were being careful not to identify ourselves and cause a time paradox."

That was true, if only part of the truth. Landin did not seem to notice the evasion.

"I remembered when you disappeared," Landin said, looking at Kryslie. "What happened?"

Now Kryslie moved her gaze to stare out the window to the garden, where several people were now sitting eating and talking. She was considering how much more to say.

"We helped uncover a lot of programmed agents, and then it was time for us to move on. When we returned next, the war had been over for almost two decades."

There was ten months that she glossed over. There was no need to mention her son…

Instead, she went on, "Tamir Grainger had been dead two years when we finally finished bouncing in time. Each of our landings, so to speak, involved him."

"You were at Washington Uni," Landin realised. "Some years after me. I had thought it must have been your parents but…"

"No, it was us," Kryslie admitted. "We left…"

"Before you graduated…why?" Landin interrupted.

"Personal business," Tymos summarised. "We had needed to be there. Grainger left something for us."

"The Grainger Exhibit! You helped Doc Emmanuel solve it," Landin recalled.

"That was what we had to do, but it made people too aware of us, of our intelligence," Tymos told him.

This time, Landin's conclusions were entirely accurate.

"You don't want to be in the spotlight, because for some reason you are not showing your age."

"Yes," Kryslie admitted. "And too much would be expected of us. We would not have the freedom to act as we sometimes must."

"To act as you must…can you explain what you mean?"

Kryslie shook her head, not intending to even hint at what she and her brother were to the Tymoreans. "I pledge you this, Sir, if we act without orders, beyond our authority, it will be because it is necessary."

"The WSRA structure doesn't allow for mavericks, especially on a space base," Landin began, and again waved his hand to forestall comments. "I trust that if you cannot explain your reasons before acting that you will afterwards? I heard about the incident the C-I-C was involved in, and the quick action of two un-named Samaritans…it seems to me that your reverence for preserving life, speaks well of your intentions. I believe that having staff capable of quick thinking and effective action can only be an asset at Lunar 1, should any major problems occur."

"We certainly hope no life threatening events occur there," Kryslie said, earnestly. Yet the shiver she felt then had the feeling of a premonition.

"You have given me a lot to think on," Landin admitted. "I have one last question, two really. Do you consider yourself Terran or Tymorean?"

"Tymorean," they both stated without hesitation.

"And what is your foremost loyalty?"

"To the cause of Peace," both spoke together, again without hesitation.

Landin nodded, as if satisfied. "I hope you and I can always talk frankly and I appreciate your honesty and trust. Will you be telling this to the CIC?"

"Do you think he would take it well?" Tymos asked, his assessment was that he would not.

"He was headhunted for his position by Tamir Grainger," Landin told them.

That information surprised Tymos, for there had been no mention of that in Grainger's notes or diaries. "I hadn't been aware of that…"

He shared a brief discussion with his sister, "Should we?"

"Not while he is already unsettled by us. We would be watched, and restrained from being able to act freely. I don't think he would fully trust us."

"We might have to in the future."

"Then we wait until we must," Kryslie decided, and she knew Tymos agreed. She then answered Landin, speaking softly. "Not at this time. If it becomes necessary in the future, then we will speak to him."

"I won't mention this discussion to anyone without your permission. I also understand your desire to work inconspicuously." Landin saw his new technicians relax. "Have you any preference for which section you would like to work in?"

Kryslie shook her head. Tymos shrugged and proposed, "Where ever we are needed."

Landin considered. "I'll put Kryslie in the Controller Division, and you in the Computer Division. But since you have a wide range of abilities, be prepared to be reassigned to where ever your skills are needed."

Kryslie and Tymos both smiled and shrugged.

Much later, when Landin had time to think further on that odd discussion, he wondered if Tymos and Kryslie realised he knew more about them than he had let on. He considered everything they had admitted to him, and it agreed in all essentials with what he had talked out of his grandfather. At the time, it had been an intense curiosity, but now … now he was sure of one thing. He could trust them, and he, and the WSRA, were lucky to have their intelligence and skill to call on.

Five years later

"You are quite the hero," Tymos whispered over his sister's shoulder. "That little incident in the shuttle bay made the newsfeeds down on Earth."

Kryslie Ward scanned the data scrolling down her computer screen and rotated her chair to face her twin. He was still in his uniform, although his shift in Lunar 1's Computer section had finished three hours ago. The shifts in Main Mission were offset from the other departments since the controllers were overseeing all other departments as well as the environment outside the base. Her own shift had three more hours to run.

"How?" was all she said, meeting her brother's unsmiling face. Tymos gave a slight shrug.

"There were no media reps here," Kryslie commented in a low voice.

"Daniel sent a message. Can you take a break and come to my quarters?" Tymos asked her. His voice was so quiet that the controller at the adjacent console could not hear him.

"I'm due for a break," Kryslie stood up. She nudged her co-worker. "I'm going for a coffee, keep an eye on my screen?" He turned and gave her a nod, before returning to his own work.

He wouldn't need to do more than glance at it occasionally. At present, she was just scanning the data coming in from a drone probe that she had programmed to shadow a meteorite passing a safe 100 million kilometres from Earth. If anything changed, the computer would ping a warning.

As she moved around the arc of the walkway to the nearest door, she spoke to the Duty Controller, Bevan Fowler, in his chair in the central 'well' of the circular deck. "I'm taking a ten minute break, Sir."

He swivelled his chair to give her a nod, and then turned his attention back to some simulations being run by the engineering section. These were currently filling the main view screen.

None of the other duty controllers paid her any attention, as they were all focussing on their assigned tasks.

Once the door slid shut behind them, they both walked quickly to the nearest turbo lift. Normally they would walk to their quarters, but Kryslie had limited time and the lift would transport them around to the far side of the base, and down a level quicker than walking. Tymos pressed the summoning plate and they soon heard the rising hum as the lift car approached.

The lift doors opened, and they were surprised to see Commander Landin step out. He said quickly, "Hold Lift" and added, "Technician Ward, I was just on my way to see you."

Both Tymos and Kryslie looked at him, so he specified, "Kryslie."

"Well, I'm on a break right now, Sir, if you'd…." She was about to offer to talk to him now, but he waved her to silence.

"After your shift will be soon enough," Landin told her. "And you might as well come too," he looked at Tymos with a neutral expression. He stepped aside and let them enter the lift.

Kryslie noted that he was still looking at her as the doors closed and she wondered if he knew about the media leak of the shuttle bay incident. She's sensed he was tense, but he wasn't annoyed with her.

Tymos gave her mind a mental nudge. "You need to see something."

Kryslie didn't sense what he was referring to, since he had his mind shielded. It wasn't intentional to block her as well, more of a reflex as they were occupying a base of limited size, with over 500 personnel. That he didn't tell her what he was referring to only meant he didn't want anyone else overhearing them.

The speed of the lift was deceptive, inside the chamber, you were hardly aware of the movement, except there was an indicator panel showing a schematic of where the lift was in respect to the base plan. Within half a minute, the lift was slowing and then there was the feeling of going down, stopping, and the door whooshed open.

They might have been back where they began, for the passageways were similar in all areas. The main difference here was the colour scheme of the wall panels – pale green instead of metallic grey. Tymos's assigned quarters were only ten metres further on, just past one of the 'you are here' schematics. Kryslie was aware of the short amount of time she had, and would have hurried, but several crew were walking along the passage, and running would have created comment and curiosity. As it was, those that passed them, merely gave her a polite greeting or a grin.

"Well, my fame hasn't spread here yet," she murmured to her twin.

They'd reached Tymos's door, and he pressed the palm locked touch pad to open it. "I've got Earthbase doing damage control, but I doubt they can do too much."

Once inside, the door closed behind them and Tymos said, "Lock door." A faint click was the only indication that the voice command had worked. He strode past the tiny lounge area – two arm chairs and a low table – and down to the desk opposite his bunk. He turned on his computer terminal, and during the second or two it needed to wake up, he pulled out his standard issue WRSA communicator, and activated a definitely non-standard app that he had programmed into it. Kryslie felt the sudden cessation of the faint hum of the air circulation system, and the faint ticking of her brother's wall chronometer. It meant that any sound inside the sphere of the effect, would not be heard beyond it, so no listening device if there happened to be one, would overhear their conversation.

The screen on the terminal changed from black to a scene Kryslie recognised instantly – the shuttle bay. Tymos stepped back to give her a clear view.

"Watch and listen," Tymos instructed. "This is what they are showing in the news feeds."

The video that began showed the shuttle bay as it had been before the previous day's 'accident' and was obviously a duplicate of the security monitoring film. There was also a voice over from a reporter, who described the events occurring on it.

It began with a view of the half hexagon entrance, framed by narrow white panel lights, and although most people couldn't see it, the pale blue of the force field that kept in the base atmosphere.

Kryslie saw herself, standing by the duty officer at his pedestal supported console. She and he were watching as the nose of the shuttle emerged through the force field. To get the through, the pilot need to apply a controlled amount of power, and once within, the shuttle was quickly powered down to minimum speed to follow the glowing yellow line on the bay floor to the glowing red circle.

She saw herself jerk, at the moment when she knew something was wrong.

Tymos remarked, "The direction of the nose jerked just then – setting the shuttle up like a snooker ball for a pocket shot."

"Yes, and he couldn't power down," Kryslie agreed, her attention still on the video replay. "Casey is blaming himself."

"He shouldn't," Tymos said flatly.

The racing figure in the red controller's uniform, was faster than the out of control shuttle, faster even than Commander Landin, who was standing near the president's guards. Kryslie saw herself knock the President down, recalled that Landin had yelled to the guards – he and they had landed on the floor just as the nose of the shuttle impacted on the wall beside the little anteroom.

Fuel had begun to leak from a cracked tank, and this ignited, sending a wash of searing heat over the prone group.

The fire suppressant system had come on, quickly dousing the flames and drenching both Landin, and herself with the chemical retardant. The other three men had already been in the protective flight suits, and were hardly affected by either the heat or the chemicals.

Once the flames were out, Kryslie had helped the President to his feet, while the shuttle bay emergency crew were assisting Casey and his co-pilot from the blackened and crumpled shuttle.

The focus of the monitor was on the shuttle, but she and the others were in the side view, and could be seen leaving the anteroom.

After that, Kryslie and Landin had been hustled through to the other shuttlebay, to the decon shower, where they had the chemicals washed off them, and uniforms replaced by clean overalls.

The reporter's voice spoke as the film played out, explaining that yesterday, the shuttle that was to return to Earth with Joel Adamson, President of the United World Nations, had entered the bay and then skidded out of control, heading directly for the position where he and two of his bodyguards were waiting.

He described the fire, the miraculous way in which the President had been saved. Her name wasn't mentioned then, but after the video finished, and the reporter's face filled the screen, a picture of her was on a screen behind him, and he had identified her.

"Damn," Kryslie summarised her unease. She had acted without thought, thinking only of the need to save the men from harm. Now there was this visual proof of how fast she could move and her name and her face were being spread around the globe below. "I don't suppose your scavenger program works on an image or can garble a voice?"

Tymos shook his head. "No, a computer can't recognise you specifically, though as far as Earthbase can tell, your name is not showing up in the print media, or the print based e-news services."

"That is all very well, but somebody had to have leaked that video. I wonder who it was," Kryslie said, her mind filling with a myriad of questions. She moved a step backwards and sat on her brother's bed.

"Someone with access to the security records, or who is a damn good hacker," Tymos summarised, turning to keep talking, and in turn leaning against his desk.

"How far this news has travelled, bro?" From his expression, she didn't need an answer, verbal or mental. "Could you trace any message going from here?"

"Not yet, I spent the last couple of hours trying. If the person who sent it is as good as me in getting into the computers, he or she will be able to cover their tracks. I have a few more ideas to try, but I am not meant to have access to those records either."

"You know, if the endangered passengers had been anyone but the President, the incident probably wouldn't have made a stir – except in the American convocation."

Tymos simply shrugged. "Daniel is monitoring the news net to get a feel for the reaction," he told her. "It is being called a tragic accident that was averted. The two body guards have relatively minor injuries. But, there is some interest in learning more about you."

"If I was merely human," Kryslie said slowly. "I would probably enjoy being in the limelight."

But she wasn't. As Tymorean missionaries, she and Tymos preferred to keep a low profile. If anyone was to make a thorough investigation – they might find some very odd anomalies.

"I couldn't let him be killed," Kryslie said, but she did not have to justify herself to her brother.

"No, of course not. But at least, up here you won't be swamped by reporters."

Kryslie laughed. "Maybe not, but they are a minor concern – I could probable twist a tale to satisfy them. I am more concerned about the gremlin. Do you think he or she intended to kill Adamson and might target me now?"

The person they had nick-named 'the gremlin', was the perpetrator of a series of serious incidents that had been occurring on Lunar 1 for the past few months. They had started after the latest intake of new staff, but all the new comers had been thoroughly checked. The intense screening processes should have weeded out any pretenders before they even arrived on Lunar 1.

Their own investigation, shared between them, had found nothing about the twenty four newcomers to be suspicious of. Security film from the areas where the 'accidents' and 'malfunctions' had occurred showed no suspicious activity either.

Tymos shrugged. "The shuttle going out of control fits the pattern, though so far the incidents have merely wasted manpower and interfered with the base's observational capabilities."

"But if the gremlin did it, bro, it might point to someone who is in sympathy with the Imperium."

"Or some of the anti-tech groups within the UWN - people are afraid of the WSRA's push to get into space."

"They'd have no reason to target the President. He has no jurisdiction over any of the WSRA bases or what they do." "But if he died up here there would be a widespread uproar," Tymos countered.

"Then the Investigative committee would investigate. Did you find anything wrong with the shuttle?"

"The computer system was fine and the engineers found nothing wrong with the mechanics of the shuttle either."

"So what does that tell us?" Kryslie asked. "Did you see anything odd?"

Tymos drew something out of his pocket and handed it to his sister.

Kryslie studied it. It was small, barely two centimetres long and one wide, with a thin wire protruding from one end.

"It has a remote signal receiver," Kryslie identified part of the object.

"And a transmitter and a micro pulse generator," Tymos confirmed. "It could have sent a signal to the shuttle to adjust its course before it sent the EM pulse to deactivate the shuttle's computer controls. Its insides are all burnt out, so it was intended for a single use, but I tested the materials. It was made on Earth. I have asked Daniel to try and trace the technology. There is nothing like it in the WSRA archives."

"Imperium archives?" Kryslie suggested.

"They are not so centralised – I will leave them to Daniel," Tymos told her.

"Have you shown that to Landin yet?"

"No, I wanted to show you first, and do some checking. I am about to go see him now."

"It explains why the monitoring cameras saw nothing amiss." Kryslie noted. "That could have been put on the shuttle back on Earth - or if the gremlin planted it – it could have been done anytime."

"Exactly, and the same can be said about each of the other recent malfunctions. I suspect that was what Adamson was up here about – even though the WSRA bases are neutral territory."

"He is a partisan of what the WSRA stands for," Kryslie admitted aloud. "He would be able to get the police in the American Convocation to look into it."

"And those anti-techno types would be the first people to be questioned," Tymos agreed.

"And if it were them, surely they would also be targeting other WRSA bases. This is the most difficult of all to get to and all the other bases are also involved in the build up to space exploration."

Kryslie was aware of time passing. "I need to get back to work. Though I don't think I will be concentrating on that. Have you considered, that although this base is part of the meteorite early warning system, and will be the major tracking base for the future space probes – that it would be no great leap of logic to presume that the orbiting satellites up here would pick up hostile actions from below."

She felt a shiver as she spoke, and her brother was aware of it.

"I will ask Daniel to check on your old friend," Tymos promised.

"I thought I fixed him the last time we met," Kryslie muttered. She did not want to think about Abdul bin Halil, leader of the Imperium. "I had better get back to work."

"Watch your back," Tymos warned.

The privacy field did not stop Kryslie leaving, and Tymos kept it on while he prepared a message to Earthbase. If anyone decided to sneak into his room, it would give him warning.

Since he didn't know who the gremlin was, he couldn't be sure that the person was completely ignorant of his low-key investigation. Nor could he be sure that his quarters were private, and his personal computer was secure. He quickly composed the message on his computer, sent it to his communicator – his personal one, not the WSRA issued one – and sent it to Earthbase as a microburst transmission. While he waited for an acknowledgement, he erased the message from his computer and communicator so that no one would be able to recover it.

His personal communicator, in theory, did not work from Lunar 1, since it was too far away from the planet based comm network. What only he and his sister knew was that there were extra apps built into it that did still work from the moon. The signal sent to Earthbase was relayed via a cloaked orbiting Tymorean satellite, and as it didn't go through the base computer – was not detected and saved. Messages coming from Earthbase were received by the relay satellite, and stored there until Tymos or Kryslie linked to it and downloaded them.

He did not have to wait long for a reply, and it was so short it didn't need to be compressed. It simply said, "No information available immediately".

Tymos turned his communicator off, knowing that Daniel would have one of the missionaries check for the information, and he would send it as soon as possible.

Only then did he deactivate the privacy field, and consider the questions that had occurred to him whilst talking to his sister. He needed to consider them, before taking the odd device he had found to Landin. He strolled to where he had his chairs placed and flopped into the one nearest the wall.

These chairs, requisitioned when he had decorated his quarters, were of a brown vinyl that blended with the beige wall panels. They looked like arm chairs, but they swivelled. Tymos redirected the one he sat in to face the nearest wall panel, and he used his toe to tap a control pad and bought up a darkened OLED screen. He said, "Image 1" and his voice activated the screen so it showed a geometric pattern in pastel shades. The image was a copy of a Tymorean meditation focus.

He could sense his twin's unease, not in his mind, but though the deeper twin bond, but the focus helped him to block that from his thoughts, so he could think effectively to bring together myriad details.

He wanted to consider the probability of another conspiracy originating in the still un-aligned countries. Sixteen years ago, he and Kryslie had broken up a cabal intent on destroying the peace of the UWN. Forty-two years ago, she had given the leader of that cabal a child, and this child was meant to be a seed of peace. However, her leaving back then had made her an enemy of the leader, Abdul bin Halil. The man was charismatic and had forged strong alliances between most of the countries that had chosen not to join the UWN. He was now considered much like an Emperor. The more recent failure of the cabal had not noticeably affected him, but that had not surprised either Kryslie or himself. The man was too smart to be directly involved, and quite prepared to denounce the overt leaders as traitors.

Both times, Kryslie had effectively bested him, and since the last encounter, she had been keeping a low profile. However, should her picture be seen by bin Halil, he would recognise her and he would not have forgiven her. Moreover, on their last meeting, she had 'treated' his mind, and if he could find a way to work around the commands she had laid on him, he would. In sixteen years, those commands may have weakened.

Tymos and Kryslie were right to feel uneasy. The newscast of the shuttle mishap had been picked up by the news media within the Imperium. More specifically, a message had been sent to the leader of the Imperium advising him to watch it. Since it involved his detested 'equal' in the UWN, he was already angry that the 'unfortunate accident' had not produced fatalities. The message had not mentioned the name of the 'saviour' – but the sender was unaware that certain names sent by computer text message were mysteriously deleted. However the message had mentioned red hair, and that had roused vexatious memories.

Abdul bin Halil felt his anger growing in intensity as he watched the rescue. The red headed person, dressed like a man, moved unbelievably fast. He let the film run to the end and then watched it again, stopping it on the one clear shot of the woman's face.

Bin Halil glanced from the screen to a picture hanging on the wall. The two images could have been of the same woman.

"It cannot be! The bitch should be dead!"

"Father?"

The Imperium Leader twirled around, like a snake twisting to strike. He glared at his son, who was staring at the face on the screen.

"I see you recognise that foreign agitator too," he challenged.

"How can it be? You said she had died." Arthur had thought she must be dead, and had grieved privately. Now he was hiding elation.

"She should have been. I was assured that she was, and if those lying, incompetent guardsmen were not dead now, I would order them to be castrated."

Abdul bin Halil was capable of ordering exactly that, but Arthur did not want to dwell on the thought, so he said, "Where is she?"

"On that obscene lunar base. That woman saved the infidel President of the UWN. I should have killed her myself."

Although he wanted to ask his father what he intended to do, he also didn't want to hear the answer. Instead, he took the remote control his father had set on a table and watched the news video from start to finish. Seeing her in action, convinced him that is was the woman from sixteen years ago. He knew things about that woman that he had no intention of telling his father.

Whatever she had done to his father back then, had the power to raise a killing rage in him. For a time, he had been different – his anger leashed

– but that had not lasted long. Now that he had proof that she was alive, he would be scheming to have her killed.

His father had hated her from first sight, because she was the image of the woman who had given birth to his son, and vanished before he could have her killed. The woman had been tortured on is orders, because he could not torture that older woman, his missing consort.

Arthur knew, however, that in spite of the fact that the red headed woman looked younger than he did now, that she was both his mother, and the woman who had come sixteen years back.

His father had tried to teach him to hate his birth mother, but his early tutors had shown him that she was worth his respect. He wanted to talk to her.

If she had been alive all this time, why hadn't she set the World Council Investigators onto his father – or rather, revealed what he had done to her? Surely the fact that she hadn't, meant something.

A voice in his head seemed to say, "She still believed he could help bring peace." Arthur knew his father too well now and he had doubts but he kept tactfully silent and waited for his father to continue.

"Arrange for me to tour that facility," bin Halil instructed his son.

"Is that wise?"

"Is the WSRA bases not neutral territory? Do you not work at Terra 5, which is here in our country? What could be safer?" bin Halil seemed to chide his son.

Arthur wondered what his father was thinking, and his eye went to the stilled newscast. He had stopped it on the image of the burning shuttle.

Bin Halil guessed some of what his son was thinking. "There will be no danger to me."

Arthur was suddenly sure that that incident with the shuttle was no accident and his father had arranged it, or at least knew in advance that it might happen. He hid his thoughts and asked, "What if it is the same woman?"

His father hissed, "I will expose her for the unnatural freak she is."

Rather than argue, Arthur bowed to his father and retreated. He spoke to his father's advisors and protocol ministers and told them what he was doing. They would arrange the details with the liaisons of the WSRA.

He was going to insist on accompanying his father. Even before this incident, he had wanted the chance to work at Lunar 1. Now he had even more reason to want to go there.

Landin was pacing his office, his mind trying to think of a way to weed out whoever was responsible for the nasty 'accidents' that had been plaguing his base. Tymos Ward had nicknamed him 'gremlin' and it certainly fit. That he admitted to doing investigating of his own, although without success, eased some of the fear eating at his mind. If no one else could find the perpetrator, he was sure Tymos Ward and his sister would eventually succeed. He intended to keep their involvement quiet, and let their quarry think that only the small security squad were investigating.

After the previous day's incident in the shuttlebay, when he and the UWN President had narrowly missed being killed, he'd had nightmares. If Kryslie Ward hadn't been there, and he hadn't stopped to ask why she had been, world opinion might have turned against the WSRA.

Already, he'd had questions via the comm link to Earth, from the Investigative Committee. They would have representatives coming up on the next shuttle. They wanted answers, but then – so did he.

Shuttlebay 1 would be out of commission until the wall where the shuttle impacted was checked. The partition between the anteroom and the bay was cracked and warped. The wall though, that had been reinforced with a force field, so they might be lucky and have minimal damage to the main structure of the base.

The shuttle was likely to be out of service permanently, and that meant the huge expense of having a new one built.

President Adamson had been severely shaken, but once he had recovered, had been courteous about the delay whilst another shuttle was sent up from Earth to get him. He had offered whatever help was needed to reverse the damage and discover the cause.

Part of the answer to 'how' was on his desk, only the object had raised many more questions.

When his door chime warned him of someone wishing to see him, he glanced at his wrist chronometer. Time had passed while his thoughts had circled uselessly. He walked back behind his desk and was seating himself as he called, 'Enter' to activate the door.

Kryslie Ward entered, her shift having just ended. Somehow she was still looking as fresh as if she had just begun work. Following like a shadow, her brother entered after her. Landin noticed that he had changed from his uniform since their earlier talk. He now had on overalls with numerous utility pockets. Neither of his expected visitors showed any particular expression.

"Sit!" Landin gestured to the extra chairs. One was positioned in front of the desk. Kryslie took that one, while Tymos dragged a second one into positon next to the other. In that short interval, Landin used a touch pad on his desk to secure the door and deactivate the standard monitors.

Only a quick glance at the touchpad by the door, where three red lights blinked in a row, betrayed to Tymos that Landin had activated the privacy mode to keep other people out. The subsequent glance that Kryslie gave him was accompanied by the thought that the indicator on the standard monitor was off. He had already seen that the burnt out device that he had given Landin earlier, was in plain view on the desk.

As he sat, Tymos commented, "If anyone has access to the monitor films from in here, they might have seen that, Sir."

"True," Landin agreed. "And would have heard me ask my department heads what it was."

He implied, by adding no other comment, that none had. His silence was a request for any information these two could give him. His mind said as much.

Tymos didn't answer him straight away, instead he said, "Blanking out the monitors in here might raise suspicions and questions from various parties. I appreciate the gesture, but…" instead of finishing the sentence, he took out his communicator and activated the app he had used earlier in his quarters. He knew that the base commander could later delete the sound from the monitor film – in cases where the conversation needed to be kept private, but usually the visual record was retained.

As if to simply have the device out of his pocket, Tymos put it on the corner of Landin's desk and from the narrowing of his Commander's eyes, guessed that Landin recognised what he had done. After a moment of thought, Landin reactivated the standard monitors, and murmured, "I really must have a closer look at your communicator."

"We can talk and not be overheard, Sir. The temporary blackout will be considered another inexplicable glitch, and since we appear to be unaware of any problem, the gremlin may not suspect anything."

Landin might have been tempted to think that Tymos Ward was paranoid, and at first he had been sceptical that any one person could be causing so many 'accidents'. There was no proof that pointed to any particular exprerson. Yet, Tymos had pointed out some trends that his security team had missed. Some of the events could not possibly be random faults. The safety protocols had to have been circumvented. If that unknown person wanted to have warning of any suspicion directed his way, the commander's office was one place he would want to watch. An un-monitored interview might cause that unknown perpetrator to wonder if Tymos was onto him. He wondered though, if Tymos had considered whether the unknown could lip read?

He swivelled his chair so that he was more directly facing Kryslie and so he was facing one of the monitor sensors.

"I have had the Investigative Committee asking questions. One was – why was there an unauthorised person in the shuttle bay when the shuttle was coming in?"

Kryslie had been sitting back in the chair, and now she leant forward, opening her mouth as if to make a protest, shutting it and then saying, "Are they trying to accuse me? I save the President, for heaven's sake. If I was trying to kill him, would I have done that?"

Tymos moved his chair, casually, and just happened to lean forward enough to block the monitor's view of his sister as Landin asked, "What were you doing there?"

Kryslie knew he had to ask the question, and her earlier reaction was a ploy to mislead the Gremlin – just in case he was somehow watching.

"The tracking program for monitoring the incoming shuttle was giving trouble. I was sent to look at it, since the President's shuttle was just coming back from its post service check flight."

"Why you? Why didn't the duty controller send someone higher than a Tech 3?"

"I was right there when the request came through."

"What did you find?"

"Everything seemed fine. I didn't actually have a chance to finish checking. I realised there was a problem and then Security took over."

Landin decided to stand and move around. He was looking at Kryslie when he spoke again, but his question was directed at Tymos.

"When you came in earlier, you didn't say anything about that device. I understand why. However, none of the senior staff have seen anything like it. What makes you think it was involved?"

"As I said earlier, I found it on the floor of the shuttle bay, about where the shuttle bounced off the wall. It was probably stuck to some surface – most likely the shuttle. The impact could have knocked it off. It doesn't belong in the shuttle bay."

"You know what it is," Landin stated, not asked. He moved to sit on the front of his desk, studying both technicians.

"Yes, Sir. It is a remotely activated micro pulse generator."

Even though Landin had never heard of such a thing, he instantly deduced what must have happened. Such a device could have caused the shuttles electronics to reset and in the very short period afterwards the shuttle would be out of control.

Tymos nodded again, confirming the unspoken surmise.

To Kryslie, Landin asked, "How did you know the shuttle was out of control?"

From anyone else it might have sounded like an accusation of complicity.

"I just knew," Kryslie said. "I have seen enough shuttles landing to know what is right."

She went silent, searching her memory for the clues she had added up in an instant. "An ultrasonic beep just as the shuttle was at the force field, the instant of panic from the pilot, and...anticipation."

She looked at Landin. "The rest was an instinct for spatial physics."

Landin's mind said her comment was an understatement. He knew they were both something more than merely human, but had promised not to reveal it.

"So, was that device planted here?"

Tymos answered that. "I have no proof," Tymos qualified. "But I believe so. The shuttle that had brought the President up had reached its mandatory service hours. It went into the service bay. The one that came to return him had just finished being serviced."

"I will have security check over the monitoring archives," Landin proposed, but he caught a quick flick of something in Tymos's eyes. He waited to see if Tymos added anything.

"Do so, by all means," Tymos agreed. "Other eyes may spot something."

Landin sighed inwardly and decided to be blunt. "You found nothing?"

He did not mention that Tymos's position of Technician Third Grade in the Computer Division, did not give him the relevant access rights to view those films.

"No, Sir. Not yet," Tymos admitted. "The device could have been planted well in advance. It might have been added at Terra One and there might be others on other shuttles."

Landin tensed at that thought, and stood again to return to the chair behind the desk. "I will need an official at statement from both of you by tomorrow. The IC are checking all of the recent arrivals, and they may widen the investigation to all staff."

He didn't need to imply they would be questioned, they probably expected that. He was giving them a heads up, on the other questions that might be asked – about their background.

With Tymos still hiding her from the monitor camera, Kryslie said, "I know it looks like one of the new arrivals, since you are rotating them through all the departments, but our Gremlin might be acting through someone who has been here a while."

Tymos added, "Surely though, the applicant screening procedure would have weeded out anyone unsuitable or dubious."

"Bro, the last big screening job was before we started here. A lot can happen in five years. Anyway – it was mainly looking for skills." Kryslie knew her brother had picked up on her unspoken, "Look what it missed about us."

Landin nodded, but added, "That last lot were a mix of Uni graduates, and those who were pre-selected last time but didn't make the intake limit."

An inner prompting caused Kryslie to ask, "Did you have a limit this time?"

Landin gave her a thoughtful stare before answering. "I had 25 places to fill, but one of those I selected pulled out at the last minute. I decided not to worry about that until the next intake."

Tymos suddenly straightened as an idea occurred to him. Landin noticed, but didn't ask what he had said to cause it. Instead, he let his posture relax and announced, "On a different subject, since I have you both here. Do you remember Don Gilchrist from the Washington Uni?"

Kryslie nodded, aware that her brother was thinking hard on an idea suggested by Landin's previous comment.

Misleadingly, she said, "We spoke to him when applying to the Uni."

Landin took two data pads from a compartment in his desk and pushed then towards his visitors. Kryslie leant forward and took both, and passed the one with her brother's name to him.

Although Landin said nothing, his mind was projecting, "Gilchrist sends his regards and commendations to you."

Kryslie kept her head down, as if reading the data padd, but projected back to Landin, "The news cast?"

She felt his confirmation. "And?" She wondered if anyone else had made the connection, as she was feeling a definite warning tingle of a premonition.

Again, Landin allowed her to read his thoughts as he merely seemed to watching her read. "He is certain that you are the same Krys Ward who walked out of his University. He noted that you look no older now than you did seventeen years ago. He hoped that I would have better luck holding on to you."

Kryslie relaxed fractionally. "Could you thank him for his kind regards, and add our apologies for leaving without a word. Perhaps he will now understand why."

"I will," Landin promised. "He admitted to being angry at the time, but has had much time to consider your probable reasons. He concluded that like your mentor, Tamir Grainger, your reasons would have been of the highest merit – even if incomprehensible."

What Kryslie was reading on the data padd was unrelated to the verbal and mental conversation about Gilchrist. It read, "The President was here, concerned about those little accidents and malfunctions. Not that the UWN has anything to do with us. But in spite of our openness about our operations and reasons for existence – a lot of people from the UWN and the non-aligned countries still fear we are some sort of big brother spying on them. I have reported this to Adamson, with pictures and description, so he can warn his people. The Investigative Committee are involved, naturally. Basoli will have an alert sent to all WSRA bases. The section heads here will look out for other odd devices. What will you do now?"

Kryslie asked, "Do we need to complete this now?"

Landin looked back at her and said, "If you could."

Tymos pulled his thoughts back to his surroundings and made motions of adding data to the padd. Kryslie was actually answering for them both.

"That device won't work again – it was single use and now its electronics are fused. We will have to look for more, but if the Gremlin knows we are, he will remove them. You will need to have someone monitoring the security films – but so far that hasn't helped."

When Kryslie finished tapping the padd, Landin said, "I am to set you a research task as part of the process. You can work together, but must write separate reports."

Kryslie smiled faintly, Landin could be deceptive too. The Gremlin, if he was watching, and if he could read lips, wouldn't know what process was meant, unless he was thinking she and Tymos wanted to go to the WSRA University.

"So, you have one in mind?" Tymos asked.

Landin pointed to the device on his desk. "You found that thing. I need someone to search the archives. See if that device is mentioned there, if so – what it is and how it works."

"Can I have Tech 2 computer access?" Tymos glanced at Landin, with a pretend hopeful look.

"A Tech 3 can access all the Scientific Journals." Landin's mind said then, "I suspect you already have full access."

Tymos grinned, and Landin abruptly finished the interview. "Once you are done, you can go."

Kryslie handed the data padds back and Tymos retrieved his communicator. He pocketed it after pretending to check for messages. When they reached the door, the privacy field was gone.

Once they were gone, Landin left his office through the door that bypassed main mission and led to his quarters. As he walked, he recalled Gilchrist's parting comment in the private message he had received earlier that day. The old man had said, "Those two could be aggravating, but they would do as asked and didn't seem to want to be in control – overtly. But I always felt that they had their own agenda and would pursue it without letting others stop them."

In the past five years, he had not noticed any such tendency…well, maybe he had. They were pursuing their Gremlin and he hadn't asked them to. And he was certain that Tymos had gained access to the computer at a level beyond Tech 3.

It really didn't matter. He trusted them, unreservedly.

Kryslie emerged from the closet sized sonic shower cubicle in her quarters and gave her hair a vigorous brushing. By the time she finished, her hair was nearly dry. The sonic shower used a fraction of the amount of water that a normal shower did, but cleaned and refreshed to a greater degree. It was one of the things about living in the moon base that some people took a long time to get used to. However, Kryslie was already familiar with the concept for the same type of showers existed on Tymorea where water conservation was as imperative as it was on the moon.

Even though it was just past the end of Alpha shift, which meant about 3 am Lunar time, she had not long returned from a vigorous workout with her twin in the base gym. At that time of the moon's 'night', (even when the base was in its two weeks of sunlight) very few people wanted to use the fitness equipment, and she and Tymos did not have to hide their greater than normal physical abilities.

Feeling too awake to try to sleep, she decided to do some research using Earth's information web, and so twisted her shoulder length hair into a pony tail. She liked to keep it off her face when she was working. During delta shift, when she was on duty, she turned it into a more formal coil at the back of her head.

In her quarters, which was laid out to a different plan than her twin's, her computer terminal was near the head of her bed rather than across from it. She sat in her chair and unlocked a compartment where she kept details of various personal research projects that occupied her in her off duty hours. She was most interested in ways to improve the resolution of images obtained from the tracking telescopes.

It was her habit to check her daily schedule every time she logged on. The week at a glance view showed her duty shifts, 2 to 8 pm Lunar time each day, as well as any other scheduled appointments like the monthly medical checks, or requests by other members of staff for a meeting.

The schedule usually mentioned the semi-regular visits by WSRA officials, politicians, statesmen, entertainment luminaries and anyone else who was notable. Often members of the senior staff would need to be available. Generally, lowly Tech 3s were not involved.

However, the regular third day shuttle was due later that day and she noted her name was now included as part of the greeting party. No particulars were given to indicate who the shuttle passengers were.

Knowing that her twin was awake, as a sense of him deep in their twin bond, she thought at him, "Any idea who will be coming up on the shuttle today?"

"No, why? Anyone the latest staff will get excited over?"

"No names are mentioned, but I have to be available. I am assuming it will be the IC."

"Likely. Those lot never seem to give out their names. Are you decent? I'll pop in."

Giving him the okay, for she had dressed in a leisure suit and trousers after her shower, Kryslie knew to expect him any second. At this hour, he would use his transmitter to arrive.

When he did, he was wearing a brown all in one suit, possibly over his sleeping clothes. He didn't waste time on greetings, simply began with, "I have been monitoring the news feeds still, but something Landin said earlier got me thinking about checking the shuttle logs. So I found out how to access them."

He was grinning, and Kryslie knew he had inserted his presence, once again, where Tech 3s shouldn't have access. "Just give me a few moments."

Kryslie watched and memorised what her twin was doing; for future reference.

"There!" Tymos announced as a list of names came up on the screen. Kryslie read them rapidly. Six of the twelve names were Lunar 1 staff returning from leave.

"It doesn't exactly say who the rest are…" Kryslie began, but then saw a name she did recognise. "Did Jon tell you he was coming up?"

"No, but it might have been a last minute decision," Tymos mused. "The shuttle would have left Terra One two hours ago."

"Well, it does tell us who some of those others must be. And since I don't recognise any names, they are not IC members we know from years back."

Their friend Jonko, who was using the name John Goss, had been working for the Investigative Committee for over fifteen years.

"I am surprised that Basoli didn't come up," Tymos admitted.

"Be glad he didn't," Kryslie murmured.

Tymos manipulated the touch pad again to check the info for the sixth day shuttle. Something about the way his body went tense, caused Kryslie to study the list of passengers for that one.

One glance was enough to cause a fierce shiver to run down her spine. The icy premonition came as she read the name of Abdul bin Halil, and she was blind to all the other names.

"Well, I think that proves it. He recognised me."

"He cannot insist that you leave," Tymos told her, sensing her concern about what the man might do.

"Bro, if he does actually think I am the woman he met seventeen years ago, or worse the one he allegedly married forty years ago, he might be out to prove it. And he probably still has that reward out for my hide."

"You could be the child of the woman he met seventeen years ago."

"Don't be daft! He won't believe in three generations of red heads that look the same."

"Then keep out of sight. You will be on shift for most of the time he is here."

"It won't work. I know how that wretched man thinks. You can safely bet that I will have to be around when he arrives. He will want to meet the celebrity, or have me around as a good luck token…something. What if he can prove I was around forty years ago and I don't look a day older now? His son – my son – looks twice my age."

"He can't prove it – I made sure nothing with your DNA on it remained."

"Except my son." Kryslie saw her brothers face go pale for a moment.

"No one looking at you would believe that you are the mother of his son."

"Most people perhaps."

"I don't think he will say anything here. He would sound crazy."

"He doesn't need to," Kryslie countered. "It would be more like him to find an old photo and imply things. Previously he has always had others do his dirty work, so he keeps his impeccable image. We can't control an underground whispering campaign. And even if most people discount the whispers, enough people will believe them. But there are always some who will hunt out freaks to expose them. And if I am revealed, you will be suspect too. We will have to leave here."

At that moment, Kryslie felt another fierce shiver of warning and knew Tymos a similar sensation.

There were no words or images with the warning; there didn't mean to be.

"Leaving Lunar 1 is not an option. We have to be here!" Tymos stated.

They had known that they had to be part of the moon base staff, and now, the Guardians of Peace, to whom space and time were infinitely mutable, had reinforced the conviction.

"Wear your portable force screen," Tymos advised.

"I would have to keep it on even after he goes," Kryslie said. "It is possible that the gremlin works for him. And we don't know who he, she or they are."

"It would be wise to do that. And we need to convince bin Halil that you are not the Krys Ward he knew. You were using an alias last time you met him. Did you ever give him your name?"

"No one asked for it," Kryslie said with contempt. "Bin Halil assumed my maternal parent and that was enough for him to hate me."

"Do you think you can influence his mind – you were intimate with him," Tymos proposed.

"That was forty years ago – what I did to his mind ten years ago was...more like rape. It is possible that he has found ways to counter my commands."

"Whatever we do, will have to be subtle," Tymos warned, unnecessarily, but he was thinking things through. "You will need to appear younger, close up. Perhaps adjust the shape of your nose, cheek bones, and eye shape."

"I can treat the roots of my hair to make them lighter – gingery, not auburn," Kryslie considered. "The shop here has what I would need. And I can adjust my eye colour, without using lenses."

Tymos nodded agreement. "If it were me needing to do this, I would get a DNA sample from Daniel to confuse things."

"Which wouldn't do for me," Kryslie decided to comment. "I'm female!"

Her mind flicked through possibilities. "Lexina," she said finally. "Far from perfect, but our DNA is like that of our foster father, and she is his niece."

"I'll organise that," Tymos promised.

"I have time to see to the rest before my shift today," Kryslie assured her brother. "Though I will need to get Doctor Long's assistance for some of it."

Tymos considered. "She's discreet and you can refer her to Landin."

Adjusting her hair was a simple matter that an appointment at the base beauty shop took care of. The attendant trimmed her hair and changed the style. Then the man cleverly bleached her hair at the roots, and gradually changed the rest of her hair to graduated shades of red, as if a colour dye was growing out. The finished effect looked perfectly natural.

When she left the beauty shop, she went to the base medical section and requested a consultation with the Chief Medical Officer, Frances Long. The doctor was free and invited Kryslie into her office – a partitioned off section of the main infirmary.

"So, what brings you here?" Long asked.

"I want to change the shape of my face – nose, cheeks, and forehead – so that I appear different." Kryslie met the doctor's appraising gaze without looking away.

"Is this because the IC want to see you?"

Kryslie shook her head and smiled. "No, I'm fine with them. It's just that there is someone else coming up on the sixth day shuttle that…well…um, he saw the news vid of me." She let the doctor assume it was an ex-friend of some kind that she wanted to avoid.

"I don't see you as the frivolous type – though I notice you have lightened your hair," Long picked up a stylus and began to tap on her data pad. For a few moments, she appeared to be reading the screen of the device. "I can pad out your cheeks, widen your nose with cosmetic injections, and I can add fine lines around your eyes and on your forehead. It will take a couple of hours."

"Not the lines," Kryslie decided. She wanted to emphasise 'young'. "When can you do it? I can come in tomorrow during beta or gamma shift."

"Does the Commander know about your problem?"

"Not the details. I don't expect this person to make trouble here."

"You seem to be sure you will need to be part of the reception group. Junior staff generally aren't involved there. Surely you can ask the Commander to keep you out of it."

Kryslie shook her head. "It won't work. So I just want to look subtly different – to mute the resemblance he thought he saw."

"Very well, come in at the end of alpha shift. I might have a few other ideas for you."

Long waited for Kryslie Ward to leave Medical before putting through a request to talk to Adam Landin. She wondered why he suggested that they meet over breakfast, when she had stressed the topic was private. The base cafeteria was neither quiet nor private. Still, she did need to eat, and it wasn't the first time she and the Commander had met for a meal.

However, she waited until they were finishing their coffee before broaching her concerns in a quiet voice that only carried across the table.

Landin listened to what she told him, and didn't hide the fact that Kryslie Ward's request was unexpected. Yet, he thought he had an inkling of her reason, although he was not going to share his guess. She, like her brother, were older than they looked, and they had not told him a great deal about their past.

"Sixth day? The Leader of the Imperium and his son will be coming up, along with several personal guards. Arthur bin Halil is a Tech 1 at Terra five. Perhaps Kryslie knew him…in the past."

"Are they still so insular and gender biased there?"

Landin shrugged. "I don't think we need to pry. I trust that her reasons are valid ones. I see no reason not to do as she asks."

Kryslie was perfectly honest when she had said that the IC didn't worry her. The senior of the two men, was their long-time friend, Jonko. She was smiling as the passengers alighted from the shuttle and approached the reception group. They were all still wearing the metallic gold coloured flight suits, although they began to remove the headpieces as they crossed the taxi way. Members of the shuttlebay crew approached to take them, and to help the new arrivals out of the flight suits. She moved forward once the newly installed force wall at the opening of the anteroom, blinked off.

If Landin was surprised at the enthusiasm with which Kryslie greeted the investigator, he kept it to himself. She was grinning, and the newcomer returned her hand shake with both hands.

Once the arrivals, now revealed to be wearing dark blue business suits that were almost a uniform for members of the IC, were ready to get down to business, Kryslie began introductions.

"Commander, may I introduce John Goss, Senior IC investigator. And…"

"My colleague is Martin Davidson," Goss inserted promptly. "I am pleased to meet you, Commander."

The two men shook hands, and then Goss asked, "Would it be possible for Martin to talk to the shuttlebay crew who were on duty at the time of the accident?"

"Certainly, they are standing by in the control room. Lt Commander Stanley will show the way."

Landin glanced at Kryslie, for Goss's expression had become all business.

Noticing the glance and sensing his concern, Kryslie said, "Can we use one of the small study rooms while I fill John in on what happened here? Oh, and don't worry, he won't be carting me back planetside. He and I have worked together before."

Landin betrayed his surprise by the elevating of his eyebrows. "Page me if you require me," he invited.

John Goss, or to use his Tymorean name, Jonko, took his cue from Kryslie and kept his manner business like. He already knew, from information Tymos had sent to Earthbase, that their discussion or rather the interview, might be overheard. So once they were in the study room, a quiet area off the main recreation room, he gestured to two adjacent chairs and once they were seated, he simply went over her report, and asked questions to clarify aspects of it. He didn't probe too deeply when Kryslie professed no knowledge of some things.

He brought up the strange device, but Kryslie knew that was an excuse to bring Tymos in. Her brother had his privacy field generator, so they could talk without being overheard.

Without changing his manner, Jonko asked, "What has you both so bothered?"

Kryslie smiled faintly. Jonko knew them too well.

"We have a fair idea who is behind our as yet unknown saboteur, and he will be coming up on the next shuttle." Tymos hadn't sat in a chair, he was perched on the edge of one of the tables.

Jonko guessed at once who they meant, but his expression didn't change. "And still no ideas of who the person is here?"

"No," Kryslie confirmed. "However, now that my face has been on the newsfeeds, I'm probably going to become a target."

Tymos spoke before Jonko could express his concern. "We can handle things up here – I have a number of ideas to help disabuse them of the idea. I have asked Vincent to obtain a few things, and when he has them ready I will transmit down and get them. However, I do have something you could look into."

Jonko nodded, and waited for Tymos to explain, only the words he heard were inside his head, not coming in through his ears.

"Jon, this is just an odd idea. Something Landin said got me thinking. I have been checking a few things, but haven't got very far yet."

Tymos paused to consider how to propose his idea and then went on, "Landin was expecting 25 new staff, when the last intake arrived. However, when the shuttles arrived, only 24 had come up. Terra One's records say that only 24 came up. See what you can find out about that last minute pull out – why he didn't come, what his specialties were, everything you can."

Jonko merely nodded, but his friends could easily sense his confusion.

Tymos tried to explain. "I just had the feeling that the matter of the missing man was important. My other reasoning is convoluted. I was looking into the shuttle flight logs for the two shuttles that brought the people up. Each log shows that 12 people came up, excluding the crew. However, one of the shuttles used more fuel than the other – as if it did have an extra passenger's worth of weight. I have checked and rechecked my calculations. The difference in the fuel used was outside the normal variation."

"I see," Jonko spoke aloud. He was trying to get a grip on Tymos's logic. "So you think someone came up, in the place of that missing man, slipped away and later changed the shuttle logs?"

"Something like that," Tymos agreed aloud. "I have a lot more checking to do to get any proof."

Jonko's mind asked a question, "Are you looking for a stowaway up here?"

In the same manner, Tymos answered, "Whoever it is, is a genius at computing, hacking, and adjusting records, but so am I and I will find his trace."

With an abrupt gesture, Jonko stood up as if the interview was over. His mind asked, "How much of your ideas can I pass on to the IC?"

Tymos considered and with a few terse thoughts, told him.

Kryslie began her shift in main mission without more than a passing comment on her change of hair colour. Most of the others on delta shift arrived just before the five minute handover and then got right to work. Some of the 'colour blindness' might have been the result of her subtle mental compulsion of 'I look no different to normal'.

However, since they didn't know who the gremlin was, Tymos had replaced the image in the base personnel file with one of how she looked now, and would change it again when Dr Long had helped with the other changes.

Of equal importance, Tymos had reassured his sister that no one had tried to access her personnel file. His little program that prevented people from casually accessing their files, would have warned him. Now, he had tightened his protections.

He could do nothing about the base 'gossip net', and from monitoring that, Kryslie's actions of two days before that had appeared on the Earth news feeds, was now common knowledge on the base.

"I hear you're famous," Oliver Branson, who occupied the console beside her on delta shift, stated.

He had started some program running and was leaning back in his chair.

Kryslie, still engrossed in the tracking data being relayed from the semi-automated equipment at Lunar Two, answered without turning to face him. "Too bad there is no 'rich' to go with it."

Branson chuckled, "You were fast though. My folks remarked on it when I spoke to them on the comm-link. They saw you on the news."

"That's because they are Earth plodders. They tend to forget we work at point eight gee here. You should try filming yourself here and there. I might be a tad faster than some, but only because I had years of quality physical training." That was the story she had created and Branson believed it.

"You have a point," Branson agreed, turning back to his screen and making some adjustments to a scanning program.

He wasn't quiet for long; a few minutes later, he said, "Scuttlebutt said the shuttle this morning had the IC aboard and you were one of the reception team. Did they want to talk to you?"

"Are you surprised?" Kryslie evaded answering, and kept her face towards her screen. Branson was as bad a gossip as a bevy of old women. She wondered if he had been the one to start the base gossip web going on the subject.

"Well?" he prompted.

"Well what?"

Branson gave an exaggerated sigh.

Kryslie relented. "I just had to go over the report I had given the Commander. That was all."

"Some people reckon you knew one of the spooks."

"Spooks? Whatever do you mean?"

"Well, I've heard them called that. They sneak around investigating on the sly and never give their names…"

Kryslie sat back laughing. "I have to admit I have never thought of them that way. And yes, I knew one of them. He has known my father for years."

That seemed to make Branson stop to think, probably to see if he could use the information.

"I would rather that didn't get passed around. Those guys have to be discreet."

"Yeah, fine," Branson agreed, although Kryslie didn't really trust that to be a promise.

After flicking a mental question at her twin, "Is the official visit on sixth day on the schedule yet?" and getting an affirmative in reply, she decided to distract her co-worker.

"Have you see the sixth day roster yet? There's another high ranking visitor expected."

"Huh?" Branson glanced at her, and rather than asking who – he did a quick check by bringing up a small window in the corner of his screen. "Oh, yeah. Well, we had the President of the UWN last week. It is the leader of the Imperium's turn."

Kryslie smiled and got back to her work, she sensed his mental gears turning and his desire to spread the word. She had a good notion that he would find a way to do it during the shift.

"I'll let you know," Tymos's amused mental voice came into her mind. "I know his username. Anyway, just to let you know, Daniel has the things we asked Vincent to get for you. I will go down for them once the shuttle leaves. The passengers are suiting up now. I will be back before my shift starts."

Kryslie gave him a brief, "The sooner the better. I have my personal force screen on, so I'm not leaving fingerprints, and I intend to wipe down my console when Branson goes for a break. I did a thorough go over of my quarters when I went to get out of my formal uniform. However, if the gremlin decides to check on me before sixth day, having no prints around will be a little bit suspicious."

"Let's hope we are just being paranoid," Tymos told her, before letting the mental contact lapse.

They couldn't afford not to be careful, Kryslie told herself. Particularly when they were dealing with the vengeful person of Abdul bin Halil. That was why they had asked the Tymorean scientists to provide some unnoticeable gloves which were etched with a set of false fingertips and had micro-tiny glands to oil them to enable her to leave fingerprints. She and Tymos agreed that it most likely that either finger prints or saliva would be tried for if they wanted DNA. Saliva would be provided by a tiny bulb in her mouth.

However, she had considered that the gremlin might get into her quarters so she had ultra-cleaned in there to remove stray hairs or skin flakes and if her sharp eyes missed anything – a human searcher would need some high power magnifiers to find it. When Tymos returned, he would also have some of their cousin Lexina's hair to put on her brush, and to scatter on the floor.

Once Tymos returned, she would begin to leave a false DNA trail, in case the gremlin had orders to check her before bin Halil arrived.

The small security team had been augmented by some of the trained reserves. Lunar 1 had little need for a large security contingent, since the only way to get to the base was by the shuttles. Mostly the regulars dealt with minor behaviour infringements and acted as OHS auditors. For times when more personnel were needed, volunteers had been trained up to be called on at need. Tymos was one of the reserves and he was already on duty in the shuttle bay, to ensure no unauthorised people entered during the visit of the Leader of the Imperium. He had several other items on his personal agenda. The first was to watch Abdul bin Halil like a hawk, and make sure he didn't make a hostile move at his sister. His second was to look out for any of the base staff trying to get a message to him or someone in his party, though he felt that was a long shot. Thirdly, he would be looking for hostile moves towards the man – just in case the gremlin worked for some unknown third party who wanted to discredit the WSRA.

When the shuttle arrived, only the security team, in their protective armour, would be in the shuttle bay – just in case of further accidents. Once the guests arrived and entered the main part of the base, the shuttle bay was to be isolated, and the security team would be stationed around the public area of the base. Tymos intended to stay close to the official party, and so that he wasn't particularly noticeable, he had put a temporary black coloured dye through his trimmed short hair. He looked different enough that people he knew quite well, did a double take.

While Tymos watched the screen showing the shuttle's approach trajectory, he listened to the security frequency and the results of the checks being made in the reception area. He also had his sister itemising the instructions Landin was giving the off-shift staff.

When the shuttle was only minutes away, and decelerating to entry speed, Tymos gave another careful look around the bay. He had already noted that the signs of the previous week's accident had been removed. The damaged shuttle had been taxied into the maintenance bay and the blackened walls repainted. The main wall, when checked, had proved to have been undamaged.

Now, his eyes found the guard patrolling along the upper walkway, across the bay. He sensed another patrolling the one on his side. They would be watching for anyone that might come to the bay via the maintenance passages that emerged up there. He glanced at the anteroom, the partition wall had been replaced, and it, like the main wall, was force field reinforced. The protective field was on across that opening.

Tymos heard the sound of the approaching shuttle, as the yellow guide line flashed on. His eyes went to the bay entrance as the nose of the shuttle came through the force field there.

"A perfect approach and landing," he mentally told his sister.

The shuttle powered down completely before the ramp lowered and two figures in flight suits emerged. With helmets still on, the figures were anonymous. However, their careful scrutiny of the bay, and the approaching welcoming committee, followed by a comment over the suit comm, "All clear" identified them as body guards.

Most of Lunar 1's security team would not have understood the words, for the arrivals had spoken in Arabic.

The third figure that emerged, moved to one side once he was down the ramp. He removed his helmet and passed it to one of the shuttle bay crew as the fourth figure emerged.

Abdul bin Halil, had already removed his helmet, so that he was immediately identifiable. He gestured to the third man, and as that one turned his head, Tymos identified him.

"Krys, Arthur is here too!"

Kryslie was so sure that she would be summoned once the shuttle landed, that she was already in a dress uniform, though she wasn't in her quarters, but those of her brother. Her own space was set up with decoy DNA sources, and she did not want any of her own hair to be mixed up with the gingery hairs supplied by her Tymorean 'cousin' Lexina. Her personal grooming necessities were currently in her brother's quarters.

"Seems like he wants a tour of the whole base," Kryslie told her brother. "Senior staff are to be available to answer questions and grunts like us are to keep our heads down and concentrate on our work. Off duty staff are not to linger in passageways…"

"Or gawk like yokels at the notables," Tymos translated. "Shuttle should arrive in fifteen minutes."

"I will expect a summons in twenty," Kryslie countered. She heard her brother's mental chuckle.

"Don't rush to answer it – after all, no one knows that he's going to want to see you, yet. And make sure your room is locked. It would be a perfect time for the gremlin to sneak in."

"From what you have said, he won't have much trouble overriding the security code if he chose to try it."

"He'll have to work at it, since your password is truly random, but I will let you know if he tries."

"If he does, I reckon that clinches whose side he is on. If he were merely anti-WSRA, I'd say he would be trying to do us a favour and kill today's ranking guest."

"Unfortunately, we can't allow that."

The summons came just after Tymos had warned her, "Arthur is here too."

He wasn't mentioned on the passenger schedule and as a result, she was mildly distracted when Stanley, Landin's second in command, told her to come to Main Mission and wait to join the reception team. By the time she arrived, she had her reactions under control and had decided on the 'attitude' she wanted to project.

Stanley was duty controller, but even so, he was in his dress uniform. He was still overseeing all the duty stations around the deck, although the shift deputy controller was occupying the centre chair and would take over when the visitors arrived.

Kryslie watched the young man currently working at her normal station. He seemed to be running a training simulation for the Auto-track system. She didn't change her focus when she heard the doors of main mission whoosh open.

"Ward!" Stanley warned as the official party approached.

Now she turned, and seemed to study the guests, and she was. It was the test of the subtle adjustments that Dr Long had made to her face. She was still recognisable as herself, but her face was fatter than it had ever been, she had a smattering of freckles, a trace of acne. Long had also injected something into her face to make her seem younger than she already looked. That youthfulness made her rank of Tech 3 believable, and the possibility of her being almost 40 seem unlikely and of her being in her sixties utterly ludicrous.

Still, she could do nothing about her name, and that was the name of Abdul bin Halil's former consort and the man would not have forgotten that.

Landin was escorting the party and made introductions. Kryslie was feigning awkwardness at being the focus of attention for such an important guest, and seemed to be watching Stanley out of her side-vision, and copying his actions, bowing slightly, as he had, to the visitor. She was impeccably polite, seemed to blush faintly as bin Halil, using his most diplomatic façade, commended her for her quick actions the previous week. She glanced at her feet and managed a modest, "Thank you, your Excellency."

Abdul bin Halil was exuding hostility, for all he showed none of it, and it wasn't all directed at her. He had taken in the details of main mission in one sweeping hate filled glance.

"I would be delighted if Technician Ward were to accompany us on the tour of this marvellous facility," bin Halil invited, and Landin instantly agreed.

"I expect that my son will have plenty of questions about how this base differs from Terra five."

Kryslie, who had been keeping her attention on bin Halil senior, allowed herself to notice the younger man. The only one not dressed in a dark foreign looking suit.

"Feel free to ask all the questions you like," Landin invited, smiling at Arthur bin Halil. "Commander Mansour tells me you are insatiably curious, and an excellent Tech 1."

"Thank you Commander. I have always wished to work here for a time, but I must balance my work and private commitments. Coming here today is likely to be the nearest I will get. I hope I won't bore you with my questions."

"I will put Technician Ward at your assistance. As one of the original staff, she is likely to be able to answer all your questions," Landin offered.

In her mind, Kryslie heard, "He's giving you his 'women are not fit to be seen' look." She agreed with her brother. Bin Halil seemed to be looking past her, not at her, but his eyes were on her all the time. She mentally sent back to her brother, "He abhors this place, resents the fact of its existence. I am surprised Landin can't feel the hate dripping off him."

Stanley bowed again and gestured to the nearest duty station and began to explain what each one was for. Bin Halil, followed him, and was no doubt remembering everything he heard.

Once his attention was off her, she became aware of Arthur's attention fixed on her.

"Do you work in Main Mission?"

"Yes, Prince Arthur," Kryslie admitted, deliberately giving him his personal rank title. She did not intend to betray that she had ever met him before.

"Surely you will just call me Arthur."

"Sir, as a Tech 1 and a member of a visiting party, that isn't appropriate."

Arthur was courteous enough to accept that without comment. "So, what do you do?"

"I work at the tracking station. I analyse the data coming in from the probes and drones we send out, as well as from the Auto-tracks, and then direct it to the relevant sections."

"Which is your station?"

"The third one from here. Denny is running a simulator for the Auto-tracks."

"Do you mind if I ask about them?"

"No, of course not. That's what the tour is about."

Arthur paused to watch the simulation, although his father continued walking. With the extra distance between her and Abdul bin Halil, she began to feel a different kind of intensity emanating from his son. She had to ignore it.

Keeping her tone polite and formal, she continued to treat Arthur as a stranger, occasionally distracting him with a question of her own to compare how things were done at Terra 5. She used a moment when he was intent on the computer to strengthen her mental shields. Yet while she sensed less of the crew in Main Mission, she couldn't block her son's intense longing. He wanted her to be the same woman as he had met seventeen years ago. The woman he believed to be his mother, even though she had looked as old as himself. He had accepted the strangeness then, and he never even considered it now. Yet Kryslie dared not drop any aspect of her current performance, she was a young, intense technician. Nothing more. She had to make it seem ludicrous that she was anything else.

They caught up to the rest of the group as Stanley was explaining some of the unusual geology of the moon and reasons why the Sea of Serenity had been selected for the base. Arthur gave the mini lecture his full attention, and Kryslie glanced across the deck to where Tymos stood watching the visitors.

"Bro? Can you give Arthur a hint to let up? It's bad enough having his father sending mental daggers my way."

The answer can immediately. "First chance I get," Tymos promised, but they both knew he'd have to wait for the right opportunity.

The chance didn't come until the group arrived in the engineering section. Visitors didn't go right into where the working machines were housed, but only as far as an open circular area that had view screens to show all of the restricted places. The area had small groupings of chairs so that visitors could watch the presentations put on for their benefit. That day, the senior engineers were talking about the proposed rocket system for manned flight.

Tymos edged closer to Prince Arthur, until he was able to breathe several phrases into his ear. On hearing them, Arthur stiffened, but obeyed the speaker of the strange language and did not turn around. Then he went on, "The woman cannot be the one you seek."

In his mind, Arthur pleaded, "I must talk to her." He heard, "Another will come." A slight shake of his head was all the movement he allowed himself, but it indicated his thwarted desire.

"Think! Do you want her to die?"

Tymos eased back into his former position, and watched the prince. He dared to brush the private thoughts - they were kin, so it was easier to do than with a stranger.

Arthur's mind had connected this odd whispered voice with memories of other times. When he had first seen the red headed woman at a party — that voice had warned him. When he had seen his father tormenting that woman, a voice had spoken to him. Each time, the voice had spoken in the odd language that his early tutors had taught him, and which he could understand, but never used. He had learnt to obey his tutors, and he trusted their wisdom and missed them when his father had dismissed them and declared he must learn manly things.

In his mind, it proved the woman he wanted was here, but then the question registered. Did he want her to die? No, he wanted to talk to her, but he knew too well what his father thought of her — the so-called hero. Then he recalled the details of the woman's face — how young she looked, how the familiar face was speckled with brown and the eyes were different — brown, not blue. In truth, this woman looked even younger than the one years before. It couldn't possibly be the same woman.

Arthur felt himself shiver, as he recalled what his father had done to that other woman — just because she had resembled his birth mother. He did not want that to happen to this one. He put his longing aside and told himself she was just a junior tech, like the ones he worked with at Terra 5.

A reception was arranged for the visiting party that was every bit as impressive as that given to the UWN President the week before. Food and drink provided for the royal imperial party and their personal security guards as well as for the attending section heads. It was an opportunity for the latter to talk about their work to the important political leader and answer any questions that he had.

Kryslie, as a junior tech, moved discreetly back and stood against the wall of the reception room. This area was on the ground level of the base, and had a clear ceiling that enabled those within to see the amazing sight of the Earth overhead.

From her position, near one of the food tables, she could see across to the two sliding doors that led to the anterooms that opened onto the shuttle bays, and the passageway used by the kitchen staff to deliver trays of food. She watched the servers who came up to take the trays to offer the finger sizes delicacies around. Some she recognised, most she didn't, but she memorised the faces automatically.

Tymos was standing watchful and alert across the room, and both of them were able to observe the mingling. It was her own intention to keep out of Abdul bin Halil's line of sight, but she noticed that he had adjusted his position each time he was introduced to a new section leader, so as to watch her. Feigning disinterest in the proceedings, she turned and took a glass of non-alcoholic cider from one of the waiting trays, before returning to watch the groupings of speakers.

A prickle at the base of her neck made her more alert. It felt like she had another set of covert eyes on her. It wasn't Arthur, for he was engaged in talking to the Chief Engineer, and was as good as ignoring her now. Without needing to prompt her twin, she knew he too was looking for the watcher.

"Move around a bit, Krys," he suggested.

So she did, walking to where the food trays were waiting and selecting a dainty, finger sized delicacy to eat. As she devoured it, she glanced around, seeing only the watchful base security team and the waiters moving deftly between the guests. She held onto her drink, sipping it at intervals, and keeping her eye on the main group.

From across the room. Landin caught her eye and beckoned. She straightened and looked for a place to put her glass, and as if conjured, a waiter appeared next to her with an empty tray. It was one of the ones she didn't know, brown hair going grey, not much taller than herself, with the lined features of a man in early middle age. He kept his face tilted down, but all the waiters were affecting the demeanour of disinterested servants.

"Thanks," Kryslie said automatically, and the man nodded and moved away. She didn't try to watch where the man went, Tymos was doing that. However, he was also trying to identify the man, whose face was unfamiliar.

"Got him!" Tymos sent his sister a visual memory of the waiter setting his tray on a small wall shelf, putting on gloves, and then handling the glass carefully while pouring the remaining drink into a disposal chute, and then taking a sealable plastic bag from a pocket and enclosing the glass within it.

The man had looked around before doing any of this, and apparently not seen Tymos who had become still and cloaked his presence using his Tymorean power. This ability to bend light around oneself was not something that humans could do, or were even aware could be done outside of fantasy stories.

Once he had the glass protected, he held it under his tray and moved out of the disposal alcove, and back to the main reception room, where he switched his empty tray for a full one. He walked right past Tymos, oblivious to the fact that there was anyone pressed against the wall.

Kryslie had her attention on Landin, even as her brother was sending information to her.

"Kryslie, were you aware that Prince Arthur works at Terra 5?" Landin spoke casually.

"Yes, Sir. I have been telling him about the Auto-tracks. I believe that one is being built Earthside near Terra 5."

"It is not due to be finished for six months yet," Arthur agreed. "I have asked if I might visit a working one."

Landin nodded and said, "I see no reason why you can't. I will clear it with Commander Mansour."

"When might this be?" Kryslie asked, glancing at Landin.

"I have a week's leave due," Arthur said quickly. "I am hoping that I might remain here until the next 6th day."

"Well, if it all gets arranged, you will have to do the basic orientation, the EA induction and the emergency drills," Kryslie advised.

"I expected no less," Arthur confirmed. "While I am here, I hope you might be free to mentor me and accept the invitation to call me Arthur as my usual co-workers do."

Kryslie gave him a slight bow as her non-committal answer. It was clear to her that Arthur had suggested this as a way to talk to her privately. It was equally clear to her empathic senses that the idea pleased his father greatly. Did Abdul bin Halil think his son was intending to spy on her? Trip her up? Trick her into revealing herself? Was he intending to interrogate his son, once he returned? About her? About Lunar 1?

She turned to Landin. "Sir, if I am not required any further, I need to prepare for my duty shift."

Landin merely nodded his permission, and as she turned and left, she still felt the eyes of the Imperium's leader, on her.

Tymos watched his sister leave via one of the doors leading to the staff only section, and felt her relief. He was still paying particular attention to the four personal guards that hovered near the exulted guests.

He sent to her, "I have marked that waiter. Got him to give me a glass of water. He's not normally one of the kitchen staff, just one of the volunteers that were called on to help out. His mind revealed that he has a shift somewhere that he needs to get to."

Kryslie was walking quickly in the direction of the nearest turbo lift to go down to the staff quarters. "I didn't recognise him either."

"He ditched the gloves he'd pulled over the fancy white serving ones, so when I gave him my glass back empty, I'd put something on the glass. Stuff should work its way through to the skin, so that the fingers on his right hand should glow in UV light."

"Was that something Vincent gave you?"

Tymos mentally chuckled. "Yes, and now I am watching him meander around the room. I am betting that he will slip the glass to one of those four strong silent types hovering near bin Halil."

Kryslie entered her quarters but transmitted immediately to her brother's. She wanted to change from her formal uniform before going on shift, and her spare uniforms were currently occupying a shelf there.

"That guy's slick. I almost missed the exchange."

"Well, that clinches it in my view," Kryslie decided.

"That bin Halil wants to discredit you, yes," Tymos agreed. "We still don't have any proof that he is behind the gremlin. Or in fact that the faux waiter is the gremlin. He could be a covert watcher, forced into acting on this occasion."

Although she wanted to think otherwise, her brother was right. "How long will that marker stuff work? Will it wash off?"

"Vincent says that it sinks into the skin and will fade in time, as old skin sloughs off and new is formed. Long enough for us to track him, even if I lose him when he leaves here. Damn it! Where did the guy go?"

"If he's due on shift soon, he'd have to be in one of the admin or support roles," Kryslie mused. "If he was one of my shift, I'd have known him."

"Unless he is disguised right now," Tymos countered. "Although I went right up close to him and saw no signs of that."

"I will check those on my shift, if he was one of them disguised, I should pick up something."

"I'll find an excuse to visit some of the non-tech sections," Tymos decided, annoyed with himself for losing the waiter. He didn't comment on the difficulty of checking the other 700 or so staff on Lunar 1.

Kryslie tuned Auto-track 1 to follow the shuttle's course back to Earth. She kept that in a small sub-screen in a small corner of her main screen.

Branson, in spite of being higher in tech ranking, and an adult, noticed the sub-screen and asked, "Have you got an interest in that Tech One Prince?"

The comment was in exceedingly bad taste, and Kryslie ignored it. "Paranoia – after last week. Anyway, Arthur bin Halil is staying here for a week, to learn about the Auto-tracks and to compare how we do things here compared to Terra 5."

"Well, now…" Branson began, then stopped when he saw the glare that Kryslie gave him.

"And yes, I will probably be saddled with him. Which, as you seen to be implying, wouldn't be so bad if I hadn't just endured several hours of his Imperial father staring at me as if I were some unpleasant insect. Or at least too brainless or countrified to be able to teach his precious son anything."

"The Commander knows you aren't ignorant," Branson protested.

"I know that! But if I dared, I'd ask the Commander to assign someone else to baby-sit the Prince."

Kryslie was half in earnest when she said that. Part of her wanted the chance to get to know Arthur, because he was her son and she hadn't had much chance to be near him. Yet, to be constantly in his company meant having to maintain her charade of being a stranger, way below him in both technical and social rank. Any mistake she made, any slip in the performance, and if that fake waiter was around and watching, it would get back to his father.

Branson fell silent, oblivious to Kryslie's abstraction. Her mention of Arthur staying around had short-circuited his intention to get gossip fodder from her. Instead, he was considering ways to befriend the Tech 1 from Terra 5, while he was not being "Prince Arthur". His mind was in social climbing mode now – imagining how his knowing a prince would impress his friends back on Earth.

"Krys?" Tymos's mental voice distracted her. She gave a silent acknowledgement.

"He really feels he needs to talk to you."

"I know, but I don't dare admit anything and I don't know how much control his bastard sire has over him."

"He has not lost any respect for his early tutors. He heard me and obeyed. Certainly he has said nothing of his suspicions to his father."

"Maybe not, bro, but his sire was practically purring with satisfaction when he asked to stay here a week with me as his mentor. I wish I knew why."

"When Arthur gets back Earthside, I will have Daniel send someone to talk to him."

"That would be best," Kryslie decided.

Changing the subject slightly, Tymos said, "I thought you would be relieved once the shuttle left."

"So did I. Do you think we fooled him?"

Tymos didn't try to hide his inner thoughts. "You don't look old enough to be either of your other incarnations. However, you still look a lot like the women he knew. He is hoping that DNA will prove it. He may suspect a trick. He now has 'your' prints and DNA from the glass, and I checked, someone did sneak into your quarters, so we must assume that person found some hairs. Are you sure you removed all of your own?"

"Are you trying to teach your fellow Great One how to cover her tracks, bro?"

Tymos sent a chuckle. "I wouldn't dare! Anyway, since he has DNA from two sources, hopefully that will frustrate him."

"Will it work against that insidious whispering campaign?"

She felt her twin sigh. He didn't need to answer that.

Kryslie heard the faint static that usually preceded a base wide alert, and sensed her brother's attention going elsewhere as the alert klaxon began. He must have been near a computer for he told her, "recycling plant", even before the computer generated voice announced it. "System failure, environment maintenance, Level 1, section 7. Tech team to recycling plant."

While her brother raced to respond, even though he was not due on duty for another hour, Kryslie turned her attention back to her own task. The tension she had felt, that hadn't abated when the shuttle left, seemed to increase. She couldn't help recalling how Abdul bin Halil had been so intent on hearing everything he could about Lunar 1 and she knew he was a very astute man.

"Sheesh," Branson muttered, loud enough to be heard. "Good thing this didn't happen when the high and mighty was here. Think of the impression he would have of us."

Kryslie decided that she already knew what he thought of the base. As for the gremlin targeting recycling, and she was sure it was bin Halil's suggestion, he probably considered Lunar 1, and the UWN, in the same class as the more noxious things being recycled.

What she didn't understand was why he would want trouble while his son was on the base. Her mind suggested, "So he would learn how efficiently the problem was fixed."

Even if the recycling system failure was a critical problem, it wasn't as critical as a failure of life support or environment. His son was not in immediate danger.

However, her son, the highly intelligent Tech 1, would want to know everything that was being done. He would ply her with questions…some she had no answers for, others she would be unwilling to give him. Any suggestion that she and Tymos were personally hunting the gremlin would put them in danger, if indeed his father was behind the trouble.

The klaxon alarm was muted once the tech team was onto the problem, but yellow warning lights still flashed slowly, telling off duty people to return to their quarters.

Even though Kryslie seemed to be concentrating on the tracking data, her brother's thoughts were leaking into their twin bond. He was examining the computer program that ran the recycling section, as others were examining the equipment for signs of damage. She found herself thinking laterally on that problem, trying to think of ways that the 'fault' had been caused, and letting her brother take in the suggestions and add them to his own.

She glanced up as the Chief Engineer and several assistants trotted into main mission and activated the engineering and environment stations. They would be overseeing the situation from there.

Senior Controller Subra, currently the duty controller, spoke above the muted alarm, "All is under control. Your work still needs doing here."

A few of the lesser ranked controllers had been watching the newcomers, but they returned to their tasks.

Kryslie still felt tense, but only part of it was a reflection of the trouble in Recycling. Her mind had switched to other possible ways the gremlin could create the same degree of havoc. She was right in the centre of one potential target. Black out main mission and coordination between all sections of the base would be lost.

"Bro, what's the password for the Main Mission control systems?"

Tymos, knowing instantly what she intended, paused in his own analysis, rattled off a 13-character string, and returned to his task.

After considering the sudden impulse for a moment, Kryslie brought up the diagnostic screen on her terminal, and input the override password, supposedly known only by senior controllers. She had neither the authority, nor the clearance, to instigate a base wide system diagnostic. A mere tech 3 would not have the knowledge to do it – but she was vastly more knowledgeable than her tech rank implied.

She set the parameters to scan only the system backups, so that her action would not interfere with anyone's work. Then, before touching the 'execute' button, she excluded engineering and recycling.

The windows and grids on her screen were replaced by a three by three framework of screens, each rapidly scrolling through lines of code.

Lunar 1 base had built in redundancies in all the systems, and if something went wrong in the main system, the back-up should have come on line. The one in recycling hadn't.

At her own station, the back-up system was actually the recently superseded system from before the five automated tracking stations had come on line. According to the specs, the two systems were completely separate. One had replaced the other. Elsewhere, the back-up should also be separate.

Seeing Branson glance at her screen, she quickly minimised all data except that relating to her station.

"What have you done, Ward? My computer is suddenly going slow!" Branson was trying to make it work faster by repeatedly jabbing touch buttons.

Kryslie ignored him. She studied the scrolling code, but in the back of her mind was the thought that if the gremlin was now targeting major systems, the threat to Lunar 1 had escalated. She didn't know the other sections as well as the tracking station, and most people up here wouldn't consider tracking as vital as other sections. That was because up on the moon, the general feeling was that they were safe from disgruntled elements such as the anti-tech groups. However, if tracking capability was lost, the base was blind. They would say that the likelihood of a meteorite landing on the base was extremely unlikely, and that was true enough, but a missile attack was not an impossibility – though almost equally likely.

Starting at the basics, Kryslie began to think through the process. The Auto-track stations fed data to the new system, but not to the old. The earlier system had only received data from the satellites, the bulky radio telescopes and radio spectroscopes. If the Auto-tracks went offline, basic tracking via the backup was still possible. They would just have to restart the radio telescopes.

With her full attention on her screen, Kryslie did not realise that the main screen was flickering on and off as if there was a loose connection somewhere. Nor was she aware that senior controller Subra had summoned his superior, until Stanley spoke sharply from behind her.

"Ward! What are you doing?"

His tone caused Branson to glance her way, but when he saw Stanley's expression, he made sure to look focused on his own screen.

Kryslie didn't turn around. She merely said, "I seem to have started a diagnostic. I wasn't sure about stopping it and I didn't expect it to take very long."

Stanley leant over her shoulder and usurped control of the touchpad, maximising the screens she had earlier minimised.

"I don't know how you managed to do this, Ward, but this is a full system check, not just a section check."

Kryslie made no comment, not wanting to make Stanley any more suspicious than he was, or worse still, hostile.

"This is not a good time to have this running."

Kryslie glanced up at the Chief controller, and only then noticed the trouble with the main screen. She didn't offer a suggestion to fix the problem.

"Good thing you didn't black out the whole system, Ward."

Subra had also been looking at the screen and now he said, "This is but the back-up system, Sir."

It seemed that Stanley knew that and chose not to react to the statement. Several of the screens had stopped scrolling and he was reading the diagnostic reports. The main screen was still flickering.

He sent each diagnostic report to the main console and to the relevant system station and then ended the subprogram.

"If this is the back-up system, Sir," Kryslie ventured, meekly. "It should be entirely separate and not affect anything unless it is switched over."

"It should be indeed, Ward." He turned to Subra. "Can you drag a spare seat over here, and then get someone from each section up here to go over those diagnostic reports."

While he waited for the seat, Stanley opened up a new sub-screen and called up some data. His face creased into a frown, and when Kryslie looked at what he had brought up, she understood. This was a record of when the main system back-ups had occurred, and the dates when the regular diagnostics were run. What showed on the screen indicated that the diagnostics had not occurred for nearly six months. The main system, had not been backed up for three months. Kryslie knew that was not a fact, and she could, if asked, list the dates when each had been done. The timing however, agreed with the onset of the gremlin's activities.

The chair arrived, and Stanley sat, almost absently. He shut out the systems that had checked out green, looked at the problems found in several more systems and again emailed the reports to the relevant section, and then checked through a list and murmured, "I see you didn't include Engineering and recycling, Ward."

Kryslie kept quiet, Stanley wasn't demanding an explanation.

"I'll get them to do a system back up when the problem is fixed."

Finally, the only diagnostic still running was that for the tracking system, and still the main screen was flickering.

"Well, it seems that this is the program causing the trouble," Stanley mused aloud. He drummed his fingers on the console, as he thought.

"Did you notice any problems as it scrolled through?"

"I saw no red flagged lines of code," Kryslie admitted.

"I think we should let this finish, since this back-up hasn't been checked since before the new one took over – according to the log. And I will need to do a back-up of the new system…though I damn well know we have done three since I took over. I will just take this terminal out of the loop."

Suiting action to words, he paused the program, and input code to isolate that terminal. The flickering on the main screen ceased.

"Hmm, when this is finished, Ward, I think I will have your terminal checked." Stanley restarted the diagnostic and glanced at the side-bar progress meter. "This will take another two hours at least. Since you started it, I want you to monitor it. Bring me the report when it is done."

"Yes, Sir," Kryslie agreed, keeping her tone neutral. She had just let herself in for an extra hour added to her shift.

Branson proved to have been listening, by giving her a glance and a shrug of commiseration. She returned the shrug, as she watched Stanley begin a conversation with Subra, that involved glances her way.

However, in spite of the impression she gave Branson, she really did want to see the diagnostic through to the end. If there were problems, she was more likely to spot them than her alpha shift replacement.

Alpha shift was the equivalent of the early night shift, beginning at 8pm Lunar time, and finishing next morning at 2am.

When the young woman who was to be her replacement arrived for handover, Kryslie told her, "I've got to see this diagnostic through, Ellie. You will need to see the Chief to see where he wants you."

"What's going on?" Eliza Shelby asked.

"Here? I somehow started this diagnostic running, so like I said – I have to see it through."

"Oh. Right. Stanley is on his way over."

When he arrived he spoke to Shelby. "I have taken this terminal out of service. Now, I understand that you are a systems design specialist?"

"Yes, Sir."

"Good. We've a problem down in recycling. I want you to report to Chief Maskin and see what you can do to help there."

"Yes, Sir!" Shelby went off immediately at a fast walk.

Branson's replacement hadn't sorted himself out yet, but Stanley had a different job for him. "What are you currently working on, Jeffers?"

The gangly dark haired man explained, "Simulations for the orbital survey of the Gobi desert, Sir."

"Fine. That can be left. Can I get you over to relieve Li Seng?"

Jeffers bobbed his head and closed down his program, and walked to the Engineering station.

Stanley sat again in the spare chair and checked the side window — so far there were no error messages.

"Forgetting for the time being how this diagnostic was started, what possible reason is there to check the back-ups at this time?"

"The back-up for the recycling system didn't start up when the main system crashed."

Stanley jerked as if startled. "You didn't run the check on that."

"No, but I was in touch with my brother when the alert began. He mentioned it."

"And engineering?"

"They might need to access it."

"I see." Stanley had turned to study Kryslie and was giving his tech 3 a careful scrutiny. "Well, it has been useful, and turned up some minor problems, but nothing here, yet."

A faint 'ping' distracted him. "I spoke too soon. Feedback loop?" he muttered. "Section 1519 theta?" His mind flicked through the program. "Theta is the data gathering subprogram, but there is no section 1519."

A second error message flicked up.

"Division by zero error, section 1519. I have never seen these errors before."

Kryslie spoke softly, interrupting Stanley's intense thoughts. "I have. Once — before you took over from Chief Ambrose."

Stanley looked at her. "Go on..."

"A similar error occurred when one of the telescopes malfunctioned. The program expects data from there and it is not being received. The program compensates by isolating that input channel until the problem is fixed," she explained.

Stanley was thoughtful. "You must know the system as well as I do. Do you know what section 1519 refers to?"

"No. Though I have a suggestion."

"I would be very interested to hear it."

"When this diagnostic is finished, I think we should reset the program parameters to the original defaults. Then after restoring the system, reload what was at the last save point before the new system took over."

"What exactly are you implying? That there is some kind of virus or malicious code in the system?"

"I'm not sure, exactly. Was this system checked just prior to upgrading to the new one?"

"Not long before."

"And that was before all these malfunctions began to happen?" Stanley nodded.

Kryslie took a breath. "Several things. First, if you don't recognise the code – it has been added since. Second, the back-up should be completely separate to the main system, so running the diagnostic shouldn't have affected the main screen."

Stanley quickly picked up on the point she was making. "So you are thinking there may be some code linking the two systems? And it involves that mystery section?"

"I think it is an extra channel that has been added to receive data from somewhere," Kryslie explained.

"That is what I was beginning to conclude," Stanley admitted and his tone was grim. "We will do as you suggest and in the meantime I will have the backup telescopes brought up to speed and run diagnostics on them. When that is done, I will do a diagnostic and back-up on the main system, as well as copying the program to the testing computer. I want to do a line comparison of the original save point and the current code – taking into account the sanctioned upgrades. Are you willing to keep on with this?"

"Of course," Kryslie agreed, satisfied that she had infected the Chief Controller with preventative paranoia. She hoped that between them, they would find any other oddities that might have been inserted in the program.

"Take a ten minute break and go get something to eat. It might be a long night," Stanley sighed.

When alpha shift was almost over, Stanley declared himself satisfied and sent Kryslie off duty. She had no further ideas to contribute, but for some reason was still uneasy. She spoke mentally to her brother who was still tracing the problems in the recycling system, and told him what she had found.

Tymos's mind went back to his problem. She sensed he was checking something.

"Bingo," Tymos thought back. "The gremlin linked the backup system to the main. So each time we tried to restart the main system the problem code reactivated and crashed it again. Demonic little bastard to think of that. I should have thought of it – even though I checked the specs on the back up first thing. We tried to use the back up and nothing happened.

Nothing was red flagged on the diagnostic, but if the code is autonomous and not linked to the rest…the diagnostic probably didn't see it."

After a few more caustic curses, Tymos told her, "We should be able to sort this out quite quickly now. Are you sure the mission control system is clean?"

"Stanley is. He sent me off duty, but I am still uneasy. I think I will be scanning the system in my dreams. I hope I haven't missed anything."

"I think the virus is jumping from the back up by wireless transmission."

"From where?" Kryslie asked, and felt her brother mentally shrug. "Damn. Most of the input is wireless. I will sleep on it."

Kryslie lay on her bed but did not sleep. Something was nagging at her mind. She set herself to go over everything about the mission control tracking system.

Something about wireless transmissions, she thought, as she was on the verge of sleep. Not the data input – that was sent encrypted – what else?

Stanley reported to Landin in the latter's quarters before he took himself to bed.

"I am as sure as I can be that the mission control system is clean," he reported. "Both the main and the backup. I ought to put Ward on report – she should not have been able to get into the programming."

Landin managed a smile. "Kryslie and her brother have excellent instincts and from what I can tell are something of prodigies."

Stanley snorted. "Then why are they only Tech 3's?"

"I think they prefer the hands on work," Landin proposed. "And they are the ones who first concluded that we have a saboteur up here. I'm also thinking that they have a good chance of locating the bastard. Tymos Ward seems to have found the problem with the recycling system."

Stanley had to smile and agree.

"Did you do a system save, Chief?" Landin asked.

Stanley swore. "No, but I will right now."

Chapter 6

Arthur bin Halil found Kryslie at breakfast and bought a cup of coffee to an empty place at her table. He nodded to the dark haired man sitting opposite her, who was finishing off a bacon and egg sandwich. He politely asked if he might sit there as well.

Kryslie simply gestured agreement, for she had her mouth full of cereal.

"I was told that you are indeed to be my mentor," he smiled at Kryslie as he sat down.

"True enough," Kryslie agreed. "I hope you don't object to someone younger and lower grade ranked than you having that role?"

Arthur jerked, almost spilling some coffee. The statement sounded like a challenge, and truth be told, if he were back on Earth, away from work, his father would consider a comparative situation to be an insult.

"As I am something of an unexpected guest here, I expect your work will be least disturbed by my presence," Arthur suggested.

Krys kept a straight face, "I don't know about that. I think tech 3's do more work than tech 2's and tech 1's."

"You are testing me?" Arthur accused her. Kryslie gave him a disarming grin.

"Yes and no," Kryslie told him. "Tech 3's here do more hands on stuff. I will probably give you more detail than others will."

"Indeed," Arthur agreed. "I have permission to join you on Delta shift. I believe that starts at 1400 hrs here."

"Yes. So what have you planned for this morning?"

Arthur shrugged elegantly. He was trying to make up his mind about his hopes and suspicions of this red headed woman. She looked different this morning. Her face was thinner and the freckles had gone.

Tymos decided to distract him from his musings. "You will be expected to do the induction for base workers. We have some different procedures here."

"How do I arrange that?"

Tymos winked at his sister as he stood up to leave.

"I can do that," Kryslie offered. "We need to go down to reception. That's the area off the shuttle bay where you went when you arrived yesterday. That's where they keep the induction packs."

Kryslie sipped her coffee as Tymos spoke to her mind.

"My opinion of him has not changed. He is definitely more kin to us, than to his bastard sire."

She thought back, "The question is, how much of what he learns here will be unwittingly extracted by his sire."

"Trust him, Krys. He will do what is right."

She didn't need to answer that, so she finished her cereal, and timed drinking her coffee so she finished just before Arthur finished his. Then she made an act of dragging herself up.

"Late night?' Arthur suggested.

"Sort of – I didn't sleep well," Kryslie admitted. "Still, I have had two cups of coffee and a huge breakfast, so I should wake up soon. Come on, let's get you started."

During the morning, she showed Arthur plans of the base, explaining the unfamiliar aspects of living in a closed environment and explaining various emergency procedures and warning codes, and how to find the safe locks and life support pods in the case of a breach in the base. Then she took him on a tour of the full base, not just the parts permitted to visitors. She kept him too busy memorising details to think about her. He was very interested in everything.

However, once she had finished with the formalities and were headed towards the cafeteria for lunch, his intense interest in her manifested again. She felt him glancing at her frequently, more so than he had been during the tour. It was making her more than a little distracted. Time to end it before the other staff began to notice his interest.

"Arthur, Sir, I don't know who I remind you of, but whoever it is, could you stop comparing me to her? Your regard is very unsettling."

"My apologies," Arthur offered with sincerity. His mind was in confusion. He finally recalled, the words of the guard the previous day. He forced himself to be patient. One like he wanted to speak to would find him.

Kryslie hid a smile, not because of her son's confusion, which in itself was protection for him as much as it was for her, but because she was beginning to feel a mother's pride in the man her son had become. She only wished she dared to ask what was bothering him. Instead, she took her leave of him, and told him to meet her in main mission ten minutes before the start of delta shift. He could amuse himself for an hour.

"You didn't offer to arrange a uniform for him for the week," Tymos mock rebuked her as she reached her quarters.

Sending him a mental raspberry, she sent back, "Bro, he's a Tech 1, he ought to know the basic stuff by now. I told him how to requisition things…or you could accidentally meet up with him and play uncle?"

Tymos sent a mental chuckle this time, admitting they were equal in that bout of teasing. "Since we are not some kind of military organisation and the uniform is more for the purpose of job identification – he really doesn't need one. That way, no one will expect him to be proficient in an emergency."

"I expect, bro, that when he is at Terra 5, he would be extremely capable. Anyway, while we were traipsing everywhere, did you pick up on anyone interested in us?"

"No, just the 'who is this guy' thoughts."

"Well, based on our private ideas of who controls the gremlin, the person will know who Arthur is."

"Yeah, and the lack of interest tends to add weight. If he was a high rank visitor from the UWN, I would expect a level of interest in terms of how to use the person's presence to add to or cause trouble."

"Though if something else does happen while Arthur is here, his father will use it against the WSRA."

"You are so comforting, Bro. Just when I thought it will be a while before the gremlin acts up again!"

She was being facetious, but there was no denying the fierce tremor of premonition. She knew Tymos also felt it.

"I think I will head for the computer hub early," Tymos decided.

Kryslie arrived earlier than usual for her shift, as she was expecting Arthur bin Halil. While she waited for him, she studied the screen of the geology station.

"You've changed the study area," she commented to Joe Thompson, a Tech 2 who used it on gamma shift.

"Not really. The Gobi has just gone out of sensor range and the Commander thought your protégé might like to see his country from up here."

"I'm sure he would," Kryslie agreed as she read the lat and long coordinates of the scene on the screen. "You are keeping the drone geosynchronous?"

"For now. What have you had coming in from that meteor, BT507?"

Kryslie glanced at her own screen where Nancy Lieu, a junior tech 3, was tracking the small object.

"High ice composition. The trajectory will bring it close, and it will be a near miss – probably it will burn up on the fringes of Earth's atmosphere."

Arthur arrived ten minutes before the shift change. He spotted Kryslie and headed in her direction. He introduced himself to the two gamma shift workers and then saw the scene on the geology screen. Hid face glowed with delight when he realised that he was seeing his own country from so far up.

The five minute alert sounded and his attention went to where Nancy had begun the official shift handover. This was a formality, most of the time, unless there was something going on, like the current meteor or rocket tests from Terra 1. Next to her, Thompson was briefing Branson.

So it was that Kryslie was watching her screen, aware of her son's delight at the scene on the adjacent screen that was in her peripheral vision, listening to a report of an unexciting morning shift, when several things happened almost all at once. There was a brilliant flash on the geology screen, at the same time as a new blip appeared on hers. A message flashed onto her screen and the whole system went down, hers first, and then a cascading effect, and the other screens in main mission began to go black.

In that first instant of startled silence, Kryslie mentally integrated all she has observed, and spoke clearly, "Auto-track 1 is down. Missile launch, Earth Coordinates 33.33 degrees north, 33.83 degrees east."

Stanley heard her and immediately issued orders, setting off base wide alerts.

"Shut down!" he ordered the entire control room. That was to stop the problem spreading further. "Bring up the back-up system on terminals one thru five. Branson, bring the radio scopes on line – terminal four."

As he spoke, he hit the alarm klaxon, and the mechanised voice began, "All non-essential personnel to safe locks. This is not a drill."

As the red light flashed urgently, he used the base comm to announce, "Tech team to shuttle bay 2, prepare for EA emergency – Auto-track 1."

In an aside, he ordered, "Ward! Get on it. You're leader."

Kryslie grabbed her data padd and raced for the exit. She heard Branson announce, "System is up!"

Stanley followed that with, "Find that missile."

She had only a momentary glance at console four – the security station. There was no sign of a missile trail, but she knew what she had seen and it hadn't been a glitch or artefact.

As she raced to the turbo lift, she sensed a flash of anger and then cautious relief. She had no time to follow that up. Instead, she sent a mental alert to her brother who was also responding to the callout for the tech team.

"The gremlin has to be near main mission. I felt his anger over us getting the back-up system up so fast and relief that the radar scoped showed nothing. I have to lead the tech team."

She sensed her brother slowing as he returned, "I'll stay here."

The shuttle bay crew were bringing the crawler from its hangar as Kryslie arrived. The emergency crew had the rack of EA suits. Five other techs were racing in as she began to suit up. Only then did she realise that Athur had followed her.

"I want to come. I am a tracking system specialist."

"Sorry, Sir. You haven't completed the EA induction or drills and you haven't worked on Auto-tracks. Get back to main mission or get to a safe lock!"

Kryslie sensed his frustration at being sent off, and his intense need to help. She paused before connecting the headpiece, as she realised that his normally tanned skin seemed a sickly shade of yellow green. He knew where that missile had come from.

"Talk to Stanley! Tell him to check the signal log from Auto-track 1. And to reset the main tracking system from defaults and add the adjustments manually up to those prior to six months ago."

"What?" Arthur seemed in shock.

"Do it!"

In that moment, Arthur saw Kryslie in a whole new light. No longer a slightly diffident junior technician, but as he knew she could be – decisive and frighteningly competent. He wasted no more time considering the congruity, but trotted back to main mission.

The emergency crew was checking all the seals and connections on the suits, adding extra oxygen tanks into the racks on the crawler, and testing the comm signals.

Even whilst doing her own mental checklist, she was communicating with her brother and making a note of the flashing message symbol on her data padd.

"Damn it, Tym. I should have remembered this last night! I knew there was something…"

She was climbing into the crawler, making sure everyone was suited, checked and strapped in.

"… All signals from the Auto-tracks come in encrypted and our commands to it are the same. All except for the initial start-up signals."

"Why use the old restore point?" Tymos quizzed her. Impressions of his movements came with it. He was approaching a bevy of hand wringing staff gathered in the observation room overlooking main mission. He began shooing them to their assigned safe-locks as Kryslie told him, "The system was upgraded recently to allow for the four Earth based Auto-tracks that are due to come on line in six months. I can't be sure, since Stanley was checking the new system – but I think the gremlin sent the initialisation program to one of the standby or future Auto-track data receivers and his virus program was waiting there and it sent itself back to the control program. If we restore before those modifications, we close that avenue."

Tymos sent tersely, "Right!"

The crawler began to move, following the glowing green line on the floor, reaching and passing through the force field barrier that kept atmosphere in the bay. It gathered speed whilst on the short stretch on concrete roadway and hit the lunar soil at its top speed of 5 kilometres per hour. At that speed, it would take half an hour to get to Auto-track 1, which was towards the north lunar pole and near the edge of the crater that was the Sea of Serenity.

Within the pressurised crawler, Kryslie removed her right suit glove, but still had on the inner flexible one that maintained the integrity of the suit's air supply, so that she could access the orders on the data padd.

Stanley had sent the full schematics for the Auto-track, as well as the default settings from the initial set up. The modifications made since were in separate folders.

Over the suit comms, she gave the team instructions. "Once we get there, we need to set up the EA generator, in case it is the solar generator that is at fault."

One of the two Tech 1s muttered, "If it failed, it had help."

"Hence, when we go in we check for signs of sabotage," Kryslie went on. "Stanley tried a remote restart. It didn't work. So we will do a manual close down, check all parts for signs of damage or tampering. Once I have done the manual power up, I have to run the diagnostic program. If the remote restart still doesn't work, I will have to do it manually."

Once the few pertinent questions were asked and answered, some suppositions were aired. "With all the bad luck we've been having on base lately, it was only a matter of time before the rot spread."

Kryslie didn't have to counter that comment. One of the others beat her to it. "I don't think that most of the problems we've had are due to poor maintenance. Or to negligence. Anyway, the Auto-tracks were designed to withstand the moon environment for months at a time."

Another voice piped up, "The regular maintenance was done two months ago. I was part of that team and I know all was well then."

Even without the glowing name badge on each suit, Kryslie knew each speaker by their voice.

Andrews had spoken last, and she wanted to know who else had been on that inspection trip, but that could wait until the emergency was over. He was a tech 2 with maintenance, while the speaker before him was Ganesh, a tech 1 systems programmer and interface specialist. The initial comment was from one of the newer tech 3's, Merck, from engineering. He was a whiz at checking electronic circuits. The other two were James, a tech 2 from engineering and Rusch, a tech 1 from the computer division.

She let the men chat or stay silent as was their nature in serious situations. They all were aware of the urgency for getting the Auto-track back in operation. That missile, had gone somewhere. It might even be approaching the base, unseen.

"Ward? Are we getting signals from Earthside?"

Kryslie didn't know, but Tymos sensed the question through the twin bond. "No. Landin is getting the WSRA comm system checked."

Her brother didn't know any more, so she changed comm frequency and asked the question of Stanley. His answer was terse. Lunar 1 was out of contact with Earth.

The answer silenced her team until Andrews said, "Rusch, can't you make this thing go any faster?"

For the next twenty minutes, the level of tension of crew in the crawler grew to be almost palpable. Kryslie used the time to recall the layout of the interior of Auto-track 1 from previous visits, memorise the schematics of the equipment, the positions of all the auxiliary power inlets, so that she had everything she needed to know in her mind. Then she considered possible reasons why the gremlin had targeted Auto-track 1. It was the nearest lunar based Auto-track to the base, and it was on the lunar face that always faced the Earth. It was able to scan on multiple frequencies, using multiple sensors and work on several projects at once.

The geology station was using its sensors to map desert areas looking for potential sites to drill for water. Their important visitor of the previous day, knew that from the tour yesterday. If he was planning to fire that missile, he would know that the Auto-tracks would need to be neutralised.

That blackout was timed for the shift change, and the missile launched almost simultaneously. If bin Halil didn't know that the shift change routine here was different to the ground bases, he would have expected that time to be the most vulnerable.

She was the only one in main mission who would have been able to read the warning that flashed on the screen for that microsecond, and the flash on both her screen and the geology screen might have been disregarded.

The only warning, hers, happened because the power to the screens stayed live for several microseconds after the power down.

As the crawler slowed to approach the Auto-track structure, Kryslie decided that it was unlikely that the gremlin had stolen a suit and enough oxygen bottles and walked out here. She wasn't assuming anything though, so she asked Stanley, "Do the monitors show intruders?" Fortunately the monitoring system was completely separate from the tracking system.

"No, it's clear," came the assurance. He didn't ask why she had thought there might be, for he had been told of the possibility of a covert saboteur.

Even with the assurances, when she approached the entry door on foot, and was examining the lock and frame, she saw no sign of forced entry and the entry code unlocked the door without a problem, and it slid wide open. She sent her awareness into the building and sensed no one hiding within. Still, preventative paranoia was better than nasty surprises.

"Let's get to it. Keep an eye on your oxygen supply. Spare cylinders are by the entry door."

Kryslie didn't wait for the two carrying the EA generator to set it up and working, she could see in the dark and in the suit, they wouldn't see how the shape of her eyes changed. The others, coming in from the day-lit moonscape required moments to adjust their eyes to their suit lights until the generator began to power the dormant lighting system.

Tymos edged his way into main mission and avoided the frantic activity at stations one to five by going to one of the seven powered down stations. He turned it on, not linking it to the tracking system, but to access the main computer, and through it, the communications logs. No one paid any particular attention to him, for he had on his computer division work uniform and even though the sleeves were mid blue, not controller purple, anyone might think he had come up to help solve the current emergency.

He had been aware of his sister pondering the timing of the outage, even as the same thought occurred to him. At times like this, they thought as one but his mind took the idea in a different direction since Kryslie had other things to consider. The timing could have been prearranged for the shift change, but Kryslie had sensed anger – her warning had not been expected, nor the rapid successful loading of the backup system.

He set a program to search through all communications occurring during the past ten minutes, since just before the power went out. With that running, he was about to go and talk to Starley, when his sister asked about tracking from Earth. Landin had ordered a check on the dedicated Earth-Moon WSRA communications system but that was all he knew. He thought it unwise to interrupt Stanley or Landin with the query, so he sent a signal to Earth using his personal data comm link.

The Tymorean Earthbase would be able to answer his question.

"Great One, all the Terra bases are tracking blind," Daniel told him.

That, Tymos decided, was surely no coincidence. "Where's that missile?"

After a moment of silence, he heard Lexina's voice. She gave him the launch coordinates, the data on its trajectory, then added, "After reaching the edge of the atmosphere, it went to hyper speed for a few seconds, and then it stopped. It is drifting at the moment, just outside the tracking range of Lunar 1. Coordinates…"

"Can you get control of it?" Tymos demanded tersely.

"We are trying, but I don't think we can."

"Keep watching it. Warn me if it begins to track again." He ended the communication and checked his search algorithm.

"Bingo!" he murmured, copying a flagged message to his data pad and listening to it. There was no encryption, except for it being in Arabic, not English. That was no problem, he had learnt Arabic many years before. It was clear from the slight tremor in the voice that the speaker was spooked.

"They've got the back up going already and the radio telescopes shortly. They will see the missile."

See it and have orders to destroy it, Tymos thought what the man hadn't said. If he had his way it would be destroyed before it came close to harming anything on Earth or the moon but he had no way of knowing the intended target.

An incoming message was immediately flagged. This one was electronically coded, but once it was copied to his data pad, it was decoded very quickly.

"Ensure all tracking is off at 1745 UTC+2"

Tymos shunted copies of the flagged messages to a storage file, and was about to close down the terminal when he saw the flagged messages disappear from his screen. The gremlin had deleted them, covering his tracks.

Now Tymos had the deadline. Lunar time was aligned to Greenwich Time, and that was two hours behind UTC+2, so in a little under three quarters of an hour, the gremlin was going to try to strike again. He left the terminal and moved towards Landin's office at a walk just short of a trot, passing the frantically working controllers. He noted Arthur in the group, and spared a thought to commend him for doing as Kryslie had directed.

He reached the ensigns desk and began to move past it, but Landin's young admin assistant sprang into his way. "You can't go in there, Ward."

Tymos knew Landin was meeting with all the section heads, but his message could not wait. "Meyer, move out of the way. I have an urgent message for the Commander."

"The commander said…"

Meyer found himself pushed aside, as Tymos pressed the touch pad to make the door slide open on the room where a meeting was in progress. Landin stopped talking when he saw Tymos enter, and everyone else turned to see who had interrupted.

"Ward, what is it?" Landin asked.

"Sir, there will be another attack on the tracking system in less than 45 minutes."

Landin wasted no time asking questions. "The briefing is over, Please get back to your sections. Emergency staffing only."

The men and women left immediately, all eyeing the Tech 3 who had simply barged in. Landin demanded, "What do you know."

In a low voice, Tymos mentioned what Kryslie had sensed and his search of the comms logs. He didn't mention knowing that all the Terra bases were tracking blind, for the communications were still down.

Landin leant over his desk and activated a voice over message. "Security to main mission. Check all IDs, allow only shift personnel in there. Send squads to all power grid accesses."

Tymos frowned, now the gremlin had warning. He might even insert himself into one of the security backup teams being called up now.

In an aside to Tymos, Landin anticipated potential questions. "We have a relay in the wireless communications signal array. We are using channel 2 for all actions now."

He sent an update to the data padds of all the section heads warning that computer access was being restricted and then instructed the computer via voice access, "Computer lock out, except main mission, Alpha access only from now."

A series of clicks indicated that the restriction was now in force. Landin wasn't finished. "Communications. Monitor all frequencies and transmission methods. Bring up emergency system. Alpha access only."

Landin turned to speak to Tymos, the question "Are you sure," in his mind, but his Tech 3 was no longer in his office.

Even though he was within the group working under Stanley, Arthur bin Halil was politely and impersonally requested to leave Main Mission and go directly to the safelock designated with respect to his assigned quarters. At first he was tempted to protest, but the sight of a black haired man being frog-marched out, ignominiously, was reminder enough that such treatment would not be fitting for a man of his social rank. Therefore, he agreed graciously, apologised to Stanley and was allowed to leave unescorted. He reminded himself that he was not at Terra 5, and had no authority to insist on staying. It didn't help his need to do something to help…the missile that was somewhere in near space had come from within his country.

Irrespective of the fact that he had no idea who had fired it or why, he felt responsible. He had seen the flash of light before the screen went black, and he felt he could give a very accurate guess of where in his country it had come from. The Karshada Science Research Centre. He had never been allowed to visit there. His father had said the work was third rate and his rank demanded a better place for his scientific pursuits.

When Kryslie Ward had detailed him to pass a message to Stanley, his initial hesitation to get involved had morphed into determination. The previous evening, when he had waited in the cafeteria, hoping to see her after her shift, he had been aware of the talk around him.

Something nasty was happening on Lunar 1, and he was suddenly sure his esteemed father was behind it. Did the people on this neutral base realise how vulnerable they were? What a major target they were to an unscrupulous would be dictator? Taking control of Lunar 1 could give someone control over the planet below.

There were treaties in place between the UWN and the alliance his father headed – agreements between peaceful men to coexist and allow individual freedom of ideology. He had thought his father a peaceful man, once. Now, he had heard too many rumours that suggested otherwise.

He was nearing the guest quarters, still deep in his thoughts, when he caught a hint of movement, as if someone had ducked into the side passage just ahead.

The movement, as he considered it, had been furtive, so it probably hadn't been a guard and since no one should be abroad in this section during a level 2 red alert, not even himself, the person was likely up to no good.

Arthur sped up, keeping his eyes on the side opening. He reached it and looked down its length. No one was in sight. He turned into the passage took a few steps. A figure sprang out in front of him, startling him. The man had on a controller division uniform, but there was no ID bar on his chest pocket, and no collar tabs denoting approved access to particular sections. It might have been the man who had been evicted from Main Mission, or it might not. He was dark haired, medium height, not young. The face, with its olive tinged skin, was vaguely familiar. Then recognition came with staggering force and Arthur felt as if his blood had frozen. He found himself saying, "Rasti." Everything he had heard of the man returned to his mind, including the reports of his execution fifteen years before. He was both a brilliant computer specialist and a pathological killer.

The man bowed slightly, but his head was turned slightly up to look at the tall Prince, and his facial expression was hard.

"You watching me, Prince?"

Arthur knew the man was dangerous, and would attack if he felt threatened. "Not you. Do I need to?"

The man gave a feral snarl. "That red headed bitch then?"

Arthur did not confirm it. Rasti's smile was malicious.

"Is all proceeding efficiently?" Arthur imitated his father's silky tones, and saw the faintest tightening of the muscles in the corners of the other man's eyes.

"That bitch almost spoilt things," Rasti stared at his controller's son, trying to see a reaction. "I don't reckon it was an accident that she did that diagnostic yesterday. You didn't tell her anything…"

"They had other problems yesterday, perhaps that is what did it. The woman is only a Tech 3, and she was too busy trying to convince me of how smart she was. Besides, I am not privy to all my father does, I just agreed to stay here for a week to observe how they do things."

"Then if you know so much, how did that bitch see what was wrong?"

Wanting Rasti to think him an ally, Arthur told him, "The screens take a few moments to power down once the power is off."

The sudden feral grin gave Arthur shivers down his spine.

"So that was it! Still, the cursed backup system is working. Can't allow that! And the bitch ain't here to stop me this time."

Arthur nodded. As if agreeing, and said, "We should move on. We might be noticed here. Come to my quarters."

Rasti darted glances in all directions, making Arthur wonder if he suspected a trap. He wanted to isolate the man, but hadn't yet thought past keeping him in sight. The shorter man began to walk towards the guest section, fast enough that Arthur had to trot to keep up.

"Why did you tell the chief C how to fix the computer?" Rasti called back over his shoulder.

Arthur kept his voice as calm as his father's always was.

"Others heard the instructions," Arthur said without concern. "And I must seem to be helpful. I am, after all, well known."

Rasti nodded. "It ain't a problem, Prince. I got more surprises for them." He revealed a palm sized computer he had taken from a pocket. As he walked he manipulated the micro sized keypad with great dexterity. Then he cursed in vile gutter language. "I'm locked out of the computer. I am going to have to find a terminal."

"I know a place," Arthur claimed. "Come with me."

"I think not," Rasti muttered as he pocketed the computer. He let Arthur go past him, get a few steps ahead, and then he launched himself at the suited man in front of him. He was surprised when his victim turned at the last moment, twisted and hit out. The bastard whelp had not been that good sixteen years before. He'd been little more than a spoilt dandy.

Rasti was pushed off balance, and landed on his back on the floor. Before he could spring back up, Arthur was on him, pinning him down. He arched his back and pushed up with his feet, twisting at the same time to avoid, a blow to the head. He got one leg free and used his knee to catch his opponent with the oldest dirty fighting trick in the book. As his would be captor writhed in unexpected agony, he squirmed free, and wasted no time delivering a vicious karate chop to drop his opponent.

He stepped back, breathing only slightly faster than normal, restraining his bloodlust with difficulty. The whelp was his controller's son, and might be here on orders too. Might be a traitor though, since he was helping fix the damn tracking system.

His victim didn't seem to be moving, that was good enough for now. He had to run, to get to his private hideout where he had a purloined terminal. Time was against him, he had to hack back into the system. His controller would not be pleased with any more setbacks.

If Rasti had waited a few seconds longer, he would have seen Arthur stirring, and trying to stand up when pain still made him want to double up. He forced himself to his feet, but teetered on the verge of blacking out again.

Suddenly, and without hearing anyone approach, Arthur felt hands holding him up, and the blackness began to retreat.

"I'm fine," he murmured, turning to see who his helper was. He recognised the dark haired man he'd seen having breakfast with Kryslie Ward, just that morning. He had the same colour eyes as Kryslie too.

"Get to the next deck schematic panel and summon help. I'm going after that saboteur."

Arthur nodded, rather than trying to talk. He wanted to know how the man would be found, since he had run out of sight. Then, he thought his eyes were playing tricks on him, for his dark haired rescuer suddenly raced off at incredible speed.

As Landin finished acting on his warning, Tymos had felt a sense of trouble. At first he thought it was from Krys, but she was out at the Auto-track station. This trouble was close…on the base. When Landin was facing away from him, he moved back to the door and in the act of passing through the opening, he transmitted away relying on his instinctive awareness of distance and direction.

When he saw the staggering figure, in the rumpled business suit, he immediately knew it was Arthur bin Halil. That was why he had recognised the feeling – Arthur was kin to him, son of his sister.

Moving swiftly, he caught Arthur as he was about to collapse, sending healing energy into him. His special gift was not as effective through layers of clothing, but also less noticeable.

"I'm fine," Arthur murmured, turning around.

He wasn't, Tymos sensed, but he was well enough. "Get to the next deck schematic panel and summon help. I'm going after that saboteur."

The attacker was out of sight, but from Arthur's mind, he had the look of him and knowledge of what the little man was. He took a moment to seek a mind that matched what he knew, and took off at a run like a hound on the scent. He needed to find that man fast, so he didn't modify his speed. If people had thought his sister had been unnaturally speedy a week ago, it was slow compared to a Great One at full speed.

He slowed as he sensed that his quarry had gone to ground, at least for the moment. Hopefully, he didn't realise that anyone had followed him. With all his senses extended, Tymos homed in on the man, and eventually stopped outside the camera iris like door of one of the storage areas. Opening that door would alert his quarry, so Tymos took out his Tymorean transmitter, and while it powered up, he concentrated on 'seeing' through the door. He hadn't needed to use this depth perception for a long time, but it came easily, giving him a three dimensional sense of where things were stacked behind the door. He identified a covert space into which he could transmit himself.

Once inside, he approached his quarry with caution. The man was dangerous, but at the moment, his mind was occupied, trying to bypass the computer lockout. This man was both angry and frightened – of his controller, not those that he perceived as fools that were living on the base.

Yet the man seemed to have the senses of a wild creature. He started at the whisper of sound when the air purifier came on. He left his task and prowled around the stacked crates.

Tymos froze, his body half in the man's view, but the other's eyes slid right past him, not able to see the faint shimmer where his Tymorean power cloaked him. Still, he was spooked, and kept turning around every few seconds. Each few seconds, Tymos inched forward, watching the man's movements – one hand playing over a touch pad, the other reaching for something from his pocket.

When he was close enough, Tymos drew on his power and leapt at the man.

The defending blast of energy came lightning fast; the man firing as he turned, and aiming instinctively. His accuracy was off, but not by much. The heat seared Tymos's arm, but did him no damage – thanks to the hidden personal force screen.

If the man was surprised by the failure of his attack, he only had micro seconds to act, for Tymos came at him at full speed and strength, knocking the gun from his hand and him away from the computer terminal and onto the floor. Still the man didn't give up, he wriggled like an eel, twisted and bucked, and managed to draw a tiny but extremely sharp knife from his boot. He lunged the blade into the fleshy part of Tymos's thigh, unknowingly causing a point overload in the force field that had protected his victim from the energy blast.

Tymos hardly felt it, as he grappled with the man who would not admit that he was outfought, even when he was face down on the concrete floor, with a broken nose and a weight on his back. A hard punch to the man's spine, just below the neck, stilled his struggles, but did not silence him.

"Son of a sewer dog, you'll die for this, and even if you begged, I will not try to save you."

"Be still!" Tymos commanded the man's mind, and his next curse was abruptly silenced. But the man's mind was an open book as he raged and gloated that the obscene lunar base would be destroyed very soon. He scorned the ability of any backup scanners to see the missile in time to stop it. Everyone would die! But he would die first, they would not make him talk.

It was only then that the man realised that he could not even bite down on either of the suicide capsules in his mouth.

When his captor turned him on his back and forced his unresisting mouth open wider, and used two fingers to wrench out the two false teeth with deceptive ease, his mind went into a full scale panic and he did not realise that he was flitting from subject to subject, prompted by thoughts that were not his own.

When the klaxons began, and the security teams were summoned to assist Arthur bin Halil, Tymos knew he was out of time, and he ruthlessly invaded the little man's mind to get the information he needed. The man had no defences and no way to censor his thoughts – the intrusive questions, provoked images and words, and Tymos memorised everything.

His face was expressionless, so his prisoner had no clue that Tymos now knew both the primary and the secondary target pre-programmed into the missile, or that it had shocked him profoundly.

Tymos removed the 'still' command, and the little man resumed his cursing, and the blood that had pooled in his mouth from the wrenched out teeth, was ejected towards his captor's face. It missed its target, as Tymos moved his weight off the prisoner.

Only then, did he remember the tiny knife, for the pain began to manifest. He jerked it from his leg, feeling blood seeping out to soak his uniform. He dropped it so that he could place his hand on the wound and send a burst of power to seal it - enough to stop the bleeding. During a few moments of concentration, he used a biofeedback technique to block the pain.

He had just recovered the tiny knife as a security team burst in. They had their weapons aimed and ready, so he took a step back from the helpless man, who was already reviling his captor and accusing him of assault.

The team leader was Murtry, who recognised Tymos immediately. "What's wrong with him?"

"A temporary nerve stun. It should wear off in an hour," Tymos answered calmly, making no attempt to move as the security team added restraints to the prisoner.

"A bit extreme wasn't it?" the security chief suggested.

Tymos ignored the innuendo, and produced the tiny knife and dug into his pocket for the two poison capsules. "I suggest that you search him carefully before you let him move again. In case he has any more of these."

"Don't try to teach me my job, Ward. You should be in a safe lock – you aren't on duty."

"I need to talk to the Commander, Sir," Tymos said, ignoring the question. He knew Murtry had a point. He should not have been wandering the passageways. If he had not transmitted out of Landin's office, he, like Arthur, would have been sent out of main mission.

"Why did you come after this man? You should have summoned us. Then you wouldn't have got hurt." He'd only seen the blood on his sleeve, from where the little man had ejected bloody spittle.

"I didn't want him to get away. I saw him ousted from main mission, and that he was not wearing proper uniform."

"Still wasn't your job, Ward."

"I still need to talk to Commander Landin."

"You can say what you need to say to me!" Murtry was staring at him, his posture signalling his impatience to hear what was so important.

Tymos saw the other guards dragging the little man upright. He was now screaming. "Don't believe him! He made me do it."

Murtry turned away for a moment, and directed, "Put that one in a high security cell in the brig and have a medic look at him." He turned back. "I'm waiting, Ward. Say your piece, or I put you in the cell next to him."

"That missile. Its primary target is Terra 5. Its secondary target is here. That man was in here, trying to get through the computer lock out. I don't know if he was trying to send a signal or do something else."

Murtry gestured to one of his remaining men to check the computer. He came back with a non-standard data padd and the dropped energy weapon – both of which he gave to his superior.

"Ward's right sir, this padd was locked out, and there is a hacking program on the terminal."

Now Murtry gave Tymos a head to toe look over. He moved and saw the blood on Tymos's leg.

"You're lucky he didn't use this on you, Ward," he showed the energy gun. "If he had, we wouldn't be having this conversation."

"Sir, the Commander…"

"Will get to hear of this. You are going straight to medical and staying there."

"Well, tell him I think that man is the gremlin," Tymos insisted as his arm was grabbed.

"It may be Ward. We found this place because the monitoring cameras were conveniently faulty."

"That bloke may have been working with someone else…"

"Let's hope I don't find out it is you, Ward."

Tymos reigned in his anger, and sense of time getting short. There were things he needed to tell Landin, that Murtry would never believe.

Tymos was not feeling meek as he was escorted to medical. Time was getting short, and he felt he had to be doing something. There was less than twenty minutes to when that missile was due to activate, and the little man was meant to bring down the tracking system again. If there was someone else working with that first man, and he succeeded, the base would be blind.

The guards were hustling him at a fairly fast pace, and it was putting strain on the knife wound. He could have waited for a stretcher, but that would have taken a lot more time. After walking the short distance from the storage chamber to the turbo lift, he could feel that the wound had re-opened, but he did not dare try to re-seal it, since his escort might feel the surge of power. The best he could do was maintain the pace, and hide the pain.

A med tech was just emerging with a treatment satchel when they arrived.

"Can you deal with Ward?" the tech was asked.

"Go in, Sir. I'm just on my way to the prisoner in the brig."

"I'll be fine," Tymos told his escorts. "You don't need to stay."

"You know the drill, Ward," one of his escorts drawled. "Out of safe zone during an emergency, when not on duty, we escort you to your designated area, and you have two days house arrest. Or two in the brig if you don't go quietly."

Tymos clamped his mouth shut, knowing it was useless to argue. He tried not to fidget whilst another med tech cut away the fabric of his uniform and tended to the wound. He didn't need telling that it was a deep incision, or that he was lucky that it missed the main artery or that he would need to keep off his leg for several days. And he ignored the statement that he was medically unfit for duty.

By the time the med tech began to run a tissue regenerator over the wound, he was barely restraining himself from swearing with frustration.

He heard the door to medical open, and someone striding in. The tech told him to keep still.

He soon had confirmation that it was Landin, for he heard, "I will deal with Ward, you can go."

The med tech finished, and said. "Stay there. I will bring you a spare pair of trousers."

Landin moved around to face his junior technician. "Why Terra 5?" he demanded, getting right to the point.

"I don't know why. The primary coordinates are…" Tymos quoted the string of numbers he read in the prisoner's mind. "That is too close to Terra 5 to be a coincidence."

"The missile came from Karshada," Landin said.

"Abdul bin Halil's native country," Tymos said, implying his belief in the real culprit. "He has never been that close to the dirty work before, though."

"It was only luck that your sister saw that," Landin admitted. "And since all the Terra bases had some malfunction at the same time as we did, I suspect it was to prevent anyone knowing where it came from. But if the one you suspect is to blame, Terra 5 as a target makes no sense. His son works there."

"His son isn't there right now. And that bastard might have half a dozen reasons for doing this."

"Ward, you are speaking about a powerful world leader. You could get in trouble for disrespect."

Tymos didn't try to justify his opinion of bin Halil's lack of honour. Landin didn't need to know all that.

"So, I tell Terra 5 to lock down – How do we know if the missile is going to go there, or here? Your prisoner isn't talking, just trying to implicate you."

"He was meant to send a signal when the tracking is down again."

Landin didn't ask how Tymos knew that. He knew Kryslie was a telepath, and suspected that Tymos was as well, even though he had implied otherwise in the past. "He can't do that from the brig, especially as he is still paralytic."

"Don't assume that nothing will happen now. With something this big, assume a backup."

"Here?"

"Yes."

Landin drew out his communicator, gave the voice code to get a secure communication channel, and proceeded to escalate the red alert to critical, and ordered the diversion of non-essential power to the meteorite shields. The lights in medical dimmed perceptibly.

"We have to be the real target," Landin stated, and he walked off a few feet. "All this is too big for a petty act of terrorism. What worries me is where that missile went to."

Since Landin already knew that he was more than just an Earth citizen, Tymos said softly, "It is more than just a missile, Sir. It is an experimental hyper drive rocket. One that is a lot more sophisticated than the one that crashed forty years ago. It's currently drifting…" he gave spatial coordinates, "That's just beyond the range of our tracking system."

"I won't ask you how you know," Landin decided. "Can you track that missile?"

Tymos shook his head. "I will know when it livens up, but on its way back, there will be virtually no warning."

"Code 2000," Landin said quietly, and Tymos read in his mind that it was the override to access the computer. "Code seven omega five," he continued. That was the code for an immediate threat, which was usually followed by a second code to indicate the type of threat. In this instance it would be Mix – missile impact in x seconds.

Tymos nodded, indicating that he understood.

"How long will that missile take to return to Earth?"

"At hyper speed, only seconds."

Landin accessed the repaired Earth-Moon comm link and spoke to Terra 5's commander, Ben Mansour. He kept to the main points and ended the call. He sent the same warning to the other Terra bases – giving only a terse explanation. Then he studied his tech 3 and made a decision.

"After an injury such as you sustained, you should be off duty for a week, but I want you in main mission, on the weapons array. If we get those scanners up in time, and we see the missile, I think you are the best person to try and get a shot at it."

Tymos pushed himself off the trolley to test his leg. He nodded confirmation to Landin's statement. He was the best to try. He could do the maths nearly as fast as the computer, and he could get some help from Earthbase. Yet there was still a fractional signal lag from there to the moon.

"I will tell security to let you in. Take the turbo lift."

The med tech returned with the spare trousers and a vial of pain killers. Landin left as Tymos went to change into the undamaged trousers. For the benefit of the med tech, Tymos walked carefully from the area, but once in the empty passageway, he transmitted to near main mission.

He wasted no time getting to the weapons station and powering it up, He had less than ten minutes to program the link to the backup tracking system and set up the missiles ready for launch.

The slow and cumbersome radio-telescopes were all they had. His sister was working like a dervish to get the Auto-track back in action, but even she might run out of time.

The view on the weapons screen was identical to the one on the main screen, but he added a grid overlay onto his and requested updated coordinates for the drifting missile from Earth base. He plotted lines of probability from there to both potential targets.

Both main mission and the earpiece in his ear were silent, eyes locked onto the screen as they waited. All too soon, the earpiece activated, "Great One – it has been reactivated, but is still drifting."

He took a moment to call his sister. "How's it going? That damn missile has been activated – not moving yet."

"I am about to do a manual restart," Kryslie told him.

"They are still doing the updates here," Tymos told her after glancing at the busy technicians and interpreting their screens. "Five minutes…"

They didn't have five minutes.

"It's moving! Target 2."

It was coming, and suddenly Tymos was in the midst of the strongest premonition he had ever experienced.

"Krys! Get out of there NOW!"

And his fingers took on a life of their own as he calculated distance based on the shouted warning from Earthbase.

A sense of urgency was already causing Kryslie to hurry her team out of the tracking station. As her fingers moved at high speed to complete the power up and activation sequence, she was saying over the suit comm, "Drop everything! Grab the spare oxygen and get back to the crawler."

They were still moving ponderously to the door when she'd finished and all the indicator lights had turned green. She moved faster than all of the others in the low gravity and went ahead, opening the crawler and getting to the control seat to power it up.

As soon as the last person was through the door, and before they had all fastened the safety straps, she had the power up to full and the crawler was accelerating.

"What's going on, Ward," Rusch asked.

While an inner timer seemed to be counting down microseconds, Kryslie merely said, "Incoming missile. We will be better off away from structures."

She was aware that four of the five in the passenger hold were strapped in, and one was having trouble when she warned, "Hold ON!" Her voice on the suit comm was drowned out by the override warning, "Missile Impact, Auto-track 1.5 seconds."

Tymos had microseconds to take in the trajectory details relayed from Earthbase and program them. His first counter missile, a type meant to destroy meteorites, was en-route, even before the course line came up on his screen and the large main screen. He fired a second and third missile, aimed at points ahead of the rogue missile hoping to intersect its trajectory.

With the slow response from the radio telescopes, he was effectively firing blind, and the rogue missile was travelling even faster than he could program counter measures. His fourth and fifth missiles passed harmlessly behind it.

Someone yelled, "You deflected it! It's moving away from us."

There was only time for the start of a cheer, before the new track became clear. Tymos extrapolated it, but could do nothing. His eye went to the screen showing the crawlers progress back from Auto-track 1. He willed his sister to move it faster, but the screen flared into brilliance and blacked out. When it came back on line, there was no sign of the crawler.

"Reposition that satellite!" Stanley yelled.

"Medical emergency, remote access vehicle, EA med team to the shuttle bay."

"Krys!" Tymos yelled mentally. There was silence in his mind. Then he was up and running, ignoring his injured leg, as the main trackers came back on line. He raced to the shuttle bay, grabbed an EVA suit and donned it as the med techs raced in.

His presence wasn't challenged, everyone snapped their equipment pack into a rack, and strapped themselves into a seat. Moments later, the shuttle blasted out of the bay and began to gain height.

Kryslie roused first, instinctively checking her own condition. She was hanging from her safety harness, upside down in the pitch dark of the powerless crawler. Deciding she was functional, she twisted so that when she released the clasp of her harness, she landed on her feet on the crawler's upper panel. Her landing jolted her head, rousing a sharp ache. She took a moment to use a biofeedback technique to deaden the discomfort.

She checked her team then, the four who had been strapped in were hanging from their harnesses. The fifth member, Andrews, had been battered as the crawler rolled, and he was in a bad way. His helmet had taken a beating, and she could hear air hissing out of it. Without wasting an extra moment, she reached into her EVA utility pouch and drew out the sealant spray. Putting the nozzle right up close to where the wisps of air were escaping, she sealed the crack. Once the hissing stopped, she put it away and removed the right gauntlet from her suit again. While no one was aware of her action, she ran her hand along the twisted figure.

Her hand was the focus she used for sensing the trauma inflicted on the unconscious man. He was bad, and that was with the suit providing some protection. However, the injuries would not be immediately fatal if they had to move him. The suit would act like a life support pod.

Kryslie then manoeuvred herself back along the central aisle of the crawler, to where the entry hatch was located. She tried to open it, but the chassis of the crawler had been damaged and the hatch was jammed.

With all the other members of the tech team still unconscious, she risked using her unusual strength, and braced herself against the side of the nearest seat and kicked the door with her feet. Then she wriggled out of the crawler and on to the black basaltic lunar dust.

Outside, she righted herself; an awkward movement that was part of the EVA training. Her head was now just below the nearest section of the caterpillar tracks – the base of the chassis still a foot above her head. Before she tried to touch any part of it, she replaced the gauntlet she had removed, since it would protect the flexible inner glove from damage.

This part of the moon was currently in the two week 'night' cycle, and lit only by starlight, but that was enough to show her the damage caused when the shuttle had rolled. Her eyes automatically adjusted as they had inside the Auto-track building. She walked around the wreck, assessing the damage, but then her eyes caught sight of the marks on the ground. They led in the direction of Auto-track 1. She could just make it out; the blast had been powerful enough to send them rolling for several miles. They were well away from where they should have been.

The first priority was getting help, so she returned to the hatch to try to see if the communications system still worked. As she walked, she thought at her brother. "Tym?"

"Coming!" he said, and his relief infused his thoughts. "We are coming by shuttle."

One of the other crew was just in the awkward process of exiting the crawler.

"Ward, you check Andrews?" The voice she heard over the suit comm was James. He had activated his helmet light.

"Yes, his helmet was cracked. I sealed it. Help will be coming, but I think we need to get him out ready for evacuation."

She heard another voice via the suit comm. "Ganesh and I will bring him out. What else do you want?"

"All the spare oxygen cylinders. I don't know how much air Andrews lost before I got to him. And check if any of the systems will power up."

While she watched the rest of her team emerging from the wreck, she considered why she still felt uneasy. Rusch reported the crawler systems were dead, although she had expected that.

"Tym, we are quite a way distant from out intended track, and all systems are dead. We are probably four or five miles to the left of the direct track out from the base."

"Tell me if you see the lights on the shuttle."

"Will do."

To get a better height advantage, she decided to climb up the side of the crawler, using the ladder that usually gave access to the crawler's roof. She had her head above the undercarriage and was looking towards the base and for the promised help when she and caught sight of a rapidly blinking red light.

Without thinking, and only just in time, she flung herself towards Andrews and his rescuers.

The explosion should not have happened. The crawlers did not use volatile fuel, nor was there oxygen to feed a fire.

Mertz and James had been standing; they were pushed over and shoved several yards away. Kryslie knocked Ganesh and Rusch down as she fell on the prone Andrews.

Kryslie felt something hit her ankle. She tried to move it, but it was pinned to the basaltic ground. For a moment she needed to get the breath back in her lungs, for the blast had slammed into her. Then she twisted to see what had happened, shocked to see that the metal body of the crawler had been peeled back and blown open like a popped kernel of corn. The two men she had knocked down were getting to their feet, and when they saw the trapped foot, grabbed the metal and worked to free her.

They heard the suit tear, as a large patch of fabric ripped off with the metal and the air begin to hiss out.

Ganesh reacted quickly, grabbing the suit above the tear, it didn't stop the air escaping, only slowed it. He had his sealant spray out and was trying to make a seal. He called to James and Mertz, to hurry to get the foot free the rest of the way, and to add more sealant. It didn't seem to be helping.

Kryslie felt her air getting scarcer, and knew they needed to hurry. "Spray the whole foot!" she directed, but her voice was weak, just audible.

"It's not meant…" Mertz protested.

Ruche, the most senior technician, insisted, "Do it. It might just work. The docs can fix any flesh damage later."

Kryslie heard the hissing stop, she was hanging onto consciousness with a stubborn concentration. She didn't resist when she felt herself being rolled onto her side so that a fresh oxygen cylinder could be snapped into place. Once she felt her mind retreating from the darkness, she said, weakly, "Check Andrews."

"Ward, I'm taking charge!" Rusch told her, and she was glad to let him, since she needed to try to damp the pain in her injured ankle. Already he was directing the others to see if the box with the emergency flares could be reached, and for them all to be careful of the jagged metal.

A short time later, she saw that one of the special flares and been ignited, and heard in her mind, "We see you."

The shuttle landed, blowing up black dust from its VTOL landing jets. Within moments, the med team were dropping to the surface, and doing a quick bouncing walk to the damaged shuttle.

Tymos headed directly for his sister, and in the blinding glare of the shuttles landing lights, saw the first aid measures and blanched. Adjusting his eyes, he saw with relief that her PFS still glowed faintly green under the already hardened clear sealant. He checked her suit monitor and noted that her vital signs were satisfactory.

"You sure made a mess of yourself," he sent to his sister's mind, but got no reply.

Two of the med techs pushed him aside, one ordering him to, "Go fetch two stretchers." They knew he wasn't a medic, and probably guessed that he wasn't meant to be there. He didn't argue, he needed to do something to ease his frustration and guilt. His sister wouldn't be unconscious, with a nasty gash on her ankle if he hadn't deflected the damned missile this way. He wanted to help heal her, but of course he couldn't until she was out of her suit.

The stretchers delivered, he went to examine the crawler, to try to determine what had happened. He took out the utility scanner from the EVA pouch and began to record what he saw, and to test the hull for residues. When he walked around to the far side, he saw the marks where the crawler had rolled, highlighted by areas of darker shadow, thanks to the shuttles lights.

As there was little dust or particles in the atmosphere, those lights penetrated a long way across the flat surface of the old crater. Tymos, with his eyes adjusted for both distance and low light, could just make out the new crater where the missile had landed, and something that seemed to reflect some of the light back, about where the crater wall would be.

It might have been part of the missile casing, but he doubted that.

"Ward! Back to the shuttle, or walk back," the med team leader ordered.

The shuttle took off vertically until it was twenty feet up, and then went to horizontal flight mode. Tymos had strapped himself into the seat nearest his sister and kept trying to reach her mind.

It only took ten minutes for the shuttle to reach the base, and Tymos could tell from the speed that they were returning 'hot'. He sensed when they flew through the force field that maintained the atmosphere in the shuttle bay, and when the baffles opened up and down to slow their momentum. It was the quickest way to bring the injured back, and avoided the need to slow the shuttle to just above stalling speed before entering.

He stayed seated as two of the med techs released his sister's stretcher from its harness, and lifted it out onto a waiting trolley. They kept the patients' suits sealed and would until they reached the infirmary. He hopped out on the heels of the last medic, intending to follow the trolleys to medical.

Several of the landing bay crew were taking helmets from the med techs' suits, and from the uninjured members of the initial tech team. When he felt hands grabbing his suit, and disconnecting the helmet, he accepted their help, but when he tried to follow the trolleys, they held him back.

"We have orders to ensure that you stand down, Technician Ward!"

Tymos's eyes blazed in extreme annoyance and he twisted around to see who was holding him. He recognised the red trimmed brown uniforms of the base security officers and was, for an instant, tempted to wrench himself free. A wiser part of his mind reminded him of the penalty for resisting the directive. He couldn't help Kryslie if he was in the brig.

Realising that part of his problem was anger, at himself, he forced some of the power he had drawn into himself to dissipate as his escorts divested him of the rest of the EVA suit.

Before they had finished, Landin strode over to him, and although he feigned calm and control, his anger leaked and was sensed by Tymos as he said, "Ward, you are officially off duty until further notice." He glared until he saw Tymos nod in acquiescence. Then he said to the security men, "When you have finished getting him out of that suit, take him to my office."

Landin didn't wait for them to reply, he strode off in the direction taken by the med team.

Tymos remained passive until out of the suit and obeyed the order to "Come on". He didn't try to fathom Landin's anger, except to accept that everything that had happened in the past two days would be enough to make any commander angry. It didn't occur to him right then that part of it might be Landin's concern for all the base staff, and in particular for him and Krys. He was used to looking after himself.

After a few steps, Tymos realised that his escorts hadn't tried to locate the shoes he had removed before suiting up. He made a token request, but as expected, they ignored it. They continued to hustle him, with each of them grabbing one of his arms, towards Landin's office, and Tymos tried not to think of how anyone that saw him like this would know he was in trouble. And he could only blame himself.

Chapter 9

His escorts kept him standing until Landin returned from medical twenty minutes later. By then, his injured leg had begun throbbing, and he could not concentrate enough to damp the pain. He kept his face as expressionless as possible, but he realised he was probably pale in the face.

Landin strode in, still emitting anger, and told the guards, "You can go!" He didn't invite Tymos to sit, even when he did sat behind his desk, making sure his Tech 3 knew this was disciplinary matter.

"What hair-brained logic caused you to join a medical evac team, for which you are not trained or authorised, especially when both I and the doctor made it clear that you were not fit for duty?"

Tymos's almost blurted out that he was a healer, and he had to help his sister. He only cried, "I nearly killed Krys!" He willed Landin to understand how he felt, but Lunar 1's commander saw things differently.

"No! A rogue missile nearly killed her. You saved the lives of everyone on this base."

"But I sent that missile…"

"Damn the missile! It was a miracle that you even got one of ours close enough to deflect it."

Tymos swallowed what tasted like bile, to stop himself protesting again.

Landin waited a moment to be sure Tymos would listen to him. "I spoke to the tech team. The missile explosion made the crawler roll multiple times. Your sister was the first to regain consciousness, was able to save Andrews's life by sealing a tear in his suit. It seemed that she did that again by landing on him just as the crawler exploded. It was that explosion, not the missile impact that injured her."

Tymos told himself he should have realised that, now his mind began to work again. "Those crawlers don't use volatile fuel. It shouldn't have been able to explode."

"My point exactly. That explosion might have happened at any time."

"I took some data of the scene. The scanner is in the EVA suit I used."

"While that will be of great interest, getting it could have waited for the salvage crew. You did not need to go there for that either!"

Landin had not finished being official. "I am not going to spare you the consequences of your flagrant disregard of base regulations. I expected better of you."

Tymos heard echoes of the Tymorean President, from back when he was new to his power. Now, the President would not criticise his actions, because he was a Great One, and for an instant, Tymos almost disputed Landin's right to do that.

"Whatever you and your sister are, above and beyond what you act like here, when you took on your current roles, you agreed to abide by the rules and procedures here. Your sister did not need you. She was in excellent hands."

Once again, Tymos heard echoes of the Tymorean President, "Your bond with your sister is both your greatest strength and your greatest weakness. As things stand now, an assassin need kill one of you to make both of you die."

He felt the rest of the blood drain from his face and felt on the verge of nausea. He had simply reacted. He had not stopped to think. What if he had got to that crawler just as it exploded – and died? What if Kryslie was already dead as he had feared? There would have been no one left at Lunar 1 to help fend off the danger still to come. His mind began to spin in circles, like his head.

He came back to awareness as Landin was easing him back into a chair, then obediently grasped a glass that was pressed into his hand.

"Drink that. It will stop you going into shock. Then eat."

It wasn't shock, Tymos knew. It was the realisation of the depth of his stupidity, but the drink helped as did the sweet bread on the plate. It restored him enough to realise that he must have eaten the commander's snack and that made him embarrassed.

"I'm fine now, Sir. Really."

"How's your leg?"

It was throbbing fiercely still, but it wasn't bleeding, so he said, "Well enough. A bit sore, that's all."

He wanted Landin to believe that, but his Commander was giving him an appraising look.

"I will accept that as truth for now," he said as he went back to sit behind his desk. "Because I have plenty of unanswered questions, and Basoli is on his way up to grill me for issuing lockdown commands to all bases. Not to mention that he will demand an explanation of why all bases lost scanning and tracking capability at the same time. Somehow, I am quite sure you know more than you are telling me."

"And more than you can explain," Tymos sighed and forced his mind to begin to think again.

"Indeed," Landin acknowledged. "And have you considered the fact that, for someone who prefers to keep a low profile – you weren't today?"

"What is the status here?" Tymos asked, not wanting to admit that Landin was right again. "Stabilising," Landin told him blandly. "You have done enough for one day, and the rest of my crew are highly efficient. So – are you going to stand down and tell me what I want to know or am I going to have to cool your heels in my brig?"

"I'll be good," Tymos promised. "What do you want to know first?"

"I would like you to explain why you decided..."Landin began to question Tymos intently until he understood the thought processes and logic that had led this enigmatic junior tech to deduce the needed actions.

"It is still a leap to go from one missile to a moon take-over," Landin commented finally. "And your questioning of that saboteur was unsanctioned."

"Is he talking yet?"

Landin shook his head, yielding that point. "Only to demand his legal rights."

"Have you studied the creature's data padd?" Tymos asked.

"It is encrypted or in a foreign language," Landin told him, and he saw Tymos's face tighten.

"Sir, if there is trouble over my questioning of him, you do not have to cover for me," Tymos told Landin, meeting his eyes.

"I hope it won't come to that and so far I only know you had from what you told me. There is no evidence you did more than capture the man," Landin warned. "The main problem is that no attack was made on Terra 5."

"There probably won't be now." Tymos thought over the information he had wrested from the little saboteur's mind. "I think we were the real target all along. I don't think that gremlin had a chance to reprogram it. He was frantic enough to get back in the system to get the back-up tracking system down. And surely, that missile must be a prototype, or the IC would have heard of someone building illegal missiles."

"I will have the Chief ask the IC to investigate that possibility. Do you think that missile was programmed to reactivate at a specific time? It came at us after you caught the gremlin."

"My no doubt overactive imagination, that proposed the takeover idea – reminded me not to presume only one agent," Tymos admitted. "That missile might have been able to be controlled from Earth, or that might have been done from here. The control or activation signal may not have needed to go through the base computers."

"We have had a full lock down on information about what happened here. The Chief knows of course, but the other commanders got my warning, but don't know what happened later. Might an agent be able to send a signal without us knowing?"

"It is not impossible," Tymos admitted, but didn't say that he had.

"Earlier you were implying the identity of the mastermind behind this. How do you reconcile that with the presence of our guest here?"

"I can't, yet."

Tymos had the sudden idea to recheck the trajectory data, and try to predict the exact place the missile would have impacted if it had been allowed to reach the base. If it had been aimed at the solar panel array that generated power for the base…maybe no one will have died, but the base would have had to be evacuated until the array was replaced.

He went on talking with only the merest of pauses. "That man's mind is as convoluted as a bag of eels. Hell, he might have decided to risk Arthur to prove it couldn't have been him! Anyway, I do know one thing about that man, and it is that he never has just one purpose behind what he does."

"You implied that earlier. You also implied that our prisoner may have had a backup. Do you think that back up is Arthur bin Halil?"

Tymos's answer was immediate, and definite. "No."

"Then we need to find out if there is one."

Landin waited to see what Tymos would suggest, but his junior tech seemed to be just staring across his office. "Never mind that for now. What I need is backing information for what you learnt from that creature in the brig."

Pulling his mind from the problem of why he had been so certain that the gremlin had a backup, and trying to pin point the elusive piece of information he needed, Tymos said, "The creature's name is Rasti. Arthur recognised him."

Landin leant forward, "So was that why he was attacked, or was that misdirection, so that we keep trusting our royal guest? So far Technician bin Halil is being as close lipped as the prisoner."

Tymos murmured, "He doesn't dare say anything. Would you let me talk to him for a bit and be ready to offer him sanctuary?"

Landin considered what was being implied. "Why?"

"A guess," was all the answer he got. Tymos decided that it would be too complicated if he were to mention Krys's relationship to Arthur or his Imperial father.

"He requested voluntary detention," Landin revealed. "He is under guard in his assigned room. I will have him come here."

Arthur glanced around the room as he was escorted in. Even when he was invited to sit, he sat on the front of the chair seat, back rigidly straight. His eyes followed the guards as they retreated from the room, and then studied the dark haired man in the other chair, wondering at the oddity of the junior tech's presence. Then he him as recognised the man who had found him and then followed the saboteur, Rasti.

Thinking of the assassin, put his mind back into turmoil. Long before he was accused of many terrible murders, Rasti had been his tutor in maths and computing. He had been an honoured member of his father's household. Now he believed that the man was acting on his father's behalf, and part of him abhorred the fact that Rasti had been free all this time, working unsuspected. He had to have had high ranking protection.

Even so, Arthur could bring himself to speak out against his father. That was something that had been trained into him since he was a young man.

Oh how he wished for the wisdom of those who had been his earliest tutors. He did not want to answer Landon's probing questions, even though he knew that refusing would go ill against him.

He looked down at the floor, not wanting to see the suspicion in the Commander's eyes.

His head jerked up when the dark haired man spoke, casually, not accusingly. "That creep that assaulted you is in the brig."

"That relieves me," he admitted quietly, not daring to say more.

"I'm surprised he didn't try to kill you, since he certainly tried to get rid of me." Tymos was leaning back in the chair as if he hadn't been nearly killed. "You recognised him, didn't you?"

"Yes," was the equally quiet answer. "He used to be one of my teachers."

Landin was quick to pick up on the confirmation of Tymos's idea. "Do you think that your father is behind the acts of sabotage here?"

Arthur's face hardened, and he looked at Landin. "I really do not know, and I will not accuse him of such treachery without proof."

Tymos changed the direction of the questions, sensing that Arthur was about to refuse to answer any more.

"Why did he decide to visit here?" Tymos asked.

That seemed a safe question to answer, so Arthur said, "It is because he saw that the President of the UWN had come here. My father holds a position equivalent to President Adamson and felt he too should come here and be treated the same."

"Was that the only reason?" Tymos asked gently.

Arthur looked down at the floor, and forced himself to answer. He did not want the red headed woman to be in danger.

"No," he said softly. "He came because he saw a woman he thought he recognised. The one who is said to have saved the President."

"Kryslie Ward?" Landin asked for confirmation. He saw Arthur nod, even though he was still looking at the floor. "Where does he think he knew her from?"

Arthur wrung his hands together. Tymos spoke a short sentence in Tymorean, "Tell him! She needs to be warned."

Arthur pulled himself together and looked at the dark haired man. He spoke the same odd language as his old tutors. He could be trusted.

"He knew a woman who looked like her – forty years ago. She ran away from him and he was angry. Ten years ago, a similar woman also angered him. He thinks this Kryslie Ward is that later woman."

Tymos knew, Arthur had not said that his father was convinced both of the earlier women were the same person.

Tymos met Arthur's gaze and nodded slightly, deciding it was time to reveal his kinship to Kryslie.

"I hope he did not decide to take his anger out on my sister. Because someone sent a missile towards the base. It missed here, and landed near to the vehicle she and five others were travelling in."

Arthur let out a moan of despair. "Are those who were in it well?"

"Krys is alive," Tymos said relieving him of that concern. "And only one of the team was hurt badly. Does your father know scientists capable of constructing rockets?"

"Yes," was they very quiet reply. "But I do not think he would have used one to kill a woman he had only just met. How could he know where she would be?"

"That creature in the brig could have known," Tymos said.

"Rasti?"

"What do you know of him?" Landin asked directly.

Answering that was getting back to accusing his father, and he couldn't make himself answer.

"If he has a previous record, the Investigative Committee will deal with him. We now have some serious crimes to charge him with." Tymos waited for Arthur to consider that.

The answer came slowly. "He was supposedly executed fifteen years ago. I was with my father when it was done. He had been my tutor in maths and computing and he was brilliant, but I learned that he was also a killer."

Tymos glanced at Landin to see if that was enough, and saw the faintest of nods.

Arthur did not see the exchange, he went on talking. "What I don't understand is why this place was targeted." He looked up glancing from Landin to Tymos, trying to understand. "If it was, and I cannot believe it, why send that missile when I am here?"

"Could your father have enemies?" Landin proposed. "Someone wanting him discredited?"

Arthur shook his head.

"I find that hard to believe," Landin persisted, as Arthur turned his head away. He could still not force himself to accuse his father of anything.

Tymos was not so reluctant. "The only enemies that man has are dead ones. If you value your life, you do not make him your enemy. It does not matter even if you are a friend. If you fail while carrying out his will, your life becomes significantly shorter."

Landin sensed that Tymos knew this from personal experience, not just hearsay. That made him thoughtful. He decided that it was obvious, although neither Tymos nor Arthur were acknowledging it, that these two had met before.

Tymos was still lounging back in the chair, as if this was a friendly chat. It seemed to be helping.

"So what does your father say about you working at Terra 5?"

"He says, that I might as well be doing useful work, since he claims that I have no head for governance. I like it there, and he does take an interest in what I do. It will be many years yet before I will need to inherit his position. And it was my idea to stay here and study your procedures. I did not think he would allow me to do that."

Landin shifted his position, thinking that Arthur might be an unwitting spy – passing on what was commonplace to him at Terra 5. He waited to hear what Tymos was leading up to.

"I had a few words with Rasti, after I immobilised him and before the guards arrived. He promised me that I was going to die. I took that to mean that since I had stopped him getting his access to the computer again, the missile would definitely be coming here. He was waiting on a signal to send it to coordinates near Terra 5."

Landin knew that Tymos had twisted things around, but said nothing. For some reason, Arthur bin Halil was more willing to talk to Tymos than to him.

Arthur frowned, and his face had gone pale under his olive complexion. "Why would it go there?"

He did not get an answer, forcing him to think harder.

"If someone was trying to compromise my father, I can see why they might launch it from within my country, and to send it to land where it might endanger Terra 5 would bring the attention of the world onto my country."

"Arthur, you are a loyal son, but you are not a child. One day, you will have to decide if you are in one mind with his ways or not. If you choose to give him your total trust, you will suffer the same fate as that which is due to him."

Landin decided to comment. "Every place with the ability to locate that launch site, was blacked out. That includes the WSRA bases as well as the infrasound monitoring stations. No one should have seen where it came from. Who would be protected by that?"

Arthur began to shake. "My father is displeased with the Chief Minister of the region where Terra 5 is located, but I do not think he would destroy one that he needs as an ally. The threat, that of seeing the missile launch, would, I think, be enough to frighten him into compliance."

After a few failed attempts to say more, he managed to say, "I do not know why he would send that missile here, particularly when I am here, but he has said that this place is like a hawk watching prey."

Tymos pushed himself out of the chair, and moved to stand behind Arthur in a gesture of support. He gently laid hands on the prince's shoulders, as a reminder that he had other kin.

"Does that narrow the leap of logic, Commander," Tymos asked.

Landin stared at his technician, who was not acting like one of lowly rank.

"To a point, but I did not know this beforehand, and it does not explain why I sent the warning to all the bases."

With a dismissive shrug, Tymos suggested, "As a precaution. We could not be sure the bastard wasn't lying."

"Please, you will not tell anyone what I have said," Arthur blurted. He felt the gentle hands squeezing his shoulders.

Landin wanted to protest, but the pleading in Arthurs eyes was impossible to mistake. He was truly frightened.

"Do you want the perpetrator of the damage here to continue escalating the damage?" Tymos asked. "Whether it is your father or not."

He felt Arthur shudder, and risked touching his nephew's mind. There was no doubt there of his father's complicity, but he said, "I do not have proof that he is doing anything bad, and I do not wish him to lose face by being questioned if he is innocent."

"The Investigative Committee is very discreet," Landin began, but Tymos interrupted him.

"Whoever launched that missile, whether your father authorised it or not, he cannot argue that it was illegally launched from his country. If we can access Rasti's computer, we would have proof, but even without it, it can be construed as an attack on him, since you, his son, were here at the time of the attack, and hence in danger."

Arthur's shaking stopped as he understood the line he could take. "All that is true and so, you are keeping me in protective custody, yes?"

Landin relaxed. "Yes, indeed. Thank you for speaking to us. Please accept an escort back to your quarters."

When they were alone again, Landin challenged Tymos with, "Do you truly think Abdul bin Halil would try to harm your sister?"

"It depends if he truly thinks she is the same woman who scorned and then embarrassed him," Tymos said, choosing his words carefully.

"Is she?" Landin dared to ask. He knew Tymos and his sister had been around longer than their appearance suggested.

Tymos met his eyes but said nothing. Landin decided he knew and if he was right about the truth, and it came out – even if it was never proved, it would mean adverse publicity. So it was probably as well that she worked up here – away from prying reporters. Then he wondered - did Rasti have any orders to kill Kryslie Ward? That was a dreadful thought, especially as they did not know if Rasti had backup.

"I think, we have talked enough, Mister Ward, and that you should go down to medical and get your leg checked."

"Its fine, Sir," Tymos insisted, but he saw Landin slowly shaking his head.

"I saw how carefully you have been moving. So I am making it an order, Mr Ward. I also believe that you should stay there overnight with your sister."

"She's conscious and well enough," Tymos assured him.

"Do not assume..." Landin began to say, but Tymos suddenly stood up and went to the door.

He was cursing himself again, for he had suddenly recalled the waiter at the reception, and in an instant compared a memory of that man with Rasti. Both men were late middle age, one with brown hair going grey and brown eyes, the other black haired and grey eyed. When he had caught Rasti, he'd subconsciously assumed Rasti had also been the waiter, and disguised. What if he hadn't been?

"You are right, Commander. I am tired."

Tymos disturbed the Chief Medical Officer, Frances Long, when he entered the infirmary. She woke from a doze in front of her computer and noticed his entrance – how he looked around like a scout in enemy territory. She went out to talk to him.

"Tymos Ward isn't it?" she greeted him. "You have dyed your hair, I see. Are you here to check on your sister?"

"Yes. Doctor. How is she?"

"She is doing well, although she has some symptoms of exposure to vacuum. I am treating that. I do not think the damage is irreversible. She also has a fractured heel."

As they spoke, Long moved to the bed where Kryslie seemed to be asleep. "I have her sedated."

Tymos knew better. She was only feigning sleep.

"I have one concern," Long said. "Her suit was lacerated at the ankle. They used sealant all over the foot and into the suit to form the seal. I was told Kryslie told them to do it."

"It worked. Is that a problem?"

"Yes and no," Long admitted. "No because the sealant hardens and is at the moment supporting the bone – like plaster would. I scanned the bone; it is not broken – only fractured. We didn't need to set it. The problem is that the sealant is not meant to be used on skin, and there seems to be flesh wounds under the sealant."

"But you have left the foot alone," Tymos commented neutrally.

"She said I should, and the damage should heal. Although if I need to, I can regrow the skin there."

"Ah," Tymos said, more to himself. "That is good to hear. Can I sit here for a while?"

"Ten minutes, then get yourself to bed."

She returned in ten minutes, but had crawled onto an adjacent bed and fallen asleep.

Chapter 10

He woke several hours later, to find his sister watching him.

"Fine guard you are, bro," she said quietly when she saw he was awake. Then she switched to thinking at him. "You didn't have to come and get me…"

"As if…" he retorted silently.

"Yeah, I know…I'd've done the same if it was you out there, but…"

"I should have stayed here in case something else happened."

"I wasn't chastising you."

"You don't have to. Landin already tore into me…he might have been taking lessons from Governor Reslic."

"I wanted to know what you saw. Last I recall was seeing a rapidly flashing red pin light on the base of the crawler, and jumping down onto Andrews."

Tymos recalled what he had seen when he was at the overturned crawler, and let his sister see those memories.

"Why did he set it off then? It would have made more sense to do it before we reached the Auto-track, not after we had fixed it."

"It wasn't the gremlin, unless, as I suspect, he had help. I'd got that bastard earlier, after he'd had a go at Arthur."

"What happened?" Kryslie's alarm was apparent. Tymos decided it was a mother's reaction.

"He's fine. He was just stunned for a few moments. He recognised the bastard as someone who used to work for his father and who was supposedly executed fifteen years ago. All things considered, the guy could have killed him. He certainly had a good go at me."

"I would have thought that Arthur would be safe. He is his father's only son."

"Unless, his father does not trust his loyalty. However, I agree with you. His bastard sire, would not want people to think he cannot keep his son's loyalty. Anyway, Arthur is now in protective custody."

"Good. But what can we do about the other agent? Neither of us are mobile, or allowed to be."

Tymos growled in frustration. "It has to be that waiter, at the reception. The one I marked. I had forgotten about him. When I caught Rasti, he had gloves on, skin tight ones and I didn't have time to check if his hand was marked."

"Can Jon find out?"

"I'll ask, but he may not be able to get close enough to the prisoner."

"Are you sure there is another agent. That explosion could have been pre-set."

"We don't know that," Tymos growled.

"Is that why you were asleep in here? To protect me?"

"Do you have to rub it in? No, Landin ordered me here, and I am on stand down." He grinned wryly at his sister, and added, "And I deserve it for stupidity, or so I have been telling myself."

"Well, you could get into the computer and try to find a trace of this other person. How long have you been stood down for?"

"Until further notice, I think, or until Landin cools down."

"Or needs you," Kryslie suggested. "Either way, you should be able to do something while I get bored in here."

"Do you want me to give that ankle a hurry up, just in case?" Tymos offered.

Kryslie considered that, and nodded. "This time, I think you should."

Tymos eased himself of the bed, and walked over to his sister's bed. He was stiff where his injury was.

"Just worry about the bone fracture – in case I have to walk on it."

Tymos would have preferred to heal her ankle directly, but the doctor had put a protective cage over it. So, he placed his hand on her forehead, while she concentrated on the bone fracture.

Kryslie had felt the sensation of speed healing before. It felt like a cool breeze blowing through her. Her ankle, which had begun to throb again, in spite of the pain meds the doctor had given her, stopped hurting, and then began to tingle. After five minutes, Kryslie pushed his hand away.

"It's lucky that you had your PFS on," Tymos told her. "It must have absorbed a lot of the power of what ever got your ankle. And it probably means that the sealant won't have stuck to you."

"It still made a mess of me. Although most of it is bruising. When they got me here, I turned the PFS off while they checked me out, but I put it back on before they took my clothes away." Kryslie took a moment to sense how her brother was feeling. "So, how did that bastard get you?"

A mental chuckle was the only way Tymos admitted that she had won that point. "I did have my PFS on, before you say anything." He recalled the fight, and shared the memories movement by movement.

Kryslie told him soberly, "He got lucky. That close, and with that sharp a knife, he caused a point overload in the screen. Do you want me to help you?"

"Yes, I think you should." He had to move so that she could reach his forehead, and hold his hand at the same time.

Kryslie couldn't speed heal the way her brother could. She could stabilise wounds, start them healing, but that was all, and he couldn't speed heal himself. However, they had discovered that she could manipulate and direct the healing – when he supplied the power – and so heal him that way.

It seemed to be a factor related to their twin bond, since their brother, the third Great One could not do it.

"I'll work from deep, out. Tell me when to stop," Kryslie told him.

Tymos was aware of her progress and finally said, "That's enough. It still needs to look bad for a few more days."

"Oh, for when the IC come up again."

"Are they?"

"Yup. I overheard Landin telling the Doc when he came in to check on us. Basoli will be coming too."

"It is probably a good thing that you are sequestered here," Tymos suggested, thinking of her notoriety down on Earth.

Physically, Kryslie shrugged, and thought back, "We'll see. Why don't you try for some more sleep? I will be having plenty of rest for a while."

Morning came and Tymos was allowed to leave Medical after the doctor had checked his injury and changed the dressing. She was pleased with how it looked, even though he had strained the stitches during his unauthorised excursion.

"You are on medical stand down as well as official stand down, Tymos," the doctor informed him. "So you are to rest that leg for the next two days, and do as little waking on it as possible."

"What about Krys?"

"Your sister is going to stay here for a few more days. I do not want her to put any weight on that ankle for at least three days. Then I will be removing that sealant and putting a proper dressing on the foot. When I am happy that flesh wound is healing, I will put a foot support on it."

"How is Andrews?" Tymos had not been allowed into the intensive-care cubicle.

"Improving slowly," Long assured him.

Tymos was trying to delay leaving, because once he did he would have to be staying in his quarters for the next two days, possibly longer. However, he had run out of questions, and didn't want to waste the doctor's time, so he grinned and departed.

Within an hour, his room had already become stifling, and in spite of being told to rest, he was pacing the length of his quarters. When his computer pinged announcing a message, he was glad of something to do.

He actually had two messages in his personal message centre. One had come in while he was in medical. It was just the official statement that he was on stand down until further notice. The new one was to notify him that he was to present himself at the assembly area, promptly at 10 am Lunar time. He guessed it was related to the IC and Basoli coming up, but when he tried to confirm it and see who else was coming up using his back door system hack, to check the shuttle logs, he found himself blocked out. He could probably circumvent it, using the code Landin had given him, but…the commander might learn of it, and he was in enough trouble now.

He confined himself to just cursing himself for forgetting that aspect of 'stand down'.

Chapter 11

Ron Basoli, the Commander in Chief of the WSRA, strode from the shuttle bay, ordering Landin to follow him. Stanley, as Landin's second in command, was left to deal with the other arrivals.

Basoli went to the Commander's office and usurped the chair behind the desk, gesturing to Landin to pull up another chair. He noticed that his PA had quietly followed him, and said, "I won't need you for a while. You might like to wait in the outer office."

Bynan, his PA, was not put out by the directive, and simply gave him a not and retreated.

As soon as the door closed behind her, Basoli got straight to business. "The IC will be going to question that prisoner of yours. Good work there. It seems that the man is high up on their wanted list. I had to bring up a lawyer for him though, and both the UWN and the Imperium sent up observers."

"It was Tech 3 Tymos Ward who caught him," Landin advised his superior.

"Was it indeed. I want to talk to him and his sister while I am here, but that is on another matter. Now, these incidents yesterday. I read your report. I hope this means that we have put an end to all these acts of vandalism."

"I certainly hope so, Sir," Landin concurred. "However, it might not be the case."

"Explain!"

"Tymos Ward went out with the medical rescue team…"

"Him again? Is he also a medic?"

"No, but he reported on the state of the crawler. The explosion from the missile landing caused the crawler that was on its way back from the Auto-track station, to roll multiple times. However, the worst damage was caused from some other kind of explosion."

"Impossible!" was Basoli's initial reaction, but then he turned thoughtful. Something had happened. "I trust the skill of your people, so you are saying that that explosion was set off after the prisoner was caught."

Landin nodded.

"I came up here to get to the bottom of this. I am hoping that the IC will get that man to talk, but they admit that they have doubts. First off though, I want you to go through that report you sent and explain your reasons for ordering a lock down of all bases…"

When Landin filled in the details of his initial terse report, Basoli considered all that had been said. "When the IC are finished with the prisoner, I want to speak to Arthur bin Halil and hear what he has to say for myself. Then I want to speak to Ward, to hear how he found out what he told you and how he managed to catch that man."

"Yes, Sir, I expected that you would want that. They are both awaiting a call through."

"After that, I want to speak to the crawler tech crew. Are they fit to come and report?"

"Two were injured. Kryslie Ward was the crew leader. She was injured when the crawler exploded. Andrews was the other victim. He was hurt when the crawler rolled."

"So, the other of the Ward pair was out there," Basoli pounced on the information. "Is that why Ward went out there? I am thinking that it isn't a good idea to have partners or siblings working together. But that Ward pair, there's something off about them, but I can't put my finger on it."

"I have no complaints about their work, Sir," Landin felt compelled to point out.

Basoli waved that aside. "I also want to speak to all the section heads, and everyone who was a duty officer in the sections where damage was done."

"I will arrange that, Sir."

Landin leant forward to get his portable computer interface from his desk. When he had finished sending messages via the ship's internal comm system, he sat back and waited for Basoli to continue.

"What's your thought on why all this acts of sabotage were being done?"

"Looking back, I think the initial incidents were while the perpetrator was learning to control things. The past day or two, with the recycling system, and the loss of the tracking system, I can only surmise that someone wants to force this base to close. I had the computer people determine where that missile would have landed, had it not been deflected – as close as they could calculate it. They believe it would have impacted on the power array. Had that happened, we would have had to abandon the base, and have only a skeleton crew."

"Is that why you proposed a hostile takeover?"

Landin mentally sighed, and began to explain.

Tymos's summons came two hours after the shuttle arrived. He entered the assembly room, where the 'court of enquiry' had assembled. He saw Arthur bin Halil in the witness chair and unobtrusively adjusted his eyes to see his face in greater detail. The two IC investigators who were questioning him in turn, were insistent. Arthur's replies were calm. While he listened to the questions and answers, Tymos risked reaching out and touching the surface thoughts of his sister's son. In spite of the outward calm, his mind was a turmoil. Tymos decided to move closer to the front, where he could hear the answers Arthur was giving. He soon understood the problem. The representative from his father was listening intently and making notes of his answers.

Finally, Basoli spoke up. "Gentlemen, I think this is getting us no further ahead. Technician Ward has arrived."

Arthur gave Tymos a faint smile as he walked past. He was anxious to be away from the enquiry board, but willing to share a moment of sympathy.

Having to answer questions from the IC wasn't giving Tymos any concern. He had worked with the IC before, knew how they liked to have reports, and how to adjust his body language to emphasize his words.

The only trouble was, Basoli had seen him in that type of persona before, and it didn't match that of a Tech 3, junior grade. A point that he targeted with his first question, "Why was he, a junior Tech, out of a secure zone at the time."

Speaking bluntly, Tymos explained that he had just finished reporting to Landin, and was on his way to his own quarters when he had spotted a crew person acting oddly. He added that the person was not correctly dressed. He continued on until the time when the guards had taken the prisoner and he had gone to medical.

The IC was only interested in matters relating to the prisoner and they said, "An excellent report, Technician Ward. You may go."

Basoli had the final word, "I would like you to stay, Technician Ward. I have other questions for you."

Reverting to his technician persona, Tymos gave the expected, "Yes, Sir."

Tymos retreated to near the door, but listened as Basoli introduced other staff members, and the IC questioned them about the prisoner. Rasti had been very clever, he had joined various shifts, had been able to blend in perfectly. He had been one of the crew who had brought out the crawler that Kryslie had gone out on. However, he was now well and truly caught, and Murtry's team had found his bolt hole, and his supply of different uniforms, a dozen false IDs, and a collection of equipment, some of which was interdicted by the IC.

At some signal from the lead investigator, Basoli announced a short recess, and specified that the base crew that he had requested to be present, should remain available. He, Landin and the two IC agents departed after collecting the data pad that a young woman had used to record a transcript.

Tymos edged his way to the front table, and said, "Hi."

Bynan, turned quickly, recognising his voice. "Hi Tymos." She was a fellow Tymorean, but knew to omit his title of Great One when they were amongst humans.

"How much of a hard time did they give Arthur bin Halil?" Tymos asked.

"Not too much. However the missile did come from his country, you know."

"I knew that. From what I saw, he handled the questions well."

"The Boss seemed impressed," Bynan offered. Then blurted, "Why doesn't he like you?"

"He doesn't know what I am," Tymos summarised. "But don't worry, I can handle him."

When the board of inquiry resumed, it was expanded to cover all the varied acts of sabotage that had occurred. Tymos stayed towards the back of the seated staff, but from his seat, he could see the whole assembly. He noted that the representative from the Imperium arrived five minutes after the resumption and he wondered at that. The IC agents had arrived back with Basoli, but now they were merely observing the proceedings, although they had the authority to ask questions of their own if they felt there was a need.

It soon became apparent to Tymos, that Basoli had been treating him mildly. This was possibly because he was a junior staff member, for now, questioning the section heads, he was all but accusing them of incompetence. Landin was keeping a neutral face, but he was uncomfortable for his hand was fiddling with a stylus for his data padd.

Basoli's manner was abrasive, but Tymos had to admire how he challenged the senior staff, so the dredged up half forgotten details that added to the overall picture. His own name was mentioned several times, as was Kryslie's. He was expecting to be called up for another question session.

"I think I will get the doctor to knock me out again," Kryslie inserted into his mind.

"That won't save you," Tymos sent back. "What else did you want?"

"Just a heads up. Someone tried to get at Rasti. They failed of course, but two of Murtry's crew were injured."

"Well now, that's interesting. The Imperium rep was late getting back here too. And yes, I think the message just got sent through. Landin, to Basoli, to the IC. And, they are calling me again."

Tymos had to give an 'expert witness' account of the damage to the crawler. When the IC had finished asking their questions, and Basoli had finished making innuendoes, the session was declared closed. Basoli allowed the seated audience to leave, but said firmly, "I'd like you to wait, Ward."

While the CIC went off with Landin to speak to Murtry, Tymos stood and walked around as if stretching his legs, and then leant against the nearest wall to try to lip read Murtry.

The reprieve was brief, Basoli and Landin, headed back in his direction, so he straightened from his casual slouch.

"Sir," he invited his Commander, and the CIC to get to business. Landin moved two chairs closer to where Tymos had been sitting, but actually cornering him where he now stood. Clearly, this was a formal session.

"Commander Landin has told me that you and your sister were the first to come to him and suggest that the malfunctions were sabotage," Basoli commented.

"I don't know if we were the first, Sir, but it seemed an obvious possibility."

The modest answer was brushed aside. "Your efforts to track down the perpetrator are to be commended, and unlike the IC, I do not think that your treatment of the prisoner was unduly rough. Whatever you did, gave us warning enough to act. It seems, that man is a dangerous killer, and he probably would have had few qualms about causing mass deaths."

Basoli paused and studied the Tymos, before asking, "Did you think there was more than one?"

"I was beginning to, Sir," Tymos admitted.

"Was that why you went out to the crawler without authorisation?"

Tymos looked from Basoli to a spot on the floor. "No, Sir. I went out because my sister was on that crawler."

Landin inserted, "Technician Ward is currently on stand-down for that indiscretion."

"Fortuitous though. Mr Ward, how do you think that explosion was set off? Another of those remote micro-pulse generator things?"

"If it wasn't pre-set to detonate, it might have been detonated by some kind of remote signal. When I spoke to my sister last night, briefly, she mentioned seeing a flashing red light, just before the explosion. She doesn't recall seeing it when she first checked the crawler for damage."

"So, if a signal was sent, it couldn't have been done by the prisoner in the brig."

"No, Sir."

"I will mention that to the IC," Basoli decided. He shifted his position in his chair.

Tymos glanced at Landin, who seemed to be rubbing his ear. In his mind, where he was hoping that Tymos would be aware of it, was the information that Basoli had been going over his and Kryslie's personnel file.

Basoli's next statement echoed that, and went on, "There is not a great deal of information about your educational background, but you scored highly in the entrance exams. Why did you never apply to the University?"

"You need quite a few references for that, Sir," Tymos reminded him. "Krys and I moved around a lot before we applied to work with the WSRA."

Now Tymos was wary. He sensed where this was leading. How much checking had Basoli done?

"Is previous education really an issue, Sir?" Landin interposed. "The entrance exams are the important criteria and both Tymos and his sister have proved their competence and skill."

"Yes, yes," Basoli agreed. He had something on his mind and almost blurted his statement.

"I have had a lot of reporters and a lot of letters arrive in my office since your sister saved President Adamson. Most wanted more information about her. Some were from scandal sheets or the more fantastical publications – claiming she is decades older than she looks."

"What?" Tymos half stood and exclaimed. "How could they claim that?"

Tymos listened to the claims Basoli had heard or read. Most were utter rubbish, but then he looked at a picture Basoli pulled from a folder.

As he studied the picture, he recalled exactly when it was taken. It had been shortly before Prince Arthur had been born, but it did not show Kryslie's advanced state of pregnancy.

"Wow, this is very like Krys," Tymos admitted. "When was it taken?"

"Forty years ago," Basoli said promptly. "Could that woman be related to you?"

"I...can't say," Tymos said. "We can't really remember our mother."

Basoli produced another photo. "What about this woman?"

This picture was neither clear nor close up.

"Amazing! Where was this from?"

"Ten years ago, some anti-government rally somewhere," Basoli supplied. "For the sake of the record – how old are you and your sister?"

He tried to make the question sound casual, but he was waiting intently for an answer.

"Sir, without intending disrespect to you, or Abdul bin Halil," Tymos said carefully. "The idea that Krys is those women is ludicrous. I admit the resemblance is uncanny..."

"Why did you mention bin Halil?" Basoli asked.

"I learnt from Arthur bin Halil that his father had commented on the resemblance between Krys and someone he once knew – that's all, Sir."

"You had more to add?" Basoli prompted. He was still intent on an answer to his question.

"Sir, we would have to be in our sixties for Krys to be that first woman. I don't think we could pass for being in our late thirties or early forties either, if she were to be the second. If I could do that, I would be insisting on a promotion to Tech 1 or Tech Officer."

Tymos was mentally sending, "They can't be more than twenty five."

Basoli seemed to back down, but Tymos caught a fleeting thought from him. "Of course they can't be ageless aliens."

Landin however, was well aware that Tymos had not answered the question, and had cleverly and truthfully, not lied.

"Never the less, I have been requested to obtain a DNA sample for comparison," Basoli concluded.

"Sir, with due respect, my sister is not under suspicion for any violent crime. I don't think you or any police authority has grounds for such a request. Idle curiosity by powerful men is not a sufficient reason either."

"I will make the request of your sister," Basoli stated severely. "And I do not wish you to influence her, Mister Ward."

"Too late," Tymos thought to himself. He did say, with a trace of annoyance in his voice, "I doubt I will have the opportunity. I have been instructed to stay available, and the doctor does not expect Kryslie to be awake before mid-watch. However, I am sure she will tell you much the same."

Basoli gave Tymos a stern look, for the slightly disrespectful tone, and then had the last word. "I can, however, insist that you undergo a thorough physical examination. Since both you and your sister have been under a great deal of stress, it will help ensure you will return to the peak of performance."

This time Tymos ensured his body language and tone were absolutely correct. "I will arrange that, Sir. I am honoured by your concern."

While wondering if Basoli was going to give the doctor specific instructions for what to look for, he noticed Landin's ensign, Meyer, approaching. The young man's face was suitably blank, but his movements seemed twitchy with excitement. He came up to the group, passed a data padd to Landin, and waited politely for a reply.

Landin's expression was intent as he read the message, but Tymos saw his eyebrows rise. He brushed the outer part of Landin's mind, as he passed the result to Basoli.

"The crash investigators have found an alien ship that had been buried under the dust – near the crash site."

In Basoli's mind was excitement, "Aliens!" and Tymos felt disquiet. Daniel had once mentioned his belief that Basoli had latent xenophobic tendencies, yet he was excited about this find.

Landin stood and excused himself. Tymos was hastily dismissed, and merely told his Commander he would be having lunch.

Since he was meant to be returning to his quarters, and having a pre-packaged meal routed to him there, that is what his commander assumed he was going to do.

In fact, after telling his sister of the new developments, he sealed his quarters, and sent a signal to Earthbase requesting the long range beam to his location. The frequency he used was not one that would be detected by Lunar 1's monitors.

Tymos arrived, met by Morin. "The boss is in the communications room. I told him you were coming."

Morin had to trot to keep up with Tymos, and had no time to announce the arrival for Tymos began at once, "Anything new from the Imperium?"

Daniel turned from the screen he was watching. "Nothing new, just the same rumours."

"Basoli has been hearing about them, and getting reporters ringing up. Now he wants to get a sample from Krys for DNA testing. He wasn't too impressed when I quoted parts of the Citizens Rights Act to him. I feel quite certain the Abdul bin Halil is behind that request. I don't know if he went as far as accusing Krys of being a subversive agitator."

"You don't look old enough to have been twenty back then, Great One Tymos," Morin stated.

"No, and that is the problem. If we did, I'd simply go to the IC and they would state that we she was working on their behalf. It won't endear her to his imperial eminence – but he doesn't like Krys anyway."

"Using my DNA won't help will it?" Lexina asked.

"It would if you could impersonate Krys, but if we agreed, the Doctor would want to be able to swear the sample came from Krys. No, we won't allow the test."

"Well, there are other ways," Daniel said thoughtfully. "I am still your biological father, and I have some hair from your mother. All we need would be to insert records for people to find. If they come to me…not that they would be able to unless I agreed…"

"An idea for a last resort. However, the records idea is good, don't make them too easy to find. Meanwhile, we will be keeping out of the way at Lunar 1 and there is a more important matter."

"Anything to do with the message Bynan just sent? She said Basoli was unusually excited about something."

"Yes. The salvage crew that went out to recover the crawler that had gone out to fix the Auto-track, found a derelict alien spacecraft. It seems that the power blast from the missile landing blew surface dust off it."

"What happened to the crawler, Tymos? Is Kryslie alright?" Markus asked. "We lost contact with her micro transmitter."

"Yeah, well, when I nudged that missile away from the base, it impacted near Auto-track 1. Krys had already got her team out of there and were on the way back. The crawler was sent rolling with the force of the blast. She was fine, got to Andrews in time."

"Bynan said it blew up," Morin blurted.

"Yes, but Krys had everyone out before then."

"But she was hurt…" Morin went on, only to be cut off by Tymos.

"She's fine! Daniel, can you call all the base controllers in here. I will explain things to everyone at once."

"Vincent is away," Daniel explained. "I will pass the word to him. Have you spoken to Homebase yet?"

"I don't have a lot of time. Basoli might decide he has more questions for me."

That was enough to get Morin off to wake the missionaries who had been on the night shift, and for Daniel to make the base wide announcement.

Within minutes, all twenty of the missionaries currently at the base were assembled, although five were either wearing pyjamas or had hastily donned tracksuits.

"Listen up," Tymos spoke over the questions being asked between the newcomers. "There is a situation on the moon that is going to affect Earth in untold ways."

He repeated the announcement about the discovery of the alien space ship. "I intend to examine it before the engineers and scientists contaminate it. It has to have arrived before the base and the tracking stations were constructed; how long before, is something we need to discover. It has to have been there a minimum of ten years."

"If it arrived since this base was built, we would have seen it," Lexina pointed out. "So that means at least seventeen years."

"True. So I want to know where it came from, and when. I will pass on everything that I find out. Daniel, I will get you to relay what we find to Homebase. They may be able to find out where it came from."

"Great One, we will do as you request," Daniel agreed formally. "Was there something else?"

"Yes. Basoli is very excited about this, which for the head of a scientific organisation is probably not surprising. What concerns me is the comment you made about Basoli having latent xenophobic tendencies. Will you ask Bynan to report anything that makes her wary?"

"Could you be more specific?" Daniel asked.

"Sorry Daniel, I just have an uncomfortable feeling. This ship might just be a trader that got thoroughly lost – but if it isn't – and others of his kind know that we are here…"

He didn't finish the thought. All the missionaries knew the various ways humans would react to the idea of extra-terrestrial visitors.

"Okay – that's it for now."

The missionaries not actually on duty wandered off, talking excitedly. Daniel waited for them to clear the communications cavern before asking, "Now, perhaps you might tell me why my daughter wasn't fast enough to avoid getting hurt."

"Do you know what, Daniel? You are beginning to sound like President Reslic."

Tymos knew his father was teasing him, and reminding him that Great Ones were not omniscient.

"She saw a light flashing on the base of the crawler. Another of those nasty booby traps the saboteur set up. Her crew were out of it, fortunately. She dropped down to protect Andrews and a bit of the metal trapped her leg. I went out with the med team. She had her PFS on, so that helped protect her, and last night I healed the fracture. She is less injured than the doctor thinks. And I got the little bastard who was organising the sabotage."

Daniel allowed his brows to rise in surprise. "And the IC will be involved?"

"They are up there questioning him. At least Basoli was civilised about how roughly I treated him. He doesn't know what I did, but what I read in the bastard's mind gave me enough warning to stop the missile hitting the base."

"I will have Jonko get in touch with what information the IC extract from him."

"They are not sure they will get anything."

"We will see," Daniel advised. "Will you tell Kryslie that I wish her a speedy recovery?"

"Yes, Dad," Tymos imitated an obedient son, and caught Lexina hiding a grin. "Meanwhile, what's around here to eat?"

"I will get Lusana to fix you something," Daniel suggested, as he gave Morin a shove to distract him from his open mouthed contemplation of the presence of an alien ship on the moon.

"Oh, yes, food for the Great One," Morin acknowledged when Daniel had repeated the request for the second time.

"Don't they feed you properly up there?" Morin asked, as irreverently as ever.

"Oh, they do. Just not when I get myself stood down and confined to quarters." Tymos grinned when Morin's mouth dropped open again.

"Can they do that to you?" he demanded, when he recovered again.

"Yeah, they can."

Chapter 12

Tymos prowled around his quarters, frustrated by being unable to tap into the base computer from his terminal. Access from it was rigidly restricted, due to his being on stand down. He still heard base wide alerts and announcements, so he had heard that Shuttle Bay 2 was off limits to all non-authorised personnel until further notice.

The ship that the salvage crew had found, had to be an alien ship. He could recall of no ships from Earth that had crashed anywhere within the Sea of Serenity. He needed to see that ship before the well-meaning Lunar 1 specialists innocently destroyed important data. He wondered how he could get himself onto the shuttle bay crew, or better yet, the second salvage crew. They would not be sending out the same crew that was bringing in the crawler, and that crew would not have taken enough spare oxygen for an extended EVA.

His impotent ruminations got him nowhere. Even if he requested it, Landin wouldn't agree. Not while he was on stand down. The doctor hadn't declared him fit for work either.

"Or while Basoli is still here," the sleepy mind voice of his twin distracted him. "Tym, why don't you do something more than pace your quarters? You're making me jittery, and I am not even allowed out of bed to work it out of my system."

"We need to know everything about that ship," Tymos insisted.

"Which has been on the moon for years already, and won't even arrive here at the base for a while yet. Besides, you haven't even been told about it officially. Basoli won't be too kindly disposed towards you if he thinks you have been reading secure private communications."

"You're right! I am just going crazy with nothing to do," he admitted by thought to his twin.

"Dim wit! You can always transmit into my quarters. My computer isn't locked out. Just set things up in yours in case someone wants you."

"I was trying to behave according to the rules…"

"Huh! Tell that to someone who might believe you," Kryslie countered. "Most people would enjoy the chance for extra relaxation."

"So why aren't you?"

"I'm enjoying it…watching some amazing new vid film…ogling the muscle bound hulk…" Kryslie stopped teasing her brother and turned serious. "Has Basoli got back to you with more questions?"

"No, and I really hope this ship discovery has distracted him. Has he been at you about that DNA sample?"

"Not yet, but I have spoken to Doc Long about it and my reasons for refusing. She is completely with me on that."

A chime from his computer distracted Tymos. He strode over to view the message. "I spoke too soon," he mentally told his twin. "I'm to report to Landin in an hour."

"After the visitors have left on the shuttle," Kryslie predicted. She was familiar with the shuttle schedule.

"Apparently. I hope he will take me off stand down."

"Wait and see. However, if I were you, I would work off some of your excess energy first, or you won't be able to pretend to be an obedient Tech 3."

Tymos didn't try to contradict her – she was right. It was just as well no one was observing his exercise session in his quarters, for it was, in no way, 'resting his injured leg'.

When he presented himself to Landin, Tymos was not wearing his uniform. Not that it was required, but it was more appropriate in formal situations. However, since he was currently in his off-duty time, as well as been on stand down medically and officially, he decided to make them think he was following the restrictions.

As he had expected, Basoli had not left on the Earth – shuttle, and he had numerous questions about his covert investigation of the saboteur, Rasti. Even while sitting in a chair in Landin's office, Tymos decided that it was as well that he had decided to reduce his power level and that he had watched Basoli questioning the section heads. It meant that he could ignore the accusative manner and concentrate on providing the answers that Basoli wanted.

At the end of the inquisition, Basoli asked, "How is it, that you are so familiar with every part of the base, Mr Ward?"

"I work in the computer division, Sir. All the sections have them, and when they give trouble, someone needs to go fix them and I like to learn all I can."

The answer seemed to surprise Basoli. He turned to Landin and demanded, "Why is Ward only a Tech 3?"

"He keeps telling me that he likes to do the hands on work," Landin told his superior, but he had a faint smile on his face.

"He can still do that as a Tech 2. Put him to work finding out how that saboteur infiltrated the computer, and to blocking any vulnerabilities. That should keep him too busy for any more unauthorised jaunts."

"Indeed," Landin murmured in agreement. He knew enough to know that the task would be time consuming and repetitive.

"When is his sister going to be back a work?"

"Not for at least a week," Landin informed him. "Not until her ankle can tolerate a walking cast."

"Well, she can still work a computer – so get her to go over the tracking programs to check that there are no more problems there."

"That is providing the Doctor is in agreement." Landin inserted.

"I am sure she wouldn't want her patient getting into mischief, with nothing better to do." Basoli directed his gaze back to Tymos and asked, "Would you agree, Mr Ward?"

"Er – yes, Sir. I think that Krys would rather keep her mind busy."

"Right, you can go, Mr Ward. You will be back on duty tomorrow."

Tymos stood quickly and retreated immediately. He didn't quite close the door after him, and since no one was around, he paused to listen to the conversation between Commander and Commander in Chief.

"When that salvage crew returns, I want to talk to them. I do not want word of the find to spread until we know what we are dealing with."

"Yes, Sir,"

"I want only senior specialists to go out and bring in the wrecked ship. They have a non-disclosure clause in their contracts."

"We will need extra help once we begin examining it."

"True, but I only want people who won't talk about it. Give me a list of your suggestions and I will have the people double checked."

"I'd like to include Tymos and Kryslie Ward," Landin said quietly. "They tend to have some amazingly intuitive ideas."

There was silence for a while, and Tymos wondered if Basoli wanted to refuse the idea.

"Very well. I have not had any adverse reports about them, if you ignore the current media circus about the President's rescuer. I haven't been able to find out much about their private life, or much about them at all. All those rumours could be true for all I can disprove them."

"I would stake my position on their integrity, Sir."

"How so?"

"They have been working here for five years, and their work has always been exemplary. They do what is asked of them, and they have come up with a number of improvements too. They came up with the concept of the sonic shower. It has significantly reduced our water requirement."

"Well, you didn't tell Ward to hare off on that salvage run…"

Landin repressed a sigh. "No, that's true."

"Have your way then," Basoli went on. "We need people who can see beyond the expected when we look at that ship. Just make sure that everyone who is working on it is sworn to secrecy. If you are going to have both of the Ward pair working on this, you had better make the sister a Tech 2 as well."

Tymos decided that he had eavesdropped for long enough. He glanced around, as he reached into his pocket. This section of the base, was usually only used by the Commander, so it was empty of other people. He drew out his transmitter, and activated it to take him back to his quarters. Once there, he mentally updated his sister on the interview and the conversation he had overheard.

"He's making you regret going out to help me," Kryslie told her brother. "He's setting you a real nit-picking job."

"So why is he making you go over the tracking program again? You were doing your job, and saving your crew."

Kryslie imaged herself shrugging.

"Maybe Basoli is smarter than we give him credit for," Tymos mused. "I doubt that he could know that I have been trying to find how Rasti got into the system, and already well on with that. I have traps set now, so that if that fake waiter tries something I will know. I doubt that he will be as clever as Rasti."

"Do you think Rasti hacked into the password file — and discovered the override passwords?" Kryslie suggested.

"He might have," Tymos considered. "At least initially. He could then authorise himself alpha one access, and a password to get him everywhere."

"How often do the passwords get changed? I change mine each week."

"So do I, and everyone is meant to, though I would guess that most aren't. The top level ones…I don't know. I will need to ask Landin — I may even suggest a blanket password change — and enforce it."

Kryslie changed the topic. "I don't expect to find any more problems with the tracking program. Stanley and I went right over them, line by line. I reloaded the initial program, and programmed the updates out at the Auto-track — I don't know if the problem was there or not. How close to Auto-track 1 did that missile land?"

"Too damn close," Tymos told her. "If you hadn't got out, you'd have been slime on the wall when the medics got to you. I don't think the engineers will be able to repair the equipment. I think it will need to be replaced or rebuilt."

"At some stage, I will need to check the three other Auto-tracks — the two up here and the one near Terra 1 — in case there is a virus in them, just waiting to be triggered."

"You won't be cleared to go out to them until you're off medical stand down," Tymos reminded her, needlessly.

"I may not have to – Rasti would have had to send any malicious code from here – he would have no way to get to the other two Auto tracks."

"Okay, I will go over the communications logs again. Though if he had a powerful enough communicator, I may not find anything."

"What about if that other guy requests instructions?"

"Already on it. I am sure that he hasn't tried anything yet, but if word gets out about that ship – and I bet it will, the prospect of getting at some alien technology, and having his master pay well for it – would be irresistible."

"Even if they don't know what they are taking?" Kryslie suggested. "They would still have to smuggle it downside."

"It isn't impossible," Tymos knew. "Can you keep an eye on the shuttle specs? And that reminds me – I need to see if Jonko has come up with anything on that no show from the last staff intake."

"And you need to look at that ship before the scientists swarm it…"

"If they haven't done so out at the site. No, the senior staff would wait…"

"And need a rest period after they return…" Kryslie inserted the idea. "And Basoli will probably insist on some sort of organisational plan, I doubt he would want a free for all…"

"Well, it won't be for a few days at least. The wrecked crawler is first priority, then the salvage crawler will need to be restocked…"

"And it will probably take a while to excavate the ship if it is buried quite deep…"

"Yes, so that gives me some time to try and catch that fake waiter at something," Tymos decided. "Apart from the password business, I have some other ideas to put to Landin, and my Department boss."

"Have you got computer access back yet?" Kryslie asked.

Tymos took a moment to try his computer. "No. I will probably have to wait until tomorrow. I do have my notification of promotion and the reminder to upgrade my uniform."

"I probably will too, then, when I get out of here. But, I do not intend to hurry. While I am in here, Basoli can't push me around too much. In fact…I think it is time I had another sleep. The doctor keeps telling me to rest…"

"Why? Is Basoli there?"

"Yup! Just walked in."

Chapter 13

Tymos found his sister by one of the medical terminals in a chair with her leg supported on a horizontal frame. She stopped he data scrolling and waited for him to speak.

"How are you doing?" That was for the doctor's benefit.

"I'm out of bed, which is a vast improvement." Kryslie glanced at a nearby med tech who was restocking a trolley. "So what's up?"

"Oh, this and that," Tymos said aloud, but mentally he told her, "The rumour mill is already at it."

Kryslie merely looked at her twin and waited for him to continue.

"It's no secret that they brought in the crawler last night, nor that a selection of section heads were closeted in the shuttle by early today, and the same ones are not at work now. I am sure that someone will have seen the salvage crawler going out again."

"You look good in a tech 2 uniform," Kryslie said aloud for the benefit of the med tech.

"I will see if in impresses some of the new female tech 3's," Tymos grinned and went on silently, "I saw the C-I-C on my way here. He wasn't looking happy, so it is my guess that he has heard some of the talk."

Kryslie decided she could say aloud, "Branson was in visiting me today. He was asking me about Auto-track 1 and how it isn't working. I told him what you said about the missile impact point. It seemed that suddenly clarified something. He thinks that is why the senior staff went out there."

Silently, she added, "He wondered, if that was the case, why Stanley hadn't gone with them."

Tymos merely grinned. "Maybe the section heads don't want us grunts to have all the fun. Anyway, have you found anything wrong with the tracking program?"

His mind suggested that if they both seemed intent on the scrolling code, they would have a reason to not be talking aloud.

"I wouldn't mind your opinion of a section of code that I found earlier. Let me go back…"

The med tech finished his task and moved away, but by then the mental conversation had changed subjects."

"The Chief Computer," Tymos began, using the nickname he had given the pedantic head of the computer division, "Is going to put my ideas about a blanket password change to Landin and Basoli. I told him that I had written some code to match each terminal's unique ID to the person requesting the new password."

"Requesting?" Kryslie queried. "So everyone has to ask for a new password, rather than you just resetting them to random? What if they don't?"

"They'll have to," Tymos said, pretending to point to something on the computer screen. "If I just reset all, the fake waiter guy – if he is involved - will get one like everyone else. This way, a terminal won't work until a new password is assigned, and they will need to input their name, their WSRA ID number and room number."

"What about the department computers? That fake waiter could do his little games during work time."

"Users will have to log on with their WSRA ID – and if I track any abnormal activity – I can see who was logged in. And if he is using an unauthorised portable unit, and not the one in his quarters, I will know that because his unit won't have an ID in my list. I have the master list of terminal IDs and room assignments too."

"What about if someone else logs in and he takes over?"

"He will have to work fast to do anything – if my little spy programs register an abrupt change in what a terminal is doing, I will be alerted."

"Well, I expect you do have things covered then. Do you know if Jonko found out anything about that no show from the last staff intake?"

"He did. The man was a John Doe in the morgue until the IC started asking questions."

"Have you told Landin that?"

"Not yet. I don't want any chance of word getting out, or mention being overheard. But I am now sure that someone was on the shuttle that shouldn't have been. My guess is that is how Rasti got up here."

"You re-checked the information on all the arrivals?" Kryslie asked him.

"Yeah, but Rasti will have had everything covered. He could have helped to substitute someone else, altered the information about him or her, so a substitution would not be suspected. I expect all possible records will have been altered."

"Unless someone knew the real person…"

"There's ways around that…coincidence – another person with the same name."

"So, are we back to the start again?"

"I don't think so, but if this current trap doesn't work, I will try something else. Jon, can't get near Rasti, but he has said the creature isn't talking. So I doubt he will admit if he was working with anyone else. So, I will be keeping my eyes open for someone who has that UV marker glow on his hand. Even if that hypothetical someone somehow saw it, and tried to remove it, I should still be able to see a trace of it."

"I am betting that he will try to pinch something from the wreck, and he will have a way to see what comes in," Kryslie predicted. "He'd hear the rumours."

Tymos straightened and pretended to stretch. "The bay is off limits."

"To obedient WSRA staff," Kryslie countered, implying the man they were after did not fit that description.

"They have monitors to alarm guards if someone goes in…"

"Things have been malfunctioning quite regularly around here."

Simultaneously, they both thought of the maintenance tunnels.

"When they have the wreck in there, they will be sealed," Tymos considered.

"Not beforehand, and not while it is being examined," Kryslie played devil's advocate. "Someone could slip in that way."

"But the sensors in the tunnels…"

"Could malfunction…"

"Yeah, okay, but Basoli is insisting on a select few being able to examine it. Anyone not on his list will be noticed."

"Perhaps not. If Basoli tell everyone who all the other authorised people are. If someone slips in via the tunnels, the guards won't see him and challenge him, and everyone else will assume he was passed in by the guards."

"That's a point. I might see about inserting an isolated circuit- sensors and monitor back up." Tymos's mind began to consider what would be needed.

Kryslie spoke aloud. "Hadn't you better get to your duty station, bro? The shift alarm is about to go."

With all but the most important announcements were muted in medical, Kryslie would have felt cut off from the main activity of the base, if it weren't for the mind link with her twin. Yet, by observing the routine around her, without a conscious decision, she detected a subtle change.

One of the small isolation rooms, like the one where Andrews was till in an induced coma, was being set up with a portable stasis field. She mentioned it to her twin, who promised to recheck the secure comm logs.

It was the middle of the base "night", but Kryslie was not asleep. "Can you still get into them?"

"Yes, Landin told me the new override, but I am not to let Basoli know I have it."

"No, or you might get Landin in trouble," Kryslie warned him. "And he certainly won't like the idea that you know it. He will be out to put you in your place. He isn't that happy with me right now. Not when I gave my reasons for not agreeing to that DNA sample. "

"Oh, that!" Tymos sent a mental chuckle. "I think he got over it. I suggested to Jonko that he leak our IC approval rating. Not when it was issued, just that it exists."

"Well, that's a relief. Now, how did your password change go? The med techs in here are all cursing at having to keep logging in after every five minutes of inactivity."

"Once everyone has updated their password, things will improve. But so far, it has only been the relatively few people on Alpha shift that are complaining. Beta shift will be much the same, but it will be a hundred times worse once gamma shift starts."

"So you have had nothing suspicious yet?"

"I am assuming that our fake waiter sleeps during the night shift. And the only people who knew about this were Landin, Basoli, the chief commuter and myself. We sprung it just before the end of alpha shift."

"You will be busy for a while then," Kryslie predicted.

"Somewhat, so I will check the comm logs for you while I can, and get back to you."

Doctor Long and one of the senior med techs came to see Kryslie when they knew she was awake. It was early, gamma shift wasn't due to start for another three hours.

"I think we will take that sealant cast off today," Frances Long told her. "Do you mind if I have the juniors in to watch?"

"Whatever you like, Doc. I'll be heartily glad to be rid of it."

"Don't think you will be up dancing around on that foot when we do. I am going to put a walking support on that ankle."

"Then can I get out of here?" Although she voiced the question, eagerly, as if she wanted to leave, mentally she was nudging the doctor's mind to make her wait.

"Not until I see how that ankle goes in a proper cast!"

Kryslie scowled, as if frustrated. "So when will this all happen?"

"We will start getting things ready for the start of gamma shift."

Later, her reactions were only partly acting, and she was glad that she had let her brother speed heal her ankle to some extent. The junior techs were not being deliberately rough, it was just that the sealant, unlike plaster, was rock hard and extremely difficult to cut through."

"I can give you some pain relief," the doctor offered, seeing Kryslie's unfeigned grimaces of pain.

"I'll be okay," Kryslie told her, deciding to close her eyes and begin a biofeedback technique to ease the pain. Once the techs stopped jolting her ankle – when the sealant cast was off – the pain would be much less.

While she had her eyes closed, she also distracted her mind by hearing what her brother had found.

"Your suspicions were correct," Tymos told her. "When the team reported that they had the rest of the craft free from the surrounding dust and rock, they also implied that there was a desiccated body within the damaged nose section."

While continuing to dampen the pain in her ankle, Kryslie thought back, "How is the integrity of the rest of the hull?"

"Not too bad, I think. The team has managed to get the lifting slings under it. However, I am sure any atmosphere in the ship will have leaked out long since. We won't know for sure until they get it here."

"Something to look forward to…"Kryslie grimaced at a sudden acute surge of pain as the sealant finally broke open. To her twin, she thought, "Remind me, next time I decide to let my EVA suit be slashed open, that using sealant on me is a ridiculous idea?"

"Would it have any effect if I did?"

"No."

"I could have healed it more…"

"I know, but it would have been odd if you had. Once I am out of here, you can finish the job. However, as it turns out, if there is in fact a body in that wreck, it will come here. And I have an impeccable reason to be here to see what goes on."

"Yeah. Speaking of goings on, did the Doc try waking Andrew for a bit?"

"Yes, but he was groggy – even so, she told me he is slowly improving. She is thinking he is well enough to send down to the University hospital. They have the very best equipment there."

"I'd do some healing on him if only I could sneak in there."

"I know, but the Doc thinks he will recover fully, in time."

In the brief respite after the sealant cast was finally off, and before the walking cast was brought over, Kryslie managed to check if her personal force screen was still working. She had been keeping it on, since the fine wires might have been noticed if it were off. However, the laser cutter used to remove the cast, might have damaged it.

Once she had reassured herself it was still working, she lay back down again, and set her mind to dull the pain.

"I told you to stay lying down," Dr Long chided her.

"I wanted to see…"

"I told you that it looked fine."

"Yeah, but…"

"The foot is bruised, the skin is delicate, but most of the swelling has gone down. There is no trace of necrosis, and by the time I take the walking cast off, it will be healed. You are an excellent case study."

Kryslie made a faint sound, suspiciously like a raspberry, but the doctor only smiled.

"I'll give you some analgesic," the doctor told her. This time though, she wasn't asking.

"You'll make me sleep so that I will be awake all night," Kryslie protested, as the doctor pressed a hypospray against her arm.

"You have permission to use the spare terminal to do whatever the C-I-C has been getting you to do. So far it has stopped you trying to get out of here before I say you can."

"I wouldn't count on it," Kryslie warned. "I went over all the damn programs with Chief Stanley before all this…" she gestured to her foot, "…happened. He's given me make work!"

"What else might keep your mind occupied?" Long looked at her with a neutral expression.

Kryslie studied her in return and dared to suggest, "Figuring why you have the room over there set up as a stasis chamber."

France Long merely shook her head. "And I thought you were sleeping." She didn't offer an explanation, for the reason was classified. "Let me know when you figure it out, and don't share your notions with anyone else."

After a short laugh, Kryslie suggested, "The C-I-C shouldn't try to make it such a secret. The base gossip net is already full of way out ideas. By now, even the densest staff member must know that something is going on. And unless there is a communications black out that I don't know of, no one has been told not to talk about the 'nothing' that is going on. So I think that the C-I-C had better have an airtight story when he gets back to Terra 1."

"I suppose your brother has been telling you all the rumours?"

"Him, and Branson who is an old gossip from way back."

"Well, if you notice things going on here, you are not to spread them around."

"Of course not," Kryslie promised.

The med techs were returning with the parts for the walking cast, and all the other supplies that they needed.

"Have you seen one of these before?" the doctor asked.

"No, but I know it supports the leg without putting pressure on the foot itself, so I can walk."

"Exactly. Once you get used to it. Now, lie still."

Kryslie decided that she didn't have a choice. As soon as she relaxed herself, she found herself nodding off. The analgesic must have contained a sedative as well.

As she had predicted, by the lunar 'night' – halfway through beta shift, she was awake again. The medical facility was quiet enough for her to hear two voices talking quietly. She recognised them as Frances Long and her second in charge, Sam Mc Nabb. She didn't try to listen, although she could have had she wanted to. Instead she wondered why the Chief Medical Officer had not retired for a sleep period.

When she came to the conclusion that the two most senior medics were waiting for something, she let her mind reach out to sense that of her twin. She discovered that he had just transmitted back from Earthbase and was now hiding in shuttle bay 2.

Tymos felt her in his mind and sent, "Hi sleepy! The salvage crew has just returned. The crew are to be on stand down until the start of delta shift. They are going to flush the bay to be sure that the alien ship contains no contaminants or microorganisms that might make us ill. They will let the crew out of the salvage crawler - still in their suits. When the decon is complete, they will let the medics come and extract the pilot."

"Did you get a portable breather from Earthbase?" Kryslie asked him.

"Naturally," Tymos's thought sounded smug. "And a lightweight EVA suit. I aim to transmit into the ship after the crew leave the bay, and before the medics go in."

"So? What does the ship look like?" Kryslie demanded of her brother.

He gave a mental chuckle at her impatience.

"It's a two person craft, very like our own personal craft. If you insist on me giving an opinion, I would say it was Aeronite."

Kryslie had to firmly suppress an audible echo of, "Aeronite". She immediately tried to think how that was possible, but her brother interrupted her thought.

"I will get homebase looking onto that, but until I check the interior, we can't be sure. It is possible that some other race or species found it and was using it. If so, they will have modified the interior."

Tymos's mind went elsewhere for a time, but Kryslie remained a passive watcher – able to see what her brother saw once he had transmitted into the wreck. She'd had a glimpse, just before her twin had transmitted, of the salvage crew under the decon shower. However, her concentration was on what her brother was seeing – memorising it, considering it. Her attention was drawn back to her physical surroundings when Doctor Long and Dr McNabb, wheeled a trolley from a storage room, past her bed, and into the back passageway.

Kryslie opened her eyes, just a slit, and saw the long, cylindrical shape of a clear-walled stasis capsule. She sent a quick, "The doctors are on the way," to her brother.

"Thanks, but the decon cycle still has a few minutes to run. Anyway, I think I have got all I can get without being able to examine the main instrument panels. Hull integrity was compromised, probably on impact, since there was no atmosphere in here and the ambient air, and the decon gas, is getting in."

"The pilot?" Kryslie asked.

"Trapped in the control section. From what I can tell, he or she is mummified. I have done a scan, but I could not get close enough to get a physical specimen. I could access the environment controls in the undamaged section; there was a tiny amount of residual power. The settings support the idea that the pilot was humanoid."

"You couldn't access the main computer?"

"No, there wasn't enough power for that. Or it could be that the computer is damaged. Anyway, I'll come and see you later, I want to get this information to Earthbase and get back before I have to present for that physical."

Kryslie listened for the return of the doctors, who returned as they had left, via the 'back door' into medical. That access was for medical staff only and was part of the fast response passages, and not usually used by crew or the med staff except in emergencies. She didn't think it coincidence that the two beta shift med techs had gone for a break just before the doctors had left, and still hadn't returned when the doctors, dressed in full biohazard gear, wheeled the capsule into the prepared room.

Still observing covertly, she saw the two doctors emerge, begin to remove their protective suits, and after they had, Dr Long locked the door, and Doctor Mc Nabb darkened the viewing window, so that the interior was hidden. She heard Long say, "I'm going for a few hours sleep. The C-I-C can wait that long for a report."

Kryslie closed her eyes as Long began to walk in her direction. She sensed when the doctor paused by her bed.

"I know that you are awake."

Kryslie stopped pretending and said softly, "Of all the rumours that I have been told, the one that fits best is that they found an alien ship with a dead crew. Can I look at who you brought here?"

"No. However if I need any ideas from you, I will ask. The Commander seems to think that you might be helpful that way. On the other hand, even with that walking cast on, you are not a qualified doctor. So, I want you to keep resting. You can have your first lesson walking in that cast during gamma shift."

After the doctor had left, Kryslie amused herself by pretending that she could transmit herself into the stasis room and peek. She didn't intend to try, though, even if she'd had her transmitter with her and not in her quarters. If she was foolish enough to try, she would become like a fly caught in mid-flight, and encased in resin. She would have to wait to hear back from the Tymorean scientists back at Homebase on Tymorea.

Tymos sidled into medical just before the end of beta shift, knowing that his sister was awake.

"Homebase have no answers, but Governor Xyron will investigate," was his quick summary. "If I can get access to the ship's computer, it should tell us a lot."

"Earth power units won't be compatible," Kryslie reminded him.

"I picked up one of our portable power packs. I won't need long to connect it – but the computer might still be beyond repair."

"And assuming that you can work unseen…"

"And that!"

"Whether we find out for sure or not, if one alien ship found its way here, Aeronite or something else, others might do so." Kryslie voiced the thought they both shared.

"Where do they have the body of the pilot?" Tymos asked.

"Over where Mc Nabb is staring. They have a stasis field in the room over there." Kryslie shrugged a shoulder in the relevant direction. "Landin gave Long the okay to involve me if she runs out of ideas."

"Are you allowed to walk around yet?"

"No, my first practice in this walking thing will be during gamma shift."

"So, how is the foot? Want me to heal it a bit more?"

"It must be getting better, it's itching."

Tymos was aware of the door to the section whooshing open, and Kryslie warned him that Dr Long was approaching.

"Didn't she only go off duty 3 hours ago?"

When Kryslie nodded, Tymos thought at her, "Basoli must be impatient for results. I am sure she didn't rush back here to give me my physical. A med tech could do that."

As Long drew nearer, coming over to Kryslie's bed, Tymos spoke just loud enough for the doctor to hear, "I can find you a probe rod to scratch down that cast if you want."

"Don't you dare, Tymos Ward," the doctor warned. "The skin "The skin under the cast is healing nicely but it is still too delicate for your cure for the itch. That cast needs to stay on for another four weeks."

"But it itches!" Kryslie said, deliberately sounding like a petulant teenager. She had picked up on her brother's idea for reinforcing the idea that they were younger than they were.

"I will see what I can do when I am finished with your brother. The Chief wants his nose to the grindstone as soon as possible, and I do not need him cluttering up my med centre."

Chapter 14

"Have you finished the work you were given to do?" Frances Long challenged as she came out of the room with the alien corpse and saw Kryslie looking in. Mc Nabb followed his Chief, and glared at Kryslie before resetting the stasis controls. He was due off shift several hours ago, and looked ready to sleep.

"All I can do from here," Kryslie said cheerfully. "And I looked in on Andrews. The monitor readings look good."

"Is there anything that you don't stick your nose into?" Long sighed.

"He was in my team when he got hurt. I feel responsible…"

"You are, I believe," Long spoke back, and didn't let Kryslie interrupt her, "responsible for keeping him alive. And I think that you had better get off that ankle for a while, or I will give you old-fashioned crutches to use. Shoo!"

Kryslie grumbled as she obeyed, still aiming to give the impression of young and impatient. She went and sat in a chair by her bed, and contemplated the enigma of the alien corpse in the stasis chamber. She pretended to doze once Long went back to her office to record her report. This time, Kryslie drew on her Tymorean power and enhanced her hearing – directing it towards the office, and ignoring all other sounds. Even so, the soft sub-vocalisation as the doctor dictated was hard to hear.

Tymos, at work in the computer lab, going over the department activity logs, the communication logs, and the security monitor logs, paused in his task when his sister requested a way to see what the doctor was recording on her computer. Since he had the new override codes, and knew everyone's terminal ID, he told her how to make the spare terminal she was allowed to use, a mirror of the Chief Medical Officer's computer.

Kryslie moved her chair quietly, and turned the spare terminal on. From this unauthorised eavesdropping, she learnt as much as the doctors had learnt from their initial examination.

The dead alien was male, with a structure very close to human. His inner organs - detected by sensitive medical scanners – were in slightly different positions from human, and in a condition consistent with the desiccated state of the rest of the body. The limbs were slightly longer than human norm, but still within the standard range variation. Hands and feet were long and slender, but again, some humans had similar. The dried up remains of the eyes, may have lacked the white around the iris, but that could not be confirmed.

Then there were columns of figures relating to the biochemical composition of the remains, but Kryslie had nothing to compare them to. Finally, there was a list of specimens collected for a more detailed analysis. As yet, the doctors had not opened the body for a full autopsy.

The doctor stopped dictating and instigated a search program. Kryslie retreated, and her terminal screen went blank. She had a lot to think on and a lot she could tell the doctor if it didn't require her admitting that she too, was alien.

Although she had not consciously read the data scrolling from the medical scanner, she could, and did recall it exactly as she considered the differences between Aeronite and Tymorean physiology.

Her mind went back to a time before the war that had devastated Tymorea. When the Aeronites were trying to cultivate a certain plant that contained a particular element that they needed in their diet. It was an element endemic on Aerdna, rare on Tymorea, and as far as she knew, unknown on Earth. The med scanner had not identified it, but that would be one piece of evidence that the body was of an alien.

There were other differences that the med scanner had not detected. Aeronites were once of Tymorean stock, millennia before, and they, like the Tymoreans, had a denser bone structure than humans. This was the one most likely to be discovered, if the doctor thought to look. She did not want to mention this, for that difference existed within herself.

Kryslie let her mind brush that of the doctor, and learnt that Basoli wanted results and that, so far, she had no conclusive proof as to whether the dead pilot was alien, or somehow human. What might she suggest to the doctor if she was officially allowed to know the examination results? How to bring up the idea? After a moment, she thought of the spectrographic analyses she did of various near space stars and the closer planets. The base instruments were able to identify elements in the atmosphere of planets and the plasma around the stars. The composition of different stars was like a fingerprint. Maybe…

Kryslie had her eyes closed to hide the fact that her mind was busy, trying now to think how and why and Aeronite spaceship could have ended up on the moon.

"Why would the Commander think you could help me?" Frances Long spoke in a normal tone, having decided after a moment of observation, that her patient was not asleep.

Kryslie immediately opened her eyes and said, "Maybe because I have dabbled in a lot of different sciences, not just tracking. He could have put me to work in a lot of different departments."

"Really?" The doctor's brows rose slightly, wondering how someone that looked so young, and who she had determined to be in her early twenties, could know so much. "What do you know about medicine?"

"I don't have a degree in it, but I do know a lot of biochemistry and physiology." It was not an idle claim, but it also wasn't the full truth. She and her brother knew as much about medicine as the Royal Tymorean Governor, Xyron, knew.

Long continued to study the tech 3, and then came to a decision. "Come with me."

Kryslie stood immediately, and seeing a glance of concern in the doctor's expression, remembered to make her movements more careful. The truth was, her body had adjusted to the walking cast after the first practice walk. She followed the doctor over to the stasis room, and aware that when the doctor turned to watch her catch up, she was assessing how well she walked.

"You have excellent balance," Long commented neutrally. "It takes most people a few days to get used to that cast."

"I want out of here," Kryslie murmured, as Long deactivated the stasis field and passed over a bio-suit, gloves and glasses.

Kryslie had no trouble pulling the light weight all-over suit on over her casual clothing even with the walking cast on, and was ready in much the same time as the doctor.

After Long pulled back the sheet that she had covered the body with, she stood back and watched what Kryslie did.

In a single glance, Kryslie took in the emaciated, desiccated form, noting the bone structure, in the face and comparing it to the Aeronites she had met. Some of them had been almost as emaciated when she had found them and taken them back to their baseships. Now the facial structure was evident, with the skin stretched over the bone. If the doctor thought to extrapolate how the man would have looked alive, and happened to look at Kryslie herself, or her brother – she and the man might seem related.

To hide her interest in the face, Kryslie angled her head so that the doctor did not see her eyes change shape, so that she could study what she could see of the corpse, centimetre by centimetre, in great detail. She wanted to know how the man had died, but his body gave her no clues. The most logical possibility was that he died on impact, or from suffocation when the atmosphere leaked from his ship.

"Do you know he died?" Kryslie asked.

"His skull shows signs of fractures."

Kryslie nodded. If there had been signs of other trauma, unexplained burns or projectiles, the doctor would have said as much.

"He is very like us," Kryslie said, knowing Long would assume she was meaning 'like humans'. She still had her eyes down, and seemed to be thinking while staring at the corpse. After she had readjusted her eyes back to normal, she looked up.

"I don't know if this could be applied to medicine, but we identify different stars by the differences in their 'aura' which might be due to different elements in the atmosphere. If that corpse is from a different planet, might there be a difference in the cell structure or the bio-elements?"

The suggestion stirred ideas in the doctor's mind. She began working on ways to test the idea. She had noticed slight differences in what she could find of the cell structure, but the body had been desiccated.

With her mind still on the problem, Long gestured for Kryslie to leave the room, stopped replace the sheet over the body, and retreated from the room. They both divested themselves of the protective clothing, and shoved the garments down the chute to be recycled.

Kryslie went back to her corner of the med centre, and watched the doctor go to her desk, and seem to stare into space.

Basoli departed on the sixth day shuttle, but before he left, his PA, Bynan, slipped into visit Kryslie.

"He's frustrated," Bynan admitted, when Kryslie had asked about her boss. "He wants to write a paper on intelligothropy, or some such coined term. Trouble is, there is no really startling information yet."

"I thought he wanted the finding of the ship to be hushed up," Kryslie commented.

"Word has got out, but most people think it is one of the old moon probes from a century ago," Bynan told her. "He isn't going to make any formal announcements, and whatever you people find out will only be shared by senior researchers."

"He won't be able to hide the fact forever."

Bynan shrugged. "I don't know about that. However he is acting as if he is the world's expert on aliens. He has some rather odd theories."

"And just how many aliens has he met?" Kryslie grinned wryly at Bynan, before adding, "Naturally, his name will be on all the papers written by people under him. Not that anyone here has enough information for a paper yet. Well, except for the Chief Mechanic. He has studied the structure of the ship, and found some unidentified metallic elements, made guesses as to what parts are used for what and has half the guesses wrong."

Tymos arrived at that point and added his opinion, "And all the scientists here will be happily occupied for a good long time."

Kryslie was discharged from the med centre two days after Basoli had departed. In those final two days, Frances Long had held long discussions with Kryslie, making sure she understood the theory of different elements having different ratios in the atmosphere of different planets. Between them, they had determined how the med scanners needed to be modified to detect the minute differences and identify unusual trace elements.

Also during that time, Tymos had taken the time to do further healing of his sister's foot. In return, Kryslie had made it her task to help him watch for activity that would confirm the existence of another malevolent agent. They were both sure that if one existed, the person would try for an unauthorised look at the wreck in the shuttle bay, and perhaps steal something from it once the engineers started disassembling it. So far though, they had noticed no glitches in the monitoring system.

Chapter 15

On her first day back at work, two weeks after the shuttle wreck, Chief Controller Stanley called her over to the 'well' where he over saw the shift and advised her of her promotion to Tech 2. He presented her with the new collar insignia, and added his congratulations.

"A well-deserved promotion, past due if you ask me."

"Thank you, Sir," Kryslie said, accepting the compliment. Then she asked, "Has there been any further trouble with the tracking system?"

Stanley grinned, "No, I think between us we flushed out the trouble. At the moment, there isn't much activity spaceward. I've had your station relaying data from Auto-track 2, to the scientists who are studying the Iris nebula. You can leave that on automatic. I want you to liaise with the techs at Terra 1, who are preparing the parts and equipment to repair Auto-track 1. I sent a crew out to assess the damage. I will send their report to your station."

"Will I be needed to be part of the repair crew?"

Stanley glanced down at the walking cast, of which the bottom was protruding from under the leg of her uniform pants. "I don't think you will be available for EVA tasks for a while yet."

"Maybe not," Kryslie had to agree, not willing to admit her foot no longer needed the cast. She obeyed the gesture Stanley gave her to get back to work.

Branson gave her a welcome back grin, but didn't notice her new collar tabs until half an hour later, when he had set his terminal to automatic, and was ready to chat.

"Hey, congratulations, Ward," he said with sincere surprise. "A promotion! The way I heard things, the CIC was wanting you kicked down to paper shredder."

Since very little paper was used at Lunar 1, the term had come to be a euphemism for being exiled planetside.

"He may have been referring to Tym," Kryslie suggested with a shrug. "My twin has a way of irritating some people."

"Oh, like that guy he caught. The one that caused all the trouble? Did I tell you about him?"

"Some," Kryslie admitted, knowing that Branson was full of gossip that he hadn't mentioned on his visits to the med centre. "Did you hear anything more about him?"

"Sure did. It was on the Earth news net. The IC questioned him, and they are going to enforce the sentence from fifteen years ago. He was supposedly executed back then."

"Does the IC know how he managed to stay alive?" Kryslie asked, although she already had an idea, and had a more direct source of information about IC activities.

It was enough encouragement to get Branson going, and he didn't even notice when most of her attention went back to the images of the inside of Auto-track 1 that were taken after the explosion. Most of what he was saying she already knew, but occasionally he had a snippet of info that her brother hadn't gleaned first. It was quite apparent that the entire roster of the base personnel was aware that an alien ship had been found, and that the body of the pilot was in the med centre.

When Branson mentioned overhearing plans by the systems analysts to try to restore power to the computer system of the derelict ship, she sent a mental message to her twin. He was stuck in the computer lab, which was located below main mission, for the rest of his shift and had no reason to go near the shuttle bay. So far, he hadn't been asked to assist the teams studying the alien ship.

Later, after his shift had ended, Kryslie heard her brother's frustrated growl. "I knew it wouldn't work. It was blindingly obvious! Too many ham-handed attempts like that will damage the data storage module beyond our ability to get data from it."

"Can't you get yourself assigned to work on it?"

"I tried, but Landin wants me to find the other rotten apple in his crew. The damned man is as elusive as Rasti. I am beginning to doubt that there is another man. There has not been a trace of a malfunction since I caught Rasti."

"Well, now I am out of the med centre, I might be able to help. I could keep watch while you slip in."

"Except there never seems to be a time when no one is poking around in there."

"How long will you need?"

"Ten minutes. What I have heard from the specialists indicates that the ship is very like the Aeronite ships we examined back home."

Kryslie stopped a data feed on her terminal so that she could consider that statement. Then she thought back to her twin, "Surely, in over a century, the Aeronites would have improved their ships?"

She felt her brother take in that idea and think on it in turn. "I am not so sure. We know Aerdna transcended its orbit, and anyone surviving in the vaults won't have the need of the materials to build ships. The

Aeronite colonies, would have been swamped with evacuees – but only one of them had any scientific culture. But from the outside, it looks like an old design. I'll ask Daniel to get a report from Homebase. However, I still want to know how it found its way here."

"After my shift, I will help you get into the ship," Kryslie promised.

"I'll have everything ready."

Kryslie had just handed over to her Alpha shift replacement, when the alarm klaxon began and a security team was ordered to shuttle bay 2. Her first thought was that her brother had gone there already, so she called him mentally.

"Tym?" She received no response, so she sent a stronger thought.

"What's up?" he responded this time.

"Where are you?"

"With Daniel," was the reply.

At that moment, Landin saw her and approached.

"Where is your brother," he asked urgently.

"I haven't seen him since before my shift," Kryslie said, wondering what was up.

"He is not sneaking about that ship, is he?" was Landin's quiet but urgent question. He knew Kryslie could talk to her brother mind to mind and ignored her evasion of his question.

"No," Kryslie told him straight away. "Why?"

"An intruder was seen on the monitors, moving around the ship," Landin told her, and then he moved off, giving further instructions to the security team via the command comm unit he carried.

Kryslie quickly relayed the information to Tymos, who told her he was returning at once via the long-range beam. On instinct, she decided to follow Landin towards the shuttle bay. She stopped in the passageway, when she saw the perimeter of guards ahead in the taxiway that linked the two shuttle bays, and held the garages for the crawlers. She was close enough to them to hear the faint whispers of information and orders being relayed through their earpieces.

Her mind wondered how, with people always around the wreck, they even knew an intruder was there, or if they recognised an unauthorised person, they didn't immediately challenge them.

Tymos materialised beside her, and stood very still, using his power to hide his presence. He spoke mind to mind, having shared her thought. Not one of the nearby guards noticed his arrival any more than they were aware of Kryslie.

"When they tried to power the ship, something shorted. The insulation began to smoulder. They stopped the fire before it took hold, but the fumes were toxic, so they ordered the bay evacuated, and sealed, while they pump the air through the purification scrubbers."

"If someone is in there, whoever it is must have gone in before they sealed they bay," Kryslie thought at her twin. "He'd have to have breathing gear…" The air would be pumped out, leaving the bay in a near vacuum.

"Could grab an EVA suit," Tymos proposed. "Like I am going to do. Let me know if you hear they're going to move in."

Tymos transmitted away, to get what he needed for his own intended foray. He wouldn't be seen, for he would transmit directly into the wrecked ship, and if the intruder was there, deal with him too.

Kryslie listened to what she could of the conversation between the guard teams. The shuttle deck was sealed, which meant that every possible outlet for air, liquid and solid was blocked. This was to prevent fire and smoke spreading to the rest of the base if a shuttle crashed and exploded in there.

In the event of an impending 'hot' arrival, crash barriers could be swung out to slow the arrival.

Guards were checking the seals on all the maintenance tunnels as well as the normally used entrances.

From various overheard comments, all power to the shuttle bay had been cut when security had been called in. Anyone inside would not be able to override the emergency door seals to get through any of them. She didn't think the intruder, even if he had donned an EVA suit, would try to get out through the force field either. He'd need something stronger than the EVA suit for that, even if he knew of a way back in that wouldn't start alarms ringing.

Part of her mind was aware that he brother had transmitted into the wreck, and he was working to try to access the data module of the ship's computer. Obviously the intruder was not in there.

Kryslie kept listening to the reports of the guards, and kept herself unnoticed. Some of the guards were in the security office, and had the monitor cameras scanning the bay. For now, the rest were standing and waiting for the order to move in. She wondered why they hadn't.

One of the guards was sent on an errand. He trotted back towards Kryslie, and not seeing her, bumped into her. He recovered quickly from his confusion and demanded, "Hold it! Why are you here?"

"Commander Landin asked me a question on his way here. I remembered the answer," Kryslie said at once.

The guard sub vocalised into his neck communicator and then ordered, "Stay put, technician."

Kryslie wasn't going to argue, even though a high-pitched sound was beginning to pain her ears.

Her mind rapidly considered what was likely to be causing it. A remote control signal? Possible, but there was no power in there.

"Tym?"

"I hear it and I'm not causing it."

Kryslie sensed her brother leaving the copying of the data module, and moving to look out the side door of the alien ship.

"I can see no heat signatures and nothing in the UV range either."

"Could he be behind the blast doors?"

"I can't see them from here but the engineers left the portable power supply in the bay, and it's near the power nexus."

Kryslie returned her full attention to the nearby guards; they had their attention on the closed doors to the bay, and the inner ring of guards were pulling on portable breathing units.

"Tym, I think they are going to gas the bay."

"I'm done. Don't know if I have anything usable. I'll be out in a minute. Tell the guards about the noise we heard."

Kryslie trotted towards the nearest guard. Before she could be challenged again, she reported the noise she heard and immediately had his attention. He spoke into his communicator, listened, and ordered, "Stay here, out of the way."

Kryslie obeyed, moving back until she was right by the wall near one of the access passages. She had a view of the flashing orange warning light above the wide and high door to the bay. When the flashing changed to yellow, there was a 'thunk' as power was restored to the doors and they began to roll upwards.

Almost immediately after that, the order to move in was given. Kryslie lost her means of knowing what was happening as the outer guards moved in closer to the shuttle bay and the nearer squads went in.

For her part, she only had a narrow view into the bay, and could only see the crushed nose section of the alien ship. She imagined the guards would have spread out to search the bay, and studied the ring staring intently into the bay. Slight stiffening of their posture suggested that something had been found, and several minutes later, two of the armour clad guards emerged from the bay, dragging a figure in dark coveralls. She adjusted her eyes to see the prisoner more clearly across the distance. The unconscious man's clothing was soaked in the fire retardant chemicals, but his face was not visible to her. When the guards rolled him onto his back, she had a glimpse.

Alden? Her mind rebelled against the idea. The man was a tech officer from engineering, and she knew him casually. He was not tall, and not young, but surely he would not have consorted with the likes of Rasti.

The guards were giving him pure oxygen, hoping to rouse him. As consciousness returned, the man tried to struggle. He was hauled to his feet, and immediately restrained by the two guards who had brought him out. Kryslie touched his mind with hers and found he was only barely conscious – reacting, not thinking, barely able to keep on his feet.

She did not need to hear the order for the prisoner to go to the brig. The guards were coming towards her, and the passageway beside her was the way they would need to go. She stayed very still, and used her power to seem invisible. Neither guard had noticed her there, nor her sudden vanishing.

Kryslie normalised her eyes, since she no longer needed to see what was further away, but as she did that, she thought of the marker Tymos had put on the waiter. She readjusted her eyes again, but this time to see using the ambient UV light. The prisoner's arms were dangling by his side, the arms held at shoulder and elbow. Neither of his hands had a trace of a glow, only the reddish residue of the fire chemicals.

Then a faint trace of blue caught her eye, and she looked again, moving her visual examination from the prisoner to the guard nearest her.

"Tym! They have pulled Alden, the Engineering tech, from the bay and are taking him to the brig. His hands are clean, but one of the guards has the marker on his hand."

"All the guard should have gauntlets on! Can you see his face?"

"No, both guards still have their helmets on."

As Kryslie watched the three men go past her, she looked for other clues, aware that her brother was transmitting from his quarters to where he could intercept these men.

The amour of the man nearest her didn't quite fit him - the ultra-tough, ultra-flexible armoured fabric was wrinkled on the legs, as if made for a taller man. She counted to five, and slipped into the passage after the men.

The yellow evacuation lights were flashing in the passageway, and the only people ahead of her were the three she followed. They were moving faster than she could with the walking cast on her foot. They disappeared into a side passage leading off to the right, and when she reached that place, they were not in sight. She forced herself to move faster, and when she reached where the passage branched again, she took the passage that led to the nearest turbo lift.

Some sound, or instinct, warned her that she had gone the wrong way, and she back tracked, all senses alert, and took the other passage. There was still no sign of the three men, as she moved carefully – eyes scanning the way ahead.

What would that fake waiter, that other subversive agent, be trying to do? Was the other guard in league with him? Had he forced the other guard to go this way…away from the quickest means to get the prisoner to the brig?

"Tym? I've lost them. But they are not heading for the brig." She sent her location and the direction she was travelling. She sensed her brother transmitting to a point that should be well ahead of the men, but he was guessing the location. She hobbled rather than trotted, but moved as fast as she dared. The cast wasn't meant for speed, and she risked falling over. Her instincts were guiding her, since she could not sense where the three men were. She turned another corner, into another yellow lit tunnel, and almost tripped over the two bodies lying on the floor. One was the prisoner, the other was the second guard – the one whose armour fitted properly, and whose hands were covered with the regulation armoured gauntlets. To be sure that this wasn't her quarry trying to trick them again, she removed them. The hands did not glow.

Then she noticed that the guard was without weapons, and recalled what she had seen with the guards when they had passed her, and cursed softly.

Neither man had obvious signs of injury – no blood, no burnt patches on armour or clothing. The agent hadn't used a ballistic weapon, or she would have heard even a silenced report. There was none of the characteristic ozone smell from an energy beam weapon, so he must have a neural subduer – silent and fast acting. Did he know how to judge the setting? Or did he not care?

Kryslie knelt beside each man. Alden, who had no armour to block some of the effect, was breathing with difficulty, the guard was better off, but unconscious and jerking as if having a mild fit.

Both men needed more help than she had time to give them. She had to keep after the fake guard, find where he was going to hide.

She came to a comm panel and paused long enough to activate the emergency alert button, and enunciated clearly, "Medical alert, this location." A voice over followed immediately, repeating the alert and adding the actual location. By the time the message finished, Kryslie was moving steadily along the passage, pausing briefly near each door and trying to sense within for the mind of her quarry and scanning walls, roof and floor for clues to the man's escape route.

This area, behind engineering, consisted of many storage chambers, and was a maze of passageways, since the walls were able to be reorganised to suit the contents. There should be a way through, no matter how the walls were organised; she slowed and studied the wall in front of her.

There was a faint hum here, like the sub-sonic hum of an electric field. Her first thought was that she was hearing the air circulation system. She had no time for second thoughts. The painful tingling along all her nerve pathways, escalated to unbearable, and her mind verged on blacking out. She recognised the effect of the neural stun from the subduer, and fought to stay conscious.

"Your luck is out, you unnatural freak," a voice whispered, thinking her unconscious. "If I can't get the recorder, I will still have you and your brother will learn what it is like to have a sibling taken from him."

The man, short though he was, was lifting her to his shoulder in a fireman's hold, and jogging further along the passage. Then she felt him manipulating her into a hatchway. Kryslie tried to mind call her twin, but she could not form a coherent thought, and blackness was pressing closer.

Tymos had the sense of his sister's confusion as the way ahead seemed blocked. He had a glimpse of the place from his sister's mind, and then, suddenly, nothing – only the absolute surety of trouble.

He recognised the area, and dared not transmit there without being sure of the layout of the maze of chambers. Nor could he use Kryslie for his location coordinates – not with her mind affected by the neural stun. Instead, he transmitted to the outer edge of the area, and ran towards where he thought his sister had been.

He slowed when he came to a dead end, and compared what he saw with what he had seen in his sister's mind.

"Krys?"

He felt no trace of his sister's mind now, as he turned slowly, studying every facet of his current location. The flashing yellow light reflected off walls, floor and roof, throwing the inset closed doorways into places of shadow. He backed away from the wall that blocked his way, and moved to the nearest door way. He entered the command override sequence on the touchpad beside the door. When the door opened, he glanced inside. The room was full of airtight crates, and no sound came from within, and he sensed no one.

Kryslie had to be somewhere close, the passage ended and no one had come back past him. With a sense of urgency, he opened each door in turn, moving back towards the nearest cross passage. He didn't stop, even when he heard the booted feet of the guards trotting nearer.

When he was challenged, he simply stopped still, his hands held away from his side. The guards were all in light armour, but that would not have stopped him had he really need to get away. These were not enemies, and he recognised the rank marker on the figure who challenged him with, "Stop right there!"

Reading the name on the shoulder of the armour, Tymos countered, "Raoul, Krys came this way."

One of the other three figures glanced around and added, "I can't see her."

"She called in the medical emergency…"

"Ward, you shouldn't be here!" Raoul stated. "Someone attacked Darcy, and you are the only person around."

"My sister is around here somewhere. I have to find her."

"We will look for her, Ward."

Tymos debated trying to argue further, but from the stance of the four guards, decided that it would do no good.

"Ward! Move!"

They gave him no more time, two of them gripped his arms at shoulder and elbow, and began to hustle him back the way he had come. He let his body move automatically, and forced himself to think. Kryslie wasn't dead, he knew that in his very core, but she had been overcome by someone who was probably in the pay of Abdul bin Halil, and must suspect at least that his master hated her. If he got word to his master, what might he be told to do? What would he do if he were cornered? He would be more dangerous, might cause more damage to the base. Certainly he would not hesitate to use Kryslie as a hostage. They needed to find him soon. Kryslie could not defend herself if she were unconscious. Once she woke though…he was sure she would be able to deal with her captor.

Tymos's mind returned to the enigma of the dead end passage. Even in this section of flexible shaped storage space, there was meant to be a way through. He recalled to mind this section of the base schematics, his mind instinctively calculating distances and locating where he had been. He stopped abruptly, and even the tugging of the guards couldn't force him to continue. That passage wasn't a dead end! There should have been a maintenance hatch at the end. One that led to the power grid main supply board, and the central data linkages. There was a warren of tunnels leading off from there – following the power and data conduits to each section of the base. He could hide in there, escape through to wherever he usually holed up…

And he hadn't seen it! He could think of only one way that could have happened, and he had been too worried about his sister to even sense it.

Tymos spoke loud enough to be heard over the insistent demands of the guard. "I need to speak to Commander Landin."

He continued to resist being moved, and finally one of the four, at a nod from Raoul, used his Wi-Fi communicator to pass on the request.

It wasn't Landin who came, but Murtry – the head of security. He was armoured, but his helmet was off. He can't have been far away, for he arrived quickly.

"This better be good, Ward. And better include why you are in an area declared off limits."

Tymos sensed repressed anger, because the intruder had eluded his men and injured several.

"Sir, that passage should have a maintenance hatch at the end, giving access to one of the central power and data linkages and the atmosphere recycling section."

Murtry was not stupid. He drew out a data padd and checked that for himself. He issued orders via his comm unit, sending others of his team to position themselves at other access points to that section.

"Keep him here," Murtry ordered the men holding Tymos. The rest, he gestured to and they followed him back into the passage.

He returned quite quickly, hiding his perplexity.

"Where is your sister, Ward? The monitors record her coming this way, and then the signal stopped. How did you know to come here?"

"I heard her put over the medical alert, and then I sensed that she had met trouble."

"You … sensed it?"

"Sir, we're twins…"

"I don't care what you are. You are here, she was here, and I have two injured people!"

"We didn't…"

"How did you get here? I have had all passages monitored."

Tymos did not want to answer that, so he said, "I think Krys met your intruder."

Murtry's penetrating stare seemed to promise dire things, but Tymos didn't look away.

"Anything else you can tell me before I have you hauled to the brig for deliberate disregard of orders, Mr Ward?"

His reply was not what Murtry expected.

"I think there is a holographic field hiding the end of that passage."

"Do you now? How does a computer tech know about such things?"

"I spend some of my spare time in R and D. Sam Ellis is into that field. Talk to him."

"I will," Murtry promised grimly. "And you will have some talking to do to the Commander – when he has time. In the meantime, we will find your sister." He gestured to the guards still holding Tymos, and this time, they were able to force him to move.

Chapter 16

Tymos paced the six foot square, white-walled cell in the brig, trying to work through a montage of emotions and reduce the level of power that surged within him. Foremost was frustration, and knowing that his current incarceration was for being out of his quarters during an alert – again. He had been warned last time, and he couldn't argue that he was been unfairly treated. It was just that he wanted to find Kryslie and the bastard who had taken her.

The second strongest emotion was concern. He still couldn't reach is sister's mind, and it had been hours now. A stun, or a physical blow, that knocked her out would have worn off by now. Murtry had told him that his men would find Kryslie. No doubt he thought he could home in on her bio-locator, but he had said they had lost her signal. If it was blocked, or removed, or if she were dead, the locator wouldn't help them.

If they did find her, he had no way of being sure they would even tell him until morning. He had the feeling that Murtry thought she might be dead. She wasn't, he was still sure of that. No one would be able to keep her hidden if he were free to look for her. Then he forced himself to be honest. Right now, he had as much chance of finding her as the guards did. Once she woke again, that was a different matter.

Concern for Kryslie and wanting to look for her kept him from thinking of how he had been lulled into believing that Rasti had been the only malevolent agent after all. He had proposed a back-up, thought it was whoever had been the waiter at the reception for Abdul bin Halil, but that person might have been Rasti – the build had been similar. The explosion could have been pre-arranged, and nothing untoward had occurred since Rasti had been caught. None of his attempts to trace a confederate had found anything. Until the previous day…

The sudden onset of a painful tingle along all his nerve pathways caused him to abruptly stop moving. He let his power drain away, and studied the sensation. His body wasn't causing it, this was a pain echo…

"Krys?" he mind sent. When he had no response, he sent with more urgency, "Are you alright?"

His thought stirred something, he felt, rather than mind heard, "What?"

He felt a surge of relief. Whatever had struck his sister, was starting to wear off. Her mind was still addled, but contact between them was returning. He didn't try to force it.

Tymos felt like he could now sit still, but to be perverse, chose to sit on the floor, not the bed. He had been hoping at first, that Landin might summon him. Now he decided that Murtry would probably delay passing on the message until morning – if only to drive home the fact that Tech 2s were not exempt from obeying base regulations. The memory of Landin's lecture after he'd gone out with the med-evac team, returned unbidden. He slumped back against the wall. He'd been a Great Fool. He had, yet again, rushed to help his sister – without thinking of the consequences. He could have handled things better – trusted that Kryslie would be able to manage for herself, once she woke again and been more covert in his search for her. Heck, he should have thought of a holo-field, when he reached the dead end passage.

To push those thoughts from his mind, he considered what he had achieved the previous day. He had managed to power up the shipboard computer in the alien wreck, and copy a major portion of it. He still didn't know if any of it would be readable, or if the abortive attempt by the engineers had garbled it all. The problem was, that he'd not had time to take the Tymorean style portable power unit, and his recorder, back to Earthbase. Both items were in his quarters, in plain view. If Murtry deemed it necessary to search his quarters, he'd need to explain them. It would be obvious to any Earth-born expert that they were not human technology.

When Kryslie had sent her warning, he had simply put them on his desk and transmitted into one of the deserted passageways between the turbo lift and the brig. Only his quarry had not gone that far.

The man had not been carrying anything when he helped Alden out of the shuttle bay. So, what had he done while in the bay – or been doing when he was seen on the monitor film? It could be assumed that he was wanting to get his hands on some advanced technology, and he had stayed in the bay when everyone had been ordered out. He had to have gone into the safe-lock or had an EVA suit on when the air was pumped out. Where had Alden been then? Alden was covered in the fire retardant, from when they had gassed the bay…

Tymos paused to examine his memory of the interior of the ship. Modules had been carefully extracted from within, he had assumed the scientific team had done that…or had the intruder taken something as well? He would have to ask the question when they let him out. So far the senior techs and scientists had not requested help from mere Tech 2s.

If the intruder had taken some part of the ship, hoping to get a rich reward from his controller, who had scientists who might learn from alien technology, he'd have to get it down to Earth on one of the shuttles, and hide it until he could. Never mind that the alien technology might be of no use. Abdul bin Halil, the person Tymos was sure was behind the troubles at the base, would gloat to have stolen it from under the noses of the WSRA guards. He would do more than gloat if he got Kryslie in his hands again.

Was that possible? Could the man who had her, smuggle her onto a shuttle, without anyone aware of it? Oh, that was a frightening thought. It was possible. He was sure that one man, possibly two men, had been smuggled up into Lunar 1.

Tymos caught his thoughts beginning to run in circles. He could not make the facts he knew into a coherent picture. He recalled a mantra for focussing, and repeated it until his mind was still. Then he thought of the calm ageless wisdom of the Elders back on Tymorea, and recalled their lessons in logic and reasoning.

He seemed to hear one of them speaking in his mind. "You do not yet have all the facts…"

That was true. He didn't even know where Krys was…

Kryslie didn't know either, except that it looked a bit like one of the maintenance cubbies where equipment was usually stored. This one had a makeshift bed with a mattress, a portable toilet like used in the crawlers; several closed carry boxes and some oddments of preserved rations.

She was in a heap on the bare floor, trussed up like a festival roast, or that's what it felt like.

The man she had gone after had removed the guard uniform and hung it next to some coveralls and other uniforms. He was now wearing some kind of jumpsuit. He was squatting on his mattress, occasionally glancing her way, but seeming to be listening to something via an earpiece.

When she had first begun to recover, her mind had been addled. Yet she had felt her brother's mind, reminding her of who she was and what had happened. Her body had been unresponsive, and it had taken a great effort to merely open her eyes a slit. Even when she did, her mind did not take in what she saw, but with her brother's mind watching hers, he told her what to do.

Slowly, her own mind began to work, and the dreadful twitching of her muscles began as the neural stun effect began to ease from the rest of her body.

Kryslie hadn't let her captor know she was aware again. He would not be expecting her to be conscious yet, since most people took up to a full day to recover from a neural stun. Now that she was, her concentration was almost fully on making herself recover faster. Once that was done, freeing herself from the 'secure' restraints would be easy.

In the meantime, she and her brother wanted to know what this man intended, but without forcing her way in, his mind was revealing nothing that she could pick up. So she stayed quite still and tried an experiment. She sent to his mind, not thoughts, but a feeling of needing to leave urgently. Through slitted eyelids, she saw him glance at his watch, stand up and start to pace the small area.

Tymos's escorts arrived promptly at the start of gamma shift, and deactivated the confinement field. They gestured him out, and when one gripped his arm, he shook it off. This was a formality only, and he wasn't dangerous, so he was allowed to walk on his own. Both of the guards knew him well enough, as he had worked with them when reserves had been needed. They didn't tease him either, since had been working to help them.

They stopped briefly at the security console, so that Tymos could retrieve the personal effects that had been confiscated the day before. He was relieved when he had taken his communicator and personal transmitter from the locker and pocketed them. When he had his shoes back on, he began to feel he was fit to be a Tymorean Great One.

Once he had been delivered to the Commander's office, the two guards departed. After a moment of mutual appraisal, Tymos decided that the Commander was exhausted, and had probably not slept during the previous night. Landin, for his part, judged that if his maverick Tech 2 was calm, then his sister was probably well.

"Sit!" Landin gestured to a chair. Then he offered, "Coffee?"

Tymos shook his head. He hadn't slept while he was confined, but he did not feel as tired as Landin looked. He was expecting another lecture from his commander, but Landin began with what was on his mind.

"We haven't been able to find any trace of the intruder from the shuttle bay, or of your sister. What can you tell me?"

Knowing that Landin was aware of his ability to mind speak with his sister, Tymos admitted, "The man has her. He used the secure restraints he took from the real guards, so she is limited in how much she can move. However, she has had glimpses of him. Once he removed his facial disguise, which Kryslie says looks to have been made of synthi-skin, he is a lot like Rasti – possibly a relative of fellow countryman."

Landin's hand twitched, as he put his coffee mug down. "What fool notion made her go after a dangerous man when she is barely able to walk?"

"Not foolish. She did not believe that Alden was our target, and something about one of the guards caught her eye."

"Explain!"

Tymos reported on what his sister had observed, admitting that he had marked the man, back when the leader of the Imperium had visited.

Landin was too tired to glare at him. He merely said, "Had you told me this, days ago, we could have had more eyes looking out for the marker and your sister might not be in her current trouble. How did she get caught?"

"She walked too close to the holofield that was hiding the man. He got her with a neural stun before she knew to react."

Landin glanced up at the ceiling of his office and said, "You do know, that you and your sister do not have to do everything."

Tymos knew that there was no point in trying to justify being involved. It would mean revealing too much to say that only he and Kryslie could have seen the marker dye, and that they had personal reasons for wanting the man caught. He said nothing.

"Do you know where your sister is?"

Since he and Kryslie had planned a way to get the man to reveal himself, and any remaining accomplices, he side stepped the question.

"Krys can't identify the place, but it is like one of the maintenance storage modules," Tymos revealed. He didn't admit that he had a fair idea of where it was. Now that Krys was aware again, and clear-headed, he could find her if he needed to.

To further distract Landin, he added, "The neural stun takes a while to wear off. She will be able to tell me more when it does."

"I am surprised that you are no longer trying to fight everyone to get to her."

Now Landin was giving him another appraising glance, making it obvious that he was seeing the rumpled uniform, which was the result of Tymos having worn it all night in the brig.

"What changed you attitude?"

Telling him of their plan, that they as Great Ones were used to doing what needed to be done, and were going to do it their way – would not be diplomatic.

"Krys is okay. The stun is wearing off – faster than the man will expect. Then she will be able to overcome him."

"With a foot in a walking cast?"

"That is not a handicap, and she is safe enough for now – albeit uncomfortable – since the man wants her alive. She's pretending to be unconscious still, and trying to discover how he intends to get her and some crates, onto the shuttle."

"And himself?" Landin asked.

Tymos shrugged. "If he is smart, he won't try. He ought to know that you will have guards around the only way off the base. He has stayed hidden this long, he should be able to continue to do so until we stop being so alert."

"Can your sister see any crates or boxes where she is?"

For a moment, Tymos concentrated on mind speaking with his sister. He did not worry about that fact that his face would have taken on a blank expression. Finally, he said, "In her line of sight, there are two cargo pods. One is being used as a table, and the other one has ration bars in it."

He saw Landin trying to stifle a yawn and asked, "Did the man take something?"

With an almost audible sigh, Landin nodded. "A piece of what we think is a weapons array. We believe he had to be able to watch and overhear the tech crew."

"What about the recorder?"

Landin's face smiled. "No, we have that. How did you know of it?"

With a shrug, Tymos said, "It makes perfect sense that you would be recording everything the team does."

"I have the feeling that you are avoiding my question, but…no matter. When the circuits shorted, Foster grabbed it, as well as helping Haydn out."

"What about Alden? How did he end up in the bay? Didn't the warden count heads?"

"For someone who wasn't near the shuttle bay at the time and who spent the night in the brig. You know too much. I assume your sister told you?"

Tymos nodded.

"Alden was not working in there at the time. He'd rotated off for a break."

Landin switched topics, back to his earlier one. "Last night, Murtry searched every chamber, cubicle, cupboard, on the base plans, as well as every conceivable storage space in the shuttle bay, and didn't find that piece of the ship. It has to be somewhere?"

"Of course," Tymos agreed. "But let him bring it out. If he intends to get it on the shuttle, he will need an accomplice – one of the shuttle bay crew, or one of the flight crew."

"I could ground the shuttles," Landin suggested. He was watching Tymos closely as he said it.

Tymos straightened and leant forward.

"Sir, doing that might make him feel trapped. He will have Krys as a hostage, and may even kill her."

"He will expect us to be looking out for him."

"Yes, but if you don't make it a big thing that you know he has some of the ship, he may think you don't know about it. If you had a few guards around when the next shuttle is being loaded, that won't hurt. He will probably think he can outwit them, by seeming to be someone else. Having none would spook him."

"I think I understand your reasoning, but you are proposing that we leave your sister with him until tomorrow?"

Tymos nodded, and then spoke before Landin could protest. "He will expect Krys to be helpless for at least another half day, and fairly weak for a time after that. I am sure that he has a way to listen in to the searchers, but since you haven't found him so far, he will be feeling pretty safe. This way, Krys can tell us if he moves out of where he is, but if he wants to escape, the shuttle is the only way off base."

"Obviously, Kryslie is recovering from the effects of the stun much quicker than Alden and Darcy who are both still unconscious."

"Maybe, it was because of the holo-field," Tymos suggested, sitting back in his chair as if Krys's rate of recovery was nothing special.

Landin had the feeling that Tymos was avoiding his implied question and sighed internally. "I don't understand why he took her. All he needed to do was stun her and leave her like he did the others. He had to know that we would hunt him all the more to find her."

Tymos's voice was hard when he said, "I know why! That man called her an unnatural freak. He knew who she was, and I know who would like to have her discredited. I think he had to hide that piece of ship in the shuttle bay – even if Murtry didn't find it. And if, for some reason, he can't recover it, he will use her as merchandise."

Landin jerked. "I will not allow that."

"Nor will I! However, I don't want him feeling threatened."

Landin studied his red-headed Tech 2, and decided this was a different Tymos Ward than he had seen before. "You have a plan. What is it?"

Now that he was sure that Landin would agree, Tymos explained. "You are correct. Krys is recovering fast and will soon be able to defend herself. The man is not aware that she is awake and playing mind games with him. She is inserting snippets of ideas into his head and reading his thoughts, and listening to him talking to himself. She is also sending him the feeling of needing to get away as soon as he can."

"That's all very well, but what about the accomplices that you propose. I would like to see the last of the maggots in my crew."

"Well, if you order the search team to stand down and rest during beta shift, he will feel it is safe enough to sneak out then. I believe that he will stick to the maintenance tunnels for the most part, and I predict another rash of monitor malfunctions at the time."

"So, how do we identify him?"

"Well, I had the idea of installing back up monitors around the shuttle bay – ones that are controlled from a separate place, and completely independent of the main system, and will not be connected to the base computer."

"If he sneaks out, why don't we just take him?"

"If he has other stolen stuff hidden somewhere, we want him to collect it. If he is going to meet someone, we want to know who. If we let these people get to the point of loading stuff onto the shuttle illegally we have more to charge them with."

"What about Kryslie?" Landin insisted.

"After this evening, at any time that you order, she will take that man down."

Landin considered the plan. It had a high chance of success, but he didn't like it. Still, Tymos seemed to be sure of his sister's ability. He would have to trust that assessment.

"Is there anything else that you need us to do?"

"Before you get the security teams to stand down at the end of next beta shift, have them concentrate on searching the maintenance tunnels around the shuttle bays, the storage areas, and move inwards. I want them to make the man want to stay where he is."

"So you can install your extra monitors and he won't see you at work?" Landin guessed.

Tymos gave him a quick grin. "Do I have your permission to requisition what I will need?"

Landin nodded. "Report back when you finish."

Kryslie was glad to be finally moving. Her captor had known that she was awake for hours, but had completely ignored her as he prowled the small area, frequently pausing to jab fingers on the touch screen of a data padd. Finally, he had freed her feet, not realising that the energy binders – the most secure type of restraints yet invented – were almost devoid of energy. He still had a set on her wrists, which held her arms behind her, but they were in a state of charge no better than the ones he had removed. There was just enough energy left in them to maintain the magnetic attraction between the two halves.

He's stepped back and drawn an energy weapon, another of the weapons he had stolen from the guards.

"Up!" he gestured with the weapon, his voice harsh, and slightly accented.

Kryslie had been lying in the same position for nearly two days, and anyone else would have been almost too stiff to move. She was not as clumsy as she made out. Once she had been awake, she had drawn on the energy from the restraints to overcome the debilitating effects of the stun, and then to enable her to maintain tiny muscle movements – flexing and relaxing them – to be ready for this moment. There was also the walking cast to make her clumsiness seen more genuine.

The man cursed under his breath and strode closer, leaning down to drag her to her feet. For a thin man, not much taller than his prisoner, he had a solid strength. He twisted her arm when she seemed to crumple on the side with her injured ankle.

That had been a risk, but it seemed that the man did not realise that the ankle in the walking cast was better supported that the uninjured one. Though once she seemed to be standing steadily enough, he grabbed a pack from the floor and slung it over his shoulder, and picked up cargo crate about the size of a suitcase.

Then he gestured for her to move, and hissed, "Make no sound, or I will cut out your tongue."

As soon as he had released her feet, Kryslie had warned her brother that they were moving. Once the man gripped her arm and shoved her through what her eyes had thought to be a solid wall, she realised that it had been yet another hologram. He paused outside, released her long enough to do something with his data padd, and then shoved her again.

While walking as fast as most people could manage with the walking cast, Kryslie could sense the man's impatience. He had a narrow window of time to get to the shuttle that was being prepared for the trip to Earth, but had not allowed for Kryslie's slower than normal pace. He cursed again, and this time it was not in English.

Kryslie ignored him, and warned her brother that her captor had changed his face again, and sent a mental image to him. The information meant something, and moments later, Tymos said, "Hibbert, one of the Arboretum workers. He is meant to be leaving on the shuttle today, but he hasn't answered the boarding call. Has he anything with him?"

"Besides me? A pack and a crate. Have you found us?"

"Not yet...now I have. You are in the tunnel coming from between engineering and the storage section. He has done something to the monitors, so that section isn't showing on the security board. He has also done something so that random screen are blanking off for a moment and coming back on. I have the ones I installed scanning on a data padd – Murtry is looking positively malevolent."

Tymos quickly told her of the precautions being taken to prevent her captor from leaving on the shuttle, most matched the scheme they had thought up.

Kryslie was jolted to a halt in front of one of the narrow ladders that went between levels of the base. Her captor looked from the rungs of the ladder to her walking cast and made a rapid decision. His hand made a rapid gesture as if grabbing something from a harness, and suddenly, there was a knife in it, and it was slashing the bindings of the walking cast.

"That will stop you running off, freak," he hissed. "So don't try anything. My master won't care if you are damaged in transit."

If he thought he had her cowed and fearful, he was wrong. Kryslie stared back at him, as he sheathed the knife. It vanished from her sight, and the dark overalls he was wearing showed no sign of a weapons harness or sheath.

"So, you have some kind of hologram generator as part of that outfit," she thought to herself, as she listened to his next warning.

"Do not try to walk away from here. If you do, I will see that you are beaten until you beg for mercy."

Since she had no intention of letting him out of her sight, she allowed her face to show a flash of what he would think was fear, before returning to her impassive expression. It seemed that he was satisfied that she, a mere woman, was not going to escape. He quickly climbed up the ladder, carrying his pack and the case-like crate, and pushed open the hatchway. Once he had pushed his stuff through, he clambered down again.

"Climb up!"

You needed hands and feet to use the ladder, so Kryslie protested.

"How the hell can I do that? Are you going to free my hands?"

He had only wanted an excuse, his arm flew out and knocked her to the floor. And before she could try to stand, he wrenched her up and over his shoulder. It proved his strength once again, for she was not exactly a light weight, and he had to support her and shove her through the hatchway feet first, and then push her through.

In her mind, she sensed her twin's amusement. "Way to go, Krys. Don't make it easy for him."

She sent back, "I'm not. However, he is in a hurry. He's thinking it would be quicker to carry me!"

Once Tymos had confirmed where she was, Kryslie had been able to estimate her position when the man carrying her stopped. He put her down and fiddled with his data padd, he cursed softly – something about extra guards.

Just then, Tymos made an exclamation, "Where did you go?"

"Nowhere," Kryslie told him. "I think we are just outside the hatch leading into shuttle bay 1."

"Can you move a bit?"

Kryslie took advantage of her captor's momentary distraction, to slump to the floor and pretend to rub here injured ankle. She didn't fall far from her captor, but it was enough.

"So that's how he did it! He's got some kind of holo-screen generator."

"Yeah. One wall of the room where he had me was a hologram. He probably used one to hide while he was in the bay earlier."

She was grabbed with callous roughness and dragged to her feet. "Not a sound, or you will be very dead!"

In front of them, the hatchway opened and she was pushed through and yanked to a stop. Over a pile of crates, she could see the upper part of the shuttle that would be going down to Terra 1, being towed around from the hangar. The one that had just arrived had already gone around to maintenance where it would be refuelled and serviced. Her captor shoved her down, but not before she had a glimpse of someone in a maintenance section uniform, strolling towards them.

She grimaced, as if her foot was hurting, but it was a reason to half close her eyes so that no one would see them subtly change shape. Carefully, she moved her head and looked beyond her captor. As she had thought, there was a glowing area between him and the stack of crates. This must be like the field she had walked into – transparent from this side, but the other side showing the wall and hatchway behind her.

"I have told Murtry," Tymos told her. "He has a team coming in to block the way behind you."

"There are extra guards stationed in here?"

"Yes, but they are stationed around the shuttle. Obviously, they can't see you. What is the state of your captor?"

Kryslie gave herself a moment to read his body language, and to touch his mind. "He was impatient to get here, probably since he needed to answer the boarding call. He has to do that still, but right now, he's as jittery as hell."

The uniformed worker, came around the crates and gave a startled exclamation, "Where did you spring from? You'd better get into the lounge, they have security out looking for Hibbert."

The other ignored the question. "Have you got the stuff to knock her out?"

Even though she was seemingly looking away from the newcomer, Kryslie recognised him from the tone and accent of his voice. Only one person on the base spoke like he did, but she gave him a rapid glance to be sure.

"Bandik," she told her brother. "Can you see us?"

"I have you on my screen, and Landin is with me. The camera is behind you. I will move it so only your head shows. Be ready, Landin is talking to Murtry on the secure frequency."

Her patient wait was about to end, and she would have the satisfaction of showing this abomination of a man that he had chosen the wrong victim.

Satisfaction, sensed through their twin bond, prepared her for the command that came a moment later. "Landin says, to take him down."

It was the work of microseconds to rid herself of the wrist restraints. The two sections of the energy binders parted with ease, not completely because their power was nearly depleted, but because Kryslie was a great deal stronger than she seemed. Her awkward posture was converted to a crouch, and she edged sideways and leapt. She sprang further than anyone would have expected, and her full weight took her captor in the back. He staggered forward, knocking Bandik aside.

The maintenance tech quickly regained his balance and chose to scuttle away, even as Kryslie's victim twisted, intending to regain the upper hand. He saw she was free, and fired at her, saw her outlined in the energy but coming at him again. He tossed the weapon, thinking it depleted, and met her second rush, was ready to grab her and toss her — at the last second, she ducked, grabbed him and twisted. He went flying over her shoulder, landed heavily, and before he could try to counter her, found himself face down and hands like tight iron bands were holding him down, and a weight was on his back. Still, he struggled, desperately, but his attempts to buck Kryslie off had no effect. Then he began cursing her.

"Words are cheap," Kryslie told him as guards raced towards them.

More cursing, then, as the man insulted her antecedents.

"Think what you will, you son of a whore," Kryslie used his own curses on him. "But I was bait…and you hooked yourself."

The man tried again to buck her off as Murtry arrived.

"Good work, Ward. We'll take him from here."

Two pairs of arms leant over her shoulders to get a grip on the man. She eased back, keeping her weight on his legs, and fiddled with something near the man's ankle.

"Before I get off, you had better remove the rest of his weapons." Her eyes met Murtry's as she yanked on a wire that she had found by feel.

Suddenly, the dark grey clothing turned brown and a lethal array of assassin's weapons appeared – each in a sheath of a harness that clung to the man's body.

Kryslie moved back further, expecting that the man would try to kick her in the face, but he seemed to have capitulated and was letting the guards drag him up. That was until he was upright. Then, he began twisting with berserk fury, almost getting free. Kryslie moved up behind him and kicked his feet from under him, then jumped back to let Murtry apply some fully charged, energy binders to his feet. A second pair were applied to his wrists, as he tried to break his fall. He landed on the perma-crete, eyes still blazing with hatred. He was turned onto his back, and could do nothing to stop all of his hidden weapons from being removed. He watched Kryslie, standing beside Lunar 1's Security chief, and spat in her direction.

The gesture of defiance caused no reaction from Kryslie who simply stared back at him. Only her twin knew that she was forcing a compulsion on his mind. She would have some revenge, for the man would discover that he would not be able to kill himself, would not be able to stop himself answering questions and a moment later, could no longer struggle.

Watching from his office, Landin saw the implacable look on Krys's face and the sudden docility of the prisoner and decided not to ask what she had done.

"Stay here, Tymos," he directed, as he left to walk to the shuttle bay.

He arrived as the last of the prisoners weapons were being removed from within the clothing of the prisoner. He studied the face of the man and identified it. "David Hibbert!"

Since it wasn't a question, the man lied. "Yeah!"

Kryslie, still watching the prisoner, spoke clearly. "Don't be fooled. He is just using Hibbert's face. Dave is tied up in the crawler garage. He is using some actor's trick with fake skin."

The prisoner stared back at her, stunned. She knew what he was thinking and added, "You shouldn't have kept muttering under your breath. You didn't muffle my hearing."

Landin directed Murtry to secure the man in the shuttle bay's safe lock, and added, "I want him taken down on the shuttle. The IC will be advised so that they can arrange to meet him. Select two of your men to go with him."

The two men that were holding the prisoner, forced the man to walk. The safe lock was no more than three metres away, and once the man was forced inside, the door was sealed from the outside and the internal functionality reduced to simple life support.

Murtry watched the procession and finally turned back to Kryslie, removing his armour helmet and scratching his head.

"I'd sure like to have seen how you took that guy down. Only saw the end of it." He bent down and picked up the restraints that Kryslie had freed herself from. She saw him automatically checking the remaining charge. They were not fully depleted and would still hold a prisoner.

Kryslie smiled, but it wasn't a friendly smile. "People tend to underestimate me…because I am short, slight and not over-muscled. I could give you a demonstration…"

She heard her brother's warning thought. "Krys…"

He was still watching proceedings from Landin's office, where he had his extra cameras linked into his data padd. "Landin saw what you did – I couldn't change the camera angle too much."

Kryslie had a flash of an image of where her bother had placed the camera, and instantaneously calculated distances and angles. "He won't have seen all of it."

"Are you sure that it is a good idea?" Tymos persisted, as Murtry accepted her offer.

"Yeah, bro…it might make him forget to ask how I got out of the restraints."

To Murtry's, "Okay, show me!" challenge, she said, "Hold me like I was your prisoner, and you don't want me to try anything – remember, I'm dangerous."

The security guards who were not involved with the prisoner, spread out in a half-circle behind their chief, as Kryslie positioned Murtry. They watched intently as she repeated her twist, toss, grip and hold manoeuvre, suddenly, and without warning. She did however, slow the action, and with hold the full force of it.

She sensed Murtry's grudging respect.

"I'd like to learn that," he said pulling himself up and glared at the men who were grinning. "I reckon the lass could tie you lot in knots if I told her to. And I might! Jack, Mick, go pack a bag. You'll be going Earthside. The rest of you, go and reinforce the security on the prisoner."

Kryslie tried to slip away but Landin saw her.

"Not so fast! I have questions for you. I want a debrief from you. Go join your brother in my office."

He saw a fleeting look of annoyance on Krys's face, but it changed to a wry grin.

Tymos had just thought at her from Landin's office. "Be prepared to have your Great sized ego returned to a manageable size."

"Yes, Sir," she agreed meekly. "May I detour first?" He nodded, but before she walked away, asked, "How is your foot?"

"Feels ok. The prisoner removed the support thinking to make me less able to help myself."

"Foolish," Landin commented, gesturing for her to go off.

Kryslie went off at a slower than normal pace, realising that others besides Landin might notice that her ankle must have healed abnormally fast. She heard him give orders to bring the crate and bag the prisoner had carried, to his office.

"Show off," Tymos greeted her mildly when she entered Landin's office. He stood and dragged a second chair across to near his.

"I had some excess energy to get rid of. Getting caught so easily...!"

"Hmm," Tymos sympathised. "I was feeling like a great fool myself – a bit too full of myself."

Kryslie slumped into the chair. "Can I tell you that experiencing one of those neural shockers is an excellent aid to memory?"

"So is spending the night in the brig," Tymos admitted. "And I don't think that will be the end of it. We did disregard a few rules, even if we did catch that creature."

She sighed and they waited. It was half an hour before Landin returned to talk to them. When he did, she knew that he had been reporting to Basoli. His body language was tenser than normal as he asked for a report from Kryslie on her actions and subsequent events.

"Can you tell me where our prisoner kept you? Somewhere in the storage area at the back of engineering, was it?"

"Yes," Kryslie agreed. "I didn't have a good idea until we left there. Can I show you on the base schematic?"

She stood and moved to Landin's computer terminal, bringing up the plan of the base, enlarging the storage area, and pointing. Where she indicated was simply a corner of the area, which on the plan was not even fully enclosed.

"The guards searched through there," Landin said to himself.

"Did the searchers look for a holofield?" Tymos asked. "Remember, he used one to hide his escape route – must have been like a one-way window."

"I will ask the question," Landin decided. Then, "What did you do to that man? He can't answer our questions fast enough."

To save Kryslie from answering, Tymos said, "Having a young helpless female overcome you before you can fight back would be a big shock to an assassin's ego."

Landin waited but neither said anything more. "Very well. Kryslie, how did you get out of the secure restraints?"

Kryslie had no intention of trying to explain the abilities of a Tymorean Great One. "They must have malfunctioned, Sir."

Landin moved his gaze to a point above the heads of the two technicians, deciding he wasn't going to get an answer. He might have been counting to ten before he spoke again.

"I am glad to have you both on staff," he said carefully. "But you both disregarded orders given for safety reasons and were...lucky...not to have been badly hurt. Ah..."

He stopped Kryslie interrupting. "The crew of Lunar 1 are expected to obey direct orders. I do not want anyone else to get the idea that they can ignore orders. Would you want that, Kryslie Ward?"

"No, Sir," she agreed, neutrally. Her face did not betray her thoughts.

"Then you will understand why I must have you both stood down – as per WSRA rules of conduct."

"You are correct, Sir," Kryslie agreed.

"I am glad we understand each other," Landin said agreeably. He studied the two technicians, and was impressed once again. They were not at all cowed, but simply accepting of his verdict.

"The shuttle's departure is being delayed until arrangements are made for the IC to meet the prisoner at Terra 1. When it leaves, you will both be going on it. You will both need a flight bag."

"May I ask why you are sending us groundside, Sir?" Kryslie asked. Tymos thought he knew.

"Yes. Apart from the fact that you both should have some time off to recover from various injuries, you are to be seconded to Terra 1. They are still having intermittent problems with their tracking systems – since the trouble we had here. Commander in Chief Basoli requested that I send down two of my experts. I suggest that you keep out of his sight."

Tymos smiled faintly, ironically. "Was that the only reason for the timing of our departure?"

Keeping a straight face, Landin admitted, "No. I deemed it wise to have extra protection when we transfer the prisoner. I expect you to be alert for trouble."

"We understand," Tymos murmured.

"One last thing," Landin went on. "You will both report to medical for a check over. I want the doctor to check Kryslie's ankle, and your thigh wound. You are both damn fools for doing too much when you are recovering from injuries. Dismissed."

Chapter 17

The flight down was uneventful. The prisoner, who had been unconscious when he had been strapped into his seat, roused when they were six hours into the flight, but caused no trouble. Kryslie guessed that Murtry had been taking no chances, and it would have been easier to get the man into a flight suit if he was not conscious. She was aware of the prisoner's calculating thoughts, once he was aware of where he was. Ideas for escape, once they had landed, were passing through his mind. In his seat in the shuttle, he was securely restrained. He did wonder in passing who all the passengers were – he had known who was meant to be going to Earth on that flight, and had picked the injured Hibbert as the one most resembling him. He wasn't sure if one of the suited figures was Hibbert or not, but there were three more passengers than he knew of. He had to assume the extras were all his guards.

"I wonder what he would think if he knew you were a fellow passenger," Tymos thought at his twin.

"I don't really care," Kryslie decided. "I would rather he didn't know, just in case someone from the Imperium is going to represent him. All in all, I want our sojourn on Earth to be very low-key."

She was thinking of the media interest that she would have to elude, if they knew she was accessible.

Once the shuttle had touched down at Terra 1's space port, and taxied to the arrivals area, it was quickly surrounded by a phalanx of police cars. The prisoner and his two Lunar 1 guards, all still in the full flight suits, were the first to step down from the shuttle. They were met at the bottom of the extending stairs by a group of IC agents. Only when the prisoner was safely within a police van, did the remaining passengers receive the okay to disembark. By then, all of those within had removed the helmets, so they could breathe the fresh air.

On the walk across to the arrivals lounge, they carried the helmets, and kept them until they had divested themselves of their flight suits so helmet and suit remained together when they went to get cleaned and serviced. Attendants were available to help the infrequent passengers from their suits, but all of the passengers had done the trip to and from the moon often enough to need no help. By the time they were out of them, their small belongings packs had arrived.

Tymos and Kryslie waved to the three of their Lunar 1 co-workers who were going on leave, as they went towards the security check point to enter the Terra 1 base. Their WSRA IDs, in addition to a retinal scan, allowed them through with no trouble, and their first destination was the office of the base commander, Pieter Haldstadt.

In spite of it being late afternoon when they arrived, Haldstadt was waiting for them.

After a few formal pleasantries, greetings, asking about the flight, the prisoner, he got to business.

"I am really glad to have you here. Adam Landin assures me that you will be able to find and fix the problems we are having with our tracking array."

"Well, I know what the saboteurs did at Lunar 1," Kryslie told him. "I am not sure how they got access here, or others did, unless they sent a virus program by wireless transmission. We will soon sort out the problems and add a program to block future attempts."

"Excellent! Once you are finished here, the CIC wants you to check the tracking arrays at the other bases as well. There will be a WSRA jet available to take you from base to base."

Kryslie feigned a yawn, acting as if she hoped Haldstadt wouldn't see it. It had the effect that she hoped. The Terra 1 commander directed them to report to his senior controller the following morning, summoned his assistant to show them to their assigned guest quarters, and to link them into the base computer.

They could have found their own way, since they were familiar with the base from when they did the training before beginning at Lunar 1, but they accepted the courtesy.

Joe Finnigan, Haldstadt's aide, gave them the electronic keys to their rooms, ensured that they knew how to set the security seal, and gave them their passwords for the computer, grinned and left them to themselves.

Within moments of closing her door and setting the security seal, Kryslie had transmitted into her brother's room – the one next to hers. She was in time to see the mauve oval on the long range beam terminus appear. Tymos gestured for her to go first, and he transmitted immediately after.

The familiar surroundings of the Tymorean base materialised around them, as they stepped from the beam terminus. A tall brown haired man, hurried towards them.

"Jon!" Tymos greeted.

Their friend glanced at his watch, and didn't bother with formal greetings. "I can't stay here long. They have the prisoner in a high security prison outside of Miami. They are going to start questioning him shortly, and I have to be there. What can you tell me? Do you know his real name?"

Kryslie answered, "No, he was using five or six different persona. Landin should have sent Murtry's report. He questioned him up there, and we located the corner where he kept himself. We weren't privy to the questioning or the search of his hole."

"Yes, we have the reports from your base commander," Jon said quickly.

"Then all I can add is what he said when he thought me unconscious," Kryslie said quickly. She repeated the statement, and Jon's eyes widened in amazement.

"That Rasti creature was his brother! We couldn't find any relatives for him."

"Maybe Rasti wasn't his real name," Tymos suggested the obvious.

"Then he was using it for many years before his supposed demise," Jon told them. "I think I will dig a little deeper."

"Why don't you ask the prisoner…he should be very co-operative."

Jon's face creased slightly into a grin; he guessed that Kryslie had done something to the prisoner.

"We did ask him. He said his name was Nazim Farouk. However, he was resisting some questions."

"If you casually work into your questions a little foreign word…the Tymorean word for 'talk' – I think you will notice a difference."

Jon's smile turned to a grin. "Right! Thanks." He turned to walk off, but Kryslie had a question of her own.

"What is going on with Arthur bin Halil?"

"He's in IC custody. We met him on his return from Lunar 1. His father is threatening reprisals if he is not released. The general rumour is that we think he is involved in a matter under investigation. He is, however, a well-treated guest."

Kryslie nodded, satisfied, but Tymos asked, "What investigation is that? Rasti and his master?"

"It is. We have uncovered a lot of subversive activities, linked to Abdul bin Halil's country. Very complex and convoluted…"

"His foulness is that…"Kryslie muttered.

"His Eminence is denying all knowledge…"

"As usual!"

"You and plenty of others dispute the denial. Once we knew that Rasti was alive, not executed as was 'witnessed' – the perpetrator of a lot of hitherto unsolved matters seems clear. We have found links to His

Eminence. My superiors are making a case to take to the World Council, so they can get a mandate to question him as a hostile witness."

Seeing that Jonko was jiggling with impatience to get going, Tymos gestured him off. He must have had a pre-set location programmed into the long-range beam, for he remotely activated it and transmitted away almost immediately.

Tymos and Kryslie began to walk towards the common area of the base, and Tymos murmured, "I am glad that Arthur is being kept safe. I do not want to think that his father would try to blame him for all the subversive deeds."

"I wouldn't put it past him," Kryslie considered. "However, I do not think that he will. He will not want to risk the only male he sired. It is proof of his own maleness."

For a moment, their arrival went unnoticed by the relaxing base helpers, as well as Morin and Keleb who were intent on a game of draughts. The latter noticed them first, but merely grinned. Morin, seeing it, first thought that he was missing a move that would lose him the game, but then glanced over his shoulder. His eyes widened and he jumped to his feet, nearly disrupting the board pieces, twisted and gave them both the traditional formal bow. Then he trotted off towards the communications chamber.

Keleb leant back in his chair and suggested, "Take the weight off your feet. Are you staying long this time?"

Tymos sat in a chair to the side of the table and said, "We have some work to do at each of the WSRA bases."

"We will need to be back at Terra 1 tonight," Kryslie added.

Keleb sighed. "Isn't it time that you two took a vacation? I thought that was why you were here. Well, in addition to talking to Jonko."

"We have to check the tracking programs at all the bases," Tymos shrugged. "Then I guess we go back. Halstadt didn't say. So what are you up to?"

Keleb stared back at his friend as he drawled, "Me?" He decided it wasn't worth trying to argue with either Great One. "Our esteemed co-ordinator has given me the job of perimeter security. I am also the liaison to the group of missionaries who are working very diligently to have Abdul bin Halil legally deposed."

Kryslie went to another chair, and seemed to stare across the cavern. After a short while, she drew herself out of thoughts of her own and said, "He is not going to give up on trying to get at me."

A new voice advised, "Then it is all the more reason to keep away from him. Once he is discredited, the rumours he started will be forgotten."

Privately, Kryslie doubted it, but decided not to disabuse her father of the hope. "We do have to visit Terra 5," she said instead. "Though without Prince Arthur being there, we may be able to keep our visit low key. Unless his Eminence has other spies there."

"We could aim to be there during the night duty shift," Tymos suggested. "Get there earlier than expected."

"Or I could dye my hair black," Kryslie countered.

Daniel glanced upward, his children were very good at changing the subject. After possibly counting to five, he said, "Are you at least staying for a meal? We are all enriched by your company."

They returned to Earthbase just over a fortnight later. Since they knew what had caused the malfunctions to the Lunar 1 tracking system, they only needed to spend a day at each of the other WSRA bases. The intervening days were spent travelling. They went from Terra 1 in Florida, to Terra 2 – in the wilds of Russia, then onto Terra 4 and Terra 3 in eastern and Western Europe respectively. After that they went to Terra 5, arriving late evening when most of the staff had gone for the day, and working all night so that they could be gone by the morning. Commander Mansour had not questioned their choice of work times, just accepting that working when the base was nearly empty meant they could work faster and interruptions to the regular work would be reduced.

Once they were away from the city of Hadjibad, and out of Karshada altogether, and without any indication that Abdul bin Halil knew they had been in his country, both Tymos and Kryslie were relieved. They went from there to Terra 8, the newest base in China, and on to Terra 7 in England and Terra 6 in Australia. In each place, the Commanders were impressed by their skill and efficiency, and offered places there if they ever chose to make a change from Lunar 1.

When they reported back to Commander Haldstadt at Terra 1, and requested space on the next upward shuttle to Lunar 1, the request was denied.

"I am told that you are due some time off," was all Haldstadt chose to say. "You don't need to stay on base, just to stay available. I will see you are given WSRA communicators – unless you have your units from Lunar 1."

The attempts to discover why they had to stay Earthside were ignored by the Commander. So, accepting the dismissal, they sought a different source of information. It was nearly time for the mid-shift meal break, and they knew that Haldstadt's aide was likely to be taking his usual early lunch.

"So, what's the deal, Joe? We aren't allowed to leave yet," Tymos asked Haldstadt's aide as he and Kryslie placed their food trays on across a table from him. "We've done what we were sent down to do."

He didn't mention that their work was co-incidental with being stood down for a time, since that should have ended by then, and he didn't mention the need to recover from injuries, for they were already well healed.

"I'm not privy to the reason," Joe Finnigan admitted, speaking around a mouthful of hamburger and salad. His hands were holding the bun where it further muffled his voice. He finished the mouthful and continued. "The Commander has been in meetings all week – with the CIC and the IC. He said you were free to go wherever you wished, so long as you stayed available."

"Yeah, that's what he told us. He didn't say how long we needed to be down here," Kryslie persisted.

Joe shrugged, having just taken another bite. His next words were, "Hey, consider it a paid vacation. There's more to do down here than up on the moon!"

Tymos grinned, as if he agreed. It wasn't as if they had an urgent need to be back up at Lunar 1, just a preference to stay out of the attention of the media, if they were still after Kryslie.

Kryslie began to eat her sandwich, but at the same time, mentally conversed with her brother.

"Do you think this is still part of being stood down, or Landin's idea of us having a rest, or something else?"

She saw Tymos's faint shrug, and heard his mind voice, "No doubt we will find out, and if we want to avoid the CIC, we could always go and visit Daniel."

"Who will probably say we should have a vacation." When she paused between bites, Kryslie added, aloud, "So, what's the definition of available, if we can go where we please?"

Joe wiped his hands on a paper napkin and thought on the question. "I guess, so that you can get back in an hour."

"That doesn't give us much scope," Tymos said. "Well, tell the Commander that if he wants us he can have us paged. We still have the comm units he gave us before we went travelling."

Without prompting, Joe began to give them a verbal tour of places that they 'just had to visit'.

Kryslie listened with half her attention, and finished eating. Tymos was feigning greater interest, since he had only fetched himself coffee. They exchanged a glance between them that said, without either words or thoughts, that Joe's ideas of a 'good time' didn't mirror their own. The other man wanted physical excitement, not mental stimulation.

When they were back in their guest quarters, they logged onto the base computer, entered a number of tourist places they 'planned' to visit, a means to contact them, and an estimated return date two weeks ahead. Then, using their personal communicators, requested a long range beam so they could return to the Tymorean Base.

They arrived mid-afternoon, but by the same evening, Daniel had had enough of them.

"Great Ones, there is nothing going on that needs your personal attention. The matter of bin Halil is proceeding but will take time. Farouk, the man you caught, is being very helpful to the Investigative Committee who may still want to talk to both of you. This is probably the reason you do not yet have permission to return. Or it may be so your Greatnesses take a holiday."

Kryslie gave her brother a mental, "I told you so," and then protested aloud, "Daniel, we don't need a holiday. We have been in five countries in the past two weeks."

"That was work! And at the speed you whizzed around the world, I am surprised that you do not need to sleep for a week," Daniel argued with them, scandalising Morin who was listening – as usual.

"When, since you both started at Lunar 1 – have you taken time off?" Daniel persisted.

"But..." Tymos tried.

"No buts!"

"We have a job to do," Kryslie argued. "We are missionaries."

"Not ordinary missionaries," Daniel stared them down. "Ordinary Tymorean missionaries, of which I have many working under me, have been doing their jobs for millennia without the hovering presence of two Great Ones."

"But..." Kryslie tried.

"Take a break! Go and find out what young people of your apparent age do for fun, do for entertainment. So when you go back to the rarefied atmosphere of Lunar 1. You can talk about something other than astro-science and computing."

"Daniel, we don't have time for frivolous..." Tymos tried to object.

"If something comes up – I will call you back," Daniel promised.

Kryslie and Tymos exchanged glances.

"And I want you to spend the next two days at least fifty kilometres away from each other. Go! Shoo!"

From just inside the door of Daniel's private suite, they heard a snicker. Tymos glared in that direction.

"Morin," Daniel said warningly. The young man bowed his head and apologised for his disrespect.

"I still don't know what you expect us to do," Kryslie muttered to Daniel as she began to leave.

"You are both quite intelligent. I expect you will figure it out," Daniel assured them.

All Kryslie caught from Morin's mind was, "meet people, get connected, start something". Daniel waited until he was sure the Great Ones had departed before berating his aide.

"If you don't learn to keep out of my head, young Morin, I will have you assigned back to Tymorea."

"But, boss, you can't talk to Great Ones like that!"

"I can and I will, when it is needed," Daniel told him. "They have learnt to respect their elders, and I changed their diapers when they were small. Who can advise them if not their father?"

"Father? But they are High King Tymoros's children."

"Fostered, like you, because of what they were to become. They were born on this world, as was I."

Morin was stuck for words. Finally, in a more sober tone he said, "You didn't tell them about the beacon."

"It stopped. We will be alerted if a ship comes this way. There is nothing that can be done."

"I guess Daniel is right," Kryslie remarked to her brother. "We haven't explored the oceans on Earth."

They were sitting on a sandy beach not far from Terra 1, and watching the ocean.

Tymos commented, "Nor seen all the interesting places."

"We have never had the time," Kryslie remarked. "Though, right now, I feel there is something I should be doing."

"Having fun, according to Daniel," Tymos reminded her. "And I wonder what that imp, Morin, meant by 'meet people, get connected, start something' – he thought it was funny."

"Hmm," Kryslie tried to figure it out. "I guess we really are out of touch with normal humans. Perhaps that's why Daniel said to split up – we could meet twice as many different people and compare notes later."

"Well, I think I might visit that marine science place down the coast," Tymos mused.

"And I might check out that resort I heard a couple of the Terra 1 officers talking about," Kryslie decided.

Kryslie arrived back at Earthbase ten days later, mere moments before her brother.

Daniel turned to meet them and studied them both, noting that both had dyed their hair and were looking tanned and relaxed. He nodded and seemed highly satisfied.

"I hope you both met some nice young people and got connected..." Daniel commented as he turned to walk towards a hibernating computer screen. He hid his smile.

Both Tymos and Kryslie were blushing furiously. Neither glanced at the other.

"Yes, Father," Kryslie finally acknowledged with mild sarcasm. "And this time I ensured that I did not start something."

"Sensible," Daniel said mildly. "Now, while you were away, young Morin thought of a way to settle that rumour about Krys."

"Oh? Clever of him – what is it?" Kryslie asked. She was glad of the change of subject.

Daniel went to a bench near the screen - it looked like he was using it as an office. He passed a folder to Kryslie and she scanned the contents.

"I see Morin excelled at forgery and artefact ageing," Kryslie remarked. "We missed that class."

Tym looked over her shoulder. "Aren't the dates a bit out?"

"Yes," Daniel spoke seriously. "But I am your natural father. I have some hair from your birth mother. DNA tests of you, me and the hairs will prove paternity and kinship. The documents will prove my age and date of marriage. The relevant data bases have this information. I will claim I forgot to have you registered due to this and that and moving around. If they dig hard enough, they will find hospital records in a small town further east."

"Tell Morin he is brilliant," Kryslie approved. "However, I won't produce this until I have no choice. You see, I did not want to disturb my sick and ageing father."

Daniel smiled.

Tymos asked, "Was this all you called us back for?"

"No." Daniel shook his head and brought up a grid on the computer screen. It showed a line moving inward.

"We had word from the relays of a two person ship heading into Earth's system. We have just picked it up now. Prior to that it might have gone past."

"Any identification possible?" Tymos asked immediately, and his attention went to studying the screen.

"Aeronite," was all Daniel said.

"What?" Kryslie and Tymos spoke together, focussing their attention on him.

"That is what Governor Reslic's message stated."

"I'd like to know how they even knew about Earth, let alone found it," Kryslie said.

"This one and the wrecked one," Tymos emphasised. "Has there been any information sent down from Lunar 1?"

"Not that we have intercepted," Daniel said.

"We need to get back up there," Tymos stated.

"That might be why you have orders to return to Terra 1. You have little over half an hour. However, the scanners on your moon base will not detect this ship for another ten days."

Kryslie gave her father a hug, forgetting her irritation with his scheming and the delay in yelling them of the ship. "Can you activate the beam for us please, Dad."

Kryslie and Tymos went straight to their assigned quarters after disembarking from the shuttle at Lunar 1. On checking their schedule, both noted that Landin had set up a meeting with them for two hours after the start of gamma watch next day. Which was a relief, since the eight hour flight had been tiring, especially since take off had been delayed for several hours by bad weather. And that had allowed the C-I- C to find them and insist on a short meeting. He hadn't done so to commend them on their work, but to try once again to insist on a blood sample from Kryslie.

He had not been happy when she had quoted certain regulations about personal rights back at him.

Basoli had masked his annoyance, outwardly, but his thoughts, that he was unwittingly projecting, were unsettling. In his mind he was convinced she was some kind of 'freak'. All the publicity about her supposedly being older than she looked, was he felt, adverse to the image of the WSRA. It looked like they were hiding insurgents from the Investigative Committee. Even changing her hair colour could not alter that.

As well as having his mind shout 'freak', Basoli half believed that she had been an insurgent ten years ago, because she was prone to disregarding rules now.

Krys had had to grit her teeth and try to ignore it. What she had done ten years before was not try to start a war, but to break up a cabal that was. She knew who was behind the cabal, but Abdul bin Halil, to clear his name, had repudiated all the members of the conspiracy and claimed that she was part of it – the only one to escape. So the Investigative committee still wanted that woman and bin Halil wanted her dead

When the shuttle was finally cleared for take-off, Kryslie had managed to push aside the sour feeling that the meeting had given her, but both she and her brother were concerned by how Basoli would react to the news of another alien ship. This one would not have a dead crew. They had plenty of time during the flight up, to consider the implications of the approaching Aeronite ship and their conviction that Basoli would want the occupants locked up and treated like prize specimens.

Landin was sticking strictly to business and had only blinked at Kryslie's blond hair, which contrasted with the black colour that Tymos had used again.

"Excellent work on the tracking systems. Basoli was impressed, as were each of the Commanders," he praised them.

Kryslie flicked her brother a look that that needed neither thought or word, but clearly said, "He might have told us that himself."

Landin went on oblivious to the exchange, "I've put Shelby onto learning the radio tracking and moved Nathan up to the Auto-tracks on delta shift."

Kryslie gave him her full attention, expecting that a reassignment was coming.

"Now that things have quietened down, I have decided to reassign Kryslie to Ericson. He has some ideas on force shields that he wants to develop."

Landin smiled faintly, seeing a more intent look come onto Kryslie's face.

"And me, Sir?" Tymos prompted.

"Hmm," Landin pretended to be thinking. "I might move you to working under Chief Delaney, in Engineering. He is having trouble integrating a few computer programs to work with the scanners. It will be a bit of a challenge for you. Don't let that manner of his unsettle you."

Tymos's thought was, "Better him than Basoli."

Kryslie thought back, "Does he know? Has he had a premonition?"

Tymos's reply was forestalled by Landin taking two sheets of paper from an 'eyes only' folder on his desk and passing one to each of them.

He was watching for their reactions. Tymos hid his well, but Kryslie didn't try as hard.

What they each held was a copy of a signed and declared certificate – Doctor of Astro-Sciences. The award they had not received because they had left Washington University just before they were due to graduate.

After Basoli's blatant suspicions, the former Vice Chancellor of the University, Don Gilchrist, had just shown he had forgiven them and they had his tacit trust.

"I have read the university reports on the work done there," Landin carefully didn't say, "your work."

He went on, "I am gladder than ever to have you here. The comments of Dr Emmanuel were extremely complimentary."

"And the personal file?" Tymos asked, now studying Landin in turn.

"Still accurate," Landin returned his gaze. "As recent events have proved to the benefit of Lunar 1."

Tymos nodded and handed his sheet of paper back. "Thanks for passing that on. I don't think we need to keep a copy." Landin nodded. He understood that this 'evidence' should be destroyed. Kryslie passed her sheet back too. "When do we report to our new assignments?"

"As soon as you like," Landin told her. "However, do try to have one sleep shift per rotation."

Kryslie grinned faintly and rose from her seat, but Landin hadn't finished.

"You may, however, be reassigned if need arises. So keep the controller tabs on you uniform. Ericson will give you R and D ones. Dismissed."

"Well, that's convenient," Tymos remarked. "I didn't have to request a change of assignment."

Krys repeated her earlier thought aloud. "Does Landin know?"

"Unlikely. He knows aliens exist, aka us. We found an alien ship on the moon – others might come. He is thinking worst case and preparing for it. And he thinks we know better than he does of what to expect."

"We do," Krys agreed soberly. "And I hope the worst that follows is only Aeronite."

"Too true," Tymos agreed. Neither formalised the thought that Tymorean Great Ones were not usually involved in minor matters. And the Tymorean Elders had foretold that they had an important part to play on Earth, where they were born.

Chapter 18

Commander Landin had only been asleep for three hours when the message tones of his computer woke him with an urgent summons to main mission. Immediately alert, he rose and dressed in a fresh uniform, aware of the importance of appearing ready for anything even when it was almost at the end of alpha shift. The command suite, which was separate from his office, was situated close to main mission and connected to it by a private corridor. Even though no one would see him, he didn't run just kept to a purposeful walk. The summons was urgent, not priority.

The duty controller nearest the door announced Landin as he entered. A piece of anachronistic protocol that he barely heard anymore. "Commander Landin is on deck, Sir."

Chief Controller Stanley turned from talking to one of his controllers and met Landin as he approached.

"Our long range scanners have picked up a metallic mass approaching from sector seven, Sir."

"Visuals?" Landin requested.

"It is at extreme range," Stanley reported. He told the senior shift controller to magnify the bright 'blip'.

"Trajectory projection?" Landin asked next, and a second controller reported.

"We are feeding the data into the computer, Sir, but we cannot give an accurate course prediction or ETA yet."

"Report to me when you have preliminary predictions," Landin said tersely. "First priority is to confirm the object's composition and configuration. Stanley, get Chief Delany up here."

Landin studied the screen, but kept his face calm, in spite of the sudden surge of adrenalin.

All sightings in the past three years had been small meteorites – the majority of which had passed safely beyond Earth. Only three had needed destruction and the weapons array on Lunar 1 had attended to one and the long range shuttles to the other two. This was likely to be another.

"Communications – report the sighting to Terra 1," Landin instructed. He relaxed his stance and noticed a corresponding relaxation in all the duty crew. Not that they were not still highly alert, but now they had the subconscious assurance that all was under control.

Landin glanced around, catching a hint of movement where he had not expected it – at one of the consoles that was unmanned during alpha shift. He moved to one side and saw Kryslie Ward seated there and in the middle of activating it. This was the one that had been reserved for testing

Delaney's program. He didn't approach it right away, but did wonder where her brother was and if those two ever slept. He had insisted that Ericson and Delaney ensure that the two technicians had an eight hour break each rotation. Then he realised that he hadn't seen either of them around the mess areas or relaxation areas at all since they had returned from Earthside over a week ago. That caused a shiver of apprehension and now he walked over to Kryslie Ward and watched over her shoulder.

"I thought your brother was working on that object recognition program," he remarked.

Kryslie did not seem surprised to hear his question. "He is, Sir, but I am more familiar with the tracking programs. I have been spending a few hours each day helping out."

"Where is your brother?" Landin asked.

The answer came as a hand gesture, indicating the floor where two feet were visible. They began to wriggle and legs began to emerge from under the console. Finally Tymos brought his head into view, spotted Landin watching him and saluted with a micro spanner in his hand and a grin on his face.

Landin waited for Tymos to get to his feet, to ask for a report of what he was doing.

"I was connecting a dedicated feed line from down level to here. The Chief wasn't ready to upload his program onto the main computer yet."

"Well the Chief seems to have excellent timing," Landin commented neutrally. "How soon will the program be working?"

"Just testing the inputs now," Kryslie reported crisply. "I need to check the various subprograms after that."

"Proceed," Landin directed, moving back to where Stanley was overseeing everything.

"It is not the same sector where the three meteorites came from," Landin remarked quietly.

"No, Sir," Stanley agreed. He then added, "And I can't help thinking of that wreck in the shuttle bay."

"It is not beyond possibility that it is one of the lost probe ships returning," Landin surmised. "Unlikely as it is."

"If that were it, there will be a horde of scientists wanting at it," Stanley commented.

"Indeed," Landin concurred, thinking, that if it was an actual alien ship it would be more than just scientists wanting to see it. "I will be in my office for a while. Advise me if anything changes."

Once in his office he called through to engineering. Sub-chief Kapetti answered and agreed to come to Landin.

"What's the status of the meteorite screen over the base?" Landin asked immediately.

"Running at optimal," Kapetti reported at once. "Maintenance and diagnostics are all up to date. We are running a duplicate power grid at the moment as Ericson has some new shields he wants to try out. He has had Ward spending time constructing specialised bits for the generator."

"Kryslie Ward?" Landin queried.

"No, Sir, her brother." Kapetti didn't think that was odd, but it made Landin thoughtful.

"Did Sam Ericson explain the new concept?" Landin made a note to himself to talk to Ericson later. He knew his R and D Chief was working on ideas, but not that he was close to testing them.

After finding out all Kapetti knew about the new shields, which was little enough, he dismissed the man back to his work. He began to wonder what was driving two particular technicians and what they knew that he didn't.

He was sure that they would not withhold any vital information and would answer to his direct questions. The problem was to ask the right questions. For now, though, he would let them keep at what they were doing. He would talk to Ericson.

After rousing Ericson from his sleep period, and discovering how much 'spare' time had been filled by both Ward siblings in departments other than their assigned ones — Landin was certain that the object they were tracking was a ship and not of human origin.

He kept that notion to himself. His staff would know soon enough and probably by using that program that Kryslie was operating. Then he realised they were helping to perfect shields too — were they expecting trouble?

Ericson explained that the new shields would block energy discharges and had spoken of protecting important buildings from lightning and possibly lasers, such as the long range shuttles used on meteorites.

And, Landin now mused, possibly other things that hadn't been mentioned. Ericson said he wanted to extend the coverage of the screens to cover the Auto-tracks as well if he could ensure that they would not distort the incoming signals. That was an excellent idea when considering that missile attack. Auto-track 1 was still out of commission.

After sending the R and D Chief back to bed, Landin decided to see what Delaney's program was giving them. It would give his mind something to think on besides the desire to sleep.

Kryslie Ward, clad in duty uniform, still looked as alert as ever and her screen was flickering through 3-D projections of every kind of air and space craft ever built on Earth. On a small inset window, was a similar 3-D graph representation of the distant object which now had a vaguely elongated shape.

"So, when do you expect it to get here?" Landin asked quietly. Krys took on a listening attitude, and he noticed she had a tiny earpiece in.

"Just over two days to the point of nearest approach," she reported, still keeping her attention on the program.

"How did you..." Landin began, when Controller Moore reported.

"Object is moving extremely fast, Sir. ETA at nearest approach is 52 hours. If it maintains its current course it will pass the moon and reach Earth."

Kryslie had a faint smile on her face as Landin glanced at her. In spite of his feeling that she had known this object was coming and probably knew what it was – this time she could have made her own calculations from the track data.

He didn't comment, even mentally, and strode off towards his office. He hardly heard, "The Commander has left the deck."

Landin returned to Main Mission after getting a few more hours of sleep. He noticed that Delaney's program was now running in a quarter of the main screen.

The object was vaguely ship-like but none of the 'closest' matches was at all like it. The rest of the screen displayed a projected trajectory and a red blip at the current coordinates. A digital timer in the corner of the screen gave the ETA. It did seem to be heading to Earth, but then, that other ship might have been heading there too, before it crashed on the moon.

In a glance around, he saw all the controllers concentrating on their screens, but glancing frequently at the main display. He noticed in that glance that Tymos Ward had replaced his sister. Hopefully, that meant that Kryslie was sleeping.

Kryslie Ward wasn't. Though if Landin asked the computer to check where she was, it would say her quarters. She was actually in the Tymorean base on Earth, where there was a much clearer picture of the approaching craft on the scanner screen.

"It is definitely an Aeronite scout craft, modified for extended travel," Lexina told Kryslie. "So far, no sign of other craft."

"Have you interpolated its course?" There was a line indicating a position far back in space.

"The best estimate from data available," Lexina specified. "Puts it leeward of Zekos when Aerdna transcended Pi sector."

Kryslie considered that. "Any indication of deep sleep technology?"

Lexina nodded. "When we first detected it, we did not notice life signs. Now we are reading two – both Aeronite. Though the last I heard was that the Aeronite colonies in Pi sector were not advanced enough to pose a threat to planets here in San sector. But, lots of ships did leave Aerdna before the transcession."

"The only people with space going ships were the Aeronite Power Council and the Warlords," Krys remarked. "Who, no doubt, took over control in the colonies. Who do we have on Zekos now? Can they throw light on this?"

"There have been no reports from Zekos for over a year," Lexina said. "Stenn Reslic was assigned there."

Kryslie suppressed a shiver. She saw Daniel re-enter the chamber.

"I have requested that Homebase send another missionary to Zekos to look for information on that ship," he reported.

"Thanks. Though it might not be possible. The transcession of Aerdna occurred before the missionaries were sent out again after the war."

"It can't have been that many years," Daniel argued.

It had been a long time, but Daniel had been in the city of Dira when the Guardians had placed all the protected cities in stasis.

"Well, we will see what can be found. Though what I think might be wise is if that ship could be subtly diverted to Lunar 1."

"Certainly, Great one," Daniel agreed. He went off again.

Lexina glanced at Kryslie. "Basoli?" she guessed the reason. "Bynan says he is glued to the monitors at Terra 1."

"And will be on the first shuttle up if it lands at Lunar 1," Kryslie predicted. "But I want to keep an eye on him."

She was about to say more but heard a faint buzz. She glanced at her wrist device and a tiny yellow light flashed. Tymos was alerting her to being wanted at Lunar 1. "Activate the beam back please."

Kryslie arrived in her quarters and quickly changed into her sleep wear and tousled her hair - pretending to have been roused from sleep. Although she hadn't actually slept, she had refreshed her mind by sitting in the tiny underground garden at Earthbase for a short while, drawing on the Earth power. To do this she needed to be directly touching the ground, and she had removed her foot wear. Now she glanced at her feet and saw they were dusty. She quickly found her slippers and drew them on as the door chime tinkled.

Since she had supposedly been sleeping, she didn't answer right away. Instead she first let her mind sense who was at her door before activating the door opener.

"Sir?" she queried Ericson who was her current superior. His hand was raised as if he was about to ring the chime again.

"May I come in? I know it is early, or rather late since I saw you up late."

Kryslie nodded, and waited until he was in and the door closed before she gestured him to a chair.

"How can I help you?"

"Landin got me up and now I can't sleep. My mind is full of what ifs...since there is that unknown ship approaching. He says we can't assume it is hostile, but I feel we dare not assume it is not. Your ideas added to mine have been ground breaking, but what if it isn't enough? Have you ideas on how we can do better?"

"What type of event do you fear?" Kryslie asked before answering his questions.

"We might not have enough power for the shields to hold. They might use 'dirty' bombs like radiation bombs, and the whole gamut of ideas from a century of fantastic fiction."

"Some of those fantastic ideas exist now," Kryslie agreed, but she went on, "I get my ideas from looking back over the early works of Grainger and Emmanuel."

As she intended, that provoked Ericson to think of the 'Grainger Exhibit' as it was known twenty years before. Only since the puzzle had been solved, and Emmanuel had been credited with that, much research had been done.

"That is certainly an idea. I am sure Grainger knew more about force fields than he revealed."

Kryslie made no comment on that except to say, "I need more sleep right now, but I will let my subconscious work on it."

Then Ericson asked a different sort of question.

"Do you think the beings on that ship are dangerous?"

"Is it manned?"

"Surely it is," Ericson proposed.

Kryslie wished she knew what had prompted the question. "Sir, I don't know. If it is, I'd like them to be friendly. Who knows what we might learn from them. And if they are hostile, I'd prefer a solid defence to weaponry."

Ericson rose, saying, "I think that I agree with you." He apologised for disturbing her and walked to the door.

"Tym?" she thought at her brother, once her visitor had gone. When he returned a thought, she told him of her visitor and what he had asked. "What do you think?"

"Odd," Tymos sent back. "I know he and Landin were discussing the new shields and I don't think Landin would have said anything to make Ericson think you were different. I thought he was satisfied with what we helped him make."

"So did I," Kryslie agreed. "And I don't think one ship with old Aeronite technology can penetrate that shield. It does more than we implied, and he will realise it if we get attacked."

"Still..." Tymos was thoughtful. "The Aeronites never used radiation bombs..."

"Humans have in the past. And the Ciriot did."

"There has been no sighting of any Ciriot since the return," Tymos said. "If there had been, we would have been told."

"Yes..." Kryslie agreed with a shiver of premonition. "And at the moment there is peace down on the planet..."

"I think we need to get Homebase to send more of those crystals Grainger used," Tymos suggested.

"We can't protect everywhere planetside."

"Then we don't let any situation get that big," Tymos told her. "And that is for later. Right now, they've noticed the deviation in the track of that ship. I almost wish we had our personal ships here so go and check it out."

"I really don't think letting them suspect that Tymoreans are around would be a good idea," Kryslie countered. "We don't know what the ordinary Aeronites think of us."

"True enough. Go back to sleep," Tymos finished.

Tymos turned his attention back to his screen where the program was portraying the 3-D representation of the ship and a second window showed its course. The change in course was gradual, but it was becoming obvious that the ship would now land on the moon.

"Well, I am pretty damn sure that is nothing of ours," Dom Marks, the controller sitting next to Tymos, stated. He had helped to enter all the old Earth flying craft into the recognition program. "I think the sky watchers below are gonna be right this time."

"So it seems," Tymos agreed. "I hope we don't ruin this chance to be friends with an alien race."

"What if they want to take over Earth?" Marks shot back.

"I will think again if they return our cautious greetings with guns and lasers," Tymos told him.

"That might depend on who sends the polite greetings and who first questions them," Marks commented with a sly side-long glance towards the centre well.

"Oh?"

"Geeze, Ward. The last person who should get near them is the C-I-C. He'd arbitrarily confiscate their ship and stick them under a microscope as if they were new animals. He has some really weird ideas about other intelligent life."

"That is enough of that, Mr Marks," Landin spoke sharply

"Sorry, Sir," Marks said instantly. "I am really trying to say that the C-I-C shouldn't risk himself."

"I will take that as the reason," Landin decided. He was beginning to agree with the sentiment that he had heard mentioned more than once before this.

However, Marks' first statement was sensible. Even if keeping Basoli away was not possible. He was coming up on the morning shuttle.

Landin decided to take a lesson from Tymos and Kryslie Ward, act first, apologise later. He moved to the shift Controller, Tony Hendricks.

"Have someone with linguistic skills here at the start of gamma shift. I want to send out a message of greeting to that ship," Landin proposed.

"Aye, Sir," Hendricks agreed.

The morning shuttle docked in bay one, which was not the one where the alien wreck was. As soon as the shuttle pilot disengaged the door seals, and opened the airlock entry, Basoli strode out, still wearing the gold tinged metallic flight suit.

He was followed by President Adamson, Abdul bin Halil, and six other men. Two had the attitude of bodyguards and the other four were glancing around in varying degrees of wonderment.

The arrival was being shown on screens around the base.

Tymos was in engineering when he spotted bin Halil on the screen.

"Your old friend is here," he warned his sister mentally.

"I saw," was Kryslie's reply. "He's got a nerve coming here, since he might be arrested on his return. Still, I suppose he has to maintain face, which is probably why he was scowling coming off the shuttle behind Adamson."

She had paused the work she was doing for Ericson to watch the screen, and seemed to go back to concentrating on some calculations once the arrivals had divested themselves of the flight suits and gone off to a briefing. In fact, she was 'listening' into the mind of Ron Basoli, as he listened to the reports by the senior technicians. They were giving out all the information that was known about the approaching ship that was still twelve hours away.

Basoli had his own agenda worked out, and was considering the data he was hearing with that in mind. Kryslie knew when he left the briefing, ordering Landin with him.

Landin must have tried reminding his chief, that under emergency conditions that the base commander is in charge.

Basoli had told him, "This isn't an emergency, this is history. It is bigger than just Lunar 1. Now, send me an assistant that can understand all this technical data and not some wet behind the ears clerical aid."

Even the clerical staffs on Lunar 1 were highly skilled and understood the technical jargon - so his comment bordered on discrimination. Too bad he hadn't brought his usual PA with him. Bynan knew how to manage him.

Landin's first choice was a Tech 1, who had worked in just about every section on Lunar 1. That man lasted half an hour. It was not surprising, since Basoli wanted a drudge, not an assistant. The Tech 1 had rightfully objected to his manner.

Basoli told Landin to get 'one of those technicians that sorted out the tracking problem so quickly'.

Kryslie expected the intracom to summon her, but it was Ericson that sent her to Landin. She appreciated his tact in not reminding bin Halil of her existence. She was told to assist Basoli who was using the base commander's office. Landin said he would be back in the briefing room where Adamson and bin Halil were being cautiously polite to each other.

Kryslie had merely nodded, not completely displeased to be given the drudge job. It would give her an excuse to watch Basoli. And she could keep her temper.

Basoli kept her busy bringing data updates, sending memo's to various section heads, and generally listening to his plan of action for dealing with the visit of the aliens.

In his favour, he was not assuming they would be friendly, and he had the weapons stations on alert in case they came in shooting. If they came in quietly, acting friendly, he had plans to bring them into the base, at first only as far as the shuttle bay. He intended to cut them off from their ship, which was in Kryslie's mind, provocative. Before then he would insist that he base be locked down, with all off duty and non-essential personnel sent to quarters and sealed in. That would be tech 2's and equivalent levels down. Kryslie frowned at that. He planned on having security very obviously everywhere. It was all very well, but she could see countless flaws in his plans. Including his assumption that the visitors didn't intend to stay , that they knew anything useful, that their intent was no more than saying hello and they would willingly let themselves be examined and probed and have their ship thoroughly scrutinised.

She also had the distinct feeling that the two occupants were not going to be what Basoli expected.

The hours counted down and with the passing of time, caution had been emphasised.

There was an atmosphere of excitement mixed with apprehension and the inbred fear of the unknown.

The interception party was on standby. Basoli had insisted on leading it and he had Landin, Mick Schultz, the linguist, two of the scientists and a dozen purple clad security officers in the group.

Armoured EA suits were on hand, assuming that they would be meeting outside of the base shields.

Krys intended to be taken along. She was proving to be such an efficient aide, almost a shadow to Basoli, and anticipating his needs so that she had what he wanted within seconds of asking for it.

Chapter 19

The serious alien diplomats and scientists that Basoli envisioned brought their ship to a stop using the simple technique of pausing the auto-program.

"This is not where we are meant to be," a young, humanoid girl told her brother.

"It is where the program sent us!"

"No, we were meant to land on the planet!" the girl insisted. "Or has cold sleep addled your memory? We were to land in an isolated area and blend into the populace. This is a moon!"

"Father programmed it."

"Yes, but I kept telling you – something was dragging us off course."

"Did you try to correct manually?" the other asked.

"Of course, but the computer said that manual control was off line."

The girl and her brother would be about twenty if they were human. They looked nearly human.

Finally the boy seemed to wake up to the problem. He studied the readouts on the screen.

"There is some kind of settlement down there."

"Yes, with force shields over it," the girl confirmed. "I think they dragged us here. That message signal came from there."

"What do you think they want?"

"Us, you fool. To them, we are aliens. You don't know what they might expect of us. This might be some defence post. Though what they might be defending against I don't know. Father knew of this planet and he didn't think they were aware of aliens."

"Perhaps it is a secret Tymorean base," the boy proposed.

"Zorrin! Don't even think that!"

"We should, Vori. We don't have enough fuel or supplies to go home, even if we dared. But we still have enough to make the planet. I have no wish to have escaped from Zekos, only to die here."

"They might let us be friends," Vori voiced her hope.

Zorrin shrugged. "We don't have much choice. If we can't override the auto-program, we will have to land so we can shut down and restart the computer."

"I'd like to be sure they won't blast us as soon as we land," Vori shivered.

"We don't have to meet them," Zorrin proposed. "We could take off as soon as the computer restarts."

"Yes. That would be best. If we don't hurt them they might leave us alone."

"The craft has stopped moving," Stanley reported to Landin. He was interpreting the figures on the main viewscreen.

"What's it doing," Basoli demanded.

"Just sitting there, Sir. Observing us, it seems."

Basoli simmered. "Have weapons got a target?"

"Yes, but it is still outside the range of our weapons."

The alien ship inched forward and stopped when it was just at the extreme range of the weapons on the moon. It waited there for a long time before sending down a single lance of energy that just touched the edge of the force shield.

"They attacked us!" Basoli shouted.

"That wasn't an attack. That was a poke," Kryslie said, risking Basoli's ire.

"Why are you still here, Ward? The emergency tones went an hour ago."

"I am acting Tech 1, Sir," Krys told the Chief. She met his eyes without backing down. Basoli glanced at Landin who nodded.

"So, you think you know better than me, do you?" Basoli didn't quite snarl.

"Sir, if they were attacking us they would aim for something vital, not the edge of the shield."

"The woman speaks sense," the silky tones of Abdul bin Halil spoke up.

Kryslie didn't turn around to see why the leader of the Imperium was not in the safe quarters he should have gone to. Basoli also ignored him, by turning his attention back to the screen.

When no retaliating weapons fire ensued, the alien ship inched closer to the moon's surface. Finally it hovered just above the surface, not far from the edge of the shield. Then a beam of light shone down onto the surface, and the ship seemed to slip down the pole of light.

"Interception team, suit up," Basoli ordered. He didn't seem to notice Kryslie suiting up beside him. "Weapons at ready."

The group exited the base and walked to where the shield was almost at the ground. It was visible as a faint glowing gridwork.

Over the suit comms, Basoli told the security men to fan out around the ship. In front of them, an opening appeared in the shield. The group moved out walking with deliberate movements and spreading out into a line. The security team went ahead of the rest of the group.

The armoured suits were bulky and required a small power supply to help propel them along.

Basoli followed after the security men, moving with a more awkward gait. Once outside the shield, Landin moved up level with his chief.

Inside main mission and indeed, all throughout the base, attention was fixed on screens showing both the alien ship and the suited humans. The humans were making no threatening moves, but there was no mistaking the fact that the purple clad figures were armed.

Tymos Ward, currently staring at the screen in engineering, as intently as all his shift colleagues. His attention was fixed on Basoli, who at that time was mentally wishing the aliens would hurry up and come out.

The external monitors were picking up a hum that Tymos knew to be the idling space drives on the alien ship. The aliens were very wary and no little afraid. Kryslie was sensing some things from them. More emotions than thoughts.

"Making us wait. The arrogant creatures," Basoli was thinking. "Ah, finally."

A ramp lowered from under one of the ship's stubby wings, and light shone out. Two figures in silvery suits, with only a darker patch at the eyes, stepped out.

"They think they are our betters do they?" Basoli was thinking.

Each of the alien figures had a weapon; they each fired a beam just ahead of the guards moving to encircle the ship.

Basoli raised his weapon, but Landin pushed it down and ordered the guards to hold position.

"They are not stupid, Sir," Landin spoke over the comm. "We have yet to gain their trust."

The two figures had stopped and now watched the purple clad guards lower the weapons they had raised. Only then did they begin to move forwards again, but both seemed to be watching the guards. They stopped at a distance from the humans and the slightly taller figure took a flat object from a pocket in his suit and glanced at it. The other continued to watch all of the humans.

Into the helmet comms, came gabble.

"We can't understand that," Basoli announced.

"Quiet, Sir," Mick Schultz requested. "They are trying different Earth languages."

After a while, Schultz announced, "It is repetitions of 'we want to be friends and we want to be free' in different languages."

Shultz stepped forward and held up a hand in a 'stop' motion. The gabble stopped.

"Can you understand English?" Schultz asked, assuming they were picking up the suit comms.

"We...some," came a tentative answer.

"Get them to come in. We can't stay out here all day," Basoli directed tersely.

Schultz spoke slowly and clearly. "We invite you to visit our base, inside," he tried.

Kryslie carefully projected a thought of the group walking back inside and the two newcomers following.

"Ship?" came a question.

"The ship will not be harmed," Landin said. "You might want to close the hatch."

Kryslie pictured them doing that, and the taller one touched the grey box again.

"You are out of order, Commander," Basoli said in a tight voice. "I want to look at that ship."

"There will be time for that, Sir," Landin said calmly. "If we are invited - these visitors are not our prisoners."

There was an 'hmpf' over the suit comm, as Basoli made an effort to mind what he said. Krys sensed his annoyance and his intention to challenge Landin's instruction. Most of her attention however was on the two aliens.

"IDIOT!" Tymos's disgusted thought came into Kryslie's mind. He was referring to Basoli. She didn't need to ask what he was thinking. She had the gist of it and it was agitating both silver clad aliens. She was trying to project reassurance. Tymos turned his attention to the aliens.

"I don't think they can understand voice thoughts," he thought at his twin. "Only those with pictures. Basoli is thinking with pictures and emotions. They are getting those."

Kryslie didn't dare say anything lest she set Basoli off. She changed her projection to 'safety inside'.

Schultz was still trying to communicate, but didn't seem to be having any luck. "Sir, perhaps if we get the guards to start moving back towards the base. Then if we start moving back and use gestures to get them to follow."

Kryslie was probably the only one who realised that the two aliens were ignoring him in favour of discussing what they should do.

"Tym, are they talking on some frequency?" Krys asked, mentally. Her brother's mind went elsewhere for a moment.

"Yes, and it isn't good. The deeper voice is angry. They both seem to know what Basoli wants and think that the other minds are trying to trick them."

Tymos could understand their speech since Aeronite was derived from the Tymorean language.

"Shields, Krys!" he suddenly thought, but his warning wasn't fast enough.

He felt, through his mind link with Krys, an extreme headache, with overtones of terror.

Kryslie planted her feet and forced mental shields up. Her head felt like it had a piercing ache. Landin seemed to be reeling and Basoli crumpled to the ground as he was pulling his weapon up.

Several of the guards were also affected for their weapons had dropped from ready. One guard took a shot before Landin managed to say, "Hold fire! Do not fire!"

Kryslie moved closer to Landin and tried to shield his mind a bit. Her own mind was 'yelling' at the two aliens, "STOP IT!"

Tymos could finally think at her. "One of them is injured."

Kryslie focussed on the scene.

Schultz was leaning over Basoli, with Landin saying, "Get him back inside. Send for a crawler."

One of the aliens was down too, and the guards were ready to fire.

Now Kryslie sensed panic from the alien who was kneeling next to the other who was on the lunar dust. That one was trying to press down on the arm of the other. She began to walk towards the aliens, slowing when the crouching alien raised his weapon at her.

"Ward," Landin warned.

"One is injured," Kryslie said. She was trying to project, "Help you."

"Get away," she heard over the suit comm. It wasn't in an Earth language, but she understood it. She stopped and pulled out the tube of sealant from her suit and showed it to the alien aiming the weapon at her. Then she pictured, and spoke, "Seals hole in suit."

Deliberately she touched it to her suit and showed it wasn't a weapon and he would see the coloured gel.

The alien slowly lowered the weapon. Kryslie moved as fast as she could, hopping to get along. Her head was still 'splitting' but she could ignore the pain for a time.

Without further interaction, Kryslie found where the projectile had torn the suit fabric, and applied the sealant. Then she brought out the spare cylinder of oxygen, slipped it in tandem with the one she was using and closed off the other and detached it. This one she handed to the alien.

He understood her gesture, and rolled his companion over and revealed where they connected portable air. As Kryslie had surmised, the fittings were completely dissimilar, but she knew what to do.

Putting the two fittings together, so the tube holes were opening onto each other, she placed sealant around to hold them together. As soon as it set, she opened the valve on her cylinder, and the alien did something on the suit. There was no cloud of vapour indicating a leak.

The alien placed a gloved hand gently on Kryslie's arm, in thanks, and then glanced up in fright.

Kryslie turned enough to recognise the suit of the base Commander.

"I have transport coming to take us inside," Landin said gesturing.

Sensing the fear of the alien, Kryslie put her gloved hand on the alien's arm. "You will be safe," she spoke aloud and in her mind.

The alien glanced around and seemed to relax when he saw the guards retreating into the base.

"Let us help you," Landin offered.

"Try and picture your meaning, Commander," Krys suggested.

The first crawler was already on its way back to the base. The second was just pulling up near Landin.

"Who?" the alien pointed at Kryslie.

"Krys," she answered, sending a mental picture of her face.

"Who?" This time the alien pointed at Landin.

Kryslie identified Landin as the base commander and also sent a picture of his face.

"Let me help you get your friend inside." Kryslie pictured the standing alien helping her to get the other alien into the crawler.

The standing alien holstered his weapon. Kryslie had already stowed the sealant. Between them, they lifted the injured alien into the crawler.

When they stopped in the shuttle bay, Krys glanced belatedly through the front view window. She felt a wave of relief when she saw that the wreck had been covered over. She wondered who had suggested that. For sure, seeing a wrecked Aeronite ship would not be a good indication of friendliness. Landin opened the crawler door and stepped out.

"I'll send medics here," he told Kryslie. "Wait here for now."

To the driver of the crawler and the guards who had materialised on their arrival, he said, "Give our guests some space."

"Sir, what of the..." one began.

"Ward will be fine. She has gained the visitor's trust and is quite capable of handling herself. If there is any problem, call me. Stunners only at ready."

Kryslie stood near the doorway and unlocked her headpiece. She was glad to remove it and intended to let the alien know that it was safe to breathe in the shuttle bay. The conscious alien was studying her face, but as yet not ready to reveal his or her own.

"Doctor Long is coming," Tymos told Kryslie mentally. "Basoli is still unconscious. Be careful, that male has a nasty little kinetic trick."

Kryslie didn't think back at him. This close to the aliens, they might pick up her thoughts.

"The doctor is coming," she said, picturing the doctor in her jacket. "Healer? Medic?"

The alien nodded, still crouched beside the other.

Long entered the crawler, ducking her head and cautiously, glancing from Kryslie to the stranger.

"What happened?"

"Suit was nicked," Kryslie pointed at the hardened sealant. "Maybe stunned as well. I wasn't able to notice at the time."

"How is your head," Long asked Kryslie as she approached the suited figure. She was getting her diagnostic tool out as she spoke.

"I'm fine, Doc," Krys claimed. "Nothing I can't cope with."

Long held a diagnostic tool over the suited figure. "I will need to get this suit off," she said in a neutral tone.

Kryslie touched the conscious alien on the arm, then used her other hand to try to mime undoing the suit. "Will you help take the suit off, so Dr Long can help your friend?"

After several tries at mime, the message got across. Kryslie was allowed to help the alien to do strip off the silvery suit.

When Long brought out the stethoscope, the alien put out a hand to keep it away.

"Show what you want to do on me, Doc," Kryslie suggested.

In that way, Long was able to gently examine the young female alien.

"Ears and eyes look okay. I don't think the air leak was too bad. Breathing and heartbeat are regular. A bit faster than ours. I don't know what is normal for them. The eyes are odd, no white, so I can't tell if she was stunned or not. I guess she was. It will have to wear off."

"Is there somewhere better than this for them?" Kryslie asked.

"I'd like to put them in that set of rooms off medical," Long proposed. "It would give them some privacy and I can keep an eye on the girl."

"Can you suggest it to the Commander?"

"I will, but I have a sickbay full of people right now. Headaches and blurred vision, Are you sure you are alright?"

"I said I was."

Long departed and Krys tried to tell the male that his female companion was fine.

At last, the male removed his head covering and revealed a thin, pointed face with olive skin and thick black hair. The woman had longer hair, just as thick and black and the same skin complexion. They had to be related, perhaps brother and sister.

"I am Krys." She pointed to herself. "Who are you?" She pointed at the male.

He thought, and said, "Zorrin, I am."

"Who is she?" Kryslie pointed at the girl.

"Vori, is she."

Kryslie gently corrected his grammar, and for a while played the game of point and name objects. Occasionally, Zorrin volunteered names in English, sometimes not.

Vori had still not stirred when Landin and two orderlies with a trolley reached the crawler. One of the orderlies was Tymos who was moving with a relaxed stride and a grin on his face. His body language, more than anything he said, reassured Zorrin.

Kryslie pointed to each person and named them. Landin nodded approval and smiled when Zorrin introduced himself.

Tymos announced, "We have arranged some rooms for you. Better than here. The trolley is for..."

"Vori," Kryslie supplied. Tymos repeated the name.

Zorrin eyed each of the newcomers and nodded, letting Tymos help bring Vori out onto the trolley. Krys folded the silvery suit and put it at Vori's feet.

The group moved through corridors devoid of other people. The flashing yellow lights, which meant 'evacuate the passage' were on. Tymos gave a running commentary as they went along and explained where they were going.

The first people they encountered were the last few of the EA team still in medical.

Landin spoke to Krys, "Get unsuited and have yourself checked. That is an order. Then you are off duty until tomorrow. I have arranged a replacement for you. Since you and your brother have a knack for getting the trust of our guests, I want you spending time with them."

That suited Krys, so she agreed by nodding. Now that she was not concentrating so hard on reading Zorrin, her head was back to pounding. She needed time to employ the pain relief technique she had learnt.

The last few guards gave Zorrin a wary look, but there was curiosity there as well, along with a sense of 'they look like us'.

When Zorrin saw Basoli, still unconscious on a bed, his mind seemed smugly satisfied.

Once in the suite of rooms, Long sent her orderlies off for food, water and several other items to make the guests welcome.

Kryslie stayed out in the main part of medical.

"What did you mean about a nasty kinetic trick?" she silently asked Tymos when he emerged.

"Oh, not much," he answered aloud, and then went to thinking at her. "That Zorrin is keeping Basoli out. He has to be. The rest of the EA team has headaches at most." He shoulder shrugged to indicate to start walking.

"Saves us the trouble," Kryslie muttered. "Zorrin will probably keep it up until his girlfriend wakes up – or longer."

"I will let them settle in first and then I might help things along," Tymos decided, speaking softly. "I will have to be careful. If I try to heal the girl, the other might notice."

"Don't rush," Kryslie advised. "Basoli deserves a lesson and he will be angry when he wakes up."

"And finds we have overstepped ourselves again," Tymos agreed with a sigh. "I would rather find out what these two want here before he destroys hope of co-operation."

Krys separated from her brother to return to the shuttle bay to unsuit. She reflected that they had timed it well, getting the aliens to their quarters. The passages near the shuttle bay were now busy with crew coming off shift.

Tymos was the last to leave the rooms after the food and drinks had arrived and Zorrin had been shown how to use the amenities in the suite.

The alien male had ignored the food, even after Tymos and Landin had tasted each item to prove it was safe.

Looking through the glass window from the main part of the medical suite, Tymos saw Zorrin position himself at the door of the inner room so he could watch the outer door and the room where the girl was.

"Dr Long, do you have smelling salts?" Tymos asked.

She looked at him thoughtfully. "Who for?"

Tymos glanced at Basoli. "Shouldn't he be awake by now?"

Long gave a faint shrug. "I can find nothing wrong. I have normalised his blood chemistry, and no one can really say what happened except their heads suddenly hurt. And it wasn't everybody."

"If you excuse my disrespect," Tymos went on. "I think Zorrin did something because he sensed danger to himself and the girl." He glanced at Basoli again. "And the Chief probably won't wake up until the girl does."

"Do you have any proof of that?"

"Ah, no. It's just a hunch," Tymos admitted.

"I will get you what you asked for," Long decided. "It's an old remedy, but sometimes simple is most effective."

Tymos took the small vial and re-entered the smaller suite. He gave no indication of noticing the guards stationed in medical who were keeping out of sight of the big window. He showed Zorrin the vial, removed the lid and carefully wafted some fumes towards his own nose and pulled a face. Zorrin did the same and jerked back quickly in alarm. Tymos spoke and gestured to explain. "Might help Vori wake up."

Even though Zorrin followed him, his attention was on the girl's face and the hand waving the vial under her nose every so often. However, it was the hand that Tymos was using to hold the girl's hand that was letting him make use of his healing gift. He had to be careful and slow, so his hand would not start to glow faintly mauve. It was possible that Zorrin would notice that.

When he felt the girl's hand jerk slightly, Tymos withdrew his own and stoppered the vial. He sensed a surge of fear from the girl, until Zorrin spoke to reassure her. He didn't let on that he understood the speech. Instead he turned away and watched the medical infirmary.

Faintly, from the room beyond the window, he could hear Basoli speaking loudly and sensed from nearby, the renewed fear of the two aliens. Not all of it was fear of Basoli, but that was foremost. Beyond that were fears of what they had fled from and a fear they would not be allowed to stay on Earth and fear of being hurt here.

"Uh, Oh," Tymos said casually. "Our Commander-in-Chief is awake. I don't think that I will be able to stay here with you."

Zorrin grabbed his arm.

"Doctor Long won't let him bother you for a while." Tymos kept his voice calm to reassure him. "He will probably try to keep me away though. Except, Landin assigned me here. If we can teach you English, we can learn from each other, much better. Um, he will probably get Mick Schultz to teach you." Tymos pictured the man just as a guard entered the room.

"Ward, the C-I-C wants you."

Chapter 20

Kryslie was returning towards medical when she sensed someone behind her. She swung around and saw bin Halil's bodyguard and a smiling bin Halil step out of a cross passage.

"Did you think I would not recognise you like that?" the silky voice was full of menace.

Krys went still and stayed quiet.

"I see you remember how I like my women. Silent and obedient."

"I am not your woman," Kryslie told him evenly.

"You are disrespectful," bin Halil rebuked her. "No, your Eminence? Or even a sir?"

Deciding that her best course of action was to say nothing that would anger him, she kept her thoughts to herself and hoped that bin Halil would explain his intentions. If he or his bodyguard attacked her she was prepared to defend herself even if she was put on charges for doing so. The men themselves were disobeying the 'lockdown' of all non-essential personnel.

"Do you know, Krys Ward, that should you come to my country today – my police have orders to apprehend you so I may pronounce the death sentence on the last of the seditionists of the uprising?"

"I can prove I am not the person you claim."

"More tricks and lies?" bin Halil accused. "I will not be taken in by them again."

"I have no intention of going to your country."

"I know. That would be foolish, wouldn't it? And I know you aren't foolish. You are a freak of some kind, an anathema that plays with men's minds so they believe your lies."

He saw no change of expression on Kryslie's face and went on. "I could kill you now and those pathetic aliens will get the blame. There is talk that they tried to kill the Commander - too bad they didn't succeed there. For you, it will prove to be a delayed reaction. Too bad the hero fell."

Kryslie stared back at bin Halil and tried to press her mind on his as she stated, "I am not the woman you claim and if you or your man touch me I will have you charged with assault."

"I don't think so," bin Halil started to contradict her, but then his face contorted and he seemed to be feeling the same agony Krys had experienced before. He gripped her arm, his hand squeezing tightly. This time Kryslie had some shields on her mind, but not all. She had her mind partly unshielded to try and gauge bin Halil's intention.

What she was feeling most now was terror! Overwhelming terror!

Krys suppressed the vision of flames and tortured people that the emotion had evoked in her mind. Instead, as bin Halil gripped her arm so tightly the circulation felt stopped, she sensed his terrors – the fear of certain bodies being found and of people learning of his secret sources of wealth. If he was found guilty of certain things he would lose many privileges and much prestige. His people would revolt against him and the life of luxury he had built would be forever out of his reach. His mind flicked through faces of people he had ordered killed, since they knew too much.

Kryslie pulled her arm free and the images faded, but not the piercing headache or the nausea at seeing so much of his callous disregard for people's lives. Then suddenly she felt a sharp pain at her neck, and felt herself blacking out.

Bin Halil gave his bodyguard a nod of approval, for it seemed that when the woman with the dyed blonde hair collapsed, the dreadful terror he had felt, stopped abruptly.

"Take that unnatural female somewhere and make it look as if she fell and broke her neck. Then return to the insulting suite that we were given."

"What were you doing in there, Technician Ward?" Basoli ranted. "No one is to approach those aliens without my say so. Is that clear?"

"Sir, I was assigned to medical," Tymos explained. "I was able to help the girl recover and made some headway communicating with them. I think they trust me a little and surely that will make learning about them easier."

"Are you finished, Ward?" His anger was like a banked furnace.

"Yes, Sir," Tymos said after a brief pause. He did not give Basoli the courtesy of straightening from his casual stance, but he kept eye contact. The C-I-C was too angry to be receptive to subtle mental hints.

Vori and Zorrin had come to the glass and seemed to be aware of the confrontation.

"Your assignment here is terminated, Ward. I do not want you returning here, while they are in there, without a damn good reason. And if I see you near them I will have you transferred groundside."

Tymos did not shrink under the glare.

"Do – you – understand – me?"

"Yes, Sir, I do." He had just turned to leave when he felt the terror. He turned back to glance at Zorrin and saw him concentrating. Then a sound like a mewing kitten came from Basoli and for an instant he saw through into the Chief's mind. Basoli was seeing a snarling, growling and enormous black cat.

Tymos ignored Basoli and stared at the aliens. "Stop it!" he thought fiercely, staring at Zorrin. "It has got to be you doing this. This will not help you! Oh damn! I can't go and tell them."

Basoli was babbling. "Make sure they are locked in. Double the guard, get trank guns ready."

Vori pulled on Zorrin's arm. "I heard that. He told us to stop it. Do you think he is a telepath?"

Zorrin stopped his mental attack on the horrible man who wanted to do unpleasant things to them. The man was a cowering wreck – pitiful. He would make the creature too afraid to come near them.

"No," Zorrin assured her. "At least I don't think he's aware I can pick things up from him. He was teaching me a bit of their language. He was thinking in pictures – like he was trying to teach a child to read. I don't think he realised what he was doing. I think he was just focussing. That time he was just hoping I would hear. He must have to take orders from that monster."

"You made that man angry with him. You said you trusted him, but now he won't be allowed to help us."

Zorrin sagged a bit and moved away from the window to sit in a chair facing the outer infirmary.

"I do not like or trust that horrid man out there," Zorrin told her. "You felt what he wanted to do to us. And the guards fired at you."

"Because you mentally shoved them," Vori reminded him. "If they figure out that it was you, they will be afraid of us."

"Good!"

"No! Wouldn't it be better to make them think we are vulnerable and no threat?"

Zorrin shrugged. "What's happening?"

"The one in white is doing something to the man. He is cowering on the floor."

"Huh!" Zorrin said in disgust. "The young man Tymos is worth two of that one."

"I think they put him to sleep," Vori guessed. "They are lifting him on to the bed again."

"Good riddance," Zorrin concluded.

Vori stared at the back of Tymos Ward. Something about his stance unsettled her. It had gone rigid and she thought angry. He strode from the room. "I think we should take turns sleeping," she said. "I am scared. Are we locked in?"

Landin strode towards Medical, but was nearly knocked over in the doorway by Tymos who was coming out.

"Sorry, Sir," Tymos apologised, as he kept walking.

"Ward!" Landin spoke loudly, stopping Tymos in his tracks. "A word."

"Sir, I can't now..."

"I wanted you on duty in Medical," Landin reminded him and he saw Tymos's rigid stance.

"Sir, the C-I-C countermanded the assignment, and I have to go..." Tymos turned his head as he spoke, but he seemed to want to keep heading away.

"What is so urgent?" Landin had never seen Tymos Ward this agitated.

"Krys..." Tymos said.

"She hasn't come in to be checked?" Landin guessed.

"No, Sir – she should have come by now."

Landin studied Tymos for a moment and then gave orders via his wrist comm, instructing his security team to look for Kryslie.

"I need to talk to you," he told Tymos.

Tymos sat quietly in the doctor's office as Frances Long told Landin of the events concerning Basoli. She admitted that for a moment she had felt terror and seemed to see everyone around her as horrible nightmarish creatures. Tymos, who was trying to reach Krys's mind, had to be nudged by Landin to tell his version.

"Yes, I saw odd things too – and Basoli saw me as a huge, snarling, feral black cat," he reported after the question was repeated. "I am sure it was Zorrin's doing and I am sure he is aware of what the Chief wants to do with them."

"Which is?" Landin prompted.

"Sir, Krys learnt this doing confidential things for the Chief," Tymos protested mildly.

"Hardly confidential if you know," Landin commented. "Do you require me to make it an order, Technician Ward?"

Tymos shook his head and spoke softly.

"Much as I expected," Landin observed when Tymos had finished. "How much do you think Vori and Zorrin understand?"

That made Tymos thoughtful.

"I think they had a way to learn some Earth languages and at the moment have to sort English out of the rest. They seem to be learning very quickly."

Landin nodded and then asked, "Are they telepaths?"

Tymos glanced at Landin and flicked a glance to Long and decided to answer cautiously.

"A little I think."

"Explain," Landin prodded.

"They seemed to understand better when I thought in pictures – not so much if I just used words. It is possible that they can think at each other, like Krys and I can."

"Is that what they did to us out side? Think at us?"

Tymos shook his head. "Not exactly. From what I felt through Krys then – it felt like some nasty telekinetic trick – like a punch in the side of the head. In here, just before, I would say projective empathy."

"Fascinating," Long observed, keeping her surprise at Tymos's revelation to herself. "What range do you think he has?"

"I don't know," Tymos admitted. "Outside he was terrified and that probably increased his power. In here, I suspect he was focussing on the Chief and the doctor and I caught the edge of it. The guards seemed unaffected."

Yet that answer did not feel quite right to Tymos and as Landin talked to Long about the condition of the guests, he considered it.

The effect could have gone further, he didn't know. Most of the surrounding area was under yellow alert and deserted. Outside, not all the people were affected. The guards here now might be totally unreceptive to telepathy and empathy. It might be, if a person had a touch of mind gifts they were affected more. And maybe, the stronger the gift, the worse the effect.

"Krys?" he thought again. She had been on her way back, and she still had a headache from the first incident. The second may have made her black out – but surely security would have found her by now. He needed to go find her.

Landin stood, distracting Tymos. "I will go and talk to them and reassure them. Tymos, I think you should come with me."

He didn't want to, he wanted to find Krys, but with a glanced out to where Basoli slept, and beyond to the door, he merely said, "Yes, Sir."

Zorrin stood quickly and smiled when Tymos returned. "You are allowed back?" he said in slow English.

"For this moment," Tymos agreed. "Commander Landin wants to talk to you."

He forced his concentration towards helping Landin and Zorrin to communicate, but he kept glancing at the window. Vori it seemed, was sleeping again.

Zorrin finally ignored a question of Landin's to ask, "I ask, Tymos, worried you are?"

Tymos turned back to face Zorrin. "Yes."

"About us? Someone might hurt us?"

"No," Tymos told him and Landin repeated his assurances.

"For that man's angry with you?"

"No, I can handle him. It isn't the first time he's been angry with me."

Recalling what Tymos said about Zorrin's possible telepathic actions, Landin remarked, "Many of us who met you outside received severe headaches. Kryslie was one and she is Tymos's sister. She was on her way back here to be checked by the doctor. She might have blacked out like Chief Basoli did."

Tymos managed to picture events to explain Landin's words.

In turn, Tymos felt Zorrin's remorse that others besides the man he meant to hurt, had been affected. "I ...regret...the Krys – helped Vori."

Landin's communicator pinged and Tymos went tense. He heard, "We have located her, Sir." A voice over requested a med team in the shuttle bay. Landin stopped Tymos dashing out by gently holding his arm.

Only after ensuring Zorrin knew how to call for medical aid, and have Landin himself called, did he turn to leave.

The emergency medical response team pushed open the doors of the infirmary and wheeled the trolley directly to an open section containing resuscitation equipment. Tymos tried again to pull away from Landin, although not with his full strength.

"Sir, I must go to her." The tone was not that of 'worried relative' but decisive, like an order.

Landin released him but stayed where he was to watch. Long was already there, as Krys was lifted across to the diagnostic bed. A defibrillator was open and the leads connected to Kryslie.

Tymos forced his way to the bed and went to the side opposite Long and seemed to fiddle with his sister's communicator as the doctor felt for a pulse and began to frown.

A moment later, Long announced, "We have a pulse." Half the EMR team retreated from the room to wait nearby. Tymos released his sister's wrist, but refused to leave.

Long scanned Kryslie with her equipment and studied the read out. Then she examined her patient's head and neck with her hands.

"Where did you find her?" Long asked the remaining team members.

One described how they had found her with her neck against a strut of the wrecked alien ship.

"Looked like she collapsed and hit her head," was the observation.

"Visual report," Long asked and a picture was transmitted to a small screen.

Long felt over Krys's right side again and moved her hair. "No sign of a head injury and the anomalies I found in the other EA team members are minor in her. There is bruising on the neck here. Bring over the x-ray scanner."

Tymos took his sister's wrist again and closed his eyes. It was easier then to visualise the energies in her. Looking at the afterglow like image behind his eyelids, he directed his attention to where Long had found bruising. The bruising went bone deep. If Krys had managed to reverse the earlier effects of the mental punch and normalise her biochemistry – she would not have fainted or collapsed. And even if she had, that bruise was too deep. That bruise was caused by a strong, deliberate blow intended to break her neck.

Probably the only reason it hadn't was that Kryslie had still been wearing her personal force screen. That would have blocked a lot of the force.

Tymos felt a slow burning anger. Someone had intended to kill her and make it look like an accident. A fall due to the after effects of what most people would assume was the aliens attack on the EA team.

Not everyone on the base wanted to welcome the aliens unreservedly and some were latent xenophobes. But he was positive that none of the crew would try to kill Krys for helping them.

That left visitors from Earthside – all of whom should still be in lockdown, except that Tymos knew of two who had ignored the lockdown orders.

"Spine is intact," Long announced.

The scanning machine was removed and Tymos sent a trickle of healing energy into his sister, as Long began to treat the bruising. He sensed when the pressure due to the bruising reduced enough for nerve signals to reach her lower extremities and shortly after, her mind roused.

"Stay still," Tymos though to her, still sending his healing energy into her.

"He thinks I'm dead," Kryslie thought back, although her mind was not as clear as normal.

"Anyone else would be!"

"He'll get what he deserves. His dirty secrets. I know them."

"Ah!" Tymos's anger turned to slightly malicious determination.

"Get Vincent to come here," Kryslie's mind said.

"The base is locked down. No shuttles are to land," Tymos reminded her. "Besides, I would rather deport your friend."

"No, he's trapped here. Get Landin…" her mind faded out.

"Damn!" Tymos thought.

"I've done what I can for now," Long told Tymos. "She is stable, so I will move her into a private room. Let her rest."

Tymos followed Long out, but only because Landin was hovering.

"I need to talk to you sir, confidentially," Tymos requested.

Landin listened to Long's report before answering him. He did not like the sound of the injury, and how it had apparently happened. He nodded at the doctor, and told Tymos, "Very well. My office then."

Tymos fell into step beside Landin and said nothing until they reached there. Even so, he glanced around the room and then reached into his pocket to activate a device that would ensure no electronic monitoring of the conversation.

Landin noted his odd behaviour but went to sit behind his desk and waited for Tymos to speak.

"I want you to allow me to bring up a doctor that knows Krys. To look at her." Tymos spoke more like an equal than a subordinate. He hadn't sat down, but was looking directly at his Commander.

"Why not simply send Krys down to him?" Landin countered. "Assuming I lift the lock down."

"No! We both need to be here."

"Why is that?"

Tymos began to pace in front of Landin's desk.

"Sir, you deserve an answer, but the truth is - I don't know. It's a bit like looking at the sky and knowing a storm is coming."

"A storm is coming," Landin echoed. "Very well, this doctor – who is he?"

"His name is Vincent," Tymos stopped and returned his gaze to Landin. "He is a consultant. He specialises in brain disorders."

Landin typed the name into his computer and waited. He read what came up on the screen. The man's biography was impressive and there was no suggestion of a non-Earth origin.

"And he will come on your say so?" Landin queried.

"It might have more weight if you requested it, Sir," Tymos suggested. "But he does know our father."

"I suggest you don't need me to ask, and are polishing my ego," Landin said deliberately.

Tymos grinned faintly and shrugged.

"You are correct, Sir. But he might also be able to check on the Chief and..."

Landin waited.

"Give me an opinion on the sanity of bin Halil."

"Now I see where this is going. Are you accusing bin Halil of trying to kill your sister?"

"Not officially," Tymos said carefully. "And I doubt you would get an admission or find proof. But, yes, and he did disregard the emergency lock down."

"And you think he might try again?"

"I think it would suit him as well if Krys is 'inert', if not dead," Tymos considered.

"Inert?"

"In a coma. At least while she is in Medical, the guards can watch out for her too."

"So, what if our Imperial visitor refuses to let your doctor look at him?"

Tymos waved that aside. "Vincent is good."

"Who else would be interested in such an analysis?"

"While we were Earthside, I heard that the Investigative Committee is scrutinizing bin Halil and may soon issue a warrant on him. Vincent's analysis will be important. Meanwhile, he is trapped here."

"And Kryslie? Are you that worried about her? The doctor feels she is well enough."

"She can't sense her in the way I usually can. Vincent will be able to tell if anything is really wrong," Tymos assured Landin. "And advise a treatment."

"Very well, I will organise that. Then..."

Tymos sensed Landin was trying to decide to ask something. "Sir?" he prompted.

"I hope you will give me an honest and useful answer. Do you know more about our guests than you have let on?"

"Some things you don't need to know, but in respect to your question...yes, but not a great deal. We don't know anything about them personally and anything we learn we will tell you."

Landin nodded, "What can you tell me?"

"The ship they came in is Aeronite. They do look to be of that race but I do not think they came from Aerdna itself. It is more likely they came from one of the Aeronite colonies."

"Are they dangerous?" Landin managed to ask without betraying his incredulity at what he was hearing.

"On their own, unthreatened, no," Tymos said with conviction. "However, I know they have mind gifts – like I described. And I do not think they have had any training in the ethics of or control of those gifts."

"Do you know why they came here?"

"No, except I had the impression of them fleeing someone who wanted to hurt them. I want to know how they knew to come here. That is a very important reason to speak to Zorrin and Vori and also to find out who they were fleeing from."

Landin understood what he meant. "Do you think others might be following them?"

"If those they are fleeing from learnt where their ship was going, it is a strong possibility."

"Can we defend against these people?" Landin asked.

"It depends who they are."

"That is not a comforting answer," Landin remarked.

"Life isn't," Tymos responded. "However there are a number of things you might consider putting in place."

"I'm listening."

"Get permission from Zorrin to bring his ship into the shuttle bay, so it is not an obvious clue to their presence."

Landin tapped a finger on his desk. "And?"

"Provoke Ericson into recalling the Grainger Exhibit. The crystals have useful properties and were supposedly found here on the moon."

"You want some?"

Tymos nodded.

"Anything else?"

"Yes, but it would be better if you don't know," Tymos said seriously. "The C-I-C will be unpleasant enough as it is."

"At least you have an impeccable reason for being in the infirmary," Landin suggested.

"Yes, I want to get back."

Landin dismissed him, having a great deal to think on. Foremost was Tymos's casual knowledge of worlds he had never heard of.

Chapter 21

Tymos spent the rest of the evening sitting or pacing the side room where Kryslie lay, hooked up to a number of machines and a fluid pump. When he sat, he sent healing energy into his sister and whilst that seemed to improve her physical state, her mind still seemed blocked from him. She wasn't reacting to the thoughts he sent her and her mind didn't feel as if it were asleep, or truly unconscious.

He made his presence inconspicuous when UWN President Joel Adamson came in to ask after Kryslie. His concern was genuine, but the doctor did not tell him much. However, it was the second man who had entered that Tymos kept his eye on. The one who kept back near the door, like a bodyguard, but who had the skin tone of the natives of the Imperium, and was not wearing the suit and ubiquitous dark glasses of Adamson's protectors. It was quite obvious, by the intent way he looked at the doctor and the President that his attention was on the conversation between them.

A faint smile betrayed his reaction to the news that Kryslie was still unconscious and would probably need to be evacuated to the WSRA University hospital. After hearing that, whilst Adamson was expressing his regret, the swarthy man slipped back out the door.

Once Adamson had gone, Tymos checked his sister once more, and took himself to the bed nearest her side room, covered himself with a blanket that had been left there for him, and settled himself for sleep. However, if anyone approached the side room, be it medical staff or any other, he would wake up, instantly alert.

He woke after an uneventful six hours of sleep, while medical was still in 'night' cycle. The shift medic, was in the duty office, and the two med techs were just beginning to prepare for the day shift. The security duo, were just coming back from a check of all the inner sections of medical. He did his own check on his sister before the techs came to check Kryslie's condition via the machines. The bruising around her neck was a vivid black, but the accompanying swelling had receded. Her mind though, still felt as if she had decided to block him out and frozen in that instant.

He felt that it was safe enough for him to go back to his quarters to wash and change out of the borrowed med tech uniform and into one of his own. He didn't need to be on duty in the computer lab at the normal time for his shift, as Landin had attached him to medical, but when the shuttle arrived with Vincent on board, the uniform would be a subtle confirmation of the importance of the visiting medic.

He was challenged on the way to his quarters, for the lockdown was still in effect. However, Landin had given him clearance to be moving about. He would no doubt be challenged again on the way back, and he did not intend to be away from his sister for long, because he did not trust either bin Halil or his guard.

He waited until he had returned to medical to order his breakfast, and while he ate as he stood by the bed he'd used, he could casually study the unhurried routine of the med techs. In addition to Kryslie and Basoli, there were currently two other patients. Both men had been affected by Zorrin's, mental attack, and injured themselves as a result. They were both awake, as a result of the med techs checking on them. His eyes scanned the rest of the ward, and he caught movement in the room where Vori and Zorrin were staying, but none from the bed where Basoli was sleeping. With merely a thought, Tymos adjusted his eyes so that he could read the monitors above Basoli. He was sedated, but all his readings were normal. There was no indication of when they would let the sedative wear off, but he decided he did not want to be the doctor when Basoli realised how long they had kept him asleep.

The gamma shift staff came in and began the handover with the night shift, and during this time, the relieving security team came in. A face at the window of the visitor's room, Vori's, decided him on going over there to reassure her. He caught her eye, gave her a jaunty salute and a big grin. She was startled, started to smile back, but then trotted back towards the door of the inner room. He didn't go in, since he hadn't permission to do so, but her fearful reaction made him wonder whether it was fear of the people at Lunar 1, or the person or people that might have followed them.

Well, if there were followers, the Tymorean relay ships would give him warning. He had people on the base that were a more immediate threat.

Non-essential personnel were not meant to be wandering the passages during a yellow-alert lock down, but bin Halil and his guard had already disregarded those instructions. As had Adamson when he had come to check on Kryslie, but the President had likely requested permission from Landin first.

If he had his way, both of the Earth Leaders would have been restricted to their quarters. The alien ship might have been hostile, and having both of the world's leaders here could have proved to be absolute folly.

Now that it seemed that Vori and Zorrin were not going to cause trouble, the lock down seemed to be more of a formality, than necessary. His impression was that the two visitors would only be trouble if they felt threatened, but the security men were around to prevent any one threatening them, as much as to block hostile actions from them.

For some reason, the words, "at the moment" came into his mind, and Tymos moved to a nearby computer terminal, and brought up the program that tracked all base personnel by their bio-monitors, and the guests by their visitor tags. That told him that both bin Halil and his guard were in their assigned quarters – or rather their IDs were there. He tried to access the security monitors, but the Imperium Leader had invoked the privacy override, as was his right. He switched his attention to the passage monitors, and checked the night's recording. From that, he was reasonably sure that once the guard had returned the previous night, neither had left the suite again.

It didn't mean they wouldn't, since he was sure that both of Earth's leaders would want to be present when the alien visitors were questioned. Though that would need to be when the two Aeronites had a better grasp of English.

On that cue, Mick Shultz, the base linguist, strolled into medical and looked around. Tymos quickly shut the terminal down, and went to meet him.

"Commander said to have you with me when I go in to talk to our guests," Shultz greeted.

"Sure," Tymos agreed, and he fell into step with the linguist.

He knew it was because he had managed to befriend the two visitors, and his presence did reassure them. They had tensed when Shultz announced himself, even though the linguist was more like an exuberant puppy than an enemy. Vori and Zorrin, were keen to learn more English, and Shultz had a device which contained a dictionary of Earth English. So once they knew what this intrusion was for, they relaxed. Tymos wasn't needed for that, in theory, so he lounged against the window, where he could listen to the lesson, and watch the main part of medical. It made it seem as if he was not paying attention to the lesson, but his mind did project images to suit the words and concepts that Shultz was trying to teach the visitors. He did not dare to try to probe the thoughts of the two Aeronites, as Zorrin might well sense him if he did. However, that did not mean he ignored the thoughts both were projecting. His own mind was shielded, except for his 'idle' consideration of the lesson. He did not think Zorrin had any idea of shielding, or that anyone else on Lunar 1 might be a telepath. He spoke mentally with Vori as the lesson went on, and Tymos heard snippets that related to their past and their fears. Nothing more, for they hardly needed to discuss in detail what they both already knew.

When Shultz called a halt, half way through gamma shift, he was little wiser. All he felt sure of was that there was a powerful being who terrified them, and their father had programmed the ship with coordinates of a place that was supposed to be their sanctuary.

The linguist left his dictionary hooked into the computer terminal, but he had ensured that it was disconnected from the main base computer. He glanced at Tymos as he left, but Zorrin had grabbed Tymos's arm gently, as a request for him to stay.

'I'll see you later, Mick," Tymos assured the older man, and he turned his attention to Zorrin.

"Was there a problem?"

Zorrin said, "Prisoners are we here?"

"No, not at all," Tymos said immediately. "We put you here so that we could be sure Vori was recovered from the trouble yesterday. And we didn't want you to have more attention than you wanted. If you want to look around the base, I can ask the Commander to let me show you. I know he'd like to talk to you first, hence the lesson in our language, and you might prefer to let the fuss die down as well."

Since Tymos had pictured a crowd of faces all trying to look at them, Zorrin understood.

"Hurt us? People might?"

Tymos considered his words, and allowed the other to see the ideas he considered. Finally he said, "I don't think so. I believe everyone up here is fair minded, it's just that there has been so much imaginative fiction about evil aliens amongst Earth's literature. And now that you are here, live aliens, well…everyone here is curious."

Vori had been listening to the conversation, but still needing to have Zorrin translate, since she was less of a telepath and slower to learn the new language. "Better I am, now."

"Great!" Tymos said, infusing his tone with satisfaction. "Why don't you both request something to eat and drink? "

"You eat?" Vori asked.

"I will, but I want to check on my sister."

"Yes. The Krys…is better? She helped me."

"She is, sort of," Tymos allowed them to see his memory of Kryslie in the extra care room. "There is a doctor, coming up from the planet to see her. He will know what to do for her."

"Horrid man, will he help?"

Tymos had to consider what Zorrin meant. Finally he grinned, "I guess, he might be able to check the Chief, but is isn't my place to suggest it. But the Chief will probably settle down when he realises that you both are friendly." The comment was meant as a suggestion, although his mind didn't betray that.

"Come here, we didn't mean," Vori blurted. "To the planet, we intended. Mix with people, not be stranger. Learn about Earth, how to be, we did."

Tymos hid most of his surprise, and commented, "You studied our transmissions, I suppose? On your way here?"

Zorrin's said, "Fact that is," but his mind revealed that they had the information in their ships memory before they left, but that he would use that explanation if asked again.

"Why here?" Tymos asked?

"Our father programmed the ship. Knew of the world he did. Said, safe we would be." Zorrin's mind had doubts, based on the fact they had landed on the moon.

"Why didn't he come with you?"

A fleeting look of unhappiness crossed Vori's face, linked to the fears they were keeping to themselves. "Away he went, ten and five…" she paused to find the word she wanted. "…years ago. Away and not back."

"Oh," Tymos kept the sense of pity in his public mind, but behind his mind shield he was thinking, "Fifteen years? If that wrecked ship we found was their father's ship, it had to have been buried in the lunar dirt longer than that." Something wasn't right. His mind calculated distance and travel speeds, and the answers didn't fit.

"Um, if you don't mind me asking, how long did it take you to come here?"

The question startled Zorrin, who challenged, "What matter is it?"

Tymos felt the spurt of suspicion, but defused it with a self-depreciating grin, "Just curious. Though the Commander will probably ask you anyway."

He heard in his mind, the quick exchange between the two Aeronites.

"The program said we sleep for years," Vori commented. "We can say that."

"I don't know…" Zorrin disagreed. "I worked out the course myself and I thought it would take less than that."

"Tell him years," Vori insisted.

Aloud, Zorrin said, "We were asleep, for years. Woke up when planet close. We listen to transmissions…"

Tymos smiled again, and said, "Might be good that you came here first. A lot of those transmissions are pure fiction. Act like people in them and you be laughed at."

His mind imagined one of the most ridiculous comedy tri-vid shows, and how silly it would be if these newcomers acted that way.

"Go you should, to the Krys. Back you come?"

"Yes, I want to check Krys, and I will be back when I am allowed."

He sensed that Vori and Zorrin wanted to discuss something in private, and they would not know that they were broadcasting. He could sit with Krys and still be aware of what they were thinking. That wasn't invading their privacy, and if they were afraid, he wanted to deflect any potential trouble.

They began as soon as he left.

"Vori, my calculations said we were only travelling for about a year."

"That can't be right. Or why would we need all those supplies?"

"Well, we'd need something to live on until we found a way to live with the humans."

"Yes but…if what you say is right, maybe the High Lord's enforcers are still coming after us. I thought…if it had been years, then we were safe."

"Until we landed here!"

"Maybe here is better. These people will protect us."

"They are innocents. They probably have no weapons. They didn't fire back at us, did they?"

"What are we going to do?"

"We hide here, while I work something out."

"If the Enforcers come, they will make these people hand us over. We won't be as important as their own kind."

"Vori! We need to think, and make these people like us. I will think of something."

At that moment, the base comm system came alive, and the message alert preceded the announcement of the cancellation of the lock down. Additional announcements informed the base that the area around medical was off limits to unauthorised personal as was shuttle bay 2.

Tymos continued on into Kryslie's room, aware that Zorrin was watching him through the window of their rooms. He emerged when he sensed that the Aeronites had finally decided to eat, and he went to the unused medical terminal. There were many thoughts running through his mind and the time paradox was foremost. He needed more information, and so he sent a microburst transmission to Earthbase, with questions he wanted answers to. Once he had the acknowledgement, he erased the record of both transmissions. The problem occupied him until he heard the routine announcements related to the arrival of a shuttle. He closed down the terminal and went to greet Vincent.

Landin was already waiting in the glassed in reception room, watching the shuttle taxing the last few metres to the disembarkation pad. This was a special shuttle, with only the one passenger, although it had a full cargo payload as well as an evacuation pod.

Once it stopped, the landing crew moved in to open the hatch and position the low steps. They helped the passenger off with his headpiece, and directed him towards the reception room. However, by then both Landin and Tymos were walking to greet the arrival, was moving with no sign of stiffness from the long flight.

Vincent nodded to Tymos, modifying the traditional greeting to one of higher rank, but clear in his mind for Tymos to read was the honorific, "Great One" and the request for Tymos to make introductions.

"Commander Landin, may I introduce Doctor Vincent," Tymos spoke quietly. He added all of Vincent's medical degrees, then stepped back to let the two men talk.

Landin, expecting that Tymos would want the newcomer to see his sister as soon as possible, kept the initial conversation short, saying finally, "I'll leave Tymos to see you out of the flight suit, and escort you to medical."

When they had left the shuttle bay and were walking along one of the deserted corridors towards medical, Vincent requested, "Please tell me what occurred, Great One."

His voice was soft and only carried to Tymos, who replied in an equally low voice.

"You should refrain from using the honorific here, Vincent. It isn't appropriate," Tymos insisted first. Then he related what he knew of how Kryslie was when security had found her, mentioning the mind attack by Zorrin and the later, less intense attack. Then he mentioned his suspicions of the real attacker."

"So, she was awake for a while," Vincent mused.

"Yes," Tymos confirmed and repeated what she had said.

"Thank you. You may introduce me to the doctor here and leave things to me."

"Ah, there are a few other people I hope you will meet and look at," Tymos suggested delicately.

"Your will..." Vincent acknowledged, omitting the "Great One" this time.

"Perhaps you could examine the Chief of the WSRA, Ron Basoli. I feel that he was particularly affected by the two Aeronites who arrived here. Vori and Zorrin have mind gifts, which I believe are completely untrained."

"Was there another?" Vincent suggested.

"I don't know if you will be able to do this, but I want your opinion of Abdul bin Halil."

"I will do what I can. Naturally, I have heard a great deal about the leader of the Imperium, I would like to meet him. Leave matters with me," Vincent acknowledged. "Where will you be?"

"The doctor will know how to summon me," Tymos said.

Vincent returned to being the esteemed consultant, carrying himself with confidence, but in no way arrogant. Doctor Long took to him right away, and Tymos felt immediately superfluous, and slipped away, deciding to go to work in the Computer section until he was needed.

Vincent conferred with Doctor Long, examined her test results, ordered different tests and explained what he hoped they would show. He already knew the problem, or rather, what Kryslie was doing. It would be easy enough to make her wake up, but he did not want to belittle Long's efforts by making it seem an obvious cure. The delay whilst the tests were performed gave him time to pay attention to Basoli, and incidentally observe the two Aeronites.

Long had organised MRI scans for Basoli and Kryslie, and Vincent was prepared to wait for the results. He listened courteously to the reports of headaches and other problems suffered by people affected by the alien male.

"Kryslie's biochemistry is nearly back to normal," Long noted. Vincent picked up on that and requested a comparison. It gave him reason to suggest a treatment that might allow Kryslie to rouse.

As the procedures would take some time, Long suggested that Vincent might like to settle into quarters prepared for him.

"Indeed," Vincent agreed. "I believe my luggage allowance will be there by now. My young friend, Tymos Ward suggested that you would know how to summon him. He has offered to give me a tour of the base, but I think a chance to refresh myself would be my first preference. Would you be so kind as to ask him to meet me there?"

Finding Tymos in a chair in the public area of the suite when he emerged from the sonic shower, did not surprise Vincent. Nor did he comment. As a Great One out ranked all Tymoreans, and Tymos did not usually intrude uninvited, so he simply accepted it.

"I transmitted in," Tymos explained. "As I was heading this way, I noticed bin Halil's guard where he could watch the entrance to this section."

Vincent had changed into a fresh suit, and the one he had worn up was hanging in the clothing alcove when it would air out and the creases smooth out.

"Great One Kryslie will be fine," Vincent stated as he sat down. "Your sister is, I believe, mind-watching her would be nemesis."

"Him!" Tymos blurted. "But why won't she acknowledge me."

"Perhaps, as she is also recovering from that near fatal attack, what she is doing requires all her attention. It is well that she had her PFS on."

"With that bastard around, we dare not give him any advantage," Tymos allowed his voice to deepen, but he kept it controlled. "At least, as far as I can tell, he hasn't left his quarters since last night."

"Your sister's doing, I suspect," Vincent said. "Is bin Halil aware of you?"

Tymos shook his head. "I have kept my hair black, and his guest suite is in the other wing. Your near neighbour is President Adamson."

"He is a supporter of your sister," Vincent noted. "Tell me about the young Aeronites."

Tymos began to relate all that he knew, but part way through, he stood abruptly and went over to the compact galley and began to make coffee.

"They are going to need training," Tymos stated as he waited for the water to heat.

"In that you are correct. They both have a trace of Tymorean power."

Tymos became still and then turned back to look at Vincent.

"I should have looked for that when I realised their mind gifts. I know some of the Aeronite warlords had a trace of it. Could these two be children of one of them? But…in the Warlords, Krys and I sensed the warped power. We would have sensed it if Vori and Zorrin were like the warlords."

"These young ones are only just beginning to come into their power. Though, like you and your sister, they likely had the telepathy much earlier. It is possible that contact with you or Kryslie, when they got here, was the catalyst."

"Then it is our duty to teach them," Tymos realised. "However, Krys and I can't train them. We have gained their trust, but if they felt threatened they could be dangerous. If we revealed our own mind gifts, or if they realise that we are Tymorean, I don't know how they would react."

"Adversely, I fear," Vincent warned. "Olassa has gone to Zekos and the general attitude there is that Tymoreans are the evil enemy that allowed a whole planet full of people to die."

Tymos turned back to his task, but he didn't continue with it for a long moment. He had to force away a sense of impotence. There was little that he could do about the misinformation that was rife on the Aeronite colony worlds. "Has she found out anything about Vori and Zorrin?"

"The oldest records that she has accessed, are barely legible. The computer files from that period were corrupted. Finding any information from around the time of the transcession will be difficult."

Tymos picked up the two filled mugs of coffee, and returned to sit opposite Vincent.

"When Earthbase first detected that ship, what speed was it doing? It had slowed to below warp one when Daniel told us about it."

"Warp four," Vincent supplied instantly. "It slowed just after we detected life signs from the crew."

As he placed his coffee on the table, Tymos asked, "Why are we assuming that it left Zekos about the time of the trancession?"

"Great One, at warp four, it would take…"

"Nearly a century to get here. I had already worked hat out. But it doesn't agree with what Vori and Zorrin told me, nor with my estimate of when that other ship crashed on the moon."

"Perhaps, Great One, you would share your thoughts?"

"I have already asked Daniel to try to find out certain things, but that was while you were on the way up. I was talking to Zorrin, and also aware of the thoughts he was sharing with his sister. Their father programmed their ship, before he went away. That was fifteen years before they fled. They believe that they had been in cold sleep for a year. That other ship, if it was their father's ship, has to have been here longer than fifteen years."

Vincent sat back, holding his cup but no longer sipping. "I was permitted to look at the analysis your Dr Long did on the dead crew of the first ship. I have to agree with you, even allowing for the desiccating effect of this airless world. Have you any theories?"

"A few, but I lack data. I have been trying to work out if they are likely for the past few hours."

Vincent recalled his drink, as Tymos stood and began to pace.

"I haven't been able to examine the drive compartment of the first ship, so I can't judge if it was capable of anything greater than warp 4. What if it was?"

"All the small Aeronite ships we examined during the war were not capable of greater speeds."

"But ours were. Possibly the Ciriot ships were. Some of their technology might have been available on Zekos."

"Perhaps, but only the upper echelon would have access to ships."

"Then I need to find out more about their father. If his ship was able to go faster than warp 4, it could have got here more than 15 years ago – Zekos years are longer than Earth years. What that still doesn't explain, is how his children got here so fast. They did not leave before the trancession. It also does not explain how their father even knew where Earth was."

"Stenn Reslic went to Zekos," Vincent revealed. "He would have known."

"Has Olassa been in touch with him?"

"Not yet."

"Did we have missionaries there before the war?"

"Not to my knowledge."

"I will have to get into Zorrin's ship. At least Landin got the okay to have it moved into shuttle bay 2, after the wreck was moved into one of the crawler garages. Trouble is, even though the bay is off limits, most of the crew have the feed from the bay monitors streaming to their terminals. And I can't just transmit in, since I can't assume that this ship is set out the same as the other. I will need to get really close before I try to go in. Anyway, that is not my most urgent priority. Have you examined Basoli?"

Vincent followed Tymos's pacing with his eyes as he spoke. "I have discussed his case with the doctor, and suggested a medicine to calm his temperament. It should make him more pleasant to work with. From the scans that I asked to be done, I have concluded that he is a latent telepath and as a result badly affected by the young Aeronite's mental attack. I would not be surprised if he has always blocked the ability by denying it."

Tymos met Vincent's look as an idea occurred to him. "Maybe it is not all that latent. I think he can sense something about Krys and I, when he is close to us. It might be why he has always been a bit antagonistic towards us – ever since the first time we met."

"I would need to talk to him and gain his confidence to find that out. Is it important?"

"Probably not, more of an oddity." Tymos dismissed the thought for later consideration. He finally recalled his cooling drink and reached down to get it. For a while he sipped it, stopping his pacing, as if lost in thought. Finally, he said, "We need to get bin Halil to leave Krys alone. Are the IC any closer to arresting him?"

"With a man of his Eminence's status, the IC must move carefully," Vincent reminded Tymos. "However, I do believe there is a way. I have suggested a treatment for your sister, and when I go back later, I will insist that the Great One can leave that unpleasant man to me. There is no medical reason for her to be unconscious, when her brain activity is off the scale. Even the doctor here remarked on that."

Tymos began to smile. "It will be a relief to leave bin Halil to you. Just thinking of what he did to Krys this time, as well as on previous occasions, makes me angry. However it would be folly for me to let him know that."

"Rightfully so, Great One. To both sentiments. However, he does not realise his own mistake of wanting to own, or control, a Great One."

Tymos made a sound like a low growl, but Vincent continued.

"It is fortunate for us that he is oblivious to the work of those who revere Great Ones, for they will be the cause of his justly deserved punishment."

"Fortunate because he doesn't know to run and hide," Tymos agreed, and then recalled, "Krys said that she had learnt secrets from his mind. Things he would rather were never discovered. Have you the means to record the information?"

Vincent merely smiled. "I am at the Great One's service."

"I am really glad to have you here, Vincent. I am learning that I can't do everything myself."

"Perhaps you would like to hear my plan to thwart his Eminence?"

"Yes, I would."

"I plan to have Lexina come up here by beam, and take Kryslie's place. She will be seen being evacuated down to Earth whilst Kryslie hides. If I bring her earlier, she can help you examine the ship."

Tymos felt a weight off his mind. "Lexina would be a great help. And that reminds me, did you bring up more of those energy mutating crystals?"

"They are in my luggage. Are you expecting to need them?"

Tymos shook his head, but his words belied the gesture. "I am hoping that we do not, but I have a feeling that we will."

"Would you share your premonition with me?"

Trying to verbalise what was really only a nebulous feeling, he said, "I think I sensed something about the person or people that Zorrin is afraid may be after them."

"There is still a chance that what you fear will not come to pass. Though, you are Great Ones and are more sensitive to the minds of the Guardians. Do you wish our fleet to stand by?"

"Perhaps a discrete watch for ships approaching here?" Tymos said slowly. "And perhaps to be prepared to get the young Aeronites to safety."

"I will see to it," Vincent promised, finishing his drink.

"You need to get back to medical," Tymos guessed. "Do you need me to show you the way?"

"I will be fine, Great One. You will have other matters to attend to."

"Actually, I have been excused from my duty shift today, but I will outwit bin Halil's guard by transmitting back to my quarters to prepare for my foray into Zorrin's ship."

Chapter 22

Vincent went in to see Kryslie at a time when Dr Long was on a break. Her staff had become used to his presence and no longer felt the need to hover around him. He took Krys's wrist as if checking her pulse for himself.

"Great One, you may stop giving that man prophetic nightmares to keep him cowering in his room. You have more important things to do," he chided gently.

Kryslie's eyes opened immediately, and she eyed Vincent without expression. Then she smiled wryly and didn't admit that he had been right.

"Tymos tells me, Great One, that you know secrets from the mind of bin Halil. Do you wish to share them?"

She nodded. "Do you have a recorder?"

Vincent drew out what everyone on Landin's staff thought was a diagnostic device.

"I have adjusted it to your thought pattern, Great one. You may proceed."

He studied the tiny screen while Kryslie closed her eyes again. It showed thought visions, converted into visual images. Her description thoughts were being recorded as sound data, but these he was hearing in is mind as Kryslie narrated the visions. There was no sound coming from the device.

Names, faces, events, deaths, and locations of those that were missing – usually dead. Vincent was impressed by how much information Kryslie remembered from what was a very short melding of her mind to that of bin Halil. Or had she been provoking more of these memories while she had been deep tranced?

"I will pass this to Jonko, and he will have the committee investigate. Some of the places will take time to find – but some will not. Is there any other thing you wish of me? The Chief of the WSRA will be more amenable when he wakes and that will be soon."

"The two Aeronites?" Kryslie asked.

Vincent told her what he had told her brother. She had a different thought about how they might have inherited power.

"Could a Tymorean missionary have married one of their forebears? Consider us for example."

"Great One, you and your brother are exceptional cases. Normally children of mixed matings take after the native parent, and at most only inherit the stamina and intelligence of the Tymorean parent."

"Normally?"

Vincent considered things he had learnt over time. "Few writings tell of the lives of previous Great Ones. They appear on our world, act as they must, and when it appears that they do not age, they go out amongst the stars. It is believed that should they engender children, there is more chance of the child being blessed by the Guardians."

Kryslie considered that. "Arthur?"

"The Prince, who I have spoken to and reassured, has such potential. Were you not aware of it when he was born? His potential is blocked."

She thought back to that exquisite moment. "I think Tymos was thinking more clearly than I, at that time."

"There is no shame in that," Vincent reassured her. "I will be leaving to return to Earth tomorrow. It will be seen that you are being sent with me. President Adamson and the aide, plus the scientists will be leaving as well."

"And bin Halil?"

"Will of necessity need to remain a few more days – until the next shuttle. Tonight he will feel the need to seek me out."

Krys didn't ask the reason. "So, I am to appear comatose until the shuttle departure, and then...?"

"I think you will agree, Great One that you must not be seen while bin Halil remains. Your Commander will perhaps send you to find more of the crystals Tamir Grainger studied. Great One Tymos has some."

"It seems like wasting time."

"Great One Tymos has instructed our President to place ships of the fleet in positions to watch for anyone approaching Earth. You will have time to do what is needful."

"But, lying around here..."Kryslie began to complain, but sensed arrivals in the main infirmary.

"Now you are awake, you will be further protection for the young Aeronites, and when your Commander begins to ask them about themselves, you will be close."

"Have you a cure for slow wits?" Kryslie asked, feeling that her mind must be sluggish.

"Yes, Great One, meditation and the first four mantras for focus and concentration."

"Uncle, that honorific does not seem to suit me right now, will you please omit it?"

"As you wish," Vincent agreed, but she felt the words in her mind as he departed.

"Tym?" Kryslie sent to her brother and felt in return his wordless relief that she was better. "You've been busy. Vincent has told me much of what is intended. What are you doing?"

"I am assigned to Ericson during your indisposition. I have almost finished crafting the parts for the new generator and have attracted the interest of the Chief Engineer and the curiosity of Ericson. He is working out the science for what we plan - from Grainger's published papers. I nudge his thinking at times. He is well on the way. The controller for this generator will be based on the existing ones and programming it will not be difficult."

"I am to find more crystals," Kryslie told him.

"Don't make it too easy," Tymos teased. "Just so you arrive back after your friend departs."

"How is it planned to sneak me off the shuttle? Vincent didn't mention that."

"Lexina transmitted up and is in my quarters," Tymos told her. "She has what is needed to copy the data banks of the Aeronite ship. When Landin is able to question Zorrin, she and I will attempt to sneak aboard. That is likely to be later today. She will replace you on the shuttle. Vincent will handle the other end."

"What of the wrecked shuttle?"

"I thought to suggest that Landin mention it and perhaps Zorrin might help restore its power to try to find out what happened. If not, I will be able to do it."

"Sounds like you managed fine without me."

"I had to. But at least I didn't have to worry about your friend venturing out of his quarters for a bit."

"Yes," Kryslie mused. "I think, even when I confronted him last, that I realised the time would come when his desires diverged from what I had forced on him. Still, no one else could have kept those warring little states together."

"And Arthur is ready," Tymos assured her. "Let me know when the conference with the visitors begins, will you?"

When Landin first arrived in the infirmary to escort the Aeronites, he visited Kryslie to express his gladness at her recovery. She had asked him then, if she could 'listen in' to the meeting by lightly linking to his mind. In spite of a degree of apprehension, he agreed. Though he asked for assurance that his private thoughts would stay private.

"Are you still able to talk to my mind?" Landin had asked, recalling that she had at their first meeting.

"Yes," Krys sent as clearly as she could. Landin's Grandfather had been a telepath, but the commander had only a latent potential.

"Good. If you have any questions you wish to have asked, I will do so."

The rest of the group that had come to escort the Aeronites to the meeting were Mick Schultz and Murtry of Security. The two familiar faces were reassuring, and by now both Zorrin and Vori could recognise the guards. As a gesture of trust, Landin detoured through some of the departments between medical and the meeting room, and offered a longer tout of the base later.

Kryslie sensed Zorrin was keen to see the base – out of genuine interest and with no ulterior motive.

Tymos was ready. His shift had ended and all he had to do was get back to his quarters and transmit Lexina and her equipment into the shuttle bay.

"We will need to arrive between the ship and the bulkhead. There are no electronic monitors there, but there will be guards moving around," Tymos explained to Lexina. "The ship has attracted a lot of curious gawkers. So when we get there, stay close to me and very still."

Lexina nodded.

"It will take me a little time to 'see' where we have to go next," Tymos finished.

Lexina didn't quite know what Tymos meant, but she trusted that he knew what he had to do.

Their timing was a little out. They arrived just as a guard glanced behind the ship.

"Freeze," Tymos told Lexina's mind. He held her close, and both were perfectly still.

"Hey!" the guard shouted. Then he rubbed at his eyes – he thought he had seen someone. "Hey Jacko – where are you?"

A second guard called from the other end of the ship. "What's up?"

"Nothing. I thought I saw someone here, but it must've been you moving down there."

Both guards returned to prowling the bay.

Tymos gave Lexina a grin and then turned to stare at the side of the ship. He was concentrating on seeing what was beyond the outer shell and where there was a space he could transmit into.

It was an odd ability that he had not needed to use for a long time.

"Ok, ready?" Tymos finally had a clear enough picture and transmitted both of them into the ship.

The guards outside had no way of seeing them or knowing they were in there.

Lexina went to the bridge and began to do her task. Tymos went to explore the craft and assess its capabilities and weapons. Neither wasted a moment, or stopped to discuss anything.

Tymos found the two deep sleep tanks, noted that they had been used, but not serviced for re-use. He accessed the computer that had controlled them and what he found was interesting. He examined the two cabins used by the Aeronites and found very little of a personal nature. He did not allow himself to feel guilty about accessing their personal logs and requesting Lexina to copy them.

He moved on to check the remaining food and fuel supplies. There was very little of either, and what he found made him thoughtful. Aeronite preserved rations were little more than compressed protein paste, in vacuum sealed foil packets. Or they had been on the Aeronite ships during the war. The rations on this ship, resembled modern Tymorean emergency supplies - some in vacuum sealed tubes or jars, others with actual compressed and freeze dried vegetables.

The weapons, all in perfect working order, were definitely Aeronite and of the type used when the Aeronites had invaded Tymorea. He must find out how they compared to weapons being used on Zekos now.

He was coming to believe that the ship had somehow been preserved since before the transcession of Aerdna. Surely the population of the Aeronite colonies, even Zekos, could not have built this recently. But then, Zekos had been a scientific colony where much of their new weapons had been developed.

Lexina found him. "I'm finished."

Tymos gave a final glance around and was about to leave when he felt Kryslie in his mind.

"Zorrin has asked to be allowed to go to his ship – to show them some information. They are on the way now."

"We are going now," Tymos returned mentally. He again held Lexina next to him and this time transmitted directly to his quarters.

"Can you start looking at what you got," Tymos requested. "I want to know what Zorrin might show them."

"Yes, Great One," she agreed. "Do you think they are dangerous?"

"Only if cornered," Tymos said. "They know only the basics of flying that ship. It is fortunate that they encountered no trouble. They did not service the sleep units when they emerged and they had no idea of conserving fuel either. But that is not the main concern I have. They were not in deep sleep for very long and I don't think they realise that. Nor has that ship the range to have got from near Zekos to near here, even if they flew it to conserve fuel."

Lexina considered that. "But how is that possible?"

"We can do it?" Tymos said. He wondered if she would see the conclusion he had come to.

"They don't have long range beams or mass transmitters. Ah! Tymoreans do, the missionary might...Stenn?"

"I hope so, but why? Why send them here?" Tymos wanted to know.

"It was somewhere so far away that he hoped pursuit wouldn't find them?" Lexina proposed. "And Stenn knew you and Krys were here."

"Both good points, but any world with Tymorean missionaries would do." That was what Tymos thought, but something was nudging his mind, like the start of a premonition.

When Zorrin and Vori arrived at the room with a low table and chairs, three men were standing watching them enter. They glanced at each, but while Zorrin concentrated on the man in the centre, Vori studied the other two men. That they were standing more than a double arm's span apart suggested that they were not all close friends. She wasn't sure if that was a good sign or not, and she dared trying to sense more of their feelings.

The central man, the shortest of the three and the one she'd seen before, wasn't as jittery as before. That surprised her, since if she had been standing between two powerful men, who had no real liking for each other, she'd have felt even more jittery. Both of the strangers reminded her of members of the High Council on Zekos. The stood straight and tall, held themselves as if they were aware of their own importance.

She turned her attention to the man she knew as Landin, as he made introductions. The President of the United World Nations, the Leader of the Imperium, the men's names meant nothing to her, they were just sounds. Then he added, "And you have met Commander in Chief Basoli."

Zorrin spoke to her mind, "What do you make of these people?"

She answered the same way. "Basoli is much calmer, the man on the right, the President, seems interested in us, but the other one – the one with the darker shade of skin - makes my skin crawl. I think, he thinks, we are fakes."

"That is actually a good thing," Zorrin decided. "It means that we could easily blend in with these people as father said."

"I don't like him, and the guard by the wall is watching him…when I thought he would be watching us more."

Landin invited then to sit, and directed them to seats at the table. Vori was glad to have the friendly Mick Shultz on her left, and Zorrin on her right and he didn't mind having Landin on his other side.

The seating arrangement, with an empty space between Mick and the President, the President and Basoli, Basoli and the other Leader, referred to now as Eminence, and that man and Landin, intrigued her, but she didn't see the reason for it.

Once they were settled, a parade of three people dressed in less impressive versions of Landin's uniform, place trays on the table so that one was within reach of all the guests. They departed, and this time returned with glasses – placing three differed shapes ones in front of each person.

"I'd stick to just water," Mick Shultz whispered into Vori's ear. "The other drinks come from various fruits and grains grown on Earth. Most of them are fermented, and I don't know if they would adversely affect you. All the food on the trays should be okay for you to eat."

Zorrin heard the advice and mentally told his sister, "Don't eat anything until you see the others eating some."

Vori glanced at the trays, and the drinks and felt that this 'meeting' would not be as bad as she's feared. The room was nothing like the inquisition chamber on Zekos when the Leader there had wanted answers from them.

Landin, who was now saying, "Vori and Zorrin arrived here in a two person scout craft containing deep sleep technology. It is in our shuttle bay. The slight sound of static made her turn to see a pictures of their ship projected onto a wall. In her mind, she heard, "At least the guards are keeping everyone away from it."

Zorrin, too, had glanced at the pictures, but he quickly returned his attention to the important Leaders. The one referred to as "President" was interested in their ship. The once called Eminence had not bothered to look at the screen. He had not taken his eyes off himself and Vori. The regard was unsettling, and Zorrin recalled some of his uncle's advice. He returned the man's gaze, the way he had when it had been the high born brats of the Warlord's descendants that had tried to bully him. He thought as he did that the clothing worn by the two leaders weren't uniforms. It had the same general appearance as Landin's uniform, but without the fancy stuff indicating rank and in both cases, the actual look was different. He had thought 'uniform' since the attire was unlike the flowing robes favoured by the High Councillors of Zekos, and more like the attire worn by the Imperial Enforcers.

His mind translated Landin's words, realised that they were directed at him, and he took his eyes of the Leader of the Imperium and turned them to Landin.

"Thank you for agreeing to talk to us. Perhaps you would tell us about yourselves and where you come from."

Before Zorrin answered, he thought at his sister, "You watch everyone – I'll do the talking."

He did glance at each of the humans present before talking. "Our home was Zekos. It scientific colony, settled by people from Aerdna."

"Tell us what it is like," Landin prompted when Zorrin had paused for a long moment. Vori had said to his mind, "I don't know that they really believe you."

"Has many, many people. Has tall buildings, lots of them, close together."

Vori, despite her brother's suggestion, spoke up. "Our uncle said it was beautiful once, before refugees from Aerdna arrived in flood. That was many years before we were born, generations, but he had picture from that time."

Zorrin went on quickly, "All people that came needed places to live, all idle land was needed for housing, or for factories to force grow food for all of them. The scientific enclaves, need many guards now."

"No one goes outside much, unless they have own air to breathe," Vori added.

Adamson, who had been listening with an open mind tinged with a degree of fascination, asked, "Is that why you chose to leave?"

"No!" Vori shuddered. "Had to we did, or dead we would wish to be."

"What crimes did you commit," bin Halil drawled, as he leant forward to take a delicacy from one of the trays. When the answer wasn't immediate, he went on, "Surely, you would not risk the dangers of space travel for something trivial."

Landin kept his face neutral, even though he was recalling how Zorrin had reacted before.

"We…our father…," Zorrin began, searching for the words he needed while feeling that all the humans were turning hostile.

"Our father was called a saviour," Vori said. "Improve things he did, Try to clean air, make our world nicer. People liked him, followed his ideas, of those of Power Council."

Zorrin added a quick explanation, "Power Council made of those whose forebears were warlords. Think themselves little gods. Take best of everything, as right, they think."

Landin nodded with sympathy. "So, he was persecuted?"

Zorrin glanced at Schultz, who provided an explanation in simpler words. "Yes, persecuted. We too young then to know, but our mother said, he fled, so could not be made work for Power Council."

"She said, people tortured, so he be made to do dreadful things," Vori added.

"Leader of the council was angry, and went after him," Zorrin said in turn.

Into Landin's mind came a question from Kryslie. "How did their father flee, and where did he go?"

Landin's mind immediately recalled the wrecked ship and its dead pilot. He asked the question aloud.

"Told we were, he left in space ship. One of two he had found and fixed," Zorrin revealed. "One of ships from Aerdna, came with one of Warlords before Aerdna transcended. Been in chamber buried by lava from eruptions at that dire time."

"Where did he go?" bin Halil asked. "Here?"

Vori's eyes widened and her face seemed to take on a greenish shade. In her mind, Zorrin said, "Don't tell them that!"

She replied the same way, "I think they know of another ship before ours." All she said aloud was, "When we ask, years later, many rumours were there," her voice was shaky. "Even our mother did not know."

Basoli finally spoke up. "If your council leader went after him, did he return?"

"Not for years, when fifteen we had become," Zorrin told them.

"While he gone, Zekos better place," Vori said. "When back, people taken again, tortured." She was shaking now, as memories she had tried to forget returned.

"Had he not found your father?" Basoli asked, in a gentle voice, and it drew Vori's eyes to him.

"No, said people, and he angry and wanted to find all who helped him. Then he found out we were children of our father."

"Ordered us to see him," Zorrin added, as he too shuddered at the memory. "Thought it lie, we did, that magic he could do. True it was. He hold us like pinned bugs, without touching us. Made us talk, though we willed it not."

"Made us hurt! Since knew we not, the answers he want," Vori confirmed. "Sick we became, and dirty we felt. Hoped we did, he'd leave us be."

"Our uncle learnt that he wanted us then, as slaves, as puppets. Took us Uncle did, told us where to hide. We run away just as the Justifiers came for us," Zorrin said.

"Why didn't you just stand up to him," bin Halil drawled.

Basoli gave the smirking leader of the Imperium a glance.

"Him, fight we could not. Said that I did. No one who try, lives more. If he want you dead, you die."

"So, you had a convenient space ship," bin Halil continued with a faint sneer on his face.

"Uncle knew of it. Promise Father he did, to protect us."

"So…why are you more important that he was? You are mere children."

Kryslie murmured in Landin's mind, "That's a good question."

Landin asked, "What became of your mother and uncle?"

Now Zorrin seemed to slump, and he looked down at the table. "Learn we did, our mother died. Tell where we were, she could not. Uncle to flee, once we gone, or he die too."

"Why didn't he come with you?" Basoli asked.

"Ship only for two, and long way to go, only two sleep tanks," Zorrin explained.

"So, how did you know how to control the ship?" Basoli asked. "Since your father left when you were very young."

"We know of ship. And father make program and we practice."

"But how did you know where to come? How did your father know?" Basoli persisted.

"Father knew! He program ship, we just follow program." Zorrin was back to glaring at Basoli, as he was sounding hostile again.

"So, he stole two ships," bin Halil drawled again. "No wonder he was wanted. What else did he steal?"

"Father, a thief NOT!" Vori's voice rose in pitch. "He good man!"

Landin decided that it was time to distract his guests. It wasn't hard to tell from their facial expressions that they were beginning to be afraid.

"You used a word before… transcended… what did you mean?"

Zorrin turned to face him. "Explain, I will try. Taught we were, that Aerdna, our people's home, was flung out of orbit by cataclysm. It now wandering lifeless, dead, in space. Happened it did, and ground quakes rocked Zekos for years, and volcanos erupted. Only those who fled Aerdna, like those who came to Zekos, lived."

"Father find ships in old lava," Vori said, staring defiantly at bin Halil. "War and cataclysm long over, then. Ships belong to no one. Find them he did. Find and fix so they could fly again."

In Landin's mind, Kryslie remarked, "Their father expected trouble…I wonder why?" He didn't have a chance to ask the question, because Adamson posed a question.

"Why do you think that your father was called a saviour?"

The two Aeronites looked at each other, and Landin, having occasionally noticed Kryslie and her brother do that, wondered if they were silently communicating.

"Our mother said it was because he came when the council had forced harsh rationing on everyone, so the lesser citizens went hungry and the council got all they wanted." Vori seemed to be trying to recall a long ago conversation. "He was illuminated scientist, he figure out how to grow food in caves, in water, in any place there was."

"Why didn't he do that earlier?" Basoli asked. "Before people were desperate."

Zorrin fidgeted. "Some people say he waited, so he seem like saint. Uncle say, people were praying for help and that's when the ship was found."

"By your father?" bin Halil interrupted.

"No, father was asleep in it."

Bin Halil snorted a laugh. "This sounds like a fairy story – concocted for children. Please, do go on."

With an eye on the Imperium's leader, Zorrin did. "It is said, that when he woke up, heard how things were, he said he could help, and did."

From her bed in medical, Kryslie murmured to Landin, "Cold sleep."

Landin responded by asking, "Do you mean that he had been asleep for many generations?"

"Yes, like we were asleep for many years coming here. We told that journey would take so long and ship too small to hold enough food."

Zorrin was still looking at Landin as he asked, "Can you tell us where Zekos is in relation to Earth?" Landin saw the subtle eye widening of his guests, and even though they did not glance at each other again, he had the feeling again that they were talking.

Kryslie, listening from medical, heard, "Why do they want to know that? They should not go there. If they do, others may come here. I wish we could contact father. I should have taken off again and gone to the planet."

Vori's response was, "You said we couldn't."

Zorrin added silently, "I have an idea." Then he spoke aloud. "Ur, we could if we were on our ship."

Basoli repeated an earlier question, but his mind held a picture of the earlier wreck and the dead pilot. "But how did your father know how to get here?"

Vori stared at him, "Did he come here? Is he here?"

When Basoli didn't answer, she turned to Landin, and he could only think her look was of pleading.

"We recently uncovered a ship – similar to yours – that had been buried for un-guessable years under the lunar dust," Landin told her gently and with sympathy.

"Can we see this ship?" Zorrin asked. "Was our father asleep on it?"

Landin shook his head. "The pilot must have died many years ago. We have carefully removed the remains and have them in stasis. Would you be able to tell if it is your father?"

"The computer should tell us that," Vori stated. "Can we access it?"

"There is no power on the ship." Landin told them.

"You must let us see it – go to it," Zorrin demanded.

Landin saw Basoli about to object.

"Certainly," Landin agreed. "Later though."

He had heard Kryslie's warning. "That has got both of them upset. They really expected to meet him on Earth."

Once again, Landin decided to distract his guests. "You have not tried any of the refreshments. My cooks have made a selection of well-liked Earth sweets, and surely, after talking so much, you will be thirsty."

Zorrin greeted the change of subject with, "Yes, I would have water, please."

Yes, water is good choice," Vori agreed.

Landin gestured Murtry over, to pour from the carafe of iced water, adding, "I'll have the same."

"What do you like, Commander Landin?" Vori asked.

He gave his suggestions, and indicated each on the nearest plates. However, he noticed that they each took only the ones that either Adamson or bin Halil had also tasted.

Kryslie murmured softly into Landin's mind. "They think that they would not poison food that two important leaders might eat." On a much deeper level, she shielded the thought that she could easily poison bin Halil.

Landin thought in his mind, "Did they really expect to find their father alive?"

In reply, "Perhaps hoped is a better word. They are quite young, still idealistic. Don't under estimate them though, they are both clever, and very intelligent – but not used to fending for themselves. What concerns me is – if their father was the pilot of that wrecked ship, and if the person who followed him was away for some years, did that person give up and return home, or catch up to their father, kill him, and then return. It is possible the pilot of that ship was dead before he crashed."

Landin considered that, his mind going over all the reports to date on the wrecked ship.

Finally, he decided to ask a question, as he needed to know if his base might be in danger.

"If your father was followed, is it possible that you were?"

Zorrin considered that. "I do not think so. We travelled for two weeks before going into deep sleep. Our ship sensors detected no other ships in that time. If any had approached while we slept, I would have been woken.

When we did wake, we travelled for another two weeks and saw no other ships."

Basoli accepted that, but Landin sensed that Krys, in his mind, wasn't so sure, though she didn't choose to challenge it.

Adamson asked, "Having come here, what are your intentions?"

Vori glanced around. "We just wanted to be able to have a good life and use what few skills we have to be useful citizens here."

"What skills do you have?" Basoli asked. He had a few ideas he wanted to explore.

"We studied history, philosophy, and science to be like our father," Zorrin said proudly.

"What can you tell us about your ship?" Basoli asked, he leant forward to better hear their answer.

Zorrin glanced at his sister again. "We would like to live on the planet below," he said. "We will tell you what we know in exchange for a safe haven down there."

Bin Halil, seeing an opportunity to examine this supposed alien technology, was quick to speak up, "I would be honoured to offer you a home in the Imperium."

Adamson spoke right after, "As would I in the United World Nations."

"I think it would be up to our visitors to learn more about the diverse people and cultures on Earth before they should decide," Basoli commented, keeping his tone neutral. "And I must point out that the WSRA is a neutral body with the aims of advancing science for the benefit of all people."

For a few moments, the attention was off the two Aeronites, as the three visitors from Earth sent unspoken looks at each other, in a sort of battle for supremacy.

Landin looked away from his Chief and the two leaders when Kryslie warned, "I think such talk of divisions in Earth's culture is upsetting them. Or it might be that they sense that bin Halil now covets them."

He took the hint. "Until these newcomers have had a chance to learn more about us – all invitations will, I assume, remain open. They may decide to go elsewhere."

Kryslie advised him, "They have neither enough food, or fuel to go anywhere and Zorrin knows it. He will bluff if he can. There is no harm in letting him think he has succeeded."

As if seeming to continue the earlier conversation, Landin asked, "You mentioned that your people had a war. What do you know of it?"

The question made both Vori and Zorrin sit up straight, faces blank. Finally, Zorrin, said, uncertainly, "Every Aeronite child learns about it, but of what matter is it here? Long, long, long ago it was."

Landin explained, "Until recently, Earth's only knowledge of worlds distant to ours was what we learnt from telescopes and probes. None had been found with a civilisation on it. On Earth, it is generally believed that we are the only world that contains life. Now, having met you, he thought of a war, implies enemies who might find Earth one day. I would like to know what we might expect, so that we can be prepared to defend ourselves."

Vori silently told her brother that the chance of them being found was virtually zero, but if she was wrong, she wanted the humans to be able to protect them. Her bother thought back, "Then there is no harm in telling them about the old war, and we gain good will for telling them."

Vori pictured herself shrugging.

"The enemy of that war would not bother to come here," Zorrin proclaimed with outward certainty. He wasn't going to go into detail of the aeon's long enmity resulting from the Aeronites separation from the world that had birthed their race. "Our scientists knew that our world was in trouble. The leaders sent envoys back to the world where our people had originated – begging for help. Their pleas were rejected. Our leaders asked if our people could return, and that too was refused. They had large areas of unclaimed land, it used to be the home of the Aeronite people, we had the right…"

"Are you saying that your people invaded that other world?" Adamson asked pointedly.

Zorrin only then realised that it could be seen that way, but all his life, he had been told that that had had the moral right – their own world was dying. He ignored the question and jumped ahead.

"Our enemies, who were once kin, didn't try to help us – they sent us away and those who dared to stay were slaughtered. Even our allies, the Ciriot, who tried to change the minds of the leaders, were killed."

Vori added with passion, "Only a fraction of our people made it safely to the colonies. The rest of the Aeronites died horribly, as the planet was flung into space, the atmosphere ripped away, the ground frozen."

Landin heard a sound like, "Hmpf" in his mind, and thought, "Are they lying?"

From her distant location, Kryslie had to admit, "It is what they believe. It is what they were taught. It is possible that the people who reached the colonies did not know the full truth, or wish to admit it. There are other views of the conflict."

Basoli was already asking, "So, who were these enemies that would not help you?"

"Tymoreans!" Zorrin hissed. "They are evil incarnate, although their leaders claim to be so intelligent, so important to the universe. But they are greedy, venial, killers…"

While Zorrin told of the evil done by Tymoreans, Vori was mentally babbling, "Landin, he knows of Tymoreans. I don't think, the others do. I think there are Tymoreans here."

Zorrin paused to think back at her, "Probably some of their spying missionaries. We must find out who they are if they are still here."

"What if they are? Surely they are just biding their time, waiting to kill us. They must have tricked Landin."

While Zorrin went on about Tymoreans destroying Aeronite food crops, omitting to say the crops had been planted illegally on Tymorea, and how the Tymoreans had sent mind warping gases and used other weapons on the Aeronites, and quoting his teachers, he told Vori, "I will insist on being allowed back onto our ship. I'll offer to show them where Zekos is, and while I do, you grab the weapons. Then I will make them show me that other ship, it must be fathers, and there will be more weapons there. Even ones that will work on Tymoreans."

Adamson questioned his view of these enemies, but Zorrin remained adamant. The Tymoreans were guilty of genocide.

Basoli had more questions, but decided to hold off and simply offered them a chance to exchange knowledge – earth sciences for theirs – and a promise of protection and help to get settled. He hoped that they would decide to work for the WSRA.

Bin Halil refrained from further comments, merely stared at the two aliens. His expression was not quite a smile, since he was trying to decide between being thought a gullible fool for believing such fantastic drivel, while coveting the chance to get access to advanced alien technology.

Landin felt that it was time to end the meeting and take up Zorrin's offer to find out where Zekos was in relation to Earth. He neatly side-stepped the desire of Adamson and bin Halil to follow them out to the ship by pointing out that that the alien ship was quite small.

Zorrin added, "Honoured Sirs, my ship only has small bridge and to understand, need you would, knowledge of astro-science."

Adamson was not insulted. "Young man, you are correct. It would mean little to me. However, I would welcome another opportunity to talk with you."

He waited until Landin had led the two aliens from the room, and found himself thinking that it was hard to think of them as aliens, since they looked near enough human – except for those odd, whiteless eyes. Then he turned to Basoli and asked, "Are you going to keep those two here for now?"

"Yes, Mr President. I do not think that they would wish to be separated from their ship, and I hope they will help us solve the mystery of the wrecked ship."

"Will you tell us of all that you learn from these…aliens?" Abdul bin Halil's tone insinuated that he thought that Basoli would not.

"Certainly, your Eminence. However, you may wish to consider if all the people of the Imperium need to know of this visit."

"Most of them? No. Have you plans to bring them and their ship down to Earth where the world's scientists may study it?"

"If we get the agreement of our guests, yes, although we would need to rig a towing pod for it."

Murtry, who had not left his position by the wall since acting as waiter, used his Wi-Fi headpiece to summon the escorts for the two leaders. He was uncomfortable at being in the same room as both the world's leaders, in case anything happened to either. He couldn't wait for them both to leave, but that would not be for a further two days, when the next regular shuttle was due.

He refrained from scowling only by an act of will. He recalled Landin's private belief that bin Halil had somehow contrived the injury to Kryslie Ward. He couldn't imagine why the man would do such a thing, to someone he couldn't possibly know. The med-evac shuttle would be departing downside later in the day, perhaps one of the leaders would go on it? Adamson by choice. But no, while the aliens were here, neither would want the other to have a clear field to influence them. Though why they were so trusting, he couldn't understand. That male had somehow given lots of people a blinding headache, so there was more to him than he was showing now.

The C-I-C had risen a notch in his estimation though. He wouldn't want to be the one to have to stand between the leaders, who were showing by the distance that they kept from one another, that they were not close friends.

As Landin escorted the two aliens towards the shuttle bay and the ship, with Schultz following behind and two discreet guards joining them once they were outside the room, he thought, "Was it true?"

He was aware of Vori looking at him and wondered if she had heard the thought.

Back in medical, Kryslie knew she had and she did not respond to Landin's thought straight away. Instead, she considered if her other communications with Landin had been sensed.

No, she decided. The two Aeronites had too much else on their minds, and now they had less, and were close to Landin.

Finally she sent, "Talk later."

She felt Vori react to her thought, and she them kept her own mind silent until Vori decided that the thought must have been Landin's. Only then did she withdraw her mind from the Commander's – so smoothly that he did not notice.

Tymos was already aware that Zorrin was heading for his ship. He had been scanning the ship from end to end, seeing what his detector could tell him of its structure and capabilities. He had also received his sister's warning, "Vori and Zorrin believe there are Tymoreans here, and intend to get weapons from their ship and more from the wreck."

"If we keep our PFS on their weapons won't affect us," Tymos shrugged off that worry. "Anyway, if they use them on the base, they will find out about the energy damper field."

"And if they freak again?" Kryslie had challenged.

"We have more guards than they can disable with a damped down energy weapon. I think in that case, Zorrin is more likely to use his mind tricks. However, if he has a weapon, he may feel secure enough to control the mind punch. Look, Krys, we are almost finished here, and only got until the start of beta shift, when you are supposedly leaving, to analyse this data."

There was no sign that anyone had been on the ship when Zorrin arrived and activated his ship's computer. As he began to give Landin the basics of astro-navigation, Vori went off to get their weapons. She wasn't aware that her inner agitation was enough for Kryslie to locate, and use to anchor her mind. The Aeronite, girl rather than woman, had picked up Landin's surprise when Tymoreans were mentioned, and jumped immediately to the worst case scenario. Would she believe that the person who had saved her life was an enemy? Hard to say, since they firmly believed that any Tymorean would kill them. Well, Kryslie decided, as someone who was 'critical' in medical, about to be evacuated to Earth –

Vori could not consider her a threat. They liked and trusted Tymos, at the moment, and he did not need to be with them constantly.

Her attention was returned to her own surroundings when Vincent arrived with the evacu-capsule and two med techs. She closed her eyes and forced her body rhythms to mimic a state of unconsciousness. By the time Vincent had finished explaining aspects of the capsule to the med techs, the machines attached to her were showing appropriate signals.

Kryslie had never seen one of the capsules before, but had all the knowledge she needed come into her mind. These were developed on Tymorea, and after this 'test' this unit would be presented to the WSRA. The capsule was very like a deep sleep chamber, and Kryslie knew to expect the tubes for fluid in, fluid out, oxygen in, carbon dioxide out, and the electro-dots to connect the monitors to. She let the med techs do their work, aware from Vincent's mind that he intended to swap Lexina into the capsule as soon as enough people had seen Kryslie in there.

Dr Long entered the side room with a message.

"Vincent, the commander would like a word with you – you can use my terminal."

With a slight bow of acknowledgement, and a quick glance to check the work of the two techs, Vincent departed.

Long waited for the techs to finish, dismissed them, and then spoke to Kryslie.

"Are you sure this charade will work? It would only take someone getting close to this capsule to see it is empty."

"It will be fine, Doc. People will see what they expect to see."

"Perhaps, but it is an expensive exercise, and I believe that the President has had word of an emergency situation and must leave with you."

"You worry too much. Everything will go as planned, no one will realise that I am still here."

Long forced her concern aside, and reverted to routine, checking all the vital signs of her patient, and telling her to get some sleep.

Tymos sent her a thought. "Vincent is getting Lexina ready now. It seems that Adamson needs to return as soon as possible, so he will be on the evac shuttle too. Plan is to swap you and Lexina, while he is hooking the capsule up in the shuttle. Adamson won't be allowed to board until that is done. You will be launching ahead of schedule."

"All the better. What did you find?"

"Our analysis was interrupted, so I will have to get Homebase to go over the logs to be sure, but I believe that Zorrin's ship came part way here by long range beam. There is a jump in the auto position recording."

It took an effort of will for Kryslie to stay lying calmly, and not try to sit up. "If that is so, a Tymorean must have helped them…so why would they fear us so much?"

"Start with brain washing from infancy and the fact that our missionaries usually do not proclaim what they are. I have told Daniel and Vincent my theory, and they will pass it to Olassa. Maybe she can find the answer."

Chapter 24

The changeover went smoothly. No one saw Lexina arrive, for she transmitted into the shuttle, swapped her black wig for a blond one that resembled Kryslie's current hair colour and style and took her place. Vincent quickly attached her to the capsule, and sealed her in, and gave Kryslie a glance to remind her to transmit away.

Only then, did he give the okay for the President and his guards to board. They were already clad in the gold coloured flight suits, and only had to attach the helmets. The flight crew had completed their checks and were ready to depart.

Tymos had inserted himself into the shuttle bay crew, watching out for bin Halil's guard. He waited there until the shuttle had launched, before walking back to his quarters.

Kryslie had not been idle in that short time. Her hair was now dyed black, and cut short to match the ID of her temporary alias, Janelle Daniels.

"I think your friend will be convinced of your departure. His spy was smiling," Tymos told his sister, who was using his quarters to hide in.

"I hope he has no plans to infiltrate the University Medical facility to have me finished off," Kryslie countered.

"Let Vincent worry about that. We have work to do here. I have your temporary ID. Apart from Landin, only Ericson, his second, and ourselves know about it. Vincent will organise your return in a suitable fashion."

"Fair enough," Kryslie decided. "What orders do you have for me?"

"Landin told me he wants you out with the crew searching for more of Grainger's crystals. They will be going off as soon as the maintenance crew finish preparing the spare shuttle for an extended search – they are adding sleep pods for everyone in the cargo hold. I have upgraded the analytical devices to detect smaller amounts of the crystals."

"Do I need to stay here? I could help with the shuttle prep."

"Wouldn't it be better to stay here until you need to leave?"

"I am not afraid of being recognised, and I will not let bin Halil scare me into hiding."

"Please yourself."

The maintenance crew leader was glad to have an extra pair of hands, and once he was sure she knew what she was doing, let her get on with the work. She was bringing extra supplies to stow in the various hatches in the cargo pod.

She was wearing maintenance coveralls and wheeling a supply trolley towards the shuttle when her empathic senses warned her that bin Halil was near. She did not look to see where he was, and waited for her fellow workers to tell her that the Imperium's leader was having a tour of the shuttle bay. She was in plain view, going in and out of the shuttle with supplies, as Stanley explained what the shuttle was being prepared for.

Mentally, she gave her brother a pre-warning. His immediate response was, "Is that guard of his with him?"

Kryslie allowed herself a quick glance at the party. "Seems not. Why?"

"If he is here, being obvious…"

An idea, possibly coming through the twin bond, prompted her to comment, "All my stuff has been taken from my quarters…" She felt Tymos's chuckle.

Thanks to his sister's warning, Tymos wasn't surprised when the tour brought bin Halil to the R and D lab. He kept working, not being important enough to talk to the Imperium's leader. Ericson had that dubious honour. However, he was the object of scrutiny for a few minutes as his current project was explained. Since he was doing a final test of all the upgraded detectors, Ericson mentioned the search for more of a specific kind of crystal that was to be used in screens to block energy discharges. This idea must have interested bin Halil, for he asked several sharp and pertinent questions.

Tymos ignored the conversation and kept working, as well as speaking to his sister. "I wonder if he will be invited to watch the shuttle launch, since he was not present when the med evac shuttle went."

Kryslie sent back a picture of herself yawning. "Thank the Guardians that he will be gone when I get back. What will you be doing while I am gone?"

"I am to help the attempt to repower the wrecked ship, since Zorrin and I get on so well. Though I really don't expect him to be much help. He has only basic knowledge of his ship, and he knows nothing of our systems.

Vori had opted to stay in their quarters off medical when Zorrin went off to help with trying to power the old ship. The previous evening, she and her brother had been shown the preserved remains from the wrecked ship. The body could not be readily reconciled with their memory of their father. The face and hands were nothing but dried skin stretched over bone. The sight still haunted her. To distract her mind, she went in search of the doctor.

Like her brother, Vori was allowed some freedom of movement, albeit under the watchful eye of some guards. She accepted that, since to her mind, the caution of the humans towards aliens made good sense. Besides, she had sensed that some of the humans were suspicious and fearful of them and would edge away from them.

So far, she had not sensed any that wanted to hurt them. Covet them though, yes she had. As if having them around would give them more prestige and power. She had met one of the leaders from Earth, after their talk, and he had made promise of vast riches, if she and her brother came to the Imperium. That unsettled her. If he was offering riches what did he expect they could do for him?

Her other fear was that there were Tymoreans around, waiting to catch them alone. Would the humans protect her and Zorrin from them when the vile Tymoreans were good at looking like the natives?

Vori found Long supervising the preparation of the 'critical care' unit for future patients. She kept out of the way until the doctor saw her and came over.

"Hello, did you need something?"

"I..." Vori began. "I don't want to be trouble to you, but I not seen Krys Ward since we come here. See her, can I?"

Vori sensed a mixture of things from the doctor. The first was that Krys had been the room's previous occupant, and had been badly hurt. The second was that she had supposedly gone down to Terra 1 that morning. This is what Long told her verbally.

"What happened? Will she be all right? She was kind to us," Vori spoke carefully. Her own thought of making Krys an ally was thwarted.

"An accident we think," Long had no intention of being specific, but her mind flicked to the effect these aliens had had on some minds and briefly to the mark on Kryslie's neck that could have been from a fall or an attempt to kill her. "We are concerned about a spinal injury."

Again Vori sensed more than was said. The doctor had not lied. Krys had been that bad, but Krys had recovered fast - unusually so.

"There is a good chance for recovery," Long finished.

Her thought that Krys was still on base, reassigned to a department of lesser importance until someone departed, made Vori thoughtful – especially after the thought of Kryslie's rapid recovery.

"Was she hurt because of us? Zorrin heard she blacked out. We didn't mean to hurt people just...warn them off."

"It might have been from that," Long admitted. "Many of the guards that met you had severe headaches. But to be honest, her injury suggested more than just blacking out and falling."

"Are you saying someone hurt her because she helped me?" Vori asked.

Long hadn't considered that. "I don't think so, even though I know there are some xenophobic tendencies. The psychological profiles of everyone considered to work here are carefully analysed."

Vori fleetingly thought of the other visitors on the base – the two Earth leaders, the scientists, and the doctor who had spoken briefly to them. They had all gone now, hadn't they?

She dismissed that concern, as her mind returned to the fact that Krys Ward had recovered fast and was still on the base – covertly.

What subterfuges were these humans intending or were they being manipulated by the Tymoreans? Vori shivered and decided to re-join her brother. Her hand moved to feel the weapon in her pocket.

Tymos was just one of the team trying to repower the wrecked alien ship. Zorrin was trying to explain what was needed but while his technical knowledge of his ship's systems was adequate, it was based on everything being Aeronite. And, as Tymos suspected, the way the Aeronite thought about things was quite different to how the humans had come to understand the same principals.

Zorrin wasn't unintelligent, and the Chief Engineer, Atticus Flannigan, was using a wall sized data padd to teach him the basic principles as learnt by humans. As Tymos had found before, it was the diagrams that helped the most.

However, the main problem would remain, that the connections used on the Aeronite ship were physically incompatible with the human style. If though, he was known for what he truly was, Tymos could have obtained a generator that would have been powered human style, but have connections that were nearer to Aeronite that human ones.

Well he wasn't, Tymos reminded himself, so the humans would simply have to re-invent the way to merge the two technologies. He knew, when the others did not, that the ships computer was useless. What he had succeeded in copying from it was unreadable.

He wasn't going to make that stop him, since other parts of the ships system, might still work if able to be powered, and he would just have to make an interface using human computers. It was a perfect way for the scientists and techs to discover new ideas.

After two days, Flannagan had decided to try to break the two technologies down to basic details. Tymos could see that the process would not work, as Zorrin did not have enough knowledge.

"Could we bring the computer unit from the dead ship and plug it in on the working ship," he suggested. He already knew that Zorrin had vetoed the idea, but he hadn't been officially present at the time. He also knew from the same unofficial source, that Zorrin didn't want to let Earth scientists look too closely at his ship yet.

The previous evening, he had only let Landin enter. He had brought up the navigation computer and shown the programmed journey and starting coordinates. He had needed to give Landin a basic orientation in astronavigation to understand it. Now the Lunar 1 navigation experts were studying the data, including the coordinates of the way points. Tymos had already decided the information was flawed.

Flanagan's communicator played a few bars of an old nautical tune, and he pulled it from his pocket. After reading the message, he apologised and explained, "Zorrin, I have to attend another matter. I will leave our wunderkind, Tym, in charge here until I get back."

When he had gone, Zorrin echoed the unfamiliar word to Tymos.

"He has other duties that can't be delegated," Tymos explained. "He doesn't want you to feel reduced in importance. What he called me was a German word that translates to wonder child in English."

Tymos let his mind reveal that there were many other languages on Earth besides English.

"Are you so much smarter than everyone else?" Zorrin asked.

Tymos shook his head. "I have a knack for this sort of thing, that's all. In terms of smart, everyone that works in the scientific departments here are of the top percentile of applicants to the WSRA. The best of the best we say."

He sensed that some faint suspicion in Zorrin's mind had been allayed, and he quickly got back to the job in hand. He asked, "Do you think there might be a power generator on the wrecked ship that we might study?"

The search team under Leonard Chung, who was Ericson's second in the R and D section, had set up camp in the area of Mare Orientale, a prominent impact basin almost 1,000 kilometres wide. This was the area where the Grainger crystals were purported to have been discovered and the current search area was determined by close analysis of the data from the lunar probe that had found them.

They were working on the theory that at the time of the original find, the instruments in use were not as sensitive as they were now, and so smaller pieces of the unusual conglomerate, unnoticed by the probe, might be found. Indeed, the original crystals were fist sized conglomerates and it was conceivable that when the meteorite they had come from, broke up on impact, smaller pieces might have been scattered.

Kryslie was answering to Janelle Daniels during the search, and since they were all required to live in their EA suits, no one was able to tell that she wasn't just a WRSA tech on temporary rotation to Lunar 1.

Landin had agreed to her short-term alias, and independently decided that having her away from the base while she was meant to be Earthside was sensible. Moreover, if he had suspicions about Ericson's request to look for more of 'Grainger's' crystals – and where the idea had come from, he kept them to himself. He knew that she and her brother had handled the original crystals, had contributed significantly to old Prof Emmanuel's ground breaking work, even if their names did not appear in the credits, and probably knew more about the crystals than anyone, except perhaps Tamir Grainger himself.

The proposal for new shields, incorporating these crystals, was described in logical terms, and certainly seemed like a prudent line of research. Somehow though, Kryslie was certain that Landin was not deceived by Tymos's statement that it was merely a contingency plan, and half believed it would be a necessity. That being so, he probably believed that if anyone could find more of the crystals, she could.

That the search area was currently in darkness, was making the search harder. Even though each day's search grid was lit by battery powered floodlights, the team had to rely on their instruments rather than their eyesight. Every little piece of rubble, threw long shadows, and the searchers themselves threw bigger ones. They used the satellites that circled the moon, to keep their line search moving ahead in the right direction.

It would have been more than a little suspicious if the group located crystals on their first day out, or even their second, so Kryslie made no move to seed terrain with the crystals she had brought with her until late on the third day. At that time, she had contrived to be at the far end of the line abreast search, so that she could toss each crystal away from her to fall in a random pattern. They would be far enough away from the day's search grid that it would be the following day, or the one after when they would start to be found. On those days, she would once again be in the centre of the line.

The fingernail sized pieces of rough crystal were Tymorean – the originals had been seeded on the moon to disguise their origin, but Grainger had known they were there, and had probably found a way to affect the search program of the lunar probe.

Knowing how many of the small crystals she had thrown around, Kryslie added her encouragement to the idea of seeing how many they could find before needing to return to the base. That gave them two more days after the first finds – three of the eleven crystals – to find the rest. Six more were found the following day, and the last two, late on the sixth day. The group returned to the camp, satisfied with the outcome of the search, and quickly packed up the camp to return to the base. They left a marker in the search area, in case they needed to return.

As it happened, they arrived back late in the Lunar day after the regular shuttle had departed for Earth. So when the team was dismissed by Chung, Kryslie went directly to her quarters, where all her belongings had been returned, and immediately made use of the sonic shower. A week living in an EA suit, left one in dire need of a wash.

During her deodorising shower, while she removed the black dye from her hair and redyed the blond to a red nearer her normal shade, she let her brother know she was back, and asked for any news that he had not imparted to her during her absence.

"Flanagan has his techs making an interface to convert our power system to the Aeronite one. Zorrin finally stopped playing dumb and thought to show us some schematics he had in his ship's memory. And that might have been because the power in his ship mysterious drained to just enough to run the computer…if we get the interface working, he hopes he can charge his ship's storage batteries," Tymos summarised. "Once that was settled, Landin sent me to work with Ericson. He had four more generators made to the schematics of the prototype – and I'm working on a sixth. That should be enough to power a shield to cover the whole base. Chung has just come in with the crystals, and he has Ericson engrossed. I had to remind him that they are slightly radioactive, so he made sure they were shielded before he got Landin to come to see them."

Kryslie felt her brother's attention going elsewhere, and quickly finished drying herself and getting into a newly laundered uniform. She intended to join her brother, but decided to wait until Landin had left the R and D section. The search team would be expected to be on stand down until the following day, and if Landin saw her, he would likely enforce it. Instead, she turned on her computer to check for messages. There was nothing of importance, which was not unexpected since almost everyone thought she was down on Earth. When she logged in, the computer noted her return, and would be updating the 'currently on the base' personnel list.

Once she went back to work, most people would assume that she had returned on that day's shuttle.

Delta shift were just leaving the R and D main lab as Kryslie walked in. Her usual fellow workers were happy to see her back and stopped for a brief word. She finally made her way to the corner where her brother was working.

"Took your time," he teased. "You missed seeing the amazing crystals Chung found."

"Missed being seen by Landin, you mean. Do you have much left to do on that?"

That was the sixth in a row of newly built generators, the first five all had a side flap open, waiting to have a piece of crystal inserted. The last did not yet have its outer casing on.

"Not really, I'm just putting the cover on this one. Then they need to be started up, calibrated and linked to the computer. We can't test them fully until the crystal is in, but the shield modes that are standard should work then."

"What do you want me to do," Kryslie asked.

"Probably start them up and initialise the internal program."

Tymos hadn't stopped working as he spoke, and he didn't need to tell his sister what to do. She went to the first of the generators they had built, their prototype, scanned through the settings Tymos had saved, memorised them on the instant and began to work on the next unit in the line.

"You will need to facet those crystals," Kryslie remarked. "Unless you allowed for a rough surface in the specs." Her fingers kept busy in the touch pad, entering the figures, but her mind was able to do that and follow other conversations.

"No, that will need to be done, but Ericson is still awed by them. I believe Tamir Grainger was one of his early lecturers."

"So, what else has been happening here while I was away?"

"They sent a team out to Auto-track 1. The shuttle that took bin Halil back came up with the pre-constructed replacement parts. They should be finished in another day or two."

"You built six units, are you planning to have six units for the base. I thought that we calculated five."

"I thought it a good idea to have a spare…"

"That's an idea, but if Auto-track 1 is almost operational…"

"It will be a target…I'll suggest it to Landin and Ericson. I don't think they have thought of that. If anyone is coming after those two Aeronites — we will need all the tracking and detecting capability that we can get."

"Any word from the Fleet ships?"

Tymos shook his head. "No, but there are only six of them and a lot of space to watch. I can't contact them directly, only through Earthbase."

"What about Vori and Zorrin? If he's helping Flanagan, what's she doing?"

"When I met her last, she said she was learning about Earth customs from the computer. She asked after you, and I think she suspects that you didn't go down to Earth. I didn't confirm it, or deny it."

"Ward! Are you still here?" Ericson's unexpected comment startled them and they both looked up. "Kryslie, I didn't expect to see you back at work until tomorrow morning."

"I wasn't ready to sleep, Sir," Kryslie said quietly, for he had come closer to see what they were doing.

"You should be. You look it. Chung was certainly glad to go to bed."

"Really, I'm fine." Kryslie's protest was met with a stern stare.

"Ward, where are you at with these generators?"

Tymos repeated what he had told Kryslie, and added what she had been doing.

"Then I think you can leave that for tonight, and you can both go to bed. I promised the Commander that I would see that you had one sleep shift per rotation."

"I don't have much more…" Tymos protested.

"Leave it until tomorrow morning. Come back to it when you are fresh. I don't want mistakes due to tiredness, and I know how long a day Kryslie has had, on top of just recovering from a serious injury."

Kryslie hid her annoyance at being ordered to bed, and didn't need to think at her brother to know that he agreed with her. They weren't going to win.

Tymos sighed, put his tools down, and wiped his hands on his uniform. He shrugged as he glanced at his sister and said for Ericson's benefit, "Might as well."

The feeling of needing to get the generators finished and working had them both back in R and D during the hours of beta shift when no one else was around. They both set to work, knowing what to do without needing to discuss it.

All six generators were completed, activated, calibrated and ready to test by the time beta shift was almost over. Tymos was in the process of linking the generators into the base computer when he murmured, "We've got company." He didn't look at Zorrin, who he had seen in his peripheral vision.

Kryslie did, and smiled at the Aeronite.

Zorrin accepted the implied invitation, and strolled over to see what they were doing. He stopped to study the schematic and specifications showing up on a flat screen built into the bench top.

"A force-shield generator," he remarked without needing to ask. He studied the specs further while Tymos and Kryslie continued their task. "To transmute energy it will? Do that how?"

Kryslie had not expected Zorrin to know that, since he had not seemed that familiar with the technology on his ship. She decided that there was no reason not to tell him.

"We have some crystals that we need to insert that enable that?"

"Crystals of what?"

Kryslie gave him the chemical composition, and added, "They are radio-active at a low level."

Zorrin was thoughtful, then said, "Heard of them I have. Then stop matter and energy these machines will. Know I didn't, that humans could make these. This base does not. Reduce it to atoms, I could have."

On a very tight thought frequency, Kryslie sent to her brother, "Sounding arrogantly confident this morning, isn't he?"

Replying the same way, Tymos sent, "He is carrying two energy weapons. Hasn't realised that they are practically drained of power. I made sure that the ones on his ship were no longer lethal."

Aloud, to Zorrin, Kryslie said, "Well, I am certainly glad that you did not. Anyway, is there a way we can be of assistance to you?"

"Curious I am, why building it know you are."

"Your arrival opened the eyes of a few people," Tymos said quietly. "And made them a bit paranoid. Like you said, you could have turned the base to rubble. Until now, no one saw the need for protection stronger than the meteorite and UV shields."

"To stop us leaving, is it?" Zorrin demanded.

"No," Krys assured him. "If you wish to leave, you can. If you wish to settle on Earth, though, I suggest you talk to Landin. He will be able to help you get a start."

Zorrin growled. "A big fuss we didn't want. Thought we would find father here – but he is dead. He killed long ago. Ship crashed here."

Krys glanced up at him. "Was that ship we found his?"

"Yes," Zorrin admitted, emitting anger. "The ships systems were pretty well burnt out. When Tymos helped me get power to it – sparks went everywhere."

"You were busy while I was recovering," Kryslie commented to her twin, as if she had not known it already.

"Recovering? What from?" Zorrin asked.

"An accident," Tymos said quickly.

Zorrin recalled what Vori had told him and decided there were other things he wanted to learn from these two.

"Did you design this yourselves?"

"No," Kryslie said with a wry smile. "The theory has existed for over twenty years. Tamir Grainger, one of the founders of the WSRA knew a lot about force shields and such. Prof Emmanuel built the first generator a decade and a half ago."

Zorrin thought on that. He didn't sense the answer was a lie. "Expecting trouble you are?"

Kryslie continued making minute adjustments as Tymos checked his computer screen. "This is more as a precaution," He said with a shrug. "Are you as certain that no one is looking for you?"

"If were, found we'd be already. Travel we did for long time, sleeping. Had ship been near, waked I would have been."

The Aeronite might believe that, Kryslie decided, but the sense of urgency she felt - to finish these shields – belied that confidence. "Are you going to test it, bro?"

Using the lowest power setting, and defining the parameters to form a dome that only covered the generator and a circle of the bench top, Tymos activated the shield from the computer. On the screen was what looked like the grid-work of a geodesic dome – it matched the glowing shape now covering part of the bench.

This was merely the power grid, the basis for the shields. Tymos made adjustments to the parameters on the computer, and the glow seemed to spread to become a glowing half sphere. He nodded to his sister, who had picked up a plastic ruler and a metal probe rod. Zorrin's eyes were flicking between the screen and the glow.

Kryslie knew not to touch the glow directly, and was careful when pushing the ruler to touch the glow. It seemed to be going through with no resistance, but when she withdrew the plastic, the part that had touched the screen was gone. Then she tried the probe rod, and this time there was resistance, and when she pushed harder, a shower of sparks.

"Shut it down, bro. It works, and it isn't safe to have going in here. The big test will be when we get those crystals in."

Zorrin's eyes had widened as he watched the test, and the computer screen. "Be here, I should probably no be," he announced abruptly, and without a further parting comment, he turned and trotted from the room.

Kryslie sensed Zorrin's sudden agitation, but could not discern the cause. She was about to go after him, but saw Ericson entering. Maybe that had been the problem.

"Why am I not surprised to see you both here already?"

As the warning signal for the imminent start of gamma shift sounded, Ericson studied the computer screen, which still showed the shield matrix structure, even though the generator was no longer emitting.

"Is it ready for testing yet?"

"This unit works. I expect the others will as well. We just need to insert the crystals to make it fully functional," Tymos reported.

"You can get some from the shielded vault. How big a crystal do you need?"

Tymos used his fingers to indicate size.

"You will probably need one for each of the generators," Ericson mused. "I presume that you know how to facet them to fit?"

"Yes, the method is shown in Prof Emmanuel's notes," Kryslie told him.

Ericson gave a deliberately dramatic sigh, rather than berate them for using their own interpretation of "a one shift cycle sleep period" and "do it in the morning."

"While you two have been shorting yourself on sleep, I have been going over the specs again – still trying to grasp the physics of this shield. It seems to be a step beyond what Prof Emmanuel produced."

"Well, Sir," Kryslie spoke up, "His pioneering work is over fifteen years old."

"Are you trying to say that I don't keep up with the latest developments?" Ericson's expression was amused, not annoyed.

"No, of course not, but the normal defensive screen generators have been vastly improved since then and not many people really understand how the Grainger crystals work. Emmanuel's notes indicate that he thought that they might actually transmute energy, in addition to changing the wavelength."

While staring at his technicians, Ericson said, "Yes…" Then he said, abruptly, "Ward, how long will it take to have it ready for a full scale test?"

"As soon as Krys finishes preparing the crystals and in."

"Two hours? Three?"

"Two," Kryslie supplied.

"Three," Tymos countered. "I will need to place the generators around the base and check the signals to them, and then synchronise them. I will have one spare, so that I can do a small scale demonstration. Where do you want to do that?"

"Make it the reception hall. While you are setting things up – I will get Stanley to set up a feed to the screen in main mission so we can see the effect from the view of the outer monitors and the lunar satellite. What will you want to do to test it?"

"Can you get one of the shuttles out to test it with the defensive lasers?"

"Already organised. Casey and Allen are preparing a shuttle now. They are both keen to see this work. I will go and advise the Commander and the C-I-C."

The group who assembled in the reception hall also included the Flanagan of Engineering, Murtry of Security and a tech one from Computing. They all took a seat in the ring arranged around the portable bench with the generator.

"Tell us about this device, Mr Ward," Basoli directed.

Tymos glanced Ericson, who merely gestured for him to go ahead. He hadn't prepared a formal lecture, but he didn't need to. He knew what he needed to say, could recite sections of relevant journals to explain the theory and was not shy about standing in front of an audience of the senior staff. He spoke confidently and kept his speech to the point and did not take all the credit, as he referred to the work of other people and attributed ideas from base staff and congratulated Ericson on initiating the project. As he spoke, he gauged how much of the technical details were being understood by the degree of concentration each listener displayed and whether they were frowning or not.

Landin was the one who was listening with the greatest concentration, since he was concerned with the safety of his base, and Tymos directed his gaze towards him, more than any of the others.

"We tested it in the lab as a semi-spherical shape," Tymos went on. "It can in fact be programmed for any regular 3-D shape. The matrix is represented by the 3-D grid on the screen. This is the framework of the shield that is projected from the unit. Once that is set up and power is put through the grid, the shield becomes operational. The area enclosed by the shield can be expanded or contracted within limits. I can show you the effect in here."

Kryslie interjected a comment. "You will need to keep back from the table. I will lock the doors during the demonstration. Please don't allow anything to touch the screen."

The senior staff obeyed the instructions, understanding why when Kryslie demonstrated the effect on wood and metal. She had an additional prop this time, a hand held laser cutter, and she aimed this directly at the screen, at its lowest setting. All that happened was that the screen glowed brighter. She increased the power to maximum and this time, some of the beam was reflected, at an angle away from her, and the screen itself brightened even more.

The gaze of nearly everyone on the little group went to where the laser had been deflected. They all knew the effect of a laser cutter at full power, and expected to see a hole in the wall.

There was more than polite applause when Tymos turned the defensive screen off. He was controlling the unit from one of the Engineering data padds.

"The matrix framework is invisible and harmless until the power is put into it," Tymos noted. "I am still attempting to reduce the light emitted during operation. It is effectively wasted energy."

The department heads began a discussion on that point. Having the screen visible as a warning to keep clear was preferred. Landin suggested it made it obvious where a target was. Tymos and Kryslie simply stood back and let the others talk. Finally Landin returned to the next stage of the test.

He spoke into his communicator, giving the shuttle the directive to launch. When he saw the shuttle was aloft, he said, "Continue, Mr Ward."

Tymos went on to describe the procedure for operation the generator, working from the familiar instructions as used for the current defensive screens and then explaining the differences. With precise instructions, he explained how to adjust the output for full coverage. He ended with,

"Sir, Chief Ericson has arranged for the full scale test to be observed from main mission."

Tymos stayed back, ostensibly disconnecting the generator from the power, and readying it to be returned to the R and D lab. He wanted the senior staff to go on ahead, and for Ericson to take over the next part of the test. The R and D Chief had other ideas.

"Kryslie can take that back to the lab. I want you running the full scale test. That way I will know it is at optimal efficiency."

"Of course, Sir," Tymos agreed. "Was there something else?"

"Yes. I want to see both of you after this demonstration is over. Back in my office in the lab."

"Fair enough," Tymos agreed easily. He glanced at his sister, there were some other tests that they had wanted to make during the main demonstration.

Mentally, Kryslie assured him, "I can do what is needed. You just stall each stage as much as you can."

Tymos had all eyes on him as he began the demonstration. On the big screen, the information was now that of the combined field from the five generators. The base appeared in outline, with the grid-work of the shield matrix as a much larger dome over it. He brought up a smaller screen, showing the view from the monitors outside the base, and a third that was the feed from the shuttle. He then looked at Ericson and said, "They can begin the test, Sir."

The feed from the shuttle showed a circular glow. Allen's acknowledgement came through with a lot of static. Then the hovering shuttle moved away and came back as if on a bombing run.

First the shuttle dropped a bomb so it fell at the edge of the shield. It exploded on impact with the shield. The external view showed the massive explosion and the fleeting instant of fire. The internal view showed a flaring of light at the point of impact as the screen resisted. Tymos appeared to be fine tuning the controls for a time, and then he nodded to Ericson.

On the second run, Allen fired projectile weapons at the shield. The ammunition hit the shield and bounced off it. Once again, Tymos stalled by adjusting some of the parameters. On the third run, he used the newer beam weapons, hitting the shield with the raw energy released by the weapon. The energy was partially absorbed and partially reflected as blinding light. Nothing came through. The final test was to see what happened when the shuttle tried to land through the shield. It hit and bounced with a shower of sparks. The shuttle lifted away and returned to a hovering position.

Ericson told Tymos to lower the shield and then told Allen to land and come through to main mission. The on-duty shift controllers applauded enthusiastically.

Tymos studied the computer controls and when he saw his sister enter main mission, slipped past the group congratulating Ericson, and met her by the door.

"As it is now," she whispered. "I could still transmit through the shield. We will have to add an override to block that. It will block the dangerous radioactive elements – the crystals will absorb and transmute the radiation."

"Communication through the shield wasn't the best," Tymos told her.

"We can fix that," she commented.

"Ericson is happy. It blocks energy, it blocks matter and it will block radiation. He hasn't conceived the idea of matter/energy transmission yet," Tymos told Krys. "Did you contact Earthbase during the test?"

"No, but I boosted the signal and got through to the fleet ship nearest here. Loud and clear. None of the ships have seen any indication of alien ships in the region."

Landin suggested that the group of senior staff move out of main mission to allow the controllers to return their attention to their normal duties. Tymos was about to slip out and return to R and D when Basoli stopped him.

"Technician Ward, excellent work once again."

"Thank you, Sir."

"I believe that you have an idea for that extra generator…to protect Auto-track 1."

"Yes, Sir, that was my idea."

"It is an excellent suggestion. How soon can you arrange that?"

"I won't be able to connect it up until the repair crew is finished."

"That will do. So, see to it. I do not wish to have to find more funding for more repairs."

"Yes, Sir."

Tymos allowed the rest of the group to pass him before he suggested to Kryslie, "Let's get back to the lab."

Their return prompted questions of how well the tests went, but once their colleagues had heard the excellent report, they were allowed to get on with their own work.

"Do you want me to help with that?" Kryslie gestured to the generator that was to go out to protect Auto-track 1.

Tymos shook his head. "I think one of us should stay and keep an eye on the visitors. Now that they are being allowed to wander around…"

"Am I right in thinking that people are now feeling that they are harmless?"

"Not everyone. I know what they could do if they want to – that's why I drained their weapons. They still have guards following them, but it is more of a courtesy now. Landin and Basoli have agreed that they can have access to their ship."

"They still have guards around it," Kryslie noted.

"Of course, but I have convinced Zorrin that it is to protect it, and again, is a courtesy. Not sure if he fully believes it, but he isn't complaining."

"Are they pushing to go down to Earth?" Kryslie asked.

"Not yet. I think they want to know more about life there. I think bin Halil scared them."

"Anyone with an ounce of empathy would be wary of him. He can present a very convincing front of being pleasant and considerate, and we both know that is all it is. Have you heard any more about the IC investigation from Jonko?"

Tymos shook his head. "Do you want to send Earthbase a signal and ask the question?"

"Later. That is one process that we can't hurry. And bin Halil will be indicted. There is no doubt in my mind."

That question would have to wait anyway, for they both spotted Ericson returning, and moved to meet him at his office. When he reached there, he simply gestured for them to enter.

"Sit!" he said as he went behind his desk. Once there he eyed the two technicians for a while before stating, "You implied, earlier, that you both understand how Grainger's crystals work, unlike most people. I am not going to ask how it is that you, who never went to the university, do. I am certain, however, that these new shields do more than you have claimed. Kryslie's comment about transmuting energy, as well as changing wavelength clarified what I had been trying to focus on. From the schematic and specs, it is possible to deduce that once energy – be it from a physical explosion or an energy beam - hits the shield, it is directed along the grid matrix, through the generator with the Grainger crystal, it is used in turn to make the shield even stronger. Is this the case?"

Asked a direct question, Tymos answered, "Yes."

Ericson suddenly relaxed and leant back in his chair. "Am I right in that it would also transmute radiation directed at it?"

Again, Tymos answered, "Yes."

Ericson nodded, pleased with this confirmation of his theories. "We have had shields against radiation, and against physical objects, and now energy. Will these new generators you have designed, work against combinations of those things?"

This time, Kryslie answered, but not with the simple 'yes'. Instead, she asked, "How would you test for a combination? The only way I can think of is to use one of the 'dirty bombs' from way back during the last war. If it works, well and good, if not…"

Ericson waved the obvious, "we'd have a radioactive mess" away.

"We can try it on a small scale and contain the radioactivity," he said. "I am thinking matter-energy."

"No one on Earth has managed to master that idea yet," Kryslie said.

"No one on Earth, no – but now we have proof that we are not the only species in the universe. If there are others, besides that of our guests, who knows what they might be capable of. Some of what we have today was only an idea in science fiction tales a century ago. Such talks often had the means to teleport matter from place to place, by converting it to an energy form."

Tymos, after a quick mental exchange with Kryslie, gave a temporising answer. "In theory it should be capable – if energy is blocked. It might be a matter of having to adjust the specifications programmed into the shield."

"Could you do that?" Ericson challenged.

"By trial and error," Tymos said with a shrug. "If energy at a certain frequency is loaded with matter, and the frequency is scrambled, when it reaches its destination to be decoded back to matter…it might be messy."

A gleam in Ericson's eye made Kryslie suspect he had an idea for a future project, but all he said was, "I suppose that someone needs to master energy-matter transfer, before I need to worry about blocking it. Maybe I should ask young Zorrin what he knows about the idea. He has a good grasp of science, although not of how science is translated into usable equipment."

"What is happening with them?" Kryslie asked. "I haven't spoken to them since I got back."

"They will be allowed to stay here until they have decided what to do? They will need a way to support themselves. I think the C-I-C would like them to decide to work for the WSRA."

"Personally, I'd agree with that. Having the media interested in them, as the 'aliens' would make them into freaks and the target of all the 'scared of aliens' weirdo's or the 'take me to your leader' ones."

Ericson chuckled, "I expect you are right. I heard some of the odd things being said about you after that incident with the President's shuttle. Is that why you are in no rush to take a break downside?"

"Pretty much," Kryslie agreed. She wasn't going to mention the potential attention of bin Halil's assassins. "Running from the media might keep me fit, but it would be no holiday."

"True. Well, now that you are back and the generators are operational, I will let Engineering do all the tests they think they need. Both of you are to be available for them if they have questions. Meanwhile, you can both keep working with our guests. Young Zorrin seems to have decided Tymos is a friend, perhaps you can work on the girl and see what her skills are. I will drag you away if I need your skills elsewhere."

"Is this to make me take it easy?" Kryslie asked.

"No, it is to help our guests if they wish to become citizens of Earth."

When Kryslie didn't react to that, Ericson added, "You can help your brother set up the pod with what he needs to set up that generator out at the Auto-track. I will ask Stanley if he needs you to test the sensitivity of the sensors when the shield is operational."

Chapter 25

Ericson might have decided to keep his questions about two particular technicians to himself when talking to them, but later, when he spoke to Landin in a quiet corner of the staff cafeteria, his words were not quite soft enough to stay confidential.

Vori sat quietly in a partly hidden corner of the food area, observing the humans. They looked a lot like Aeronites, except for the white around their eyes. That took a lot of getting used to. They didn't act like people on Zekos either. They seemed freer, less harried and she yearned for that. Yet they still didn't know how to act around her. Some of the males were intrusively close to her when they spoke to her. Others seemed nervous, as if she would hurt them. It only took her stilted English to mark her as alien. English, was such a twisted way of speaking. Zorrin's advice to stay here, until they learnt to fit in was a good. No one had tried to hurt them here.

Yet, her mind reminded her. Zorrin was convinced that there was a Tymorean here in the moon base, or perhaps more than one, just waiting for a chance to kill them. Forcing that fear aside, by noticing her 'guard' sitting nearby, Vori began to listen to nearby conversations again. She was understanding more and more of the words now.

As she tuned into a different set of voices, she realised that she was hearing the pleasant voice of Landin, the base commander.

"I am impressed by those new shields," Landin remarked. "And how quickly you came up with them."

"That wasn't just me. That Ward pair did most of the designing and building, in spite of the fact they were passing credit to everyone else who was involved."

Landin chuckled. "They do seem to want to keep out of the limelight, but even so, I am damn glad to have them here."

"I certainly won't argue with that, but what I really don't understand is why they never applied to go to the university."

"According to that pair, they had an unconventional education and didn't have the formal records needed for the university."

"Yet they understand how Grainger's crystals work, and that is so unlikely in anyone outside the university."

"Not necessarily," Landin disagreed mildly. "The puzzle Grainger set was solved over fifteen years ago and there are many articles about them now."

"And I have read everyone that comes out. But I never even gave it a thought that those crystals cans transmute radiation into other forms of energy. Yet when I went over the specs again, I could see it was obvious. That was not something I had specified in the early work."

"Really, so you are saying Tymos added that capability into the design? Did they tell you that?"

"Not until I asked them directly. Just like you said, if you ask the right question, they will tell you the answer."

"Or redirect the question," Landin murmured.

"Yes. Now that I think of it, Kryslie did exactly that when I asked if those crystals could block matter energy transmission — such as is being played with to transport goods around. She asked me if I knew of a way to test them for that…"

Vori heard the second speaker stop abruptly, and risked a glance at the two men. Now she recognised one of the senior people who her brother was helping.

"…but Tymos did suggest that these new shield ought to although the parameters might need adjusting."

"He could just be theorising," Landin suggested.

"Maybe, but he said, 'If energy at a certain frequency is loaded with matter, and the frequency is scrambled, when it reaches its destination to be decoded back to matter…it might be messy.' It made me think that he knows more about the possibility than he was going to tell me. I didn't quiz him on the subject, I already had the feeling he wouldn't tell more, and he may have said more than he intended to."

Now, Vori felt as if the temperature in the cafeteria had dropped ten degrees. A clammy chill seemed to envelop her when she heard what Tymos Ward, their friend, had said. He could almost have been quoting from an Aeronite scientific text book. Matter-energy transmission could be described as he had said…and humans didn't know that science yet, but…Tymoreans did!

She had to get to their private place and tell her brother. Getting up slowly and edging out from her table, she caught the glance of her guard, and began to move through the crowded tables towards the corridor. She was grateful when her guard stood up immediately and began to follow her. She sensed that he no longer considered her to be dangerous, and hoped that he would protect her if the Tymorean tried to kill her. Trouble was, the Tymoreans were frighteningly clever and well liked too, and would probably be believed more readily than two alien strangers.

When she arrived back at medical, she smiled shyly at the man, and thanked him. He smiled back and went to his normal position near the door, to wait.

Zorrin was pacing the inner room, but he stopped and twirled when she blurted, "I know who the Tymoreans are! I overhead Landin talking to one of those men you are helping."

Vori went on to tell him what she had heard, but he didn't seem to be as surprised as she expected.

"I saw that shield generator they built. I looked at the specifications. We studied one just like it in our lessons and it was a Tymorean design." Zorrin began to swear in his native language. After a while, he said, "I challenged them about it, but they just said the technology had been around for years. Which agrees with what you heard. I didn't want to think that they are our enemies. Krys Ward saved your life! Why would she do that? So she could torture you later?"

"You were hurting most of them, perhaps she felt it too and wanted you to stop. She may not have known who you were then."

"No, I am sure they knew. I think they didn't kill us then because they would have to explain why and that would mean revealing themselves. By now, no one would think that they hated us, so if something happens, they won't be suspected."

"Then they must want to know what we know." Vori shivered. "Perhaps even where Zekos is, so they can send people there to kill everyone. They must have got the commander to ask about it."

"Yes, I would do that if I were them. But I didn't tell Landin exactly where it was anyway, or give him the full directions. That's also why, when Tymos was trying to power the computer and other things in father's ship, I made it seem like the circuits were compromised, and shorting out. I didn't want the humans trying to go there, and now I am even gladder I did it."

"So what can we do? We are stuck here. We can't leave without help from the humans."

"Father was right to come here. The planet below may not be perfect but at least the people look much like us – in fact some of the people here look stranger than we do. The healer here says that she can make us lenses so that our eyes will look like those of everyone else here. And I want to go down there and look around. Some of the younger ones from Engineering have offered to show me around. I can take the other message capsule and set it off. What if father is actually alive, down there and it wasn't his ship that crashed here?"

A fleeting hope crossed Vori's mind before it vanished. "If it isn't, it means that he was followed here and others know he was here."

"I will do it anyway, but I think that body was him. I bet the Tymoreans found him and killed him. They could have moved his ship here and buried it. They wouldn't want it on the planet."

"If we do get to go there to live, what is there to stop them following and finding us? There would be more places to hide bodies down there."

"We get them first. Disable them until we are gone."

Vori paled, she sensed that her brother meant to kill them. He in turn sensed her revulsion but went on. "Tymoreans aren't immortal."

"In our history classes, they said that Tymoreans had some special powers…"

"Only the high ranking ones, and the old warlords had a weapon to counteract that," Zorrin reminded her. He turned thoughtful. "Father's ship had to be one of the old warlord's personal ships. Ours too, I think."

"Do you think there might be one of those weapons on it?"

"Ours? No. Not unless we missed some compartments. I think everything we wouldn't need was removed to make more room for food and fuel."

"What about the wreck? Do you know what one looks like? I never studied old weapons."

"I have an idea. I know it didn't look like a normal weapon."

"What if they know what it looks like?"

"Those two? They'd not be old enough."

Vori wasn't convinced. "You dare not assume that."

"No, you are right, if we do find one, we will have to plan our moves carefully. Let me think about this."

Vori gave up watching him stand like a statue and think. She went to the food dispenser and ordered some of the human foods she had come to like.

"First thing, I will find a reason to have to check over the whole of that wreck. If I see anything that might be one, I will sneak back later and get it."

"And if you don't?"

"I'll get to that. If I find one, we will invite them onto our ship and offer them some of the sweet stuff uncle put here for us. You know, like as thanks for helping us. And then we turn the weapon on. It won't kill them, but it will stop them trying to escape."

"I don't like it," Vori told him.

"If we don't, they'll keep after us."

"And if we do, the humans will be after us. Up here, we can't get away, and down there, we still don't know enough to hide from them."

"What if we go down to that place where that darker skinned leader lives?" Zorrin suggested. "No…hear me out. I think that one doesn't like Krys Ward. He might get rid of them for us."

Things that Vori had overheard, and been told, suddenly made sense.

"Krys's accident. They don't want to talk about it, but people should have thought she died then and didn't. And she recovered fast and did that charade about going down to the planet, but she didn't. She came back after that leader left."

"See? That supports my idea…"

"Zorrin, if she should have died, but didn't, what if she has some sort of personal force shield? Wouldn't that negate that weapon anyway?"

"Curses it might at that! We will need to find out if she does – if they both do. There must be a way to short them out?"

"I will go through our computer," Vori offered. "I might find out ways to test for one as well."

"And I had better make sure our weapons are fully charged. We will only have one chance at this."

"And we had better have a backup plan," Vori told him.

Vori used the excuse of Zorrin being down on Earth and Tymos being out at Auto-track 1, as a reason for her suggestion, "You like to see over our ship? Some sweets from Zekos we have. You try them?"

Kryslie, who was in the computer lab, checking signals between the base and Auto-track 1, wondered at the invitation, but all she could sense from Vori was wanting to be with her. In fact, she added, "Know you better, I'd like."

Landin and Basoli would certainly want her to accept. "I'd like that," she said. "Would you like me to bring anything?"

A wistful look came onto Vori's face. "Some chocolate? Turkish Jelly?"

Kryslie laughed. "A deal. But I can't come until after my shift, though."

"Oh! Good that be. Wait I can't."

Once Vori had walked off, Kryslie sent a purely mental message to her brother.

"She might just be feeling nervous without her brother around," Tymos suggested. "And with him away, I don't think she would try anything."

Even with her brother agreeing that Vori wasn't likely to try anything, Kryslie was being careful. She knew that Vori was as intelligent as her brother, but she had been keeping a low profile, that keeping her eyes down around men, made everyone think of her as shy and demure. Even the guards were coming to think of her as a woman needing protection, even if they were still unsure about Zorrin.

Vori trotted across the shuttle bay as Kryslie approached with her package of sweets.

"Quickly, you came," Vori greeted, smiling like a young girl. "Come see our ship."

Kryslie had to increase her pace to keep up with her, but she said as she went, "I had to ask Commander Landin if this was okay. He had orders that none of us was to go into your ship."

"Stop you, he can't. My guest you be."

"Yeah, but he had to tell the guards it was okay."

"Now, no matter," Vori said, as they reached the open hatchway of their ship. "Something I have, show you I want."

She grabbed Kryslie's hand and urged her to hurry up the lowered ramp. "On Earth transmissions, I see this."

Vori led the way from the open area around the outer hatch, through the narrow passage section, and into the area where the sleep capsules were. These were now closed, Kryslie noticed, aware of the state they had been in when her brother had made his covert foray. Now too, a table was set up, with plates of varicoloured cubes. While she glanced around, Vori went to a box that was also on the table. She fiddled with it, and suddenly, the light in the ship went from the natural white, to reddish orange.

"Like this, do you?" Vori asked, grinning like a child involved in mischief.

"It's an interesting effect, but why orange?"

"You don't like? Change it I can." She moved a dial on the box and the light changed to yellow and then green, watching Kryslie's face, frowning slightly. She kept it there for a moment before continuing to change it to blue, then purple, then red.

When it was green though, Kryslie felt as if something was crawling on her skin, and for that brief moment felt as if her body was sluggish. It didn't last, but the feeling, coupled with the colour, and brought back a memory from a long time ago. She kept her sudden suspicion under a tight mental shield, and merely said, "Which colour do you like best?"

Vori turned her attention back to the box and switched the light to yellow. "Like this, but like green too. Green like growing things, but yellow like your sun, warm and welcoming."

With a mercurial change of subject, Vori said, "Come here later, we will. See ship now."

Kryslie finally put her package on the table and let Vori act as guide. She didn't let on that she already had a good idea of the ship, just flowed

Vori all the way through the various sections to the bridge, which was like the cockpit of a passenger jet and just as compact. There were two seats there, but indications – screw holes in the floor, that the area immediately behind had once held two or more seats. The bulkheads and walls of this section had all the instruments that controlled the ships functions.

After Vori took time to point out various instruments and what they did to her guest, they returned back through the narrow passage lined with storage hatches to the entry area, and continued through to the rear of the ship. Kryslie noticed, although Vori made no mention of it, that each section could be made airtight. They passed through yet another narrow section, with fewer storage openings, to an area that might be a mini workshop and gym, and onto the engine compartment.

Kryslie didn't hide her interest, although it was not the interest of one who had never been on a ship like that before. She was instantly comping everything she saw now, with what she remembered of Aeronite ships of a century ago.

They returned to the compartment with the table and the sleep pods, and Kryslie asked to have a look at them. Vori seemed to tense a little, but immediately began to prattle.

"Find I did, how to service them. Just now recharging control computer. Why it drained, know not. Should have lasted, 200 years. Your brother, help make interface to power here."

Kryslie knew he had, but his intention had been to try to access the computer in the wrecked ship. She saw the little modified generator, and the power lead going to the nearest pod.

"Look you can," Vori invited. "Tell how it works, I will."

The instant Kryslie touched the capsule, she felt the electrical shock. Her PFS quickly neutralised it, and the generator stopped.

Her face must have betrayed something, for Vori came over, "What happened? Hurt you?"

"No, I am okay. But I think you need to get one of our techs to check how that generator is hooked up. It seems to have livened up the pod."

"Oh!" Vori's eyes went wide. "Can you absolve me? I…"

"I'm fine, really. It was little more than a tingle. I have had worse when I have been doing maintenance on old equipment. Why don't we sit and swap sweets. I did get some chocolate and Turkish delight."

Kryslie mentioned the incident to her brother when he returned, and he promised to sneak onto the ship again once the two Aeronites had settled for the night. She had scanned the pods, the generator, even the light controller box, and from the visual survey, had seen nothing suspicious.

When Tymos transmitted into her quarters, he had nothing to add.

"The light controller is just a simple circuit, in a standard box. She requested it from our spare parts store. There is nothing I can see wrong with the pods or the generator to cause the charge on the pods. The techs found nothing either. I looked for any sign of one of those old weapons the warlord used on us, but again – nothing."

"So, are you saying I am paranoid, Bro?"

"No, but …"

"I know, it was unlikely, and possibly just an atavistic memory."

"Or the fact that we both feel something is coming, and there is no sign of trouble anywhere," Tymos sighed. "All the while we were building the generators, I had a sense of urgency, and time running out…and every time the engineers want more tests done with those shields, I have to hold myself back from telling them to turn the shields on and leave them alone. If I did say something, they'd laugh at me."

"Well at least Auto-track 1 is back in action, and even more sensitive than before. I am wondering if I should get myself put back onto Controller duties."

"If anyone is coming, it will be the fleet ships or Earthbase that will see them first. We will have warning."

"Unless they are cloaked…"

The calm continued, and instead of being lulled, Tymos and Kryslie felt tenser. By contrast, most of the Lunar 1 staff had accepted the two aliens, and no longer felt either were dangerous. After all, they had been there a month, and except for that initial incident, the Aeronites had been perfect guests.

Their sense of impending danger made their Tymorean power accumulate, and they had little way to ground it except by spending their spare time in vigorous activity in the base gym – usually during beta shift when most people were asleep, if not on duty.

Zorrin had found them there when he wanted to tell them that he and Vori had been offered the chance to work for the WSRA at Terra one, and that they would be taking their ship down there once the right kind of fuel rods had been made. He added, that arrangements to integrate them into Earth society were well underway.

In turn Tymos noticed that both Aeronites were spending more and more time on their ship, supposedly checking out all the systems ready for the flight down.

They could only wait.

Chapter 26

The only warning they had was when the screen of the hand held scanner went black at the same instant as the lights in the lab went out. They had barely turned around, looking for the cause, when they felt their muscles freeze like they were now statues.

That sensation they knew. Once felt, never forgotten but they had not thought it possible that the weapon causing it would be used at Lunar 1.

Tymos swore mentally, and tried to fight the effect. "And I called you paranoid," he thought at his twin. "What are the damn fools up to?"

He could hear the six engineering techs calling out, trying to find the cause of the problem. Since there was lights in the passage outside the lab, the problem was internal.

"Ward! Did you do something down there?"

He wasn't able to reply. The green glow that surrounded them was the source of their paralysis, but he did not know if the other techs could see it. Yet the shift leader was striding down the central walkway, heading his way. He reached a point about three metres away, and suddenly dropped.

Hearing the thud, the other five techs came running, two had grabbed torches. Tymos could only watch as each dropped in turn.

In his mind, he was hearing Zorrin giving directions to his sister. "That's all of them. Hurry up and give these two the sedative. People might be along soon to see what happened."

"Zorrin! I can't get close. That field makes my hands numb."

Able to see Zorrin, Tymos saw him fiddling with something in his hand, as the strength of the field increased. Now, he was no longer able to hear Kryslie in his mind.

She had been saying, "Something has them in a panic, and their power is getting stronger, reacting to the need to do something. They are not thinking rationally – they see us enemies, but we have never..."

He had a glimpse of Vori, just a shadow in the dimness, but he heard the hiss of a hypo spray, and Kryslie fell limply, as her muscles relaxed and no longer tried to fight the field. Tymos guessed she would have to go around the bench to get to him, and he knew he could do little to avoid being drugged – except to tell his mind of the need to metabolise the drug fast.

It had not occurred to the two Aeronites that if they too were affected by the field, then they must be like their enemies.

He felt the cold sensation of the spray, aimed at his neck, and felt himself falling as he tried to stay conscious. He fell against the bench, his scanner knocked out of his hand. He could do nothing to stop it clattering across the floor. Zorrin must have loosed an EM burst first, to cause the device to go black. It probably deactivated his personal force shield too, or that green aura weapon would not have affected him.

As he continued to fight to stay awake, he began to hear a buzzing in his ear. It was the tiny, ultra-powerful communicator he used to receive messages from Earthbase, when he was unable to look at his computer or personal communicator.

The message must be urgent, probably related to what had set the Aeronites off, but his mind was getting fuzzier…

Landin woke to the imperative message beeps. He automatically checked the time on his bedside chronometer, part of his room communicator. 0300 Lunar time. He pressed the answer button and heard the voice of Security Chief Murtry.

"We may have a problem, Sir. The two visitors are no longer in their rooms at medical. The four guards are unconscious. I have had the shuttle bay checked. Their ship is there and looks locked up. The team on duty there saw the visitors leave two hours ago, and no one else has been near it since. I have alerted my other men to look out for them."

"Any alarms in any sections?" Landin asked.

"No, Sir. All is quiet."

Landin had no suggestions except to 'keep alert'. There could be a number of perfectly innocuous reasons for the visitors to have left medical, but not for the unconscious guards. He decided to dress and prowl around.

His wanderings took him around the various technical departments. Research was dark and deserted – not surprising since it was beta shift. Computing had a small shift crew, monitoring all the systems. The same was true of maintenance and life support. He neared Engineering and saw lights on and went in. No one seemed to be around. He headed to the small 'break room' and found the six people on beta shift neatly laid out in a row on the floor. He used the private comm system to notify medical and Murtry.

He checked the computer to see if he had accounted for all those who had signed on into engineering at the start of the shift. He had, but he glanced around looking for signs of why - he assumed it was the alien visitors – had come here. He went to where the work lights were brightest and examined the neatly laid out components and a half assembled piece of machinery. Beside it was the schematic diagram. There was nothing on it to indicate what it was.

He turned quickly back to the computer and requested the full list of those logged into engineering. Two names more than the shift crew appeared and Landin felt disquiet.

Murtry and a team of guards entered, the latter went to the break room and Landin indicated two names to the security chief, Tymos Ward and Kryslie Ward.

Murtry prowled around the bench, looking for indications of trouble. "No signs of weapons fire," he said softly. "The equipment is undisturbed…" He looked further from the bench, spotted something on the floor, and bent to pick it up.

"Diagnostic scanner – not a standard model. Not working either."

Landin looked at the device, and recognized it. "It belongs to Tymos – he made it himself."

"You know what, chief," Murtry scratched his head, considering something. "I noticed that all the computers and equipment in here have been reset, and even the chronometers are flashing. I'm almost ready to believe that the base was hit by an EM pulse, except that there have been no reports of trouble anywhere else."

"It must have been localised – just in here. Perhaps set off like the device that disrupted the shuttle," Landin suggested, not liking the ideas that thought had raised.

"Odd that Tymos and his sister are missing at the same time as the two guests," Murtry said.

"Have someone check their quarters," Landin directed. He hoped the answer was that simple, his technicians, who had been very good friends to the Aeronites, might be having a farewell party.

But his gut began to tighten with concern. Vori and Zorrin fervently believed that Tymoreans were their enemies, the epitome of evil, and creatures who would kill Aeronites on sight. He did not believe that of Tymos or Kryslie, but they were Tymoreans. Had his guests somehow discovered that?

So far it looked like his technicians were the victims, but he knew how capable they were. They might very well be acting for their own reasons and holding Vori and Zorrin somewhere. As Murtry had said, it was odd that those four were missing on this particular night. The Aeronites were due to be relocated down to Terra One when the shuttle left in the morning. The C-I-C had come up to personally escort them.

Had the Aeronites, or his technicians, seen this as the last chance each had to confront their enemies? Zorrin had mentally attacked the team that first met them. Had he done it again? Was that why the duty shift had been knocked out?

Or had Kryslie and Tymos, shed their docile, pleasant ordinary personalities to show their inner selves who could be hard and implacable? He'd seen some of that when Kryslie disabled the second saboteur, and Tymos must have been like that when he overcame Rasti. There was a lot about them that he didn't know…could they be intending the guests harm?

He let his eyes scan the scene again, and this time he spotted a small round object on the floor. He picked it up and felt a vibration coming from it and a faint but urgent beeping. Not sure what it was, he took it to one of the safety chambers and sealed it inside. Then he went to find a working hand held scanner and when he returned, directed it at the device. The round object, whatever it was, did not contain any known type of explosive and although the scanner didn't identify it, Landin felt sure it was a communications device. He unsealed the chamber, and took the device out and stowed it in his pocket in his uniform.

"I have activated all my teams," Murtry told Landin. "They will do a section by section search. Where will you be, Sir?"

"Office," Landin said. "How soon will a report come from the personnel section?"

"Any minute," Murtry said as he took on a listening pose. "Both quarters are unoccupied, no sign of trouble. Ward's – Tymos that is, has a priority message notification on his computer. It can't be accessed even with an emergency override command."

"Have someone work on accessing it," Landin directed. "Though that young genius has probably added his own protections to ours. Keep me advised."

Basoli, roused by the search that included personnel quarters, strode into Landin's office. He wore a coat over his pyjamas, which was a stark contrast to his usual impeccable business attire.

"What is the reason for disturbing everyone? What is going on?"

Landin told him what little he knew and his reasons for the search.

"So you don't know if those aliens are showing their true colours or those two damn mavericks of yours are up to something," Basoli interpreted. "Those two junior techs seem to have a talent for acting to suit themselves. Maybe they tried something and those two aliens objected."

"Sir, we don't have enough information to make an informed conclusion. Neither Tymos nor Kryslie are answering their personal communicators. Why don't you return to your guest quarters? I can update you there when I know more."

Kryslie nudged her brother with her toe. It was all she could force her body to do. She had used up all her energy simply getting into a sitting position.

"Wha..." came the thought into her mind.

"Wake up, bro," she told him mentally. She heard him groan and then saw him look around at the enclosed area.

"What hit me," he asked aloud.

"Zorrin! And he has one of those green aura projectors on us." Kryslie sensed her brother's mind going into full function.

"I remember. The power went out, and Vori injected us with something. We don't have time for this. Earthbase sent an emergency signal just before I blacked out."

"I think he knows people are coming and he is in full scale mindless panic."

"He has to know we are Tymorean," Tymos decided. "But we have done nothing to hurt him."

"He isn't thinking clearly and I believe the little power he has is out of control. I don't know if he tried to kill us and failed or hopes to buy his freedom with us."

"Freedom from whom," Tymos growled.

"Figure that out later," Kryslie said. "Have you got your personal force shield on?"

"I did have, but he pulse must have neutralised it."

"That's what I decided," Kryslie admitted, mentally berating herself. "I used up my energy sitting up. When I began thinking straight I realised I should have tried to reset it. At least I have my headache down to a manageable level."

Tymos was forcing his hand to move to the activation pad for his force field. "We are going to have to convince those two Aeronites to trust us. We are the only ones capable of protecting them from whoever is following them. Particularly if we can't get those new shields up before the followers are in weapons range."

Tymos's hand reached the pad but it took an effort to press it. Once he had, he was free to move and wasted no time turning Kryslie's PFS on. The portable force screen neutralised the green aura field, in fact their PFS were actually based on Aeronite technology.

"Let's go," Tymos urged. They activated their personal transmitters, and directed their minds to where they needed to go. They felt themselves hit a wall and found themselves in a different part of the Aeronite ship.

Their location looked to be the anteroom to the drive chamber.

"Hmph!" Tymos muttered. Both of them recognised the effect of an anti-transmission field.

"Come on," Kryslie urged. "They may not realise that field does not stop us leaving the normal way."

"We've been out for hours," Tymos muttered after checking his watch that had automatically reset to Lunar 1 time. They paused a moment to check if the next compartment was empty before forcing open the sliding door. It had been, but as they entered, Zorrin raced in from the opposite opening, looking for them. He waved an odd-looking weapon in their direction.

"Stop there Tymorean scum!"

Sensing the mental instability in the Aeronite, they both paused after edging fully into the compartment. Kryslie glanced around, noting the few stacked and restrained crates near the far door, beyond the sleep pods — little to use as weapons or for defence.

"So —what are you doing? Why are we here?" Kryslie asked, moving her hands away from her body slightly. She was trying to touch his mind and calm him. It had the opposite effect. He fired the weapon at one of the crates. A huge chunk of it vaporised and the edges of the blast fused blackly from the heat.

"Keep out of my mind!" Zorrin yelled, moving closer. "Or do that to you I will. How you get free?"

"Walked," Tymos said calmly. "Like humans do."

"Tymoreans you are! Deny it you can't. Our ticket to freedom you be."

In his mind was the knowledge of twelve ships heading directly towards Earth.

"Who are they?" Kryslie snapped. "Those ships — and how far away are they?"

"What?" Zorrin asked. "How you know?"

Kryslie read the fear that the ships were coming for him and his sister.

"It's in your mind! How close are they?" Her instincts were telling her they were very close.

"Matter it doesn't," Vori told her. She too had a weapon. "If they have you, leave us alone they will."

"Are you fools?" Tymos demanded. "Landin won't let you do that. You have been treated well by everyone here, but try that and they will treat you as enemies."

"Pah!" Vori snarled. "Those weaklings won't stand against those coming. Too strong they will be."

With remorseless logic, Kryslie told her, "That is probably true if you don't let us out to warn them to turn the new shields on. Then you would have a chance — this way you don't. They didn't come all this way to find two possible Tymoreans – they came for you. If you let us go, we will defend you. If you don't, Landin won't see any reason not to hand you over."

"I don't believe you," Vori's voice was shrill. "You don't care about us! You probably intend to kill us or strip our minds. We know what Tymoreans do. They like torturing our people."

"I think you have been misinformed," Kryslie said, not prepared to be argued with. "If we are what you think, I could have killed you when you arrived, instead of helping you. I could have killed you any time since then and these humans wouldn't have been able to prove it. And you are right, only Landin knows we are Tymorean, but he only think we belong to some pro-peace Earth sect."

Kryslie glanced at her brother. This had to end quickly.

"Who is following you?" Tymos demanded.

As he spoke, both he and Kryslie moved rapidly to close the space between themselves and the Aeronites. Neither Vori nor Zorrin expected the move. Both thought their prisoners were cowed by the weapons they wielded.

Vori tried to fire her weapon but her wrist was squeezed so tightly, she dropped it. Her struggles to get free were futile as Kryslie twisted her arm behind her and pushed her to the metal floor.

Zorrin fought better, but was no match for Tymos who was not holding back his strength. He twisted the Aeronite's weapon from him and squeezed it in his hand. He dropped the welded lump of metal and plastic. He made no move to avoid a powerful kick from Zorrin, simply used the foot to twist his attacker off balance. Tymos was on him before he could twist up off the floor.

"Where is the field generator," Kryslie demanded of her prisoner. Vori swore and refused to say.

Underneath them, the floor of the Aeronite ship rocked and warning klaxons could be heard through the metal walls.

"Knock him out, Tym," Kryslie said aloud. "We will have to wreck the door, we can't stay here."

"No!" Vori screamed. "Do that you can't! Then escape we can't."

"Too late for that. Your people are here now."

Both Aeronites began to struggle desperately and with increasing strength.

"Kryslie," Tymos thought at his sister and then gestured with his head at his captive's hands. They were glowing with a purple aura.

With swift movements, Tymos rolled Zorrin onto his back, but kept him down with a grip on his hands. Kryslie acted similarly with Vori.

"Who were your father and mother?" Tymos demanded.

"Why?" Zorrin snarled. "They were not some scum spawners like yours."

Tymos slapped him with only enough force to make his point. "Look at your hands."

Zorrin did – with an expression of horror. His mind gave a very clear picture of an old man with hands that glowed green.

"Who was your father?" Tymos insisted.

"Horvath Rozzin," Zorrin finally admitted. "Why?"

"He was a Tymorean. That is why your people wanted him dead and why they want you," Tymos told him.

"No," Vori shrieked again and struggled fiercely.

Kryslie had the sense of 'no more time'. She freed one of her hands and ignored Vori's attempts to scratch her eyes out.

"Stop it!" Kryslie commanded, and Vori shivered in her grip. Then she turned off her force shield and placed a hand over the girl's eyes. Knowing how to control Vori's rising Tymorean power, she did so. Vori collapsed, sobbing.

Tymos, in the same moment, neutralised Zorrin's power and cautiously released him. Both Aeronites were now slumped in abject terror.

"Enough of that! Start thinking – neither of you are stupid," Kryslie snapped. "You should know by now that we don't intend to harm you! If you do as we say, you will be safe. Let us out and then immediately raise that shield again and any other shields you have."

"Where you going?" Vori asked, trying to cling to Kryslie. "You can't fight Hepziah. Kill you by looking, he can."

"We can deal with him, but the humans can't," Tymos promised.

The Aeronites didn't believe it but both had the idea of flying the ship out of the base and away.

"You would be suicidal fools to try it and you wouldn't get far before you were out of fuel and dead in space," Kryslie warned. "Landin has guards around the ship. He isn't intending to give you up yet. Hurry, let us out."

Zorrin jumped to his feet and ran to the ships bridge. "Off it is," he yelled from there.

Vori saw Tymos and Kryslie vanish in front of her eyes. "They are gone! Turn the shields back on!" she mentally screamed.

The base rocked from the attack that had come out of nowhere. At first, everyone assumed it was an explosion; that something in the shuttle bay had detonated. The klaxons and warning messages seemed to confirm it. Nothing at all was visible on the tracking screen.

Landin gave orders for the emergency crews and caught a flash on the main screen just before the base rocked again.

"Turn those new shields on," he roared over the noise of the klaxons.

The third flash on the screen translated into a grid of bright lines as the energy beam hit the new shield and was absorbed.

Landin caught a hint of movement and saw Kryslie Ward trotting toward a vacant console. As he moved after her, he saw her brother moving one of the other controllers aside.

Kryslie was accessing the Auto-track controls and moving her fingers over the control pad at an amazing speed. Part of his mind registered her unusually mussed appearance, but that and the question of where she had been were not important.

"Do you know what is happening," he demanded.

"There has to be a ship or ships out there," she told him. "Come for our guests. They are in their ship with shields up. They should be safe enough for now."

"What are you doing?" Landin asked.

"I am trying to find a frequency or radiation signature to give us a picture of them. It is a mixed blessing that the Auto-track is under the new shield but I might be lucky," she spoke without slowing her pace.

Landin left her to it. His attention was caught by further light effects on the main screen.

Tymos was behaving much as his sister was but manipulating the control pad of the new shields. The generators could do much more than Ericson realised. He was setting up the specifications for a third layer of shielding and one he hoped would enable the sensors aimed from the base to get a blurry outline of the ships that had to be out there and close.

"Commander," one of the controllers called out.

Landin glanced at the main screen – now there were six hazy outlines of ships. Even as he looked, one grew larger and came right at the shield.

"What is it doing?" Basoli demanded.

"Looks like it is trying to land through the shield," Landin commented calmly, as showers of sparks and more light lit up the main screen. "It is larger than the other alien ships we have here."

Tymos allowed the on-duty controller back at his console and took up a portable data pad that could access the computer system by wireless signals. He moved towards Landin.

The red alert klaxons continued to sound, but now at a muted level, and the red lights were still flashing. Tymos nudged Landin and became the target of both his and Basoli's attention.

"I think you should escalate the alert to emergency status."

Landin gave him a sharp look and acted on the idea.

Tymos ignored Basoli who was demanding to know why a junior tech was giving orders to the Commander.

"Sir, you need to go to your assigned quarters," Landin told his superior.

"I will not be ordered around by a junior technician," Basoli's eyes betrayed his anger at Tymos's presumption.

Landin insisted, "Sir, if you don't follow emergency procedure, I will have you taken to your quarters by force."

Already half the shift had departed main mission, and everywhere else only a skeleton staff remained on duty. If needed, those few could be augmented, but for now, as many as possible were proceeding to their quarters or what were effectively escape pods. Both types of places could be made air tight in case of a breach in the base. All had emergency air and water.

Basoli recalled, before needing to be reminded, that in declared emergency conditions - the base commander out ranked him. He stalked off rather than being shamed by having to be forced away.

Since Tymos was still hovering, Landin asked, "What do you know?"

"Not enough," Tymos said quickly. "These ships have come for our guests. I don't think they will accept no. I suggest you don't antagonise them."

"I don't intend to hand our guests over," Landin said. "And from what you imply, that will antagonise them. We don't have any close-in weapons. Will the shields hold?"

"Yes," Tymos assured him.

Landin reached into his pocket for the small object he had found in engineering. "Yours?"

Tymos nodded, took it and placed it in his ear and then seemed to be listening intently. His expression betrayed concern. He turned abruptly and went to a now vacant console and began another lot of rapid hand movements.

"What's happening?" Landin demanded of the people around him. "Reports!"

The energy bombardment had ceased and there was tense waiting anticipation. The hazy ship figures had gone from the screen, but most eyes were looking there still.

Murtry reported, "Minor damage to shuttle bay one. Pressure leak was contained. No injuries. All personnel are in EA suits. There is one big ship with weapons aimed right into the bay. It is sitting just outside the limit of the new shield."

"Close outer blast doors," Landin ordered.

After that, each section reported in turn with only minor concerns.

"Can we transmit a message to those ships? I want to find out what they want," Landin demanded.

The duty communications officer composed the message and began sending it out on all frequencies available to him.

Kryslie Ward moved over to her brother. "Earthbase can't raise the fleet ships," she told him.

"I know. Landin found my earpiece. There are twelve ships and we have only seen six. The big one and five smaller ones."

The light around them began to increase. Kryslie turned and saw the terminus of what looked like a long range beam – the source of the blinding light.

"Tym! Anti-transmission shield, now!" His fingers began to fly over the touchpad.

Landin was shielding his eyes. Krys moved to stand between the light and her brother. This development she had not expected.

How had someone on the Aeronite colony of Zekos, obtained the specifications for a long-range beam – and the ability to use it? It wasn't impossible that some Aeronites had the power needed, but how could they have learnt to use the ability to transmit?

Landin had summoned guards, but armed and armoured figures were emerging from the blinding light.

"Make no sudden moves," Landin warned the controllers and technicians around him. All were now staring, some with mouths agape, at the suddenly appearing figures.

Two robed figures emerged after the six armoured ones, and were followed in turn by one more in armour.

One of the robed figures threw the hood back off his face. He looked humanoid; perhaps the main difference was in the facial bone structure. The bone were clearly defined for the face seemed to have little flesh padding it. It wasn't really alien looking, just odd. This one spoke into the silence. No one moved, and no one understood his speech. The alien adjusted something hanging from a chain around his neck.

"Everyone is to move into a group away from your machines," came the instruction, now in English. The voice sounded computer generated. Still no one moved.

Landin spoke up. "What is the meaning of this intrusion and the unprovoked attack?"

"You are harbouring two dangerous criminals. We insist you deliver them to us."

"And you are?" Landin asked calmly.

"I am Volentin, Prime Justifier of Zekos," the figure identified himself.

"I am Commander Landin," Landin returned the introduction. "Why did you not contact us first, before attacking us? We are not harbouring criminals."

The second hooded figure stepped forward, but did not reveal its face.

"You are lying, human," the generated voice sounded identical to the other. "The criminal's ship is in your ship landing area."

"We found an old ship buried in lunar soil," Landin deliberately misconstrued. He was hoping the guards would arrive soon.

"Where are the criminals?"

A hand like that of an old man emerged from the sleeve of the robe and pointed at Landin. It glowed green. Landin felt pressure in his mind to answer the question and then felt Kryslie in his mind again and she was somehow deflecting it. He said nothing.

The robed figure moved his head slightly.

"You! Come here."

One of the duty technicians, found himself walking towards the alien with no ability to resist.

"Where are they? The two that came in the ship?"

Even though the man tried to say nothing, he stuttered, "In ... In ...med...ical."

"Go there," the robed figure ordered, and he gestured to the guard behind him. "Bring them to me."

The robed figure looked around. He must have caught some movement behind Kryslie.

"You! What are you doing?"

Tymos didn't stop. Kryslie spoke instead. "He is trying to maintain the atmosphere in here. Your weapons damaged the air purification system."

Volentin spoke again. "Everyone move away from the machines."

The aiming of weapons at each controller emphasised the point. Landin nodded and this time his crew obeyed – except Tymos who was still working behind his sister.

Landin did not draw attention to him. From Kryslie's look, they both knew exactly what they were doing. A weapon fired in Krys's direction.

She didn't move. Tymos ignored it too, but he had finished and slowly turned around to stare back at the intruders.

Landin wondered where his guards were. They should have arrived. Kryslie felt the thought and tried to sense them. She couldn't, but was now aware of other intruders prowling the base.

"How can you justify invading our base, holding us hostage and searching? That is an act of war," Kryslie spoke deliberately.

"So, fight us female," the robed figure challenged. "If you can. If you dare."

Krys smiled faintly, but it went unnoticed as a protesting figure was hustled into main mission.

"Unhand me! I demand you release me," Basoli was shouting.

Landin glanced that way but didn't sigh. "Chief, we are in no position to win this fight. They have come seeking two criminals."

Basoli erupted again, "We are hiding no criminals."

"Sir, they will search, not find them and leave."

Just then, an armoured figure hustled Doctor Long into main mission.

"This woman will not tell me where the two we seek have gone." The voice of the armoured figure was amplified but not obviously computer generated.

"They were free to leave," Kryslie remarked, again deliberately drawing attention to herself. "No doubt they did."

"The ship is still there," Volentin told her.

"You didn't need a ship to get in here," she pointed out. "If they are your people, perhaps they had others outside here to help them."

"They do not have the ability," the robed figure moved forward. "Nor did we notice any other ships nearby. Those we saw are floating hulks."

Kryslie shrugged, "We never saw you coming."

The robed figure put his full attention onto her. She gave no sign that she knew the creature was trying to force its mind on hers.

"Where are the criminals?" he demanded aloud.

"We know of none," she stared back at him.

The robed figure moved to reach for her neck. She put her arm up to block him. The figure stopped moving, stared at her and then spoke to his companion, Volentin.

"Order your men to continue to search the base."

The figure stared at Krys a moment longer, then dropped his arm and turned away. He gestured to the soldier holding Long. He released her and went to the robed figure and bowed. The doctor moved closer to Landin.

"Are you going to allow this, Commander?" Basoli raged. "Where are your security people?"

"Your guards are indisposed," the robed figure told them.

"Commander, just tell them where those two are," Basoli ordered.

"Sir, don't you recall, we have been looking for them since first watch. I really do think they have gone." He didn't even think in his mind that he knew better.

"Those two were missing as well," Basoli pointed to Tymos and Kryslie. "Where were you?"

"Indisposed," Kryslie told him, without looking at him.

"Exactly," Tymos added, so that the robed figure glanced at him.

The robed figure spoke a word that Krys recognised. It was in an old Tymorean dialect and translated into the name of a very unsavoury scavenging animal. He put his hand on the soldier that had fetched Doctor Long. The gesture suggested ownership. His instructions were low pitched and not picked up by the translator, but Kryslie heard them.

"Go to the ship – in the ship bay. Find out if the children are there. Do whatever is needed to open it."

The soldier ran off and the robed figure moved its head and spoke to Volentin.

"Everyone is to lie down on the floor," Volentin ordered. Once again, the weapons emphasised the point.

Basoli glanced at the weapons and began to sink down. Most of the other staff were doing likewise, while keeping their eyes on the weapons.

Landin told Long to obey, though he himself waited a perceptible moment, until a few more of the soldiers aimed at him, before obeying. In the corner of his eye, he saw Tymos and Krys imitating the other crew but they were focussing on the robed figure. Then he saw Krys tense, and seem to resist a glance at her brother. He could not see Tymos's expression.

Tymos and Krys kept their thoughts to themselves. Yet they shared an understanding that was deeper than mere thought. They did not know if either of the two alien leaders could detect telepathy – now they needed to find out.

"Fools," Krys deliberately broadcast, sensing that Vori or Zorrin had unshielded their ship and the alien had tricked them.

"They knew that one and trusted him," Tymos thought back. "These aliens have no honour."

"Fools indeed," the robed figure moved quickly and easily lifted Kryslie from the floor, and holding her by the neck, dangled her in front of him. "You, female, are something different to these others. I think I will have you as a prize. I will enjoy finding out what you are. Now, who were you thinking at?"

Kryslie stayed hanging limply and simply stared back at the hooded eyes. Without warning, her arms moved suddenly and knocked the cowl of the alien's head. His reaction was instantaneous and violent. He flung her to the floor, and placed one foot on her neck as he quickly re-covered his face.

Basoli, watching, quivered fearfully. Landin hoped Kryslie still knew what she was doing. The robed figure had looked alien. With its purplish skin and argent eyes that were deep set under thick eye ridges, it looked insane.

"Bring me...that one," the hooded figure ordered his companion.

Landin wondered if Volentin wanted to obey, though obey he did, dragging Tymos to his feet and towards the robed one. He pushed Tymos to his knees and ordered, "Bow to Hepziah."

Tymos didn't.

The robed one, still with one foot on Krys, leant forward and massaged Tymos's chin. "Two strong willed humans. You will provide me with delicious sport. I will enjoy breaking you."

Landin moved slightly and saw one of the armed soldiers kick Tymos in the back, forcing his face down, and then holding his weapon forcibly into his back.

Some sense of survival finally clicked in Zorrin's mind. "Vori, snap out of it. We need to get our armour on."

Vori shook herself, and followed him to the locker where she knew it to be. When Zorrin opened it, they both stared in shock. The metal was streaked with lines of etched and bubbled metallic oxide. The armour's joints, made of a tough resistant synthetic, were in tatters.

"It is like someone poured lenthic acid on them," Vori said. "But no one has been in here except us."

"Those Tymoreans were!"

"But we had no acid on board."

"So, they had transmitters, they must have got in before and done this. They don't want us to go. The rotten scum tricked us."

"Let's put our flight suits on then. They will protect us a bit."

"Not if they have blasters," Zorrin objected, but he followed the suggestion. Then he moved to the bridge and turned on the exterior sensors and bridge controls. He studied the engine status and then slumped in the pilot's couch. His sister took the navigator's position.

"We are trapped here," he told her. "Not enough fuel to get anywhere and guards all around the ship."

"We could shoot them," Vori suggested. "The lasers are fully charged."

Movement at the opening to the bay drew Zorrin's attention. He swore some vile Aeronite oaths. "Now we are trapped for sure – they are sealing the bay."

Vori was studying her instruments. "I've got a feed from the drone we left above. There are still six ships in far space. The others have landed at a distance from the base. One is right outside the bay. Perhaps the humans do mean to protect us."

Zorrin looked at the navigator's screen without doing more that rotating his couch. He pointed to the biggest of the ships. "That's Hepziah's ship," he said with his voice shaking. "We're gone! We're history! The people here can't protect us, the Tymoreans won't help us. There is no one here to help us."

"Close everything down," Vori said quickly. "Make it look like the ship is dead. Life support too. We will use the emergency oxygen and hide in the sleep capsules."

She was turning off switches, but just before turning off the screen showing the shuttle bay outside, she saw a figure in armour running in and firing at the ring of guards. The nearest ones fell immediately, the more distant ones fired back but the armour of the lone intruder was able to take it. He kept firing at the guards until all were down.

Vori stared in horror, and then her eyes met Zorrin's. He said, "Shut it down! Have you got your other weapon ready? He will try to shoot his way in. I don't know how much the shields can take."

They waited, crouched down between the sleep capsules. At any moment they expected to feel the concussion of a blaster beam on their ship. They felt one thud, and then nothing.

"He can't have given up," Vori spoke over the suit comm.

"No...listen," Zorrin returned. He unsealed his suit to hear better. There was tapping on the hull. "It's Hakos code!"

Vori gripped his arm in excitement. "It's Stenn! It's got to be. He can help us."

"Shh..." her brother hissed. "It is him. He said he will remove his helmet so we can be sure."

Zorrin went to a side view port and looked into the bay. He saw the blond haired figure gesturing urgently. He was close enough to the ship for his features to be clear. "It is him."

Vori ran through to the bridge and cut the shields and opened the landing ramp. "What are you doing here, Stenn? How did you do it?"

"Never mind, but I replaced one of the elite. I can get you out of here. Come on, there isn't much time. I have fixed one of the ships so only I can activate it again."

Zorrin touched his friend's arm. "There is an extra shield..."

"It's no problem. I have one of our leader's gadgets. He gave it to me to bring half the guards in. It took us through the shield. Now – come on!"

Still Zorrin hesitated.

"Hepziah knows your ship is here. He sent me to the healer's place to get you back but you weren't there. He has people searching the base here. They will get here soon and destroy your ship. You know he has weapons that can do it."

Vori dragged Zorrin out. "Come on. Brother, come on."

"Stand close to me," Stenn instructed. "This will feel weird, but it won't last long."

Chapter 28

Kryslie linked once again to Landin's mind. She was able to see what little he could see. It included her own seemingly desperate position. But, she was where she wanted to be – close to the alien. He was unaware that she was studying him and not at all helpless.

She sensed Landin's anger and frustration at the same time as she sensed Zorrin's anger and Vori's terror.

Both young aliens were struggling desperately in the grip of the armoured soldier, who was holding them both with contemptuous ease. Kryslie felt her body kicked as Zorrin struggled to keep back from Hepziah. He was like a berserker and his struggles seemed to be exciting the robed alien.

"Oh, yes," came a murmur in a language Kryslie understood. The sensation she was receiving made her feel nauseous. "Young, strong, intelligent...yes indeed. You will regret ever displeasing me."

Hepziah reached out and placed his hand on Zorrin's face and seemed to squeeze. The young alien made a weak sound and went limp.

Vori continued to struggle in the soldier's grip. Hepziah moved away from Kryslie and took her, dangling her as he had Kryslie. He struck her a blow on her face.

"You cannot trick me that way, disgusting child. I will break you and make you my personal slave. You will break easily. You are weaker than my Tymorean pet."

He hit her again and she went limp too.

"Carry that female," Hepziah told Volentin. He took Zorrin and slung him over his own shoulder.

Kryslie slowly moved her hands ready to push up. She sensed Tymos doing the same when he felt the weapon pressure easing on his back.

"Fix those two," Hepziah ordered the armoured soldier.

The soldier, who had betrayed the two young Aeronites, seemed to consider the two humans for a moment. He then used his weapon in a vicious movement, bringing it down hard on each head.

Hepziah placed a hand on the soldier's helmet. "Well done my little pet. You please me well. We leave now, bring those two with you."

Tymos and Kryslie were only pretending to be unconscious. Their personal force shields had absorbed most of the blow. The soldier lifted one in each arm, to start dragging them but it looked like he was having trouble managing it.

"What of the rest of the soldiers?" Volentin asked.

"We no longer need them. I have what I want. Come on or be left behind," Hepziah told his companion.

After lifting Vori, Volentin moved closer to Hepziah and the shimmering distortion. The four disappeared. The soldiers still remaining began to back away from those they guarded and towards the distortion.

They did not see Tymos and Kryslie twist and throw their captor to the floor. It was so fast an action that Landin missed it. He was cautiously raising his head and saw Kryslie raising the soldier's helmet, while Tymos held the struggling soldier down.

"Stenn!" Kryslie said sharply, but in a quiet voice.

She looked into the face of her friend. He looked back at her with eyes betraying conflicting emotions, hatred of them and agonised entreaty. He spat at them, still struggling and forced out a whisper in Tymorean.

"Kill me! Kill me before he makes me kill you."

"No," she whispered, but her mind was counting down fractions of seconds. "Not now."

Tymos hit their prisoner with his fist – hard enough to knock him out, just as Hepziah and Volentin returned with their burdens. Both seemed disoriented and for a moment, Hepziah teetered, and then his eyes fixed on Tymos kneeling over his minion. He dropped Zorrin and moved to him. Tymos stood up, Krys stayed crouched.

"You!" A blast of light and energy flew from Hepziah's hand and struck Tymos in the chest. He stumbled back a few paces and then stood firm, and stared back at the cowled eyes, just visible as glowing orbs.

"Having trouble, are you, Abomination?" Tymos said provokingly, still standing his ground. "I have to tell you there is a little flaw in your stolen technology."

"You! You are dead!"

Another flash of energy arced at Tymos, but he merely moved his head to the left.

"Doesn't feel like it," he taunted, watching Hepziah move closer. "Ciriot weakling."

Hepziah covered the remaining distance like fluid lightning and grabbed Tymos by the neck. He wasn't helpless. He chopped Hepziah's neck with both hands and stared into the eyes that blazed with anger. Sparks of energy sizzled around Tymos's head.

Landin's attention was on Tymos, wanting to help him. He slowly raised himself until one of the soldiers saw the movement and put the aperture of his weapon in his face. Beyond the weapon, he saw Kryslie move, lifting Zorrin and grabbing Volentin who still held his burden. She vanished. Landin blinked and heard Basoli make a quiet exclamation.

Tymos reached his hands towards Hepziah's face as if intending to poke at his eyes. They didn't reach. Hepziah threw Tymos to the ground, calling for his slave. In that moment when Hepziah glanced to see why his creature didn't reply, Tymos laughed mockingly. "You want me, old man? Find me."

The next instant, he wasn't there. Hepziah spun around, hands only half lowered. He was expecting some sort of trick, but there was no sign of Tymos, or of Volentin and the two young Aeronites. Hepziah swore vile untranslatable oaths. He ignored the weak puny humans, craving as he did the one who had stood against him. He would have that one, and find the others....he vanished.

Kryslie had transmitted herself and the Aeronites to her brother's quarters and warned Volentin not to try anything. She watched him as she sent a signal to Earthbase to activate a long-range beam. From Tymos's computer, she lowered the anti-transmission shield her brother had raised, but only for the vital moments it took Jonko and Keleb to appear beside her, take charge of the Aeronites and return to Earthbase. As soon as the beam terminus vanished, the shield went up again.

She did not stop to ponder the reaction of Volentin. At first he had been too surprised to react. Then he had only said, "Tymorean" and was perhaps resigned to an unpleasant fate. Or he might have been relieved to have escaped from an intolerable one.

Tymos didn't need to broadcast to Kryslie when he left main mission, nor did she need to be told when Hepziah did. She sensed the change in the different energies. The powerful alien, went first to the shuttle bay.

Kryslie returned moments after Hepziah had left, arriving into almost the same position as she had occupied before. Landin blinked, but didn't dare move.

"Drop your weapons!" she spoke in the Tymorean dialect Hepziah had used - but made it a command.

Eleven weapons clattered to the floor. The Lunar 1 staff wasted no time grabbing them and taking the upper hand.

"Take these aliens into the nearest storage room," Landin ordered at once. "Ensure they can't get out."

"How did you do that?" Basoli demanded of Kryslie.

She ignored the question and spoke to Landin. "It will be a very good idea if you all went into emergency quarters."

She reinforced the idea in Basoli's mind.

"My place is out here," Landin told her, but he gestured the rest of the staff out.

"Leave the weapons here," Kryslie insisted, as the crew who had secured the aliens returned.

Long took Basoli by the arm and insisted he obeyed.

When only Kryslie remained, Landin asked sternly, "What game are you playing?"

"No game, Commander. And our tactics are working. If you choose to stay here, I won't stop you – but put on an EA suit. It will be no protection from those weapons, but it is something. You might choose to find the security team and get them safe. Tymos has told me that the team in the shuttle bay is down. I will deal with them."

"And your brother?" Landin demanded.

"He has the attention of that abomination, Hepziah," Kryslie said. Her implacable tone, did not disturb him this time.

More alerts came over the comm system, indicating a fire in the shuttle bay.

"You are following a dangerous course," Landin warned her. "I hope you understand the stakes."

"I do, Commander. Better than you do."

She stalked out of main mission, and as soon as she was out of Landin's sight, transmitted to the shuttle bay.

Tymos was no longer there, as she had already sensed, and neither was Hepziah. In a sweeping glance, Krys noticed the signs of an energy blast on Zorrin's ship and the residue of fire suppressant where something flammable had ignited. The EA suits of some of the prone guards were soaked with the suppressant.

Dragging two unconscious guards at a time, Kryslie got all of the guards to the safety lock in the shuttle bay. With them all in a sitting position, the lock was crowded, but at least they were all still alive. They had each received a heavy stun.

She knew it had been Stenn Reslic who had done this when he was getting to the ship. He had obeyed Hepziah and betrayed two innocents who had trusted him. He would have known what Hepziah intended with them. It seemed the creature had warped him, turned him rogue.

Kryslie forced her mind off her friend; not wanting to think what she had to do – what his father the President of Tymorea would do if he were here. Instead she sealed the safety lock, set the independent life support controls and moved on.

Over the internal comm system, Landin ordered all hands to quarters – full lock down.

Instantly, all pressure doors slammed shut, dividing the base into isolated modules. All computer controlled systems, except life support, powered down to standby mode. Movement between sections was halted unless one knew the manual override codes. The crews still manning stations would move into safety locks in their section.

Landin didn't seal main mission. There was no point. The creature Kryslie and Tymos were hunting – and he knew they were intending to destroy Hepziah – could probably enter anywhere in whatever way he had arrived and departed. It seemed though, that Tymos had done something to the shields to stop the alien leaving the base. Basoli was probably going to be livid about that.

He glanced down at the remaining alien guard. This one didn't look much different to humans. There was blood seeping into the thick blond hair, from where Tymos had hit him, and he was still unconscious. There was something about the bone structure of the face that was similar to that of Kryslie and Tymos Ward.

Thinking of that made Landin realise that his technicians had known him...had called him by a name.

"Tymorean," Landin mused. In his mind he contrasted what he knew of Tymos and Kryslie, to the hatred he had sensed from Vori and Zorrin. Maybe there was truth in both views.

As Landin stood, a fierce grip on his ankle startled him. The prone figure had woken and the eyes were staring at him with manic intensity.

"Human, you must kill me now! You must!"

The alien spoke in English, and Landin was startled into saying, "It is not my decision to make,"

"But it is mine!" Stenn Reslic pleaded. "You cannot let me live. I will be forced to kill – as soon as Hepziah senses I am awake. I don't want to kill innocents – or my friends."

"Kryslie…" Landin began.

"Can't help me! Her duty is to neutralise me, but she is my friend. Tymos is my friend. Better that you kill me so they don't have to do that duty. They will do it though – they have no choice – even if they hate it."

Landin shivered, recalling that Tymos had acted – not viciously or callously – but because he had to.

"I will not shoot you in cold blood, but I have another solution," Landin offered. "I can keep you asleep until Kryslie and Tymos are free."

"No! Please! Kill me now."

The expression in the eyes suddenly altered, like another person now lay there. Landin shivered, sensing a malevolent evil. In the next moment, he felt his legs pulled from under him and himself falling forward. Before he could push up, he had his arm twisted up behind him.

"You will show me every section of this complex," Stenn commanded. Landin now realised what Kryslie had done to the alien guards. He could not resist the command.

Then he discovered how strong this renegade Tymorean was, as he was lifted to his feet and forced to walk to the lifeless monitors.

Even as his free hand input the override commands, and brought up the internal monitors on multiple small screens, his mind was hoping Tymos or Kryslie would sense his mind.

On one of the screens, Landin spotted Tymos moving stealthily down deserted corridors. On a second screen he saw Kryslie creep up on an alien soldier and overcome him in a brief one-sided scuffle. She and the alien disappeared from that area and a short time later appeared in a different section where Kryslie dragged the guard into a storage locker. A schematic of the base showed lights where Tymos, Kryslie and the alien soldiers prowled.

The soldier holding Landin watched intently.

Kryslie continued hunting alien soldiers, always alert for Hepziah. If he found her, he would transfer his attention to her and Tymos would seek aliens to capture, or human guards to rescue.

Landin stopped inputting commands, and watched the screens in an attempt to distance the pain in his arm and shoulder where it was being forced up behind his back.

A flash of intense light drew his attention to one monitor and he saw Tymos ducking down behind some storage crates. Hepziah prowled around, looking for him. Tymos stuck his head out briefly and a blast of light hit the place where he hid. When the monitor's auto light sensor stabilised, Tymos was no longer there.

Landin found his mind able to think again and he checked the base's status screen. Damage was minimal so far, injuries few and non-fatal. He grimaced as his arm was wrenched further.

Kryslie sent a message to her brother. "All alien guards accounted for and our people are all safe. Landin is still in main mission."

Thinking of him was enough to sense his trouble. "Landin has trouble. How are you?"

Tymos sent back, "Holding out. He has got a couple of decent shots at me, but I avoided most. He doesn't seem to be weakening any though."

She could tell he was suddenly busy again and transmitted to main mission.

"Release him!" Kryslie spoke loudly, and clearly, in the main Tymorean dialect, but did not make it a 'command'.

Stenn Reslic swung his hostage around like a shield and did not release him. Landin's face betrayed his agony.

"Are you a coward now, Stenn Reslic?" Kryslie accused.

Landin was seeing yet another face of Krys Ward, and this one gave him shivers. Cold, distant, unforgiving. Pain shot into his shoulder as the hand holding it shook, either in anger or fear.

Then he was thrown aside, falling heavily against a console and sliding to the floor. He lay there gasping in pain as the alien strode towards his accuser. He wanted to help, but he had seen she could look after herself.

Landin didn't understand the exchange – angry and spiteful from the alien, calm from Kryslie. She didn't back away or seem frightened, only deadly intent. The alien attacked her, but she was ready.

Except for the time she had disarmed the second saboteur, Landin had always found Kryslie to be polite, gentle, and peaceable even if strong willed. Until that day, he had never guessed she was capable of fighting like a commando and throwing her opponent over her shoulder and moving so fast. He had honestly thought her speed when saving the President had been desperation and training.

"You won't get me like that again, bitch," Stenn yelled at her, using English. He ran at her again, and this time she grappled with him and took three vicious punches. They didn't seem to affect her.

Landin stayed clear. He was in no condition to help, and Kryslie didn't look worried. He listened though, and learnt a lot from comments like, "The President taught me too," from Kryslie and "You are not so damn Great," from the alien.

He could tell how hard the two opponents were affecting each other from the sickening thuds of fists on flesh or bodies against hard surfaces.

"You've got a force shield on, you damn bitch," the alien accused, and he found something and yanked. "Now we will see who is strongest."

The fight escalated in degree and the alien was out for blood, out to kill. Kryslie was adept at avoiding killing blows. Landin missed the moment when she attacked, and her opponent had been tricked into thinking she was only about to dodge again. She charged him so fast, so unexpectedly, that he was flung backwards. He didn't seem able to move.

Kryslie wasted no time putting her hand on his face as Hepziah had done to Zorrin.

This alien began to struggle, but Kryslie easily held him down with just one hand. Then he began to scream, long and piercing.

"Don't resist me, Stenn," Kryslie almost begged. "You know I must do this. Deep inside you, you know."

The screaming was such that you wanted to block your ears and have it stop. There was a concussion of power and the screaming did stop, only to be replaced with sobbing that was equally hard to bear.

Kryslie stepped away and left the sobbing heap where it lay. Her expression was completely closed.

Landin saw Tymos walk up beside her. His expression was the same as he looked down at the alien.

"Activate your force field again," he said and then asked, "What did you do?"

"Neutralised his power. I need to get him somewhere before Hepziah gets to him again."

"Can you help him?" Tymos asked.

"No. His power was totally warped. Hepziah was in total control, and if he comes back now, he will be as bad as before."

"Don't let him have me again," a pleading voice said. "Great One, I cannot fight him, you must kill me. Even without power he can use me."

"We'll get you away from here," Kryslie told him. "You can live without power." To Tymos she said, "What about putting him in a stasis chamber? I don't want to activate a long range beam - Hepziah is likely to sense it."

"True. And I don't want the shield down even for an instant," Tymos agreed. "The Hepziah entity is powerful. I don't think I have weakened him any – all he has to do is reanimate his creature."

"Where is he getting his power from?" Kryslie asked aloud. Tymos stood rock still.

Landin voiced an opinion. "Could he be pulling it from the power grid? The power fluctuates when he tosses those lightning bolts."

"We can do that, but I know of no others who can, but that must be it. We need to end this fast."

Tymos leant down and hefted the alien. He turned as Hepziah arrived back in main mission.

"Put my property down," Hepziah spoke with deadly venom. He now had a weapon in his hand.

"Weaklings need weapons," Kryslie told him as Tymos lowered Stenn to the floor.

"Think that at your own risk, Tymorean," Hepziah countered. "Where did you take my prisoners?"

"Nowhere that you dare to go," she told him.

He fired his weapon at her legs, part of her uniform vanished. She didn't move or act as if the weapon had hurt her.

"I will have that knowledge from you!" Hepziah promised. "Before I kill you, slowly and painfully."

He pointed at her and energy arced at her and for an instant, she was encased by a glowing green nimbus. She stood, unmoved.

"Is that all you can do?" she asked, goading the entity. "All of your companions are dead or gone – it's time you were gotten rid of."

"Not all," Hepziah told her. The next energy beam was aimed at his creature. "Get up!"

To Kryslie's revulsion, Stenn's body jerked in a convulsion, and he began climbing awkwardly upright.

Tymos began to move to Stenn, but a beam from the weapon passed millimetres in front of him.

"This is a disintegrator," Hepziah explained. "It tends to take chunks out of whatever it is aimed at and sears the edges, so you don't bleed to death too quickly. Maximum pain, minimum danger to life. I wouldn't trust your fancy force shields to protect you for long."

"That is not our only protection," Kryslie warned him.

"Check them for weapons, my pet," Hepziah ordered the reanimated Stenn. "Neither of you move. If you do, I will prove the effect of this weapon to you."

Landin realised he was unnoticed and forced his uninjured arm to reach up for a weapon from the console above his head. He let the idea sit in his mind, hoping Krys would read it there. He thought again once it was in his hand.

"No weapons, master," Stenn's voice sounded mechanical now.

"Over-confident children," Hepziah sneered. "Immobilise the female." To Kryslie he added, "Don't try to move or it will be half your face that goes."

Landin saw the knife in Stenn's hand and thought hard in warning. Kryslie took an instant to link to his eyes.

Stenn lunged, aiming the knife at her spine, just below the neck. She dropped a fraction of a moment ahead of Stenn's movement, twisted and rolled so her attacker was in front of her. She twisted the knife from his hand; made it fly like a blur straight to Hepziah.

Even as he fired his weapon, the knife embedded in his chest. The cowled figure staggered for a moment, began to fall, then jerked back upright.

Stenn screamed again, from the burning of the discharged weapon that touched him.

"Throw it!" Kryslie mentally yelled at Landin, referring to the weapon in his hand. Without looking, Tymos caught the weapon; his mind identified it by feel as a stunner, and adjusted it to maximum, lethal, also by feel. He aimed it at Stenn and then fired. The screaming stopped.

He aimed it at Hepziah and fired again.

"Look, Krys!" he said at that instant.

Chapter 29

Once again, the cowled figure stumbled, this time falling. Where it had stood, a nimbus of energy hovered in the air. The body twitched and tried to rise. A wisp of faintly glowing green energy seemed to be sucked from the still form of Stenn Reslic and joined the larger nimbus. Again the body beneath it twitched and this time seemed to be being forced to its feet.

The lights in main mission flickered and grew dim. Tymos spun and raced to the environment controls, and without finesse, reached under the console and yanked the bundled conduits. Wires and ribbon connectors stretched and broke. The lights went out and the computers went dead.

Next instant the muted klaxons reached a new pitch of urgency.

"Life support," Kryslie said aloud.

Tymos felt for where he had earlier placed the portable wireless computer interface. In the dark, he allowed his fingers to manipulate the press pads.

The voice over warning was, "Life support failure. Oxygen depletion in thirty minutes."

"Can you see it?" Tymos called.

"No," Kryslie said calmly. "Both gone. It needs energy and you just cut it off from the base power."

Both Tymos and Kryslie were thinking intensely.

"Maintenance duct. Main mission isn't sealed," Tymos realised.

"Arboretum," Kryslie deduced rapidly. "It has got separate environment support. With the disruptor it can break through the bulkhead if it can't teleport through it."

Tymos knelt down by Stenn's body and felt for a pulse. "Follow it, Krys. Hold it there until I come."

Kryslie transmitted to the base's garden and found a secluded corner to watch. Her senses told her the entity was not there yet and she had time to wonder why it had not instantly teleported as it had been doing. She considered what she had observed, the body and the glowing nimbus.

"It needs a physical body," Kryslie realised. "The one it is using is injured now, perhaps fatally. Certainly it is old. Is its ability to teleport a function of the body or the nimbus?"

A series of seemingly unconnected facts flicked through her mind.

Hepziah, the combined entity, was using Tymorean transmitter technology. Only Tymoreans could use it - royal Tymoreans — those with the Guardian's power. The body controlled by the nimbus was old, ancient. It wanted Zorrin and Vori — who had some of the Guardian's power.

"Tym," Kryslie sent. "I know what the nimbus needs, besides energy to feed on. I know how to trap it and how to kill it. I have to be the one to do it."

Tymos found a very weak pulse in Stenn's neck. His skin was clammy and cold and he was going into shock. "Hang on cousin," Tymos said softly as he deactivated his force shield. Then he placed a hand on Stenn's forehead and sent his personal power into him. Since it was dark, Tymos adjusted his eyes to see the energy flows in his friend's body and directed his power to heal the damage done by the disruptor and stunner. He stopped once Stenn's heartbeat and breathing were at a less critical level.

Then he scuttled to where Landin lay. He felt his commander flinch.

"Sorry, Sir," he said. "Let me look at your shoulder."

"Is that alien gone?" Landin asked. Hissing as Tymos felt around the swelling where his shoulder was dislocated and sent some healing energy into it.

"No, but it fled from here. Kryslie has gone after it."

"Do you plan to kill him?" Landin asked.

"We have no intention of letting that energy entity roam free in space. And I am sorry that we are using the base as our hunting ground. It is weakened now, since I have denied it the ability to feed on the base power."

"It?" Landin queried. He hissed again as Tymos held his arm and twisted. His shoulder slipped back into place with an audible snap.

"Hepziah is not remotely humanoid," Tymos said quickly. "It is an energy entity controlling a humanoid body. Possessing it you would say."

"You switched off life support," Landin accused.

Tymos moved away and returned with the portable computer interface. On the screen was the countdown to critical failure.

"Sir, when it gets to five minutes – restart the life support system," Tymos told him. "If we haven't overcome the energy entity by then – we won't be able to. We will have to force it to return to its ship. It will have to or starve."

"I am going to have a lot of questions for you when this is over," Landin threatened, weakly.

"I guess you will, Sir," Tymos agreed.

Without further word, Tymos reset his force shield and transmitted to the Arboretum.

The normally bright down lights seemed obscured by a sickly green cloud. From it, fingers of lightning arced down to the ground. The air felt scorched.

Tymos found Kryslie kneeling beside a cowled body. As he moved around in front of her, he realised that she had a head, now uncovered, and resting in her lap.

"Krys? Are you all right?"

"Yes," she assured him. Her voice seemed husky. "Tym, this is Lorno."

Tymos glanced at the old man's face and then at the ceiling.

"It has left me, Great One," a barely audible voice whispered. "I am but a husk, my time has passed. I should have died. Yet there is that which I must tell you. I was what you are now. I served the Guardians for a thousand years. Willingly, I welcomed death, but there was one final battle – one evil we knew we must fight. Joshe died, Tormel died. I...lived. We went out against the evil entity worshiped by the Ciriot as a God. We failed; we were too old. I tried to change it, but I was too weak. Now I deserve only death and oblivion."

"No," Tymos disagreed, focussing his attention on the aged, dying man. "You are merely mortal, for all your longevity. The Guardians cannot expect you to be a god."

The old voice went on, "Sometimes, I was able to overcome the evil one for a time. I tried to free the lad, but he sensed me, locked within the evil one. He tried to help me, but I betrayed him. Spare the lad if you can. He has a good heart."

"I know," Kryslie said, still weeping silent tears.

"Sir, you mentioned trying to change it," Tymos said urgently. He crouched by the old man.

"Too weak! I was too weak."

"He is barely hanging on," Kryslie told Tym. "He forbade me to help him. I know what to do. He was like me - only more of an empath."

"Like you?"

"A mind healer," Kryslie whispered. "I have to transmute the energy – through me. I have to do it now – while it is weakened. And I need you – to drain my energy and send it back into something else."

"How?" Tymos asked.

Kryslie gave a faint mirthless laugh. "Like Jon and I did, back home – with the plants."

"Yes," Tymos understood. "Do you think Lorno influenced it to come here? Does he have planet sense too?"

"I don't know about planet sense. As for the rest – Stenn knew we were here. I think he sent Vori and Zorrin here, knowing the evil one wanted them," Kryslie told him. "But I want to know why the Guardians let Lorno suffer for so long."

Tymos felt the anger in her mind. "So do I," he agreed and he stood up straight and raised his arms high and wide. Krys, still kneeling, copied his gesture.

The lightning in the garden increased, white now, not like the sickly green, as the Great Ones called on the Guardians of Peace – and were answered.

"Why?" they asked. "Why is your servant forgotten – neglected – tortured – broken?"

The sense of the Guardians swirled around them. The green cloud fled and cowered on the far side of the garden.

"He still serves us," the sense of the Guardians said to their minds. "He contained the evil until you, who were stronger, came."

"He begs for peace," Kryslie told them. "Will you grant him that? And our friend – our cousin – who tried to help him – can we help him?"

"Yes and yes," was the answer. "You are strong and you must remove this evil."

The sense of the Guardians vanished.

"I think, if I unshield, the entity will try to overwhelm me," Kryslie said. "Lorno is dying and weak. The entity has not the strength to animate him anymore. It wants a stronger body to possess. I am ready."

The green cloud was slowly spreading out again, trying to draw energy from the heat and light source for the garden.

Kryslie reinforced her personal mind shields, took a few calming breaths and snapped off her personal force shield. She placed a gentle hand on the old man's face – to tempt the evil one to her. The old man's face, without the possessing entity, looked human, vulnerable and old. Lorno's hand moved weakly to cover hers.

A tiny cloud of green drifted down and enveloped Krys's hand, as if tasting her. She watched it, felt her brother's hands grip her shoulders, as he crouched behind her. He had his personal force shield on and his mind shields up. He would be invulnerable to the invasion Kryslie was allowing – at least for now.

Feeling him there, gave her courage. This was a dangerous move. Yes, she had a gift for mind healing, but the energy entity did not have a physical mind. And in this instance, she was letting it into her mind, though only into part of it. To transmute the energy, it would be her own mind she had to heal. That was the danger – could she?

Tymos's gift to heal physical wounds – was limited to healing others. To heal himself, he needed her. He could feed his healing energy to her, to use on him. Could this work now – with the roles reversed?

They had never tried this – but the entity could not know of the twin bond. That together they were twice as strong as apart.

Kryslie shivered though. She recalled how her mentors had warned her that this great strength was also a great weakness. She had been taught, in a way she couldn't ignore, that being wide open to her twin, as she had been, was suicidal. Hence she had been forced to forge strong mind shields. But to finish this – Tymos would have to be wide open to her. If she failed to contain the entity, he would be overwhelmed as well.

With a sudden rush, the energy cloud engulfed her, surrounded her.

Lorno felt Tymos's hand gently pushing him away and found enough energy to roll clear.

"Now!" Kryslie thought down the twin bond.

The entity thought it had won, was tasting her power. It swarmed into her mind, and found the connections to work her body. It tried to surge through her – but couldn't – but for now the steady flow of energy satisfied it.

Tymos opened his force shield, and from where he touched Krys, he pulled at her power. He drained power from her, as Kryslie had from Stenn Reslic, only much more slowly so that the entity did not notice. He felt the 'taste' of her power change; saw her mauve aura swirl to murky green as the entity filled her. He kept drawing this energy into him and through him and grounded it into the soil around him.

He ignored the new warnings being broadcast as the sensors under the thick layer of soil detected the free energy. Part of his mind caused the roots of the plants to draw on this energy, use it to grow, to flower, to seed. He watched as the last of the green cloud seemed to be absorbed into Krys.

Through the twin bond, Tymos sensed Krys's revulsion at the satiated entity that was feeding on her essence.

Tymos kept up his drawing out of energy as Kryslie snapped her mental shields tightly closed again. The entity was trapped within her, but still replete from its greedy feeding. She stopped drawing energy from the living energy around her. Only then did the entity realise it was threatened. It began to panic as it felt itself weakening again and unable to get more energy.

It bounced around inside Krys's head as it tried to find a way out. It emitted lightning to try and pierce a way out, but only weakened itself further.

In spite of a monumental headache, Kryslie focussed on her brother's mind. He opened his shields as she dropped hers. Tymos caught the entity as if it were an unnatural growth. Kryslie linked with his mind and looked at her own. She drew energy from Tymos and used her gift to change what she saw to what it should be.

The core of the entity resisted, saw its death coming and wrenched itself from Tymos's grasp, fled from Krys's mind as a tiny intense glow, and shot up, piercing the bulkhead above as it fled for space.

Kryslie still resonated to it – felt it still as part of her. It hit the shields – the scrambler field Tymos had added after the rest...

Kryslie went limp in her brother's grip. He tried to reach her mind but her mind shields were solidly in place, blocking him out. He began to send energy to her.

"No," Kryslie whispered. "Not yet."

"Why? You are vulnerable."

"I know – but – not yet. I think the scrambler field finished it. Wait. Be sure. Stay shielded. If it returns, it will seek me."

Tymos nodded, following her logic. If it managed to pull back together, then through resonance or vengeance it would return to Krys. She was depleted, but it was weak too, and he could act.

The increasing urgency of the warning alerts drew his attention.

"Go!" Kryslie told him. She activated her personal force shield again.

Tymos stood, reluctant to leave her, but needing to act. He glanced at Lorno and saw his face had slipped into peaceful lines. No trace of the alien visage remained and his withered old hand touched Kryslie lightly.

Tymos transmitted back to main mission, found Landin unconscious as the atmosphere was depleted of oxygen. He picked up the portable computer link counting down the last seconds to terminal life support failure. He restarted the system, bringing online the emergency battery back-up system and felt the pressure increase as the circulating fans also came back on line.

The alert system announced, "Life support back on line," and then quoted oxygen and carbon dioxide levels.

Tymos slumped down next to Landin and waited for him to revive. He used the time to contact Earthbase, using his personal communicator.

"I am relieved that you are well, Great One," Daniel responded. "How may I help you?"

Tymos sighed internally. He still felt unworthy of the deference, but there were things that needed doing that he could not do himself.

"What is the status of the three fleet ships," he asked first.

"Intact, but operating on emergency life support," Daniel reported. "President Reslic deployed the Joshe Rhodin to assist them. Perhaps you are aware that it is the fleet Command Ship."

Tymos wasn't, but the information had come to him as Daniel named the ship.

"Please contact the command ship. We have thirty members of the Zekos elite guard in custody and I think it would be better if they were gone before too many people here revive," Tymos proposed.

"Ah, yes," Daniel agreed. "How do you wish to proceed, Great One?"

"I have disabled the anti-transmission shield I put up here. Could you send someone via long-range beam to collect them? You can use me as a locus for the beam. I also need to remove the six Aeronite ships that landed around the base. There are six more somewhere."

"Your orders have been relayed, Great One," Daniel confirmed. "Is Great One Kryslie with you?"

"Elsewhere on the base," Tymos said without giving details. "I am going to request leave when the situation here has normalised. I will be preparing a report for Homebase. There are things that they need to know."

"Noted. The Joshe Rhodin will be in position for long distance beaming in a few minutes."

Tymos ended the communication. He looked past Landin to where Stenn Reslic lay. He didn't need to touch him to know that he was still alive, but comatose. He had no wish to tend him further, until Kryslie could examine him. That would not be until after she declared herself free of the entity and confirmed that it had not found its way back into its former minion.

He sensed Landin stirring.

"Sir, the idea of the EA suit was for you to maintain an independent oxygen supply," Tymos greeted him as he woke.

"I won't take that, even from you!" Landin growled. "Using this base as a battle ground! What made you think you could deal with that thing on your own?"

"I wasn't alone, Sir, and the base is still intact," Tymos said, with his relief and elation suddenly tempered.

"Where is Kryslie?" Landin demanded.

"In the garden, Sir," Tymos reported quietly.

"Get her here!" Landin ordered. He had a blinding headache and it was making him angry.

"She is...not fit for duty right now," Tymos told him.

Landin's anger evaporated. "Is she all right? Why aren't you with her?"

"She is alive, but she doesn't want me with her right now."

"And that entity you were hunting?" Landin challenged.

"Destroyed, we believe."

Landin tried to push himself up. Tymos sensed how much he was hurting but did not offer to help.

"Would you care to explain what happened?" Landin stared at Tymos with as much authority as if he had been standing.

"Not just yet, Sir," Tymos declined. "You have a base to run."

"I am aware of that, Mr Ward," Landin snapped. "Give me a status report and help me up."

Tymos hefted Landin to his feet and held him until he was steady. Landin hid his surprise at the younger man's unexpected strength.

"Sir, all personnel, except yourself, Kryslie and I, are either in quarters, or in the safe locks. Our people sustained only non-critical injuries. The security detail in the shuttle bay received heavy stuns. They are all in a safe condition. The roving guards were incapacitated by light stuns and are also in safe locks."

Tymos reported concisely, and accurately. He itemised the damage done to the base with more detail than Landin could have got from the computer if it could be made to work. Landin listened and memorised the details. The major damage was to main mission, where Tymos had crudely depowered it.

"What happened to our guests?" Landin asked.

"Gone," Tymos summarised.

"How?" Landin demanded.

"I haven't the full story, Sir," Tymos claimed. It was avoiding the truth, not actually lying.

"Is that the truth, Mr Ward?" Landin asked.

"There are still facts I do not know," Tymos confirmed. "And I have not considered all facts to prepare a report for the C-I-C."

"I see," Landin commented. "Your contention?"

"I believe what you told the C-I-C is the wisest outcome," Tymos commented. "They came, they searched, they took what they wanted and left."

Landin considered his technician, believed that Tymos was not going to tell everything to Basoli and said, sternly, "I want a full report from you before you report to the C-I-C."

Tymos gave him a faint wry smile.

"Have the alien ships departed and what of the alien soldiers you and your sister subdued?"

"Arrangements are in hand to deal with those," Tymos reported. He pulled out his personal communicator and sent a signal to the Tymorean Fleet Command ship.

Moments later, Landin recognised the sight warping oval and tensed.

Tymos glanced that way and said, "It is all right, Sir. This is the cavalry. You are being honoured."

A few moments later, two figures emerged from the beam terminus and bowed to Tymos, murmuring in Tymorean, "Great One, we are at your service."

Landin, believing they were greeting him, bowed back.

"Commander Landin, may I introduce Perrin Reslic, Admiral Commander of the Tymorean Peace Fleet and his second in command, Dorsh Rhodin."

Landin studied the newcomers. Both wore impeccable uniforms with noticeably empty sidearm holsters. Neither made a move to approach.

Landin was more than equal to the situation.

"Tymos tells me I am being honoured, and though I know little of you, I believe that to be the truth. You have come to relocate those who came here?"

"Yes, Commander," Perrin Reslic bowed slightly. "The time is not yet right for your world to be formally part of the federation to which we belong. Yet I hope, when the right time comes, you will greet us as friends."

"I think, I hope, that time comes soon, but yes, the time is not now," Landin responded, and then he got to business. "A number of our uninvited guests are in various storage areas."

"I will show you," Tymos offered, looking at the newcomers.

Reslic bowed again and reported, "I have crews preparing to fly the grounded craft off your base, and take over those still in space."

"What of the first one that had the two young fugitives?" Landin asked.

Tymos proposed quickly, "Surely, Sir, that would be a spoil or war – compensation for the unwarranted intrusion?"

"As the folk in question are safe in our custody and have no further need for it, I see no problem with that," Reslic agreed, taking his cue from Tymos.

"However, I do not think that the weapons we confiscated should remain here," Tymos proposed.

Reslic now glanced openly at the neat pile. "May I examine them, Commander?"

Landin nodded, and walked with Reslic to the pile. Tymos heard him identifying each type of weapon and describing how it worked and its effect.

Rhodin bowed and followed Tymos to the chamber with the first twelve prisoners. The men all recognised the Tymorean uniform and cowered against the far wall. Rhodin confirmed their fears – that they were being placed in the custody of the Tymorean Peace Fleet.

Tymos explained, "Which means, you will be questioned and if you behave well, will be returned to Zekos. You need not expect that the leader of this invasion, Hepziah, will be returning to Zekos."

Tymos sensed their relief at that, and their acceptance of their new situation, although they all expected to be tortured. "You will learn that we are not your enemies."

Rhodin and Tymos escorted these to the beam terminus, and Rhodin took them to the Command Ship, and returned. Two more groups were transmitted away, and then Tymos found a crate for the alien weapons.

Reslic bowed to Tymos when he had returned to stand next to Landin. "There was another matter?" he stated, with only his eyes flicking to the body on the floor.

"Yes," Tymos confirmed. He then thought at Kryslie, "Are you able to come?"

In answer, Kryslie transmitted into the room. Tymos sensed the effort it had taken, and wondered how she had the energy to stand.

Landin exclaimed at her pale haggard appearance. He made to go to her, but Tymos held him back.

Kryslie walked slowly and carefully to where Stenn Reslic lay. She knew his uncle had recognised him.

She sank down to kneel beside him, and touched his forehead for a long moment.

When she was ready to stand again, Tymos was beside her, helping her up.

"I wish you to return our cousin to the care of your best healers," Kryslie commanded. "Through only the best of intentions, he became affected by the entity known as Hepziah. His actions when thus controlled were not of his choosing. There were periods when his true desires were possible. He helped Vori and Zorrin, the children of Horvath Rozzin, to escape a similar fate to his."

"It will be as you command," Reslic bowed.

"There is more. I invite you to accompany me to the arboretum," Kryslie said, "It is not far."

Tymos leant his sister the energy to walk as far as the horizontal lift, which would take them to the garden. Reslic left Rhodin guarding the terminus. Landin insisted on coming with them. He trusted those that Tymos had introduced.

The first thing Landin noticed was how the garden had overgrown since he had last been there. Later he realised that all other attention was on the robed body lying in peaceful repose on a patch of lawn. "Is that...Hepziah?"

Kryslie answered him, standing on her own as Tymos slipped away on an errand.

"No, Commander. These are the mortal remains of Lorno, a Great warrior of Tymorean descent."

Reslic recognised the name. He straightened and tensed.

"I will explain, Commander Landin," Kryslie went on. "More than a hundred years ago, three warriors re-united for a final battle. Joshe, Tormel and Lorno. Their enemy was the one you met here, Hepziah, but then, he was not as you saw him here. He overcame Joshe and Tormel, and then possessed the body of Lorno, who had tried to change their enemy's nature. Lorno was old, and not as strong as he had once been. When his companions fell, he knew that he was the only one who could stand in the way of this evil. He did not let it overcome him completely. He retained enough will power to contain the worst of the entity's excessive evils, even though he knew he had damned his soul to eternal perdition. This evil had grown in power through the worship of a warlike race. Through the mind of his possession, it learnt of the people of Tymorea. It learnt how strong, powerful and prosperous they were. It wanted to breed, to divide itself into many, and it influenced its worshippers to that end with dreams of untold riches."

Kryslie saw Perrin Reslic interpreting what she didn't say.

"Lorno welcomed death. He died free of the evil taint – in peace. His last words were that we should not deal harshly with the boy – our cousin – for he risked his soul to help a Great One."

Kryslie was aware that Tymos had returned. He had a folded bundle of silver and gold fabric. He now knelt by the body of Lorno and deftly shrouded the remains.

With great deference, Perrin Reslic lifted the ancient body and carried it back to main mission. Kryslie returned with the group, once again leaning on her brother. Rhodin's expression betrayed nothing as Reslic carried the body back to the ship. In their absence, he had removed the weapons and returned the crate. He went to Stenn and lifted him as gently as he could.

"We will take our leave of you, Commander Landin. I hope we may meet again."

"As do I," Landin admitted. He watched Rhodin disappear, and the warped air dissipate.

Only then, did he turn and see that Tymos was kneeling by Krys, who was unconscious on the floor. He moved to a console, muttered when it remained dead, and recalled the portable link. He used that to reactivate the comm system, using the back-up power supply.

"Command override. Medical team to Main Mission. Priority One." The computer voice was broadcast over the communications system, audible in the silence, but coming from the speakers in the passages that led to main mission. A minutes later, as the medical team arrived, he broadcast, "Command override. All section heads to main Mission."

"Mister Ward, report to medical for a full physical examination," Landin directed. "You are on stand down until declared medically fit."

Tymos didn't blink. "Yes, Sir. I will go at once." He hoped Landin would also have himself checked over. There was his temporary blackout and his shoulder – both were excellent reasons to be 'unfit for duty' and in no condition to report to Basoli.

Basoli strode into main Mission full of thwarted authority. He subsided as he watched Landin climbing awkwardly out of the EA suit as the section heads arrived.

Once Landin had briefed the section heads, and assured them that all the aliens had gone. He requested that only the reduced crew be permitted to assess the damage in the relevant sections, he added, "You all know what to do. Report progress to the C-I-C. I am standing myself down until I have had my shoulder looked at."

Basoli straightened at having important things to do. He watched the section heads depart before he addressed Landin.

"So, the aliens have all gone – good. What happened to the power in here?"

"The main power conduits are damaged, Sir."

Basoli accepted that understatement quite innocently. "What happened to you?"

"I believe I slipped as I was trying to put the EA suit on in the dark. I know I was unconscious for a time. While I was out, Life Support went critical. I was able to reroute power. Sir, I am really in no condition to think right now. I will be pleased to give you a report later."

"Off then," Basoli ordered. He then added, "You look like hell."

As Landin walked off, he wondered what Basoli would think if he saw how Kryslie Ward had looked.

"Death warmed up and worked over," he thought to himself.

A faint tendril of thought drifted into his mind. "An extremely accurate description. I need to sleep for a year."

The thought reassured him.

Basoli finally found the time to follow Landin down to medical. He had questions he wanted answered. When maintenance had inspected the damaged power conduits and found how they had been yanked apart, he had been speechless. He had maintained enough control to refrain from speaking of what he had seen.

Repairs to the conduits were underway, but it was a major job. In his mind, he was positive that the aliens had done it deliberately as an act of vandalism.

"Doctor Long," he greeted. "How is the Commander?"

"Resting comfortably, Sir. He is sedated and sleeping right now."

"What other injuries did we take?" Basoli continued. He could see the infirmary was packed with temporary cots.

"The guard team in the shuttle bay believe they were hit with some kind of stun weapon. The last were rousing when they were able to contact medical. The other guard teams were overcome and woke to find themselves in one of the emergency safe locks. The worst affected are here, the rest I have released to rest in their quarters."

"Kryslie Ward and Tymos Ward – are they fit to be talked to?" Basoli demanded.

"No Sir," Long said firmly. "Kryslie is in a seriously depleted condition and I intend that her brother rests for a full shift cycle as well. I don't think he has a concussion, but he has some kind of burn on his chest."

Basoli clamped his mouth shut, and reigned in his annoyance. He seethed silently for a moment. "Very well. Please send me regular reports, to update me on how long people will be on stand down. I might need to request substitutes from other bases."

"Yes, Sir," Long agreed. She was allowed to return to her patients.

Chapter 30

"Wake up, lazybones," Tymos poked his sister. "You have been spending too much time in here lately. I could help you out of here faster."

"Why? Do you need help handling the C-I-C?" Kryslie challenged him.

"No, but we have six hours before the doctor will let me out of here and Landin has questions," Tymos told her. "Can I let him in here?"

Kryslie glanced at the IV drip and auto monitors and said, "Since I am kind of hooked up – probably."

Doctor Long accompanied Landin when he arrived. He was dressed, but not in uniform. While he settled himself in a chair, Long checked Kryslie over.

"How is Technician Ward," Landin asked.

"Improving, Sir."

"When will you release her for duty?" Landin asked.

"Not for another two days – if she improves as quickly as she has so far."

"Good! Please advise the C-I-C of that."

Long nodded and left them alone.

Tymos perched on the end of Kryslie's bed and waited for Landin to speak.

"Aren't you going to check the room for listeners?"

"I know it is clear, Sir," Tymos said, meeting his eyes. He didn't clarify if it was because he trusted Landin or had already checked.

"If I were to reveal all of what occurred here, would you have reservations?"

Tymos glanced down and Kryslie stared past Landin. "Yes, Sir," they said, almost in unison.

"Perhaps you would be willing to explain your reasons?" Landin invited. "You don't look alien, but then neither did most of our other visitors."

"Has Doctor Long found any oddities?" Kryslie asked.

"Only with your eyes," Landin admitted. "It isn't noticeable normally."

"Sir, by our choice, and we won't try to force you," Tymos began tentatively. "If you revealed our – parentage – you would severely reduce our usefulness to the WSRA."

"This discussion is unofficial and off the record," Landin assured them. "Drop the Sir, and speak plainly."

"We don't want to be known as freaks." Kryslie said bluntly. "Too much would be expected of us."

"What if your relationship with the last guests wasn't mentioned?" Landin prompted.

Tymos considered his words. "I think that the people of Earth will need time to accept the idea that aliens came here and communicated with us."

"Indeed, but your friends seem like the type of friends we should make," Landin proposed.

"They are already friends, or we would not be here," Tymos assured him. "When...those plans for manned space exploration bear fruit – then – contact is usually made."

"Why not now?"

"Sir, you are an exceptional man – eager to meet new races. Think on the general attitude to 'life on other worlds', 'alien visitors', and all the decades of fantastic literature on the subject," Kryslie suggested.

"Fair enough," Landin had to concede. "But when the events here get known, surely it will confirm the idea that aliens are evil."

"It isn't wise to rush off and think all aliens will welcome you with open arms and pure intentions," Tymos advised. "Although like on Earth there will be those who wish peaceful contact and those who fear strangers on most worlds. You have seen both types. Vori and Zorrin were refugees and fallible, but had no ill intent. Hepziah was a powerful entity of pure evil. As it stands, here, humans got rid of him and did his followers a great service. They left, peaceably, and thinking well of us humans."

"I am not sure that I get the point you are making," Landin admitted. "No, I doubt explaining further will help at the moment. I will think on that later. I only told everyone that the aliens had gone. The Chief knows I was unconscious for a time. It will have to seem like the aliens left while I was unaware."

Tymos relaxed.

"I have had no reason to regret my promise to keep your secrets," Landin said in assurance. "However, you both did things that were unusual."

"We will deal with those," Tymos assured him.

"That vanishing trick you both did?" Landin mentioned.

"There is proof that I can move very fast when I need to," Kryslie said with perfect honesty and complete poise. "Hepziah assumed we did what he did – not ducked behind a console. Humans can't teleport."

Landin smiled faintly. These two were adept at shading the truth. "An evasion and not a lie – behind a console, behind a wall?"

Tymos nodded with a faint smile of his own.

"Then perhaps you will preview the report you will give the C-I-C?" Landin requested.

Tymos and Kryslie spoke alternately, each explaining what they did, frankly and when questioned giving reasons. Landin learnt more about their unusual abilities than they had admitted previously, but he was still convinced there was much that they still had not told him. He decided not to ask them to explain the cryptic comment of the soldier, who Kryslie called cousin, about being trained by the President. It implied they were more important than they let on.

"You seem to have covered everything," Landin had to admit. "I will make the relevant monitor records available. However, Kryslie was observed doing that vanishing act."

Kryslie went tense.

"Those records may have been corrupted by power fluctuations," Tymos said thoughtfully. "With the system down to emergency levels, the monitoring system is not consistent."

"You are the expert," Landin mused, shaking his head.

"Sir, the C-I-C is trying to insist on coming in," Kryslie advised abruptly.

Landin stood and adopted a more official looking position.

"An investigation of events here will be undertaken," Landin was saying as Basoli walked in. "I want you reporting for duty as soon as you are passed fit, Technician Ward." He turned from Tymos to Kryslie and added, "I will be insisting you take leave downside. If possible, I want hardcopy reports of all events while they are still fresh."

Basoli nodded. "I will require all reports by first shift Friday. There will be a full board of investigation into events here. The WSRA directors, the other base Commanders, and representatives of the Investigative committee will be involved."

He drew two envelopes from his pocket, checked the names on them and handed one each to Kryslie and Tymos.

"The letters outline the charges against each of you," Basoli announced.

"Charges, Sir?" Tymos queried.

"Yes, Mr Ward." Basoli looked and sounded severe. "I suggest you review the WSRA Code of Conduct - the relevant sections are noted. Commander, I will speak to you privately."

"It's a formality," Kryslie told Tymos after Landin and Basoli had left and they had read their letters.

"Wait until he hears the rest of it," Tymos predicted. "This is only what he witnessed and it's enough to put black marks on our service record. I wonder what we did to get him mad at us."

It was a rhetorical question. They had irritated him ever since they had joined the WSRA.

Landin stood as he read the official document Basoli presented him with and controlled his reaction. Fortunately his superior didn't want a comment for he continued speaking from behind Landin's own desk.

"The Investigative Board will convene on the next first day and will be held at Terra 1. Commander Haldstadt will preside. You and those two technicians are required to attend. If other appropriate parties wish to attend, you will notify me a shift cycle in advance."

"Yes, Sir," was all Landin said. Basoli hadn't finished. "You will retain Command here, pending the findings of the Board."

Basoli rose abruptly and left Landin's office.

Landin sank into his recently vacated chair. He allowed himself a grimace of annoyance, and the fleeting uncharitable thought of, "How in hell did Basoli get to be where he was," and "Does he think he could have done better?"

The first comment was irrelevant. The second comment prompted Landin to consider all he had done.

"No," Landin mused softly. "I don't think the Chief could have done better. He would have ignored Kryslie and Tymos, probably have had them confined – if that were possible. And he probably would have got himself seriously hurt."

Landin considered that he would have to describe the situation as clearly as possible. He would need to consider the probable outcomes if things had been done differently.

"I think..." he mused again, "That this is really because I allowed junior technicians to tell me what to do. Suggestions that made excellent sense as things turned out. The real question should be how Tymos and Kryslie knew things in advance about the intruders. Not that I intend to bring that up."

Landin continued to consider the charges. He wasn't too concerned about his own position. He was more concerned about his two technicians – neither of whom he wanted to lose. They were a lot more than two 'jumped up' technicians. Yes, they were acting in a subordinate role, but they sometimes betrayed the sense of being used to being in command. They would act as they saw the need, and it was this that Basoli was really objecting to.

Nothing they had done had caused him to doubt their integrity. They might have secrets, and they knew things no human could have known, but they had handled the invasion in a way that had minimised harm to people and the base. Then he had to smile grimly – except for the power conduits in main mission.

He would have to make it clear that the danger from the entity had been extreme. The action, totally unorthodox, had needed to be taken immediately. There had been no time to re-route power by ordinary means. Though, it must have taken a lot of strength to pull all the conduits at once.

He shivered to think of that entity taking over all of his staff.

Thinking ahead, Landin requested his admin assistant to bring him the personnel records of Tymos and Kryslie Ward and to summon several of his section heads.

If Basoli was trying to be rid of his technicians, he was going to get as many reasons as possible as to why it would be negligent to do so.

Chapter 31

Landin re-entered the waiting area off the main conference room at Terra 1 and spoke to Tymos Ward. "They want to see you next."

Both Tymos and his sister stood up.

"They only want Tymos," Landin remarked with a slight tone of caution.

"We come as a set, Commander," Kryslie told him. "It will be more efficient for us to present together. They will soon realise that."

Landin declined to point out that they were providing evidence of intentional disregard of instructions. He knew that neither were the type to be intimidated when they believed they were right. Then there was the way they had dressed for this meeting – impeccable business suits instead of their formal uniforms. It seemed to be a statement implying that if they chose to, or if they were asked to resign - they could step straight into a high salaried position.

If he were a betting man he would say that the pair of them were not missing a trick and they knew exactly what they were doing and why.

If either Tymos or Kryslie were superstitious, they might have considered the thirteen pairs of eyes staring at them to be unlucky. Only one pair was staring angrily and, not unexpectedly, it was Basoli. He spoke first, even though Commander Haldstadt was acting as convenor.

"Did you not understand the request? We wish to interview you individually," Basoli challenged them.

Tymos was prepared for that. He inclined his head slightly to Commander Haldstadt, glanced quickly at the other base Commanders, the five men and women from the Investigative Committee and the representatives of the UWN and the Imperium. He did not acknowledge Arthur bin Halil's slight smile.

"Sir, my sister and I acted in concert during the period under investigation. It will make things clearer and simpler if we are both here to report."

Commander Haldstadt accepted that assumption before Basoli could comment further. "Will you tell this board what happened and what you did from the time you first became aware of the alien incursion."

Tymos took him literally. He would not mention being held by Vori and Zorrin prior to the arrival of their pursuers.

"After the first energy blast, I went to main mission. I had been speaking to the earlier arrivals and they believed they had been followed here. I knew that the damage to the shuttle bay had come from outside. I expected the Commander to raise the new shields and as I had programmed the controllers, I wished to be present in case of problems," Tymos reported.

"Your Commander reported you were busy at those controls," Commander Haldstadt noted.

"Yes, Sir," I was also attempting to find a means for the base sensors to see through the shields. I believed there might have been more than one ship out there."

"I believe that the Auto-track was working again, did it not detect the ships?" Commander Haldstadt asked.

"We built a shield to cover Auto-track 1," Kryslie answered. "However, there must have been some kind of masking field around the ships. I tried to find a frequency or radiation signature to detect them. Even so, the Auto-tracks do not pick up signals directly over the base if they are under 100m."

Commander Haldstadt addressed Tymos again. "Why did you feel the need to tell your Commander to activate emergency status?"

"My instincts were telling me that whoever was bombarding the base intended to get in and might have capabilities previously unheard of."

"Did you think your Commander was incompetent to think of it himself?" Commander Haldstadt asked.

"I understand that the WSRA is not a military organisation and offering an opinion to my Commander is not unacceptable. It was his choice to act on the advice," Tymos answered. No one missed his confidence in facing them.

"Why did you not take your own advice, Mr Ward?" Basoli asked.

Tymos was prepared for that, and quoted from the emergency procedure manual.

"The manual states that only the six most senior technicians are to remain on duty during that level of alert. On the grounds of seniority and Kryslie is rated expert on the Auto-tracks and I was most knowledgeable about the new shields, we both remained."

Basoli chewed on that in silence.

"Tell us in your own way, what happened and what you did next," Haldstadt invited.

Tymos kept to facts. He told them how he had managed to produce a hazy image of the six ships hovering over the base and how the bombardment continued until the attackers had realised the shields were strong enough to withstand it. He mentioned that the ships had landed around the base outside the limit of the shields and one was positioned facing into the shuttle bay."

Tymos went on to describe how the aliens had arrived inside the base from his point of view. "The Commander advised us to make no sudden moves," Tymos went on. "In view of the unknown types of weapons aimed at us by the arrivals – it was a wise decision."

"We have heard from Commander Landin, and seen on the monitor film, that the leader of these aliens had a way to make people do his will. Did you feel that effect yourself?"

"Several times," Tymos admitted, adding no details.

"Commander Landin also reported that the alien challenged you. What were you doing then, and how did you resist his compulsion?" Haldstadt asked.

"I was trying to tweak the shields to stop more of them coming through," Tymos told him, and that was true enough; it was more comprehensible than saying it was to stop them leaving. "My mind was fully occupied with that."

Kryslie spoke up again, startling everyone. "Which is why I moved to block the aliens' view of him."

"A rather provocative position," Basoli commented. "How did you resist the alien's insistence to move away from the consoles?"

"I was not near my console," Kryslie remarked, clearly, precisely.

"Were you not frightened by the weapon that was fired at you?" Basoli persisted.

"I judged the angle of the weapon to be directed to one side of us and the conformation of the weapon to be such that it would deliver a narrow beam or angle of effect," Kryslie told him, confident in her knowledge. "Also, if the alien wanted answers, he would not want us dead immediately."

One of the base Commanders remarked, "One cannot presume that an alien race would think like us."

"You are correct, Commander Miller, but Tymos and I had the opportunity to learn about the earlier arrivals and I based my actions on that knowledge."

Several heads nodded in agreement.

Basoli went onto his next challenging question. "Commander Landin explained that he thought the best course of action was passive resistance. Did he make this view clear to you?" He looked at Kryslie.

"The Commander said we were in no position to fight the aliens – which was true. There has never been a need to have weapons in main mission. He believed they would leave if allowed to search and failed to find the two younger aliens," Kryslie reported.

"It didn't stop you provoking the leader," Basoli challenged her.

"I was not attacking him, verbally or physically," Kryslie pointed out. "I was trying to provoke dialogue. I personally did not agree that allowing the aliens unrestricted access to the whole of the base was wise. However, stating that conviction at that time could have been seen as non-passive resistance."

Two members from the Investigative Committee conferred in a whisper. One spoke up. "Your subsequent actions show you to be deliberately drawing the leader's attention to yourself. Why did you choose to do that?"

"Passive resistance is all very well in the face of overwhelming weaponry," Kryslie began.

"Passive resistance with shrewd guerrilla tactics is better," Tymos finished.

A few of the audience realised that while Kryslie was speaking, they had forgotten her brother.

"Please explain that statement," Haldstadt requested.

"I...We," Tymos included Kryslie in his statement, "Object strongly, when bullies try to get their way at any cost. The alien leader had shown his intention when he ignored our attempt at communication and came in blasting. Without intending disrespect to our work colleagues – they have probably never had to learn to deal with bullies. We have."

Kryslie sensed some grudging agreement from Basoli, about objecting to bullies.

Tymos went on, "We know how to deal with them and in terms of risk – we were the least senior present, least experienced in terms of normal work, and relatively most expendable."

From the expressions on the faces, all of the base commanders disagreed with 'expendable', but Basoli glowered at them.

Haldstadt looked at Krys. "The alien leader suddenly went for you. Did you expect that?"

"Not exactly. I think that it could sense what I was thinking and that could have provoked it," Kryslie admitted. She allowed a faint hint of embarrassment to show. Enough to make her listeners feel she was as fallible as they might be.

"I don't think de-cowling that alien could be referred to as passive," Basoli challenged. "It got a rather violent reaction."

"Yes, Sir," Kryslie agreed. "However, it placed his attention firmly on me, and Tymos. And if what he muttered at me was correct, he was looking forward to tormenting me at his leisure. I am sure he intended that and worse for our first two guests."

"Was it your intention to be taken into that warped space that the others went into?" Basoli asked, referring to the beam terminus.

"No, Sir," Tymos answered at once. "And as strong as that slave was, we got free of him easily. He had two of us, and we are used to working together. I did have time to wonder why he was delaying – since he had no trouble lifting two dead weights. And he hadn't really hit us as hard as he could have."

"What were your intentions when you assaulted him?" Basoli verbally challenged.

"He begged us to kill him," Tymos said bluntly. "Before he was forced to kill us or others."

"Why didn't you?" one of the Investigative Committee asked.

"If he wasn't in agreement with the leader, he might have made an ally. Also, I think he must have helped Vori and Zorrin escape originally. I think they trusted him enough to emerge from their shielded ship. I hoped that knocking him out would stop the leader controlling him. I didn't trust him completely, because this time he had betrayed Vori and Zorrin."

"Did you intend to let them take their two fugitives?" Basoli provoked them, even though he had advocated that action.

"We were not in a position to stop them," Kryslie remarked.

"Because of your earlier actions," Basoli retorted.

Neither Kryslie nor Tymos reacted to that. They did not answer.

Commander Haldstadt continued smoothly, "It seems that the aliens were unable to return to their ship."

"Yes." Kryslie agreed. "It is possible that the slave expected that result and hoped to take advantage of the slight disorientation betrayed by the leaders."

"Too bad you couldn't read his mind," Basoli spoke in a low growl. "I think you angered him."

"He was angry because he couldn't return to his ship," Tymos corrected. "Since his means of transferring to his ship is unknown on Earth, his failure cannot be attributed to us."

"Did you enjoy his reaction?" Basoli demanded.

"No, Sir. That did hurt. But I was not going to let on."

"Why continue to provoke him, Ward?" Basoli demanded again.

"To get him to concentrate on me, who intended to keep him away from our people. To give our people time to get to safety," Tymos stated.

"He could have killed you," Basoli pointed out.

"He would have had to catch me first," Tymos claimed with a hint of arrogance. "I knew the base better than he did."

"How did you leave main mission?" Basoli demanded.

Tymos gave a half grin. "I don't think he stopped to think that humans can't do that vanishing act of his," he began, and then enhanced his next statement with a hint of 'command' in his voice. "I ducked out of sight." He wanted Basoli to believe that.

"I suppose you did a similar trick," Basoli accused Krys.

She just grinned slightly and let everyone assume she had.

"What about when you got the aliens to disarm?" Basoli persisted.

Kryslie shrugged. "A psych trick – using voice tone and body language." She used a trace of 'command' again, and ignored the fact that she had not spoken English to give the order to the aliens.

Basoli rubbed his forehead as if he had sensed the coercion. "It worked better than might have been expected," Kryslie added.

"We have heard of the subsequent events from Commander Landin," Commander Haldstadt told Kryslie and Tymos. "Tell us what you did after that. There are some gaps in the Commander's report."

"I kept the alien leader busy," Tymos answered, obediently. "I hoped to weaken him. Those energy bolts he emitted, I assumed would be limited."

Kryslie spoke then. "I went to find the guard team that Commander Landin had summoned. I knew how to manually open the isolation doors. When I found one of the unconscious guards, I took him to the nearest safe-lock. If I found one of the intruders, I disabled him and locked him up."

"Commander Landin was unable to account for some of the time you were gone. Do you have any idea why?" Commander Haldstadt asked.

"The slave had apparently woken up," Kryslie volunteered. "I had to overcome him again. The Commander had fallen against a console."

"Where were you all this time, Mr Ward?" Basoli asked.

"Still leading the alien a dance," Tymos stated. "I returned to main mission shortly after Krys. I needed to rethink where the creature was getting the energy to keep blasting me. The Commander suggested he was getting it somehow from the base power grid. As freaky as it sounds, I thought he could have been right. The emergency lighting did fluctuate when he tossed those energy bolts."

"Then what happened?" Haldstadt prompted.

Kryslie spoke with a tinge of revulsion in her voice. "That alien returned. He wanted to know where Vori and Zorrin were. I didn't tell him and he tried to force me but I can be very stubborn. Then he – reanimated his unconscious slave – like he was a puppet. Ordered him to do – something – while he held something he called a disintegrator on us. That sounded nasty so I kept still until I sensed the slave behind me. I acted then, the slave took the shot aimed at me, and I took from him a knife he was trying to kill me with."

"And then?" Haldstadt prompted.

Kryslie paused, deliberately creating tension. "I threw the knife at the alien."

The room was quiet. Kryslie went on. "The alien went down, but a glowing green nimbus hovered in the air where the body had stood. The body twitched like it was trying to rise but it didn't."

Tymos took over the tale. "The next moment, the emergency lighting in main mission went almost to nothing. Voice warnings announced life support was failing. That was when I pulled out the power conduits to main mission – to deny it that source of energy and protect the powered down equipment."

Tymos was prompted to continue. "It had stolen enough power to drag its physical body away."

"I went after it," Kryslie took over the report. "It hadn't left by the door or the horizontal lift. That only left the maintenance tunnels. I guessed it was seeking another energy source. The only one I could think of was the arboretum which is on an isolated circuit. That is where I found it, and the physical body was dead. I don't think it could get much power from there. It tried to take me over...I really...don't want to think about that. It really drained me. I think if Tymos hadn't come and helped me to resist it..."

Kryslie was still looking pale from the incident. The entire board of inquiry was sympathetic.

"What I saw next was a small glowing ball of green energy," Tymos continued. "It left Kryslie and seemed to shoot through the roof. I think...it's gone for good."

There was silence from the group as if they were considering the implications if it hadn't gone.

"When I had a chance, I checked the usage log of the new shields. They were still working since the power circuit hadn't been integrated into the base circuits yet. At the time I saw the glow vanish, something impacted the shields. There was an energy surge similar to when we tested the shields. The Chief has seen the effect. The energy was dissipated over the screen."

Tymos glossed over the departure of the aliens, implying he had been tending to his sister.

During Tymos's report, Basoli was making notations on a data padd. When the reports were finished, he stood and announced, "I have heard the reports, and must now add to the charges against those who stand before us."

Against Tym, he alleged, "Deliberate damage of expensive equipment" and Kryslie he alleged had "deliberately ignored safety regulations."

After the questions, Tymos and Kryslie were asked to return to the anteroom to wait. Landin joined them, but made no comments about how things had gone.

The session had a dual purpose. It was to report on the alien contact and incursion and to investigate how it had been handled. The questions had two different purposes.

The WSRA board members and Commanders were to consider the charges against Landin and the two technicians – with the Investigative Committee acting as impartial observers or consultants to oversee the interpretation of the Code of Conduct. The IC was also to recommend policies to be considered in case of further contacts.

Landin was summoned back first. Kryslie and Tymos did not try to sense the discussions within the room. They sat quietly and without fidgeting, but communicating mentally.

"If they fire us, we can walk into our choice of high paid jobs," Tymos said wryly.

Kryslie sent a laugh to his mind. "I am quite sure they won't. Basoli got the hint from our suits, and I don't think he will want to do us such a favour. I did get the sense that he hated to agree with our logic."

"What do you want to bet that he will be inwardly cringing when he has to commend us, and impress us with his authority by penalising us for breaches of conduct?" Tymos proposed.

"No bet, bro," Kryslie sent back. "All the WSRA brass were um...impressed...by your admission of malicious vandalism."

"What about your deliberate disregard of safety protocols," Tymos countered.

"They will probably think I learnt my lesson," Kryslie guessed. "Still, the Code is there for a reason and we did disregard it – even with the highest intentions. Under the circumstances, I think they will waive most of the charges. The Commanders are more of realists than Basoli."

"Still, Basoli has that petty streak, and a reasonably big ego," Tymos added. "I think what really annoys him is that we won't defer to his every word – nor grovel before him."

Finally they were recalled. Of the Board members, only Basoli, the WSRA directors and the base commanders were still present. Landin was with the other commanders.

Basoli, as Commander in Chief, addressed them. He read from a data pad.

"The Board of Investigation wishes to state their formal commendation for your actions during the recent events. Though unorthodox, the Board believes that your actions ensured the safety of personnel and minimal damage to the base. You are the sort of people Earth needs on the frontiers of science. You are able to act thoughtfully in unexpected circumstances and achieve necessary outcomes."

Basoli went on, no longer reading from the data pad. He gave a short discourse on the reason for the Code of Conduct, and how violations that were permitted, might lead to a lowering of the high ethical standard of the organisation.

"The charges tended against you will not appear on your service record," Basoli stated.

Kryslie sent a mental word to her brother. "I sense a 'but'..." She didn't try to read Basoli, just wished he would hurry up.

"Mr Ward, your action to deprive the alien entity of energy, while effective – resulted in an expensive repair bill and the blacking out of a vital monitoring position. I have recommended that you spend your spare time helping to rectify the problem."

"I had intended to, Sir," Tymos acknowledged as Kryslie mentally whispered, "Hard Labour."

"Miss Ward," Basoli went on. "On the recommendation of the Lunar 1 medical staff, you will take a month's leave, to enable you to recover fully."

Tymos sent back, mentally, "Exile?"

Basoli wasn't finished. "After that, you will be assigned to Terra 1 under Commander Haldstadt. He will brief you on your new position."

"Thank you, Sir," Kryslie acknowledged. She did not betray her annoyance.

To Tymos's mind, she sent, "Exile indeed! He is splitting us up."

Tymos sent back, "Maybe he thinks he can tolerate us in half doses."

They were officially dismissed, but Landin caught up with them before they disappeared.

"When do I effectively finish with you, Commander?" Kryslie asked. "And do I need to have a departure briefing?"

"Effectively now, and no. It is an internal transfer," Landin told her. "I am sorry to lose you, but you will be an asset to Commander Haldstadt and I expect it is time you each had to work alone."

Kryslie felt his words as a shiver of premonition. She managed to hide it from him. "You are probably right, Sir," Kryslie agreed. "And I am sorry to be leaving Lunar 1. Tymos can send my stuff down."

Kryslie walked with Tymos back to their assigned temporary quarters. "I will brief Daniel and Homebase on what happened at Lunar 1 and have

Vincent check me over," she proposed. "You have an hour until the return shuttle lifts."

"So I was advised," Tymos confirmed. "You changed your mind about being annoyed?"

Kryslie gave a wry smile. "Yes. I realised I was a Great One having a brat attack. If I complained to Daniel he would have told me as much. When you think about it, three Great Ones can do three times as much in three places. But, darn it, I enjoy your company."

"We are only a thought apart," Tymos reminded her. "And I am only your brother, not a spouse."

"Yeah!" Kryslie said aloud.

Kryslie watched the shuttle launch and turned to return to collect her travel bag. A discrete messenger stood behind her. He bowed when she turned and proffered her a message.

"I am to await an answer, Mam."

Kryslie took the envelope, studied the beautiful calligraphy and opened it. The enclosed letter was equally well written.

"His Imperial Highness, Arthur bin Halil, requests the privilege of a meeting with Kryslie Ward at her earliest convenience."

"Would you be so kind as to reply that I will be available from tomorrow morning," Kryslie said.

Chapter 32

Kryslie did not expect to be met by a stretched white limo and attendants in a dark blue uniform. She was dressed in a formal outfit, so the passers-by looked at her as if she were a celebrity. Inside the limo were all the comforts that the rich expected, but she was interested in none of them. The driver had told her deferentially, that His Excellency's personal jet awaited her at Miami International Airport. Once there, she stepped from the limo, which had driven onto the tarmac and stopped beside the executive jet. There was only a few metres between the between the two. The driver escorted her to the steps up to the door, and although she climbed alone, the pilot met her as she stepped into the jet.

That the limo driver and pilot had the olive skin of the natives of the Imperium did not make her fearful. Both men treated her with unusual deference, and had not ignored her as of little importance because she was female. She did sense that they wondered as to the reason why the new leader of the Imperium had requested her presence.

The jet flew to Washington's Ronald Reagan airport, where she again had only a short distance to walk to another white stretched limo. She was not surprised to be driven to the exclusive estate outside the capitol that was the embassy of the Imperium.

The limo took her right to the door and more dark blue liveried attendants were there to assist her out.

Arthur bin Halil met her at the door, surprising the attendants. He personally escorted her to a small but luxurious meeting room, where refreshments were waiting. When he offered her a drink, she declined.

"Should I be offering you blessings on your Ascendency, your Majesty?" Kryslie asked in Tymorean, tacitly confirming who and what she was. She had sensed great tension in the new leader of the Imperium.

Arthur, who knew without any doubt that he could trust her, still considered his answer.

"My ascension brings me little joy," he said, seating himself, so Kryslie would sit.

"Tell me how you feel?" Kryslie offered gently.

"I always knew this day would come," Arthur said. "But I did not expect it yet, but only when my father reached honourable old age. All my life I was taught to respect him and how he had done so much good in uniting all the warring little countries into a great empire."

"Your father was a great man, and he did do good in bringing peace to warring factions," Kryslie confirmed. "But he was not a saint."

"Yes. I did not know how he had achieved what he did – until recently. What I know now – sickens me. He loved you once – didn't he? How could he have changed so?"

The question was a plea from his soul.

"Arthur, you may not like what I have to say, but will you listen?" Kryslie asked.

He nodded, looking more like a forlorn child, than the ruler of many tiny nations.

"Your father is a product of a different age and a culture different to mine. He took me, without my agreement, and after he had put me in a vulnerable position. He decided, arbitrarily, that I belonged to him. As for love, perhaps he did, but as one loves a possession, or a dog or a horse."

"He spoke of you with such passion," Arthur disagreed. "He hated to have lost you."

"Yes," Kryslie said gently. "Because I left him, before he was ready to discard me. He intended to use me against what was to become the UWN. I am not angry with him for any of that – for even as he used me, I was using him. Forty years ago, the Guardians of Peace used me to sow the seeds of peace. It was their doing, not mine that I vanished when I did. I had known I could not stay, and I prepared those who would nurture my seed of peace. They did well, for you are here now ready for your future."

"And what is that?" Arthur asked.

Kryslie shook her head. "Do what you believe is right," she told him. "I created you, but you are not my slave or my puppet. You are free to do what you feel needs to be done."

Arthur considered her words in silence.

Finally he nodded, more to himself, and seemed to grow in confidence. He seemed to come to a decision.

"My father was arrested by the World Council," Arthur revealed with pain in his voice. "His crimes were made public and the trial was open to all. The people of my nations rose up in anger and denounced him. They deposed him and after much talk, I was appointed his successor."

Kryslie sensed the powerful emotions he was controlling within himself. She waited for him to continue.

"The World Council found him guilty of many, many crimes. Most were done within the Imperium, and so they conferred with the justices there when passing sentence. President Adamson would have accepted life imprisonment. My people demanded his death."

Kryslie stood and moved closer to her son as he choked on the words he tried to say next.

"He is my father, but I had to endorse the sentence."

She gently gripped his shoulders in support and sympathy.

"I am proud that he did not disgrace himself and accepted the judgement honourably," Arthur said shakily. "Then he asked if he would be permitted to take his own life. That is allowed in my country...It was the least I could do for him, so I said yes. He has until a week from now."

Arthur stopped speaking, but forced himself to continue.

"Then he asked for a last request. I could not refuse him. He asked that you be present when..." Arthur couldn't finish.

After a period of silence in which Kryslie considered many things, she said, "I will come." She felt her son's hands cover hers on his shoulder.

In the ensuing silence, Arthur regained control of himself. "I did not think it right that he demand that of you," he said finally.

"If it will give him a measure of peace or satisfaction, I will not deny him that. It will not be the most dreadful thing I have witnessed. I will come, not for him, but to finish something I started forty years ago."

Arthur gripped her hands. She would be there to support him, her son.

"My father is under guard by the World Council." Arthur managed to say calmly. "He is in a secure suite of the Imperial Palace. I did not wish to humiliate him further by having him kept in prison. I am to fly back tomorrow."

"I have a month's leave," Kryslie told him. "For that period, I am at your service."

Arthur gripped her hands once more, and then released them. Kryslie moved back to her seat, pausing to pour them both a drink of the fruity wine from Arthur's country.

"After...later...I am meant to be crowned, like an Emperor. I will not do that. I will bring together my council which I will select from the wisest men and women of each nation. I want to negotiate with President Adamson and the World Council to remove divisions between the Imperium and the UWN. I would welcome your wisdom...Mother."

"You know why that must remain secret," Kryslie acknowledged. "But, my son, I am proud of you and your courage and vision. I will do what I can, and of course you have other friends to advise you."

"I had not forgotten my early tutors," Arthur admitted. "Will you accept my hospitality? All that you require will be provided for you."

Kryslie agreed, and organised to notify Terra 1 of her intentions during her leave.

Kryslie refused to visit Abdul bin Halil after she arrived at the Imperial Palace. There was nothing that she wanted to say to him or hear from him.

She knew he had not changed his intentions towards her. He wanted this one last chance to hurt her – if not physically, then emotionally.

In the few days she had, Kryslie spent part of the time meditating – preparing herself. Up on Lunar 1, Tymos sensed her conflict, but could offer little but his support. "Reslic did say that the time might come when we must act as judge, jury or executioner," Tymos recalled. "Being what we are brings great responsibility to innocents. I will be with you in spirit."

It was appropriate that she watch him die. She had used him, urged his subconscious to conquer all the little divided nations, to bring them together. If this day was to be the result, it was also her responsibility, and if it brought her pain, then she would bear it in silence.

The observers presented themselves dressed in formal robes. Arthur supplied Kryslie with her preferred clothing. She had chosen a golden brown sleeveless tunic over long white pants and a white long sleeved shirt. She wore no adornment except a matching coloured ribbon in the formally braided hair style.

In the pre-gathering, Kryslie kept back from the important observers, and used her mind to discourage curiosity about her presence. They were all inside the World Council Building in the capital of the Imperium. They would be escorted to the death chamber when Abdul bin Halil was prepared.

When the message arrived, Arthur moved to escort her. The other observers noticed her for the first time and wondered who she was – if she was a secret wife of the condemned. They were not enlightened.

Within the death chamber, Abdul bin Halil was strapped to a chair. Straps held his head, shoulders, legs and one arm in position on the chair. The free arm was so he could drink the fast acting poison, rather than having it administered. However there was a tube going into his leg, in case he refused. There were also machines to monitor his life signs.

One of the guards that stood behind the chair, moved to speak to Arthur. Kryslie recognised Jonko and his mind betrayed surprise at her presence. She pretended not to hear the exchange which was in Arthur's native tongue. When Jonko had moved away, and Kryslie had buried his concern for her in a deep part of her mind, Arthur spoke softly to her.

"He has chosen a fast acting poison, but one that gives a painful death. He requested as his last wish, that you be with him when he takes it. You do not have to do this."

"I will do it," Kryslie spoke in a voice devoid of fear or reluctance or any emotion. "There is a statement I wish to make to him."

When it became apparent what she would be doing, there were protests.

Adamson was most vocal. "You cannot do this!" he said, aghast. "I would not wish any woman to have to witness this."

Kryslie turned just before reaching bin Halil. "Mr President, your concern is noted. However, I chose to be here. No one forced me and it is not because of concern for the condemned."

"Why?" Adamson wanted to know.

Kryslie met his eyes, saw his recognition of her and shook her head. "This is between him and me."

She moved to bin Halil, close enough to take his hands. He twisted his free hand, and Kryslie felt him trying to dig his nails into the flesh of her hand. She saw a faint smudge on them.

Very softly, in his own language, Kryslie spoke to him. "I expected this dishonour from you. You will not see me die of poison before you. I do not belong to you. I have never belonged to you. This fate that you embrace is of your own making."

"I curse you to hell," bin Halil hissed at her.

A small cup of white liquid had been delivered to be within his reach. He grabbed it, almost angrily and put it to his mouth. Then, in a rapid move, threw it into her face. She closed her eyes and mouth just in time and kept them shut. She didn't try to pull away.

Angry words were spoken as the observers realised what had happened. Kryslie sensed concern from Jonko and the others. She thought at Jonko. "Water to rinse my face." He acted quickly. He ran off as guards restrained bin Halil's free arm. He had not released her and Kryslie was not trying to get free.

Arthur was close. When the guards had moved back, he spoke to his father. "That was unworthy of the man I honoured all my life."

"You traitor's whelp," he hissed. "She will see you in hell, too."

Arthur turned abruptly, face expressionless and returned to stand next to Adamson. Jonko returned and carefully rinsed Krys's face until she mentally pushed him away.

The guard in charge of the execution came and spoke to bin Halil, telling him that as he had failed to administer the fatal dose to himself, it would be injected. He tried to move Kryslie away, but bin Halil gripped her harder and Kryslie did not try to move.

Bin Halil stared into her eyes and Kryslie met them fearlessly. She saw in them, the first realisation of the poison and the rising pain. He betrayed nothing. In moments, his face contorted, his body went into spasms of agony.

Kryslie thought she had shielded her mind, but with his gaze and his grip – the agony lanced through her too. It was as well that no one could see her face. It mirrored that of the man before her. In the moments between spasms bin Halil smiled in malicious pleasure in seeing her suffering.

Kryslie sensed the life departing from him as his body tried to breathe and could not.

"I forgive you," she sent to his mind as she sensed the end.

"Curse you to hell," his mind retorted. And his mind spewed all his hatred into hers as his body relaxed into death.

Kryslie could not move. She remained standing by will power alone. Her body still mirrored the death spasms, her mind reeled, full of hatred. But in that moment of extremity, she felt the touch of the Guardians of Peace, easing her mind, freeing her of the poison of hatred and the pain in her body. She took a deep breath and imaged raising one arm in thanks.

"He is gone," she said quietly but it was heard by all. "Let us move forward in peace."

Arthur moved forward and embraced her. He headed her away from the other observers and out a side door. Jonko moved after them, as the other observers left through another door and the body of bin Halil was released and moved to a trolley.

In a quiet room, away from everyone, Arthur offered her something to calm her. Jonko hovered by the door. Kryslie managed a faint smile, but not of mirth.

"I will be fine, your Majesty," she told Arthur. "Though if you don't mind, right now, I prefer solitude."

Arthur nodded, showing he understood. He dare not betray his grief, not openly. Later, in private, he would mourn for the father he had once loved. Instead of protesting, he took Krys's hand and kissed it gently.

"I understand. You will ever be an inspiration to me and a source of strength and serenity." He backed away and allowed Jonko to hold open the door for him and follow him out.

"See she has whatever she needs," Arthur directed.

"I will, Sir," Jonko agreed. He took up a guard stance outside the door, but only until Arthur was out of sight. Then he re-entered the room, and provided an absolutely trustworthy shoulder and a source of comfort that would never betray her, or that a Great One was still only human.

When Jonko escorted her back to the Imperial Palace, Kryslie had regained her serenity and was ready to support her son in his determination to unite the two powers of the world, the two halves of his heritage.

The End

The story of Great Ones Tymos and Kryslie will continue in
The Tymorean Trust Book 6 – Invasion

Other works by Margaret Gregory

NOVELS

The Tymorean Trust Book 1 - <u>POWER RISING</u>

The Tymorean Trust - When peace rules Tymorea —
Peace reigns in the universe.
Chosen to be the Advocates of the mystical and incorporeal Guardians of Peace,
twins Tymos and Kryslie must first learn to control and use the power rising in
them - or it will destroy them.
On Tymorea, only the ruling Triumvirate Governors are powerful enough to
guide the strong-willed alien-bred twins until they have mastered their power.

The Tymorean Trust Book 2 - <u>GREAT ONES</u>

The peace of the Guardian Planet, Tymorea, is in deadly peril. War there will
create ripples of unrest and destruction throughout the settled universe.
Tymos and Kryslie, still adolescents, have barely mastered their power and
Llaimos is still less than a year old, but they are the three chosen to be Advocates
of the mystical Guardians of Peace, to safeguard the Tymorean Trust

The Tymorean Trust Book 3 - <u>THE RETURN TO EARTH</u>

Even before the war on Tymorea, the Elders foresaw that Great Ones Tymos
and Kryslie would have an imperative mission on Earth.
But as the Tymoreans prepare to build an Earthbase to support them, they
discover that specifications for two vital protective shields are missing.
Now, nearly a century later, Tymos and Kryslie must find his work and build the
generator before the base is found

The Tymorean Trust Book 4 - <u>EARTH MISSION</u>

Just before their graduation from the prestigious WSRA Washington University,
Tymos and Kryslie Ward deliberately disappear. The Great Ones have foreseen
the capture and death of the new Tymorean missionaries and discovered that the
leader of the Eastern Imperium plans to undermine the United World Nations.
Tymos and Kryslie must protect their kin and prevent a potentially devastating
world war.

<u>THE WILD ONE</u>

Sixteen year old Jai Cassidy thought she was finally free of her family until she is discovered by her other relatives…the ones that aren't human. Jai uses her natural perversity and cunning to escape their control, but catapults herself into the middle of a deadly feud between two alien races.

<u>ATAPI SORCERESS</u>
The sequel to The Wild One

Jai Cassidy is beginning her mission of reversing the decline of the non-humanoid Atapi. As a sorceress and an Atapi-Human hybrid, she is vehemently disliked by the male Atapi sorcerers and the humanoid rulers of Korvu. Her task is complicated by the treachery of a group of alien engineers, who are inciting insurrection and harsh reprisals.

<u>WANDA: FROM BAD TO WORSE</u>
Book 1 in the Third Generation Series

If she was going to die young, like her mother, Gwen Willard was determined to die rich and she had very few years to do it. She met Hooch, who taught her some exciting and illegal skills, and she came to the attention of the police. Then her uncanny knack for predicting trouble, warned her to flee to the city and change her name. She was 15. Life wasn't easy, but her new skills came in handy.

SHORT STORIES:

<u>GRAFFITI GIRL</u>
Valerie has become known as "The Graffiti Girl" but she is more than just a street artist. She sees and paints life her way.

In Valkyrie, the second story, Valerie, blinded by an explosion, must learn to paint and see again.

<u>GHOST WRITER</u>
Edwina is a ghost with a mission - to find out why she died.
Only to do so, she must first help another girl.